W9-BUG-948

WITHDRAWN

THE ENCHANTRESS

{ *The Secrets of*
THE IMMORTAL
NICHOLAS FLAMEL }

ALSO BY MICHAEL SCOTT

The Alchemyst

The Magician

The Sorceress

The Necromancer

The Warlock

THE ENCHANTRESS

{ *The Secrets of*
THE IMMORTAL
NICHOLAS FLAMEL }

Michael Scott

DELACORTE PRESS

This is a work of fiction. All incidents and dialogue, and all characters with the exception of some well-known historical and public figures, are products of the author's imagination and are not to be construed as real. Where real-life historical or public figures appear, the situations, incidents, and dialogues concerning those persons are fictional and are not intended to depict actual events or to change the fictional nature of the work. In all other respects, any resemblance to persons living or dead is entirely coincidental.

Text copyright © 2012 by Michael Scott
Jacket art copyright © 2012 by Michael Wagner

All rights reserved.
Published in the United States by Delacorte Press,
an imprint of Random House Children's Books,
a division of Random House, Inc., New York.

Delacorte Press is a registered trademark and the colophon is a trademark
of Random House, Inc.

Visit us on the Web! randomhouse.com/teens

Educators and librarians, for a variety of teaching tools, visit us at
RHTeachersLibrarians.com

Library of Congress Cataloging-in-Publication Data is available upon request.

ISBN 978-0-385-73535-3 (trade) — ISBN 978-0-385-90518-3 (lib. bdg.) —
ISBN 978-0-375-98590-4 (ebook) — ISBN 978-0-307-97766-3 (international tr. pbk.)

Printed in the United States of America

10 9 8 7 6 5 4 3 2 1

First Edition

Random House Children's Books supports the
First Amendment and celebrates the right to read.

To the memory of my father,
Michael Scott.
Consummatum est.

I am legend.

There was a time when I said that death had no claim over me, that illness could not touch me.

That is no longer true.

Now I know the date of my death, and that of my wife, too: and it is today.

I was born in the Year of Our Lord 1330, more than six hundred and seventy years ago. Long-lived, yes; immortal, too, but not invulnerable. Perenelle and I always knew this day would come.

I have had a good life, a long life, and have few regrets. I have been many things in my time: a physician and a cook, a bookseller and a soldier, a teacher of languages and chemistry, both an officer of the law and a thief.

And I was *the* Alchemyst.

Gifted—or was it cursed?—with immortality, Perenelle and I fought the evil of the Dark Elders and kept them at bay while we searched for the twins of legend, the Gold and Silver, the sun and moon. We always thought they would help us defend this planet.

We were wrong.

Now the end is upon us and the twins have vanished, gone back in time to the Isle of Danu Talis, back ten thousand years, back to where it all begins. . . .

Today, the world ends.

Today, Perenelle and I will die, if not by the hand or claw of some Elder or monster, then by old age. My dear wife has extended my life by a single day, but at a terrible cost to herself.

And if there is some consolation, it is that we will die together.

But we are not dead yet, nor will we go down without a fight, for she is the Sorceress, and I am the immortal Nicholas Flamel, the Alchemyst.

From the Day Booke of Nicholas Flamel, Alchemyst
Writ this day, Thursday, 7th June,
in San Francisco, my adopted city

Thursday,

7th June

CHAPTER ONE

*T*he small crystal mirror was ancient.

Older than mankind, it predated the Elders, the Archons and even the Ancients who had come before them. This was an Earthlord artifact, washed up when the Isle of Danu Talis was ripped from the primeval seabed.

For millennia the mirror had hung on a wall in a side room in the Palace of the Sun on Danu Talis. Generations of Great Elders, and then the Elders who had come after them, had puzzled over the small rectangle of crystal in the plain black frame that was not wood, not metal, nor was it stone. Although it had all the appearance of a mirror, it wasn't a true reflecting glass: its surface showed only shadows, though those who peered closely claimed they caught a hint of their skulls beneath their flesh, of the impressions of bones beneath skin. Occasionally—infrequently—some claimed to catch

3

glimpses of distant landscapes, polar ice caps, expanses of deserts or steaming jungles.

At certain times of the year—at the fall and summer equinoxes—and during solar and lunar eclipses, the glass would shiver and show scenes of times and places beyond comprehension and understanding, exotic worlds of metal and chitin, places where there were no stars in the heavens and a black sun hung unmoving in the skies. Generations of scholars spent their entire lives trying to interpret those scenes, yet even the legendary Abraham the Mage could not decipher its mysteries.

Then one day, when the Elder Quetzalcoatl was reaching out to straighten the glass, he had caught the side of his hand on the edge of the frame. He felt a sting and pulled away in surprise to see that he'd wounded himself. A single drop of blood spattered onto the crystal and suddenly the glass cleared, the surface rippling under the curling thread of sizzling blood. In that instant, Quetzalcoatl had seen wonders:

. . . the Isle of Danu Talis at the heart of a vast empire stretching unbroken across the globe . . .

. . . the Isle of Danu Talis burning and shattered, rent asunder by earthquakes, the great streets and massive buildings swallowed by the sea . . .

. . . the Isle of Danu Talis just visible beneath a sheath of ice, huge spike-nosed whales drifting over the entombed city . . .

. . . Danu Talis rising pure and golden in the center of a limitless desert . . .

The Elder had stolen the mirror that day and never returned it.

Now, slender and white-bearded, Quetzalcoatl spread a blue velvet cloth over a plain wooden table. He smoothed the cloth flat with a black-nailed hand, picking off threads and dust. Then he placed the black-framed rectangle of crystal in the center of the cloth and gently wiped it clean with the edge of his white linen shirt. The glass did not reflect the Elder's hawk-nosed face: the polished surface twisted with a gray smoke-scape.

Quetzalcoatl leaned over the glass, pulled a pin from the sleeve of his shirt and pressed the tip of the pin into the fleshy pad of his thumb. "By the pricking of my thumbs . . . ," he muttered in the ancient language of the Toltec. A ruby droplet of blood slowly gathered on his smooth flesh. ". . . something wicked, this way comes." Holding his hand out over the glass, he allowed the drop to spatter onto the mirror. The surface instantly trembled and shimmered, the ancient crystal running with a rainbow of oily colors. Red smoke steamed off the glass; then the colors settled into images.

Millennia of experimentation and vast quantities of blood—very little of it his—had taught the Elder how to control the images in the crystal. He had fed it so much blood that he had come to believe that it was somehow sentient and alive. Staring into the glass, he murmured, "Take me to San Francisco."

The mirror blurred, then washed with white and gray

light, and suddenly Quetzalcoatl found himself floating high over the city, looking down over the bay.

"Why isn't it burning?" he wondered aloud. "Why are there no monsters in the streets?" He had permitted the immortal humani Machiavelli and Billy the Kid to return to San Francisco in order to release the creatures on Alcatraz Island into the city. Had they failed in their mission? Or was he too early?

The image in the crystal shifted once again and settled on the narrow length of Alcatraz, and Quetzalcoatl spotted a line of movement in the water. A shape moved across the bay, leaving the smudge of Alcatraz and heading toward the city. Quetzalcoatl rubbed his hands together. No, he wasn't too late: he was just in time to witness a little chaos. It had been a long time since he had seen a city destroyed, and he did love a spectacle.

The color image suddenly flickered and faded. The Elder pierced his finger with the pin again and then again, dripping more of his lifeblood onto the glass, feeding it. The mirror blinked to life once more and the image of the city re-formed, three-dimensional in its clarity. Quetzalcoatl focused and the image spun downward, pulling him toward choppy white-capped water. A creature lurked beneath the waves, something huge and sinuous: a sea serpent. The Elder squinted. It was hard to make out any details, but it seemed as if the creature had more than one head. He nodded in approval; he liked that. It was a nice touch. It made sense to send the sea creatures to the city first. He smiled, showing savage teeth as he imagined the monster rampaging through the streets.

Quetzalcoatl watched the sea serpent sweep across the bay and curl toward one of the piers that jutted out into the water. He frowned and then nodded in understanding. It would crawl ashore on the Embarcadero. Excellent: lots of tourists, high profile.

Light shifted on the sea. He spotted the faintest shimmer of a blue and red oily stain on the water and abruptly realized that the sea serpent was heading straight for it.

Unconsciously, Quetzalcoatl dropped lower still. His head dipped toward the glass, hawk nose almost touching the surface. He could smell the sea now, salt with the faintest hint of rotting fish and seaweed . . . and something else. Closing his eyes, he breathed deeply. A city should smell of metal and traffic, burnt food and too many unwashed bodies. But what was he smelling here—these were odors that had no place in the city: the tartness of mint, the sweetness of aniseed, the flowery scent of green tea.

Realization struck him as the monstrous creature—the Lotan—rose from the sea, seven heads darting toward the swirling red and blue stain on the water. Quetzalcoatl recognized the auras and the colors now: the red was Prometheus, while the blue was the immortal humani Niten. And the sickening odor of mint in the air could belong to only one man: the Alchemyst, Nicholas Flamel.

Quetzalcoatl saw them then, standing on the end of a pier. And yes, the woman was there also, Perenelle the Sorceress, whom he knew from bitter experience. His tongue automatically found the space in his teeth where she'd knocked out one of his big back molars. This was not good, this was not good at all: a renegade Elder and three of the most dangerous and deadly humani in the Shadowrealm.

Quetzalcoatl's hands clenched into tight fists, razor-sharp nails biting into the flesh of his palms, dripping thin blood onto the glass, keep the images alive. His dark eyes watched unblinkingly.

. . . the Lotan turning to feed on the auras . . .

. . . the creature rising from the water, balancing on its tail, all seven heads darting in to feed, mouths agape . . .

. . . the flash of green fire and the overwhelming stink of mint.

"No!" the Elder hissed as he watched the Lotan transform into a small blue-veined egg. He saw the egg drop into the Alchemyst's outstretched hand. Flamel tossed it triumphantly in the air . . . and a circling seagull snatched it and swallowed it whole.

"No! Nonononono . . ." Quetzalcoatl howled his rage, his face darkening, contorting into the flat serpent image that had terrified the Maya and the Aztec. Ragged teeth jutted from his mouth, his eyes narrowed and his dark hair stiffened in spikes about his face. He pounded on the table, the ancient wood cracking and only his lightning-fast reflexes saved the mirror from falling to the floor and shattering.

As quickly as it had begun, the rage passed.

Quetzalcoatl breathed deeply and ran a hand through his stiff hair, flattening it. All Billy and Machiavelli had to do was to release a few monsters into the city—three or four would have sufficed. Two would have been fine; even one, preferably something big with scales and teeth, would have been a

8

start. But they'd failed, and they would pay for that failure later—if they survived!

He needed to get the beasts off the island, but to do that he would have to keep the Flamels and their Elder and immortal friends busy.

It was obviously time now for Quetzalcoatl to take matters into his own hands. A sudden smile revealed the Elder's needlelike teeth. He had collected a few pets in his Shadowrealm—the humani would call them monsters—and he could allow them out to play. But no doubt the Alchemyst would deal with them in the same way he'd dealt with the Lotan. No, he needed something bigger, something much more dramatic than a few mangy monsters

Quetzalcoatl found his cell phone on the kitchen table. He dialed the Los Angeles number from memory. It rang fifteen times before it was answered with a snarling rasp. "Do you still have that bag of teeth I sold you millennia ago?" Quetzalcoatl started in. "I'd like to buy it back. Why? I want to use it to teach the Flamels a lesson . . . and of course keep them busy while I get our creatures off the island," he added hastily. "How much for the bag? Free! Well, yes, of course you can watch. Meet me at Vista Point; I'll make sure there are no humani around.

"Something wicked this way comes . . . ," Quetzalcoatl whispered. "Heading your way, Alchemyst. Heading your way."

CHAPTER TWO

Sophie Newman opened her eyes. She was lying facedown on grass that was too green to be natural and had the texture of silk. Crushed beneath her face were flowers the likes of which had never grown on the earth, tiny creations of spun glass and hardened resin.

She rolled over on her back and looked up . . . and then immediately squeezed her eyes shut again. A moment ago, she had been on Alcatraz in San Francisco Bay, the cool salt-scented air stinking with raw power and the zoolike odors of too many beasts crammed together. Now the air was clean and crisp, filled with exotic smells, and the sun was warm on her face, searing blinding afterimages on her retinas. She opened her eyes again and watched a shape move across the face of the sun. Squinting, she made out an oval of crystal and metal. "Oh!" she breathed, surprised, and reached over to nudge her twin. "You better wake up. . . ."

Josh was lying on his back. He opened one eye and groaned as the sunlight hit his face, and then, when the realization of what he'd just seen sank in, he snapped awake and sat bolt upright. "That's a . . ."

". . . a flying saucer," Sophie finished.

There was movement behind them and they both turned to see they were not alone on the grassy hillside. Dr. John Dee was on his hands and knees, staring wide-eyed into the sky, while Virginia Dare sat cross-legged beside him, jet-black hair rippling in the wind.

"A vimana," Dee breathed. "I never thought I'd see one in my lifetime." He crouched on the grass, staring in awe at the fast-approaching object.

"Is this a Shadowrealm?" Josh asked, looking from Dee to Dare.

The woman shook her head slightly. "No, this is no Shadowrealm."

Josh stood and shaded his eyes, staring at the craft, mesmerized. As the vimana drew closer, he could see that it was made from what appeared to be a milky crystal encircled by a thick band of gold. The saucer dipped and dropped to the ground, filling the air with a low subsonic buzzing that fell to a deep rumbling as it hovered inches over the grass.

Sophie climbed to her feet and stood alongside her twin. "It's beautiful," she whispered. "It's like a jewel." The opalescent crystal was flawless, and the gold rim of the vehicle was inscribed with tiny sticklike characters.

"Where are we, Josh?" Sophie whispered.

11

Josh shook his head. "Not where . . . *when*," he murmured. "Vimanas belong to the oldest of all the myths."

Without a sound, the top half of the oval flipped open and the side of the craft retracted, revealing a blinding white interior.

A man and a woman appeared in the opening.

Tall and slender with deeply tanned skin, they both wore white ceramic armor etched with patterns, pictographs and hieroglyphs from a score of languages. The woman wore her black hair short, in a style cropped close to her head, whereas the man's skull was smooth shaven. Their eyes were a bright, brilliant blue, and when they smiled, their teeth were small and perfectly white, except for the incisors, which looked unnaturally long and sharp. Hand in hand, they stepped off the vimana and walked across the grass. The glass and resin flowers melted to globules beneath their feet.

Unconsciously Sophie and Josh stepped back, squinting against the low sun and the blinding reflection off the couple's armor, trying to make out their features. There was something so terribly familiar. . . .

Suddenly Dee gasped, then drew in his arms and legs, trying to make himself as small as possible. "Masters," he said. "Forgive me."

The couple ignored him. They continued on their path, staring at the twins pointedly, until their heads blocked the sunlight, revealing their features in a halo of light.

"Sophie," the man said, bright blue eyes twinkling with delight.

"Josh," the woman added, shaking her head slightly, lips curling into a smile. "We've been waiting for you."

"Mom? Dad?" the twins said simultaneously. They took another step backward, confused and frightened now.

The couple bowed formally. "In this place we are called Isis and Osiris. Welcome to Danu Talis, children." They stretched out their hands. "Welcome home."

The twins looked at one another, eyes and mouths wide in fear and confusion. Sophie reached out and gripped her brother's arm. Despite a week of extraordinary revelations, this was almost too much to take in. She tried to form words and ask questions, but her mouth was dry, and her tongue felt thick and swollen.

Josh kept looking from his father to his mother and back again, trying to make some sense of what he was seeing. The couple looked like his parents, Richard and Sara Newman. They sure sounded like them too, but his parents were in Utah . . . he'd spoken to his father only a few days ago. They'd talked about a horned dinosaur from the Cretaceous period.

"I know this is a lot to take in," Richard Newman—Osiris—said with a grin.

"But trust us," Sara—Isis—said, "it will all make sense." Her voice was reassuring as she smiled at the boy and girl. "All your lives have been leading up to this moment. This, children, is your destiny. This is your day. And what have we always said about the day?" she asked, smiling.

"Carpe diem," they both responded automatically. "Seize the day."

"What—" Josh began.

Isis raised her hand. "In time. All in good time. And trust us—this is a good time. This is the best of times. You have stepped back ten thousand years into your past."

Sophie and Josh looked at one another. After everything they'd been through, they knew they should be delighted to be reunited with their parents, but there was something terribly wrong here. They had a hundred questions . . . and the two people standing in front of them hadn't exactly answered any of them.

Dr. John Dee scrambled to his feet and fastidiously brushed himself off before pushing past the twins and bowing deeply to the white-armored couple. "Masters. I am honored—deeply honored—to stand in your presence again." He raised his head to look from face to face. "And I trust you will acknowledge that I was instrumental in bringing the twins of legend to you."

Osiris looked at Dee, flashing a ghost of the smile he'd shown the twins. "Ah, the dependable Dr. Dee, always the opportunist . . ." He stretched out his right hand, palm downward, and the Magician scrambled to take it in both of his and press his lips to the back of the fingers. ". . . and ever the fool."

Dee looked up quickly and attempted to pull away, but Osiris had caught his hand. "I have always—" the Magician began in alarm.

"—been a fool," Isis snapped.

A shadow crossed Osiris's face, and as his lips drew back from sharp white teeth, it transformed in an instant into a

14

cruel mask. The shaven-headed man suddenly took hold of Dee's head on either side, thumbs on the immortal's cheekbones, and pulled him up until the human's feet left the ground. "And what use have we for a fool . . . or worse, a flawed tool!" Osiris's blue eyes were level with the Magician's. "Do you remember the day I made you immortal, Dee?" he whispered.

The doctor started to struggle, eyes suddenly wide with terror. "No," he gasped.

"When I told you I could make you human again?" Osiris said. *"Athanasia-aisanahta,"* he breathed, and then he flung the Magician away from him.

The Magician sailed through the air, and by the time he hit the ground at Virginia Dare's feet, he was an old man: a shriveled, wizened bundle of rags, face lost in wrinkles, gray hair scattered in clumps on the silken grass around him, eyes milky white behind cataracts, lips blue, teeth loose in his gums.

Sophie and Josh looked in horror at the creature who only moments before had been a vibrant human. Now he was ancient beyond belief, but still alive, still aware. Sophie turned back to stare at the man who looked like her father, who sounded like him . . . and realized that she did not know him at all. Her father—Richard Newman—was a loving, gentle man. He would have been incapable of such casual cruelty.

Osiris saw the look on Sophie's face. "Judge me when you are in possession of all the facts," he said icily.

"Sophie, something you haven't learned yet is that there are times when pity is a weakness," Isis said.

Sophie started to shake her head. She didn't agree. And

although the voice was Sara Newman's, the sentiment was not. Sophie had always known her mother to be one of the kindest and most generous of people.

"The doctor has never been worthy of pity. This is the man who killed thousands in his search for the Codex, the man whose ambition sacrificed nations. This is the man who would have slain you both without a second thought. You must remember, Sophie, that not all monsters wear bestial shapes. Don't waste your pity on the likes of Dr. John Dee."

Even as the woman was speaking, Sophie caught flickering hints of the Witch of Endor's memories about the couple known as Isis and Osiris. And the Witch despised them both.

With a tremendous effort, Dee raised his left hand toward his masters. "I served you for centuries . . . ," he croaked. The effort exhausted him and he fell back on the grass. His wrinkled skin had tightened across his head, emphasizing the skull beneath.

Isis ignored him. She looked at Virginia Dare, who had remained unmoving throughout the brief encounter. "Immortal: the world is about to change beyond all recognition. Those who are not with us are against us. And those who stand against us will die. Where do you stand, Virginia Dare?"

The woman gracefully climbed to her feet, twirling her wooden flute lightly in her left hand, leaving a single note shimmering on the air. "The doctor promised me a world," she said. "What do *you* offer?"

Isis moved and the sunlight blazed white off her armor. "Are you attempting to bargain with us?" The Elder's voice began to rise. "You are in no position to negotiate!"

16

Dare spun the wooden flute again and the air shivered with an unearthly keening. All around them the glass flowers shattered to dust. "I am not Dee," Virginia said icily. "I neither respect you nor like you. I am certainly not afraid of you." She tilted her head to one side, looking from Isis to Osiris. "And you should remember what happened to the last Elder who threatened me."

"You can have your world," Osiris said quickly, reaching out to rest his hand on his wife's shoulder.

"Which world?"

"Any world you wish," he said, a broken smile fixed on his face. "We will need someone to act as a replacement for Dee."

Virginia Dare stepped daintily over the ancient wheezing man. "I will do that. Temporarily, at least," she added.

"Temporarily?" Osiris smiled.

"Until I get my world."

"You will have it."

"Then we are done and I will never see you again, nor will you ever bother me."

"You have our word."

Isis and Osiris turned to the twins and held out their hands again, yet neither Sophie nor Josh made any attempt to take them. "Come now," Isis said, a touch of impatience in her voice, making her sound like the Sara Newman they knew. "We need to go. There is much to do."

Neither twin moved.

"We need some answers," Josh said defiantly. "You can't just expect us to—"

"We will answer all your questions, I promise you," Isis

17

interrupted. She turned away and the warmth in her voice disappeared. "We must go now."

Virginia Dare was about to step past the twins, when she stopped and looked at Josh. "If Isis and Osiris are your parents . . . what does that make you?" she asked. She glanced over her shoulder at Dee, then turned away to walk toward the crystal ship.

Sophie looked at her brother. "Josh . . . ," she started.

"I have no idea what's going on, Sis," he said, answering her unspoken question.

A dry, rasping cough drew their attention back to Dee. Although the sun was blazing in the sky and the air was warm, the ancient man had curled up in a ball and was shivering violently, arms wrapped around his body for warmth. They could hear his teeth rattle in his head. Without a word, Sophie pulled off her red hooded fleece and handed it to her brother. He looked at it for a moment, then nodded and stepped forward to kneel down beside Dee. Gently he draped the fleece over the Magician, tucking it in around his shoulders. The Magician nodded his thanks, his white eyes wet with emotion, and clutched the fleece to himself tightly.

"I'm sorry," Josh said. He knew what Dee was, knew what he was capable of, but no one deserved to die like this. He looked over his shoulder. Isis and Osiris were climbing into the vimana. "You can't just leave him like this," he called.

"Why? Would you rather I kill him, Josh?" Osiris asked with a laugh. "Is that what you want? Dee, is that what you want? I can kill you now."

"No," Josh and Dee said simultaneously.

"His four hundred and eighty years are catching up with him, that's all. He will die of natural causes soon."

"It's cruel," Sophie said.

"To be honest, considering the trouble he's caused us over the past few days, I think I'm being rather merciful."

Josh turned back to Dee. The old man's withered lips moved, his breath coming in great heaving gasps. "Go." A clawlike hand wrapped around Josh's wrist. "And when in doubt, Josh," he whispered, "follow your heart. Words can be false, images and sounds can be manipulated. But this . . ." He tapped Josh's chest. "This is always true." He touched the boy's chest again, and the sound of paper crackling under his red 49ers Faithful T-shirt was clearly audible. "Oh no, no, no." The Magician's face fell. "Tell me that's not the missing pages from the Codex," he whispered, voice cracking.

Josh nodded. "It is."

Dee erupted in what began as a laugh, but the effort sent a wracking cough through his body and he folded in on himself, struggling to catch his breath. "You had them all along," he murmured.

Josh nodded again. "Right from the beginning."

Shaking with silent laugher, Dee closed his eyes and lay back on the silken grass. "What an apprentice you would have made," he breathed.

Josh watched the dying immortal until, finally, Osiris interrupted. "Josh," he said firmly. "Leave him. We must go now—we have a world to save."

"Which world?" Sophie and Josh asked simultaneously,

"All of them," Isis and Osiris replied together.

19

CHAPTER THREE

*T*he screams were piercing.

A flock of parrots, green-bodied and red-faced Cherry-Headed Conures, swooped low over the Embarcadero in San Francisco. They buzzed past the three men and the woman standing at the wooden rail by the water's edge. The shrill, high-decibel shrieking echoed through the late-afternoon air. One of the men, bigger and more muscular than the others, pressed his hands to his ears.

"I hate parrots," Prometheus grumbled. "Noisy, filthy—"

"Poor things; they're upset." Nicholas Flamel didn't let the Elder finish his complaint. His nostrils flared as he breathed deeply. "They sense the auras in the air."

Prometheus dropped a heavy hand on the Alchemyst's shoulder. "I've nearly been eaten by a seven-headed sea monster. I'm a little upset myself, but you don't hear me screaming about it."

The third man, slender and black-suited, with delicate Japanese features, looked up into Prometheus's broad lined face. "No, but you *will* grumble about it for the rest of the day."

"If we survive the rest of the day," Prometheus muttered. A parrot flew by, close enough to ruffle the Elder's graying hair, and a spatter of sticky white appeared on the big man's checked shirt. His face wrinkled into a grimace of disgust. "Oh, great—that's just perfect! Could this day get any worse?"

"Will you three be quiet!" the woman snapped. She pushed a coin into the slot beneath the blue metal viewing binoculars, then tilted them toward the island of Alcatraz, which lay directly ahead of them across the bay. She turned the wheel and the buildings swam into focus.

"What do you see?" Nicholas asked.

"Patience, patience." Perenelle shook her head. Her long hair had shaken loose from its braid, and shimmered black and silver across her back. "Nothing unusual. There's no movement on land and I can see nothing in the water. There are no birds in the air over the island." She stepped away from the binoculars and allowed her husband to take her place. She stood thinking for a moment and frowned. "It's too quiet."

"Calm before the storm," Nicholas muttered.

Prometheus leaned his massive forearms on the wooden rail and looked across the bay. "And yet we know those cells are full of monsters, and Machiavelli and Billy along with Dee and Dare are there. Mars, Odin and Hel must be there by now. . . ."

"Wait," Nicholas said suddenly. "I see a boat. . . ."

"Who's driving?" Prometheus asked.

Nicholas turned the big metal binoculars and focused on a small craft that had appeared from behind the island, white waves foaming in its wake.

Niten climbed onto the lower rail of the wooden fence and leaned forward, hands shading his brown eyes. "I can see one person in the boat. It's Black Hawk. He's alone. . . ."

"So where is everyone else?" Prometheus wondered aloud. "Is he fleeing?"

"No, this is Black Hawk. . . ." Niten stopped the Elder before he could finish the thought. "Do not dishonor his name." He shook his head firmly. "Ma-ka-tai-me-she-kia-kiak is one of the bravest warriors I've ever encountered."

The three immortal humans and the Elder watched the boat bounce over the waves, heading toward the shore.

"Wait . . . ," the Alchemyst said suddenly.

"Is there something in the water?" Niten asked.

Though the binoculars, Nicholas could see a dozen seal-like heads bobbing on the surface of the waves surrounding the boat. He squinted to get a better look. Though his eyes were aging, he could clearly see that the heads belonged to green-haired young women who were beautiful until they opened their mouths to reveal piranha-like teeth.

"Seals?" Prometheus asked.

"There are Nereids in the water," he announced. "And more are coming."

Soon the boat was close enough that the group on the pier could all see the creatures surrounding it. They watched in silence as one rose out of the sea and attempted to climb aboard. The stocky copper-skinned immortal nudged the boat to one side and the hull of the craft slammed into the fish-tailed creature, sending her crashing back into the water. Black Hawk turned the boat in a tight circle, almost tipping it over, bringing it around to head back into the group of Nereids, driving it directly toward them. Water foamed as they scattered.

"He's deliberately engaging the Nereids," Niten said. "He's keeping them away from the island."

"Which means Mars and the others must be in trouble," Prometheus said. The big Elder turned to Nicholas. "We have to help them."

Nicholas looked at Perenelle. "What do you think we should do?"

The Sorceress's face lit up with a dangerous smile. "I think we should attack the island."

"Just the four of us?" he asked lightly.

Perenelle leaned forward until her forehead touched her husband's, and looked deep into his eyes. "This is the last day of our lives, Nicholas," she said softly. "We have always lived quietly, keeping to the shadows, hoarding our energy, rarely using our auras. We don't have to do that anymore. I think it is time we reminded these Dark Elders why they once feared us."

CHAPTER FOUR

*T*he Rukma vimana shuddered, engine whining. The huge triangular flying ship had been damaged in the fight outside Abraham's crystal tower. One side of the craft was peppered with scars, portholes were shattered and the door no longer sat flush in the frame. Icy air howled and shrieked through the opening. The screens and control panels along one wall were black, and most of those still working pulsed with a jagged red circular symbol.

Scathach the Shadow stood behind Prometheus. She knew him as her uncle, but he had no idea who she was. In this time stream, she had not yet been born—and would not be born until after the island fell. The Elder was struggling to control the craft. Scathach had both hands clasped behind her and refused to grip the back of the Elder's chair. She was also desperately trying to prevent herself from throwing up. "Can I help?" she asked.

Prometheus grunted. "Have you ever flown a Rukma vimana before?"

"I've flown a smaller one . . . a long time ago," Scathach admitted.

"How long?" Prometheus asked.

"Hard to tell, really. Ten thousand years, give or take a century or so."

"Then you can't help me."

"Why, has the technology changed at all?" she asked.

William Shakespeare was sitting on the right-hand side of the craft, next to the bulky Saracen Knight, Palamedes. The English immortal looked at Scathach, his bright blue eyes huge behind his overlarge glasses. "You know, I'm a curious person," he said. "Nosy, some would say."

She nodded.

"Always been my biggest failing . . . and my greatest strength." He smiled, revealing his bad teeth. "I find you learn so much more by asking questions."

"Just ask the question," Palamedes muttered.

Shakespeare ignored him. "Experience has taught me that there are some questions one should never ask." He pointed toward the circular symbol flashing red on the few working screens. "But I really do think I want to know what that means."

Palamedes rumbled a laugh. "I can answer that, William. I'm no expert in ancient languages, but in my experience, when something is red and blinking, that means trouble."

"How much trouble?" Shakespeare asked.

"It means abandon ship," Prometheus answered. "But

you don't want to pay too much attention to that. These old ships are always throwing up warnings."

The left-hand wing dipped and they heard something bang and scrape along the underside of the craft.

Joan of Arc shifted in her seat to peer through one of the broken portholes on the left side. The vimana was skimming treetops, leaving a trail of leaves and broken branches tumbling in its wake. She glanced sidelong at her husband and raised pencil-thin eyebrows in a silent question.

The Comte de Saint-Germain shrugged. "I am a great believer in only worrying about those things we have control over," he said in French. "And we have no control over this craft; therefore, we should not worry."

"Very philosophical," Joan murmured.

"Very practical." Saint-Germain shrugged elegantly. "What's the worst that can happen?"

"We crash, we die," she suggested.

"And we die together." He smiled softly. "I would prefer that. I do not want to live in this world—or any other world, for that matter—without you."

Joan reached over and the man caught her hand in his. "Why did it take me so long to marry you?"

"You thought I was an arrogant, ignorant, boastful, dangerous fool."

"Who told you that?" she demanded.

"You did."

"And I was right, you know."

"I know." He grinned.

There was another bang and the entire craft shuddered. Glossy green leaves drifted in through the ill-fitting door.

"We need to put down now," the Shadow said.

"Where?" Prometheus demanded.

Scathach lurched over to one of the portholes and gazed out. They were racing over a dense primeval forest. Enormous leathery winged lizards spiraled lazily through the skies while brilliantly plumaged birds burst through the treetops in splashes of color. Humanoid creatures that looked vaguely simian, though they were coated in feathers, scampered along the crown of the forest, shouting and calling. And from the shadows behind leaves and branches, huge unblinking eyes stared up at the vimana.

The Rukma vimana lurched again, then plunged, and the right wing ripped a narrow slice out of the canopy. The entire forest screeched, howled and bellowed its disapproval.

Scathach ducked her head, eyes darting left and right. The forest stretched unbroken in every direction until it was swallowed up by dense billowing clouds on the horizon. "There's nowhere to land," she said.

"I know," Prometheus said impatiently. "I have flown this route before."

"How much farther?" she called.

"Not far," Prometheus said grimly. "We need to get to the clouds. We just need to stay in the air for a few more minutes."

William Shakespeare turned away from one of the portholes. "Could we settle down atop the trees?" he asked.

"Some of them look strong enough to support the weight of the craft. Or perhaps if you were to hover, we could climb down on ropes."

"Look again, Bard. Can you see the forest floor? These redwoods are over five hundred feet tall. And even if you did manage to reach the ground unscathed, I doubt you'd get more than a few feet before something with teeth and claws ate you. If you were extremely unlucky, the forest spiders would get to you first and lay their eggs in you."

"Why is that considered extremely unlucky?"

"You'd still be alive when the eggs hatched."

"That is probably the most disgusting thing I've ever heard," Shakespeare muttered. He pulled out a scrap of paper and a pencil. "I've got to make a note of that."

A trio of huge black vulture-like creatures flapped up from enormous nests in the trees and flew alongside the vimana. Scathach's hands fell to her swords, though she knew that if the creatures attacked she'd be able to do nothing about it.

"They look hungry," Saint-Germain said, leaning across Joan to stare through the porthole.

"They're always hungry," Prometheus said. "And there are more of them on this side."

"Are they dangerous?" the Shadow asked.

"They're scavengers," Prometheus said. "They're waiting for us to crash so they can feast off the remains."

"So they expect us to crash?" Scathach watched the huge birds. They looked like condors, though they were three times the size of any condor she'd ever seen.

"They know that sooner or later, every vimana crashes,"

Prometheus said. "Over the generations they've see so many crashes, the knowledge is now bred into them."

Suddenly, the glass screen directly in front of the Elder turned black, and then, one at a time, all but one of the pulsing red screens winked out.

"Hang on!" Prometheus called. "Strap yourselves in!" He jerked back the controller and the Rukma vimana lurched up into the sky, engine straining. The entire ship started to vibrate once again, and everything that wasn't tied down went crashing to the back of the craft. As the ship rose higher and higher, the wispy white clouds turned thick and solid, plunging the interior of the craft into gloom, and the windows were suddenly streaked with curling rivulets of rain. The temperature within the craft plummeted, and a speckling of water droplets covered everything. The single functioning screen bathed everyone in crimson alternating with blackness.

Scathach flung herself into a seat that had not been designed for a human body and clutched the arms hard enough to crack the ancient leather. "I thought we were going down!"

"I'm going to take us up, as high as we can go," the Elder grunted. His broad face was sheened with sweat turned the color of blood in the screen's light, and his red hair was plastered to his skull.

"*Up?*" Scathach's voice was a high-pitched squeak. She swallowed hard and tried again. "Up?" she repeated, her voice normal. "Why up?"

"So that when the engine gives out we can glide," Prometheus answered.

"And when you do think that will—" Scathach began.

There was a loud bang and the interior of the Rukma vimana was suffused with the stench of burning rubber. And then the low buzzing drone of the vimana's engine cut to silence.

"Now what?" Scathach demanded.

The Elder sat back in his chair, which was far too small for him, and folded his arms across his massive armored chest. "Now we glide."

"And then?"

"Then we fall."

"And then?"

"Then we crash."

"And *then?*" Scathach demanded.

Prometheus grinned. "Then we'll see."

CHAPTER FIVE

"*N*iten." Nicholas turned to the Japanese man. "You are the master strategist. What do you suggest?"

Niten tilted the binoculars and scanned the island across the bay, moving from right to left and back again. "Did you ever read my book?" he asked. Then, without waiting for an answer, he continued. "There are three ways to counter an enemy. There is *Tai No Sen,* when you wait until he attacks and then counterattack. There is *Tai Tai No Sen,* when you time your attack to his, so that you enter battle together. And then of course, there is—"

"*Ken No Sen,*" Prometheus said. "To attack first."

Niten glanced over his shoulder at the Elder. "You *did* read my book. I'm flattered."

Prometheus grinned. "Don't be. I found some mistakes in it. And of course, Mars disagreed with just about everything you said."

"He would." Niten turned his attention back to the binoculars. "*Ken No Sen.* I think we should attack first, but we need to know the disposition of our enemy before we make our move. We need eyes on the island."

"Can I remind you that there are only four of us?" Prometheus said.

"Ah." Niten turned from the binoculars to look at the group. "But I am guessing that our enemies do not know that." He smiled. "We can encourage them to believe that there are many more."

"The ghost of Juan Manuel de Ayala is trapped on the island," Perenelle said, "forever tied to the place. There are other shades there also. They helped me escape. He would help, I'm sure of it. He will do anything to protect his island."

Niten smiled. "Ghosts and spirits are a useful distraction. But to battle the monsters we will need something a little more tangible. Preferably something with teeth and claws."

Slowly Perenelle's lips turned up in a smile that was terrifying. "Well, of course, Areop-Enap is on Alcatraz."

Prometheus spun around. "Old Spider! I thought she was dead."

"When I last saw her, she had been poisoned by the bites of millions of flies. She'd cocooned herself in a hard shell to heal. But she is alive."

"If we could awaken her . . . ," Prometheus murmured. "She is . . ." He paused, shaking his head. "She is fearsome in battle."

"When you say Old Spider . . . ," Niten began, "are we talking about a big spider?"

"Big," Nicholas and Perenelle answered together.

"*Very* big," Perenelle added. "And incredibly powerful."

Prometheus shook his head. "I knew her when she was beautiful, before the Change took her. The Change is rarely kind, but I think it was particularly cruel to her."

A large party of smiling Japanese tourists gathered nearby and began photographing the island, each other and the swooping red and green parrots overhead. The immortals and the Elder took this as their signal to move farther down the pier.

"We need to contain the monsters on the island," Nicholas said quietly as they walked. "If they're all in one place, it will be easier to defend the city."

Prometheus shook his head. "This is about more than just defending the city, Nicholas. We need to destroy these beasts. And time is not our friend. I can guarantee you that every evil thing on the West Coast of America is heading here now. Every Dark Elder and his servant are on their way. We cannot fight them all."

"We don't have to," Niten said firmly. "We should focus on one enemy at a time. Let us address what is before us first." He tilted his head toward the island. "The Dark Elders intended those creatures to spread terror and confusion throughout the city. If we can prevent that, then already we have hurt their plans. And yes, I am sure there are others coming, but they are individuals, and we are more than capable of handling them."

"And we don't have to be just four," Perenelle said. "There are others—immortals like us, or immortals loyal to peaceful Elders or Next Generation—who will stand with us. We should get in touch with them."

"How?" Prometheus asked.

"I have their phone numbers," Perenelle said.

"Tsagaglalal will fight with us," Nicholas continued, "and no one knows the extent of her powers."

"She is an old woman," Niten said, shaking his head.

"Tsagaglalal is many things," Perenelle said, "but it would be a mistake to think that she is just an old woman."

"If you have contacts, then call them," Niten said decisively. "Get them all here." He turned to the Elder. "Prometheus, you are a Master of Fire. Could you rain fire onto the island?"

The big Elder shook his head sadly. "I could, but it would be a thin rain, and would utterly destroy me. I am old, Niten, and I am dying. My Shadowrealm is lost and I have little aura left . . . enough perhaps for one final blaze of glory." He bared his teeth in a grim smile. "And I want to save that until the very end."

The Japanese immortal nodded. "That I understand."

"So we focus our efforts on the island," Nicholas announced. "But before we do that, we need to know what's going on over there."

"We could try scrying," Perenelle suggested.

Nicholas shook his head. "Too limiting and too time-consuming. We would only be able to see whatever was

reflected in glass or pools of water. We need a bigger picture."
He stopped suddenly and grinned. "Do you remember
Pedro?" he asked.

Perenelle looked blankly at him, and then her face lit up
with a smile. "Pedro. Of course I remember Pedro."

"Who is Pedro?" Niten asked.

"Was. Pedro is no more. Gone almost a hundred years,"
Perenelle said.

"King Pedro of Brazil?" Prometheus asked. "Pedro of
Portugal? The explorer, the inventor?"

"The parrot," Perenelle said, "named in honor of our
great friend, Periquillo Sarniento. For decades we had a
Timor Sulphur Crested Cockatoo. I say 'we,' though in truth,
he was bonded to Nicholas and only tolerated me. We found
him as an abandoned chick when we were searching the ruins
of Nan Madol in the eighteen hundreds. He was with us for
almost eighty years."

Prometheus shook his head. "I really do not see—" he
began.

"Parrots are the most remarkable birds," Nicholas continued, ignoring him. He stretched out his left arm and the merest hint of mint touched the salt air. His lips moved, his breath
hissing softly between them. There was a sudden flutter of
wings and a spectacular red-headed green-bodied parrot settled onto his outstretched hand. It tilted its head to one side,
and a large silver and gold eye regarded him quizzically; then
it slowly began to sidle up his arm. The Alchemyst ran the
back of his finger down its breast. "Parrots are extraordinarily

intelligent. And their eyesight is marvelous. There are some species whose eyes weigh more than their brains. They can see into the infrared and ultraviolet spectra; they can even see waves of light."

"Alchemyst . . . ," Prometheus said.

Nicholas focused on the parrot, blowing gently across its iridescent plumage. The parrot rubbed the top of its head across Flamel's forehead and started to groom his bushy eyebrows.

"Alchemyst," Prometheus repeated, a note of irritation in his voice.

"John Dee and his kind use rats and mice as eyes to spy for them," Perenelle explained. "But over the years, Nicholas learned to see through Pedro's eyes. It's a simple transference process. You wrap the creature in your aura and then gently direct it."

"Pedro saved our lives on more than one occasion," Nicholas said quietly. "It got so that he would scream at even the hint of Dee's sulfur stench." He brought his face close to the Cherry-Headed Conure and it ran its beak back and forth across his forehead, now grooming his close-cropped hair. "Prometheus, would you hold on to me now?" he continued. "I'm going to get a little dizzy."

"Why?" Niten asked, puzzled.

"I'm going flying," the Alchemyst whispered. He cocked his head and the parrot mimicked the movement. For an instant, they were eye to eye. The salt air turned sharp with mint and the conure shivered. As he stroked the bird, Flamel's fingers left shimmering trails of green that were almost invisible against the parrot's feathers. Nicholas closed his eyes . . . and the parrot's yellow eyes turned pale, almost colorless.

Then, with a sudden flapping of wings, the bird took to the air, and Prometheus caught the Alchemyst as he slumped to the ground.

CHAPTER SIX

"Are you really our parents?" Sophie asked.

"What a question!" Isis snapped.

Sophie and Josh looked at one another. The twins were sitting in two narrow seats directly behind Isis and Osiris. Virginia Dare crouched on the floor behind them. Josh had attempted to give her his seat, but she'd told him she preferred not to be strapped in. She patted his face as she thanked him, and the touch sent a flush of heat through his entire body.

Richard Newman—Osiris—swiveled around in the black leather seat and smiled. "Yes, we really are your parents. And we really are archaeologists and paleontologists—or at least, we are in your Shadowrealm. Everything you know about us is true."

"Except the Isis and Osiris, rulers of Danu Talis, part," Josh said. "Or the whole aging and immortality thing."

Osiris's smile broadened. "I said everything you knew about us was true. But I didn't say you knew everything about us."

"What do we call you?" Sophie asked.

"What you've always called us," Isis said. She was controlling the crystal and gold vimana, her long-fingered hand flat on a glass panel, tiny movements of her thumb and forefingers sending the craft buzzing through the air.

Sophie stared at the back of the woman's head. This woman looked like her mother, talked and moved like her mother . . . and yet . . . there was something different, something wrong. She glanced sideways at her twin and knew instinctively that he was feeling exactly the same way. The man who looked like her father was smiling at them. And the smile was identical to the one she knew so well in her own Shadowrealm, Earth—wrinkles creasing the corners of his eyes, little lines at the corners of his mouth. His lips were tightly shut, just like those of her father, who never opened his mouth when he smiled. She'd always thought he was self-conscious of his long eyeteeth. "Vampire teeth," he'd called them when she was a child. She'd laughed at it then, but now the words were chilling.

"I think I'll call you Isis and Osiris," she said eventually— it felt *right*—and from the corner of her eye, she could see Josh nodding in agreement.

"Of course," Osiris said evenly. "I'm sure this is a lot to take in. Let's get you back to the palace and get some food into you. That'll make things easier."

"Palace?" Josh asked.

39

"Just a small one. The bigger one is in a nearby Shadow-realm."

"So you are the rulers here?" Virginia Dare called up from her place on the floor.

The tiniest flicker of annoyance danced across Osiris's face at the question. "We are rulers, yes, but we are not the ultimate rulers. Another rules."

"Though not for much longer," Isis said. She turned her head to smile at her husband.

This time Osiris's pointed incisors appeared against his lower lip as he grinned. "Not for very much longer," he agreed. "And then we will be the rulers of this world and all the worlds beyond."

"So we are definitely on Danu Talis," Josh said, almost talking to himself. He raised his head to look out the speeding vimana. All he could see from his side was the mouth of a massive volcano, a thin thread of gray-white smoke curling into the skies. "The famous source of all the legends of Atlantis."

"Yes, this is Danu Talis."

"When?" he pressed.

Osiris shrugged. "It's hard to say, really. The humani have adjusted and readjusted their calendars so often that a precise measurement is impossible. But roughly ten thousand years before your time on Earth."

"From *our* time?" Josh said. "Not your time?"

"This is our time, Josh. Your world is just a shadow of this one."

"But you lived in our world also."

40

"We have lived in many worlds," Isis said, "and many times, too."

"Your mother is right," Osiris said. "We have walked between the worlds for millennia. Between us we have probably explored more of the Shadowrealms than any other Elders."

"So you're Elders?" Sophie asked.

"Yes, we are."

"And what does that make us?" Josh asked. "Are we Elders or Next Generation?"

"That remains to be seen," Osiris said. "At this particular point in time, there are no Next Generation. And if all goes according to plan, then there will be no Next Generation. They only arrived after the sinking of the island."

"All that matters is that you are here and that you have both been Awakened and trained in many of the Elemental Magics," Isis said.

The craft dipped and suddenly a vast circular, mazelike city appeared before and below them. Sunlight ran silver and gold off stretches of canals and waterways that ringed a huge pyramid at the center of the city. The streets were teeming with people, and the tops of scattered small pyramids blazed with fire from torches, while others were bright with flags. There seemed to be houses, palaces, temples and mansions in dozens of architectural styles. At the fringes of the city lay a vast warren of low tumbledown buildings.

"It's huge," Josh breathed.

"The largest city in the world," Osiris said proudly. "In fact, it is the center of the world."

Josh pointed toward the enormous pyramid the city was

41

obviously built around, and the sprawling palace that lay beyond. "Is that where we're going?"

"Not yet." Osiris smiled. "That is the royal Palace of the Sun, currently home to Aten, the ruler of Danu Talis."

"It looks busy . . . ," Josh began.

Isis suddenly sat forward and the vimana dipped sharply. "Husband!" she called, alarm clear in her tone.

Osiris spun around and leaned forward to stare at the pyramid. The air above the palace was busy with vimanas of all shapes and sizes, and lines of black-armored guards were taking up position on the ground. An enormous crowd milled in front of the building, and there were people streaming in from all the surrounding streets.

Isis glanced sidelong at Osiris. "Looks like something happened while we were away," she said quietly.

"Bastet!" he hissed. "I should have known she'd not leave well enough alone. Change of plans: take us down. We need to attend to this immediately."

"Down?" Isis said, even as the vimana's engine dulled to a low whine and the craft gently seesawed over a broad market square full of stalls bright with colored awnings. The space was thronged with short, squat, deeply tanned people, the majority of whom wore plain white woolen robes or white shirts and trousers. A few glanced at the vimana, but no one paid it any particular attention. Two anpu guards in leather armor, carrying shields and spears, came running toward the vimana, but when they saw who was aboard, they abruptly turned away and disappeared down a side street. Dust swirled as the craft settled in the center of the square.

"Virginia, I am leaving the twins in your care," Osiris said as the top of the craft peeled back.

"Mine!" Virginia Dare blinked surprise.

Osiris nodded. "Yours."

Isis swiveled around in her seat to look at Sophie and Josh. "Go with Virginia. Your father and I will be back soon, and then we'll have a family supper and catch up. We'll answer all your questions, I promise. There are great things in store for you. You will be recognized as Gold and Silver. You will be worshipped. You will rule. Go now, go."

The twins unstrapped from their seats and stepped out into the late-afternoon air. They breathed deeply, clearing their lungs of the dry, metallic ozone odor of the vimana. The market square was filled with a thousand strange and not entirely pleasant smells: fruit—some of it rotting—exotic spices and too many unwashed bodies crammed close together.

"Where are you going?" Virginia asked Osiris.

The Elder stopped in the vimana's doorway. "We have to get to the palace, and I don't want to bring the children into danger," he said. He pointed to where a gold spire rose over the rooftops. The spire was topped with a billowing flag, and stitched into it was what looked like an ornate eye. "That's our home. Go there. Wait for us." He looked around the square. Most of the stall holders had turned to gaze at the tall bald-headed man. Not all were able to conceal the expressions of loathing on their faces. Osiris took his time to look over the crowd. No one would meet his eyes. "No one will harm you," he said loudly, voice echoing across the square. "No one will even try. They know my vengeance would be terrible indeed." He leaned forward and rested a hand on Virginia's left shoulder. She immediately shrugged it off. "Protect my children, immortal," he said quietly. "If anything were to happen to them, I would not be pleased. Nor would you."

Virginia Dare stared into the Elder's blue eyes. He dropped his gaze first. "I don't like threats," she breathed.

"Oh, this is not a threat," he said softly. He stepped out of the vimana, and a low moan ran through the crowd. "Let it be known," he boomed, "that these three are under my protection. Assist them, guide them, protect them, and I will be bountiful. Hinder them, misdirect them, harm them, and you—all of you—will know my vengeance. This is my word, and you know my word is law."

"Your word is law," the crowd murmured. Some of the older men and women got down on hands and knees and pressed their foreheads to the stones paving the ground; some of the younger people only bowed their heads.

Osiris glared at a group of youths. "If I had more time, I would teach them a lesson for their insolence . . . ," he muttered. He stepped back into the vimana. "Go now. Do not delay. Head straight for the building with the pennant. We'll be back as quickly as possible."

The side of the Rukma vimana closed behind him and the craft hummed into the air, leaving Sophie, Josh and Virginia Dare standing alone in the center of the square. The vimana had barely disappeared over the rooftops when a tomato came sailing over the heads of the crowd and spattered onto the ground at Josh's feet. A second and a third followed.

44

"I'm glad to see Isis and Osiris really command the crowd's respect," Josh said.

"Let's go," Virginia called, catching them both by the arms and pulling them back. "It usually starts with fruit . . ."

A rock clattered off the ground and shattered.

". . . but it always ends with stones."

CHAPTER SEVEN

*C*olors.

Bright, brilliant colors . . .

Shimmering, dancing threads of iridescence . . .

Pulsating bands of light . . .

Nicholas rose over the pier, riding higher and higher on nearly invisible curling waves of air that spun and twisted beneath him. He looked down and saw the huddle of people below and recognized himself in the middle of the group.

He was flying.

And the feeling was extraordinary.

There had been a time when he had taken to the skies almost every day and seen the world through Pedro's eyes. He had never truly understood the lure of flight until he had soared over the island jungles of the Pacific, the winding, ruinous streets of Rome and Ireland's patchwork green fields and looked down through Pedro's huge eyes. Nicholas knew then why Leonardo da Vinci had invested so much time in creating machines that would allow man to fly. Maybe the rumors were true; maybe Leonardo had been immortal and had learned to see the world through a bird's eyes.

Although it was late afternoon and the light was fading, the world seen through the parrot's eyes was alive with vibrating flares and streamers of color. The Embarcadero blazed yellow and gold, sending lines of heat billowing out over the water.

Nicholas could feel the wind moving over his body, the whispering ripple of feathers flickering against one another. Years of flying with Pedro had taught him not to think, to simply focus on a destination and then allow the parrot's nature to take over. Below him, the water was cloudy with phosphorescent bubbles, alive with streaks of hot and cold channels.

Alcatraz was less than a mile from shore, which was no distance for wild parrots, but Flamel knew the bird would not be comfortable flying out over the water. Even the vague thought of land made the conure turn sharply and head back to the Embarcadero's blaze of lights. The parrot squawked, and the birds on the shore lining the roofs in washes of color screamed in welcome.

Nicholas visualized the distinctive shape of Alcatraz again and the bird swerved—almost reluctantly—and headed away from land. It rose higher, farther from the salt spray, allowing the Alchemyst to see the island clearly: a long, low, ugly shape topped by the white prison building with the tall finger of the lighthouse jutting into the sky. Behind him and to his right, the Bay Bridge was a ribbon of red and white streaks, while off in the distance, the Golden Gate Bridge was a horizontal smudge picked out in shimmering lines of heat and warm air.

In contrast, Alcatraz was in total darkness, and no heat radiated off the ground

As he got closer to the island, the Alchemyst realized that Perenelle had been right. There were no other birds in the air over the shores. The ever-present Western gulls that haunted the island's rocks, coating them in white, were missing, and as he coasted in closer, he realized that nothing was moving. There were no cormorants or pigeons. But Alcatraz was a bird sanctuary; hundreds of birds nested there every year.

Nicholas shuddered and felt the shudder ripple through the little bird's frame. Something had fed.

When it reached the rocky shoreline, the conure dipped and rose on air currents, then swooped in over the dock and dropped down to land on top of the map and guide stand. Nicholas let the bird rest for a moment. Hopping from foot to foot, it turned in a full circle, allowing him a complete view of the docks. They were deserted. Nor was there any sign of Black Hawk's boat. He took some consolation from the fact that he could see no wreckage, either, and he hoped the immortal hadn't fallen to the Nereids.

Nicholas urged the bird upward with a single thought and it flew in slow circles over the bookshop and Building 64. Going higher still took him over the ruined Warden's House, and for the first time since reaching the island, he spotted a low pulse of light. The conure landed on one of the metal beams that supported the ruined house, then sidled along the bar, claws scratching on the metal, and peered down. In the corner of the ruins, covering the tumbled walls and gaping floor, was an enormous mass. It looked like a ball of hardened mud. With the parrot's enhanced sight, Nicholas could just about make out a shape within the mud: a massive creature, tightly curled into a ball wrapped around with too many legs. It was a spider. It throbbed with a slow, regular light: Areop-Enap was still alive.

Yet where was everyone?

Black Hawk had dropped Mars, Odin and Hel on the island. They couldn't all be dead, could they? And where were the monsters? Perenelle had spotted boggarts, trolls and cluricauns in the cells. She'd seen a child minotaur, at least one Windigo and an oni. Another corridor held dragon-kin, wyverns and firedrakes.

The parrot was tiring now, and Nicholas knew he'd have to get it back to the mainland soon. He would have one quick look around and then head back before night fell. He circled the lighthouse, then, catching a sudden spark of light, soared over the prison building and dropped into the recreation yard.

The yard was awash with energy.

The ghostly remains of incredibly powerful auras snaked and coiled across the huge flagstones, writhing like serpents. There was pure gold and shining silver, the stinking yellow of sulfur and a thread of pale green scattered across the ground.

And in the center of the yard, there was the fading impression of a rectangle, shimmering with the remnants of ancient energies. The merest hint of the outlines of four swords was etched into the stones.

A door slammed open. The parrot started upward as light blazed, and Nicholas turned to see Odin race through a narrow doorway and down a flight of stone steps. The one-eyed Elder stopped at the bottom of the stairs and turned to face the way he had come, a short spear in either hand.

Mars appeared in the door and held it open, and then Machiavelli and Billy the Kid raced through, carrying Hel between them. The Elder's arms were draped over both immortals' shoulders, and her legs were dragging on the ground, trailing a dark liquid in their wake. Mars slammed the metal door shut and put his back to it. The warrior's black leather jacket hung in shreds, and the short sword in his hand dripped a bright blue liquid. Even in the gathering gloom, Nicholas could see that his eyes were bright with excitement. The door behind Mars shuddered in its frame, but the Elder braced himself and held it shut until Machiavelli and Billy had reached the end of the steps and Odin stepped out to protect their back.

The one-eyed Elder gestured to Mars and the big man launched himself away from the door—just as a spiky tusk burst through the metal and ripped upward, shredding it like paper.

Mars and Odin took up positions at the bottom of the steps, protecting Machiavelli and Billy, who were tending to Hel's wounds on the steps of the exercise yard. Billy had pulled off his belt and wrapped it around the Elder's torn legs, and his hands were dark with her blood.

Silent and invisible, the parrot circled overhead.

Nicholas tried to make sense of what he was seeing: Mars and Odin working together with Billy and Machiavelli, protecting them while the American worked on Hel's wounds. Nicholas was confused: the Italian was no friend to the Flamels or their cause and had fought on the side of the Dark Elders all his long life. Maybe Machiavelli had somehow tricked the others? The Alchemyst shook his head and the parrot mimicked the movement. Fooling Mars was a possibility; maybe Hel, too. But no one could fool Odin. Maybe Machiavelli and Billy had finally chosen the right side. What was it Shakespeare had said about misery making strange bedfellows?

It took an enormous effort of the Alchemyst's will to urge the parrot to drop lower. The bird's every instinct was to flee. The yard was now alive with buzzing colored auras, the stink of Elder blood and the stench of beasts.

The creature that filled the shattered doorway was huge. It looked like a boar, but it was the size of a bull and its tusks were the length of a man's arm.

"Hus Krommyon," Mars said. "The Crommyonian Boar. Not the original, of course. Theseus killed that one."

Odin's single eye blinked. "It's big," he muttered. "Strong."

The beast came slowly down the steps. It was so broad that its flanks rubbed against the wall on either side, coarse hair rasping against the stones.

"It will rush us," Mars warned.

"And we're not going to be able to stop it," Odin added. "I've hunted boar. It will attack with its head down and then rip upward. The muscles around its neck and shoulders are especially thick. I doubt our swords or spears will be able to do anything against it."

"And if we use our auras, that will draw the sphinx and she will feast off our energies," Mars said. He gently pushed Odin to one side. "Both of us do not have to die here. Let it charge me. I'll grab its head and hold on. You take it from the side with your spears. See if you can get in underneath. The flesh there is softer."

Odin nodded. "It's a good plan, except . . ."

"Except?"

"You will not be able to hold its head. It will gore you."

"Yes. Probably. And then you stab it."

"And you saw what it did to the metal door," Odin said quietly.

"I'm tough." Mars grinned.

"You're enjoying this, aren't you."

"I've spent millennia trapped within a hardened shell, unable to move." He flicked his wrist and spun the short sword. "I haven't had this much fun since . . . well . . . I can't remember."

The Hus Krommyon's hooves scrambled on the steps, striking sparks off the stones, and then it charged.

There was a sudden flash of green and red, and what appeared to be a small parrot darted in front of the beast, claws raking along its snout and up between its ears. The boar squealed, slowed and raised its head, jaws snapping, spraying thick saliva. The bird swooped in again, its powerful beak nipping a chunk out of the creature's hairy ear. The Hus Krommyon bellowed and reared up on its hind legs to snap and bite at the darting creature.

And Odin's spear took the monster through its exposed throat. It was dead before it hit the ground.

"Way to go!" Billy hollered.

"Billy, why don't you shout a little louder. I'm sure you can bring some more monsters down on us," Machiavelli said quietly.

The American punched his shoulder. "Sometimes you just have to loosen up and celebrate." He looked down at Hel. "Did you see the size of that thing!"

"I've seen bigger," she lisped.

The parrot flapped down to land on the Hus Krommyon's head. It tilted its tiny red head to one side, looking first at Mars and then Odin.

"Who are you, little bird?" Mars asked, and then his nostrils flared. "Mint." he said in astonishment. "Nicholas?"

The conure's beak opened and closed and then it squawked, "Flamel."

Mars saluted the little bird with his sword. "Alchemyst. It is good to . . . ahem . . . see you. We are alive, as you can see. Our numbers have swelled by two, but we are in dire straits. There are too many of them, far too many, and the sphinx is prowling." He stopped, then added, "I cannot believe I am giving a report to a parrot."

"Areop-Enap," the bird chirruped.

Mars looked at the one-eyed Elder. "Did it just say 'Areop-Enap'?"

The parrot danced from foot to foot. "Areop-Enap, Areop-Enap, Areop-Enap."

Odin nodded. "It said 'Areop-Enap.'"

"Where? Here?" Mars demanded.

The bird flew into the air and circled the two Elders. "Here, here, here."

"That's a yes," Odin said. "What an ally, if she'll fight with us." He clapped Mars on the back. "Go get the Old Spider. She can't be that hard to find. Let me tend to Hel's injuries." He grabbed the Hus Krommyon by one massive tusk and dragged it off the steps.

"What are you doing to do with that?"

"Hel isn't a vegetarian." Odin grinned. "And she loves pork."

"Raw?"

"Especially raw."

The Cherry-Headed Conure dropped out of the evening sky toward the Embarcadero, wings flapping tiredly, and alit on the Alchemyst's head. Its red head dipped and it tapped his skull with its closed beak.

Nicholas shuddered and drew in a deep breath, and Prometheus held him while he straightened and shook pins and needles from his fingertips. Then he lifted his right hand and the parrot hopped onto his fingers. "Thank you," he breathed. Mint-green mist smoked off the red and green feathers. The bird shivered and took to the air, calling, "Areop-Enap, Areop-Enap, Areop-Enap." Flamel's eyes followed its path into the evening sky.

"Within a couple of days every parrot on the Embarcadero will be screaming that," the Alchemyst said.

"Did you learn anything?" Perenelle asked.

Nicholas nodded. "The monsters are in the main cell block. I saw Mars, Odin and Hel. There was no sign of Black Hawk anywhere, and Hel is injured. But we seem to have two new allies: Machiavelli and Billy the Kid were helping her."

Perenelle blinked in surprise. "Machiavelli has been no friend of ours."

"I know that. But he is an opportunist. Perhaps he realizes that it would be better to throw in with the winning side."

"Or maybe he just rediscovered his humanity," Niten said quietly. "Maybe someone reminded him that he is human first, immortal second."

"You sound as if you are speaking from personal experience," Perenelle said.

"I am," he said softly. "There was a time when I was . . . wild."

"What happened?"

He smiled. "I met a redheaded Irish warrior."

"And fell in love?" she teased.

"I didn't say that."

"You didn't have to." She turned back to Nicholas. "And what of Dee?"

"That's the odd thing: I could smell his aura, but it was old and fading. And it was entwined with Sophie's vanilla and Josh's orange. There was the odor of sage, too. . . ."

"Virginia Dare," Perenelle said.

"They were all mixed up together, along with the energies from the four Swords of Power. But I don't think Dee's on the island anymore."

"Then where?" Niten asked.

The Alchemyst started to shake his head, then stopped. "There was the impression of the four Swords of Power on the ground," he said slowly. His hands described a square. "It looked like they were laid end to end, to create a rectangle."

"He's made a gate," Prometheus said. "I've never seen it done myself, though I know it is possible."

"A gate to where?" Nicholas asked. He looked at Perenelle and she shook her head.

"Nowhere in this world, that's for sure," Prometheus said. "In fact, I can almost guarantee it will open up somewhere on Danu Talis. Dee has taken the twins back in time."

CHAPTER EIGHT

So this was how it felt to die.

Dr. John Dee lay back on the silken grass and pulled the red fleece tightly around himself. He was cold, so, so cold, a profound chill that numbed his fingers and toes and settled deep in his stomach. There was a pain in his forehead, as if he'd eaten too much ice cream, and he could actually feel his heart beginning to slow, the beats becoming weak and irregular.

He'd rolled over onto his back, and although his vision was blurred, he could make out the impossibly bright blue of the sky, and out of the corners of his eyes, the grass was still a shocking green.

There were worse ways to go, he supposed.

He'd lived a tumultuous life in a series of dangerous times. He'd survived wars, plagues, court intrigues and betrayal after betrayal. He'd traveled the world, been to just about every country on earth—except Denmark, a place he'd always wanted to visit—and explored many of the vast network of Shadowrealms.

He'd made and lost fortunes and met with just about every leader, inventor, hero and villain to walk the planet. He'd advised kings and queens, fomented wars, brokered peace and been one of the handful of people who had nudged and urged the humani toward civilization. He had shaped the world, first in the Elizabethan Age and then on into the twenty-first century. That was something to be proud of.

He'd lived almost five hundred years in the Earth Shadow-realm, and at least that lifetime again in some of the other Shadowrealms. So he really didn't have too much to complain about. But there were still so many things he wanted to do, so many places he needed to visit, so many worlds still to explore.

He tried to raise his arms, but there was no feeling in them now. No feeling in his legs either, and his sight was beginning to dim. His Elder masters might have aged his body, but his brain was still as alert as ever. Perhaps that was their greatest cruelty. They had left him alert in this useless shell. He suddenly thought of Mars Ultor, trapped for millennia in his hardened aura deep beneath Paris, his body inert but his brain alive, and for the first time in centuries the English Magician experienced the alien emotion of pity.

Dee wondered how much longer he would survive.

Night would fall, and this was Danu Talis, a world where creatures long extinct in the Earth Shadowrealm and .

monsters drawn from the myriad other Shadowrealms wandered freely.

He didn't want to be eaten by monsters.

When he'd imagined his death—and he'd often thought of it, given the nature of what he did and the capricious humor of his employers—he'd always hoped it would be glorious. He wanted it to have meaning. It had always needled him that so much of his work had been done in secret and the world remained ignorant of his genius. During the Elizabethan Age, everyone had known his name. Even the Queen had feared and respected him. When he'd become immortal he had faded into the shadows, and he had lurked there ever since.

There was not a lot of meaning in lying shriveled and ancient on a Danu Talis hillside.

He heard movement, a dull thump. Close by. To his right.

Dee attempted to turn his head, but he could no longer move.

There was a shadow.

It was a monster, come to eat him.

So this was his destiny: to be eaten alive, alone and friendless. . . .

He attempted to call upon his aura. If he could just gather enough of it, maybe he could frighten the creature away. Or burn himself to a crisp in the process of trying. That wouldn't be so bad. At least he'd avoid being eaten.

The shadow moved closer.

But why would he want to frighten it away? It would only

return. He was merely delaying the inevitable. Better to surrender to it, to remember all the good things he had done during his long life . . . but there were few enough of those.

The shadow darkened.

And now that the end was upon him, old fears and almost forgotten doubts washed over him. He found himself humming a line from a song. "Regrets, I've had a few . . ." Well, he had more than a few. He could have—should have—been a better father to his children and a kinder husband to his wives. Perhaps he should not have been so greedy—not just for money, but for knowledge—and certainly he should never have accepted the gift, the curse, of immortality.

The realization struck him like a blow, making his breath catch in his chest. Immortality had doomed him.

The shadow stretched over him and he caught a glimpse of metal.

No animal, then. A human. A brigand. He wondered if there were cannibals on Danu Talis. "Make it quick," he whispered. "Give me that mercy."

"Was that a mercy you offered others?" Suddenly he was scooped up in strong arms. "I'll not kill you yet, Dr. Dee. I have use for you."

"Who are you?" Dee gasped, desperately trying to make out the face of the man towering over him.

"I am Marethyu. I am Death. But today, Doctor, I am your savior."

CHAPTER NINE

$\mathcal{I}$t was time for Aunt Agnes to die.

The old woman stood before the bathroom mirror and looked at her reflection. An elderly human stared back, a face that was all angles and planes, sharp cheekbones, jutting chin and pointed nose. Iron-gray hair was combed off her face and held in a tight bun at the nape of her neck. Slate-gray eyes were sunken deep in her head. She looked like an eighty-four-year-old woman. But she was Tsagaglalal, She Who Watches, and her age was beyond reckoning.

Tsagaglalal had adopted the Aunt Agnes disguise for most of the twentieth century. She'd grown fond of this body, and it would be a shame to let it go. But then, she had worn many guises over the millennia. The great trick was knowing when to move on, when to *die*.

Tsagaglalal had lived through ages when anyone who was different—in any way—was suspect. The humans had many wonderful characteristics, but they had always been and would continue to be suspicious and fearful of those who stood out from the crowd. Even in the best of times, they were constantly alert for something wrong, or on the lookout for someone who seemed a little out of the ordinary. And there had been a time when a person who remained far too young-looking was always going to be suspect.

Tsagaglalal had lived during the decades when men and women were burned as witches simply for looking odd or being outspoken and independent. But long before those terrible years in Europe, and later, briefly, in America, she had learned that if she was to survive, she had to blend in, to be such a part of the humans that she became invisible.

Tsagaglalal learned to age appropriately.

Every century had a different perception of what was right and proper. There were eras when thirty was old and forty was ancient. In some of the more primitive and isolated cultures, in which old age was revered as a sign of wisdom, she could become sixty or seventy before she "died" and moved on.

And when she aged, she did it completely, altering her skin texture, her posture, even her muscle mass, to mimic the passage of time. Generations ago—in Egypt, or was it Babylon?—she had perfected the technique of making her knuckles, wrists and knees swell to indicate arthritis. Later she'd learned to adjust her flesh so that her veins stood out thick and blue against paper-thin skin. She'd mastered techniques that turned the skin of her neck soft and loose and even managed to yellow her teeth. To complete the illusion, she had deliberately allowed her hearing to dull and her eyesight to fade. She *became* old, and therefore did not spend every waking moment pretending. It was safer that way.

Staring at her reflection in the bathroom mirror, Tsagaglalal lifted her hands to her head, fiddled with the antique pins that held her bun in place and shook loose her gray hair.

The latter half of the twentieth century had been the easiest to live in. This was the era of cosmetics and plastic surgery. This was the era when people worked hard *not* to age, when movie and pop stars looked younger with the passing years.

Tsagaglalal pushed upward and the wig came off her head. She dropped the mess of gray hair into the bath and ran her hands vigorously across her smooth skull. She hated the wig; it always itched.

There were dangers particular to this century, of course. This was the age of the camera—personal cameras, street cameras, security cameras, and now most cell phones had cameras too. This was also the age of photo identification: passports, driver's licenses, identity cards. Everything had a photo, and the immortal in those photos had to change, to subtly alter and age. A mistake brought attention from the authorities, and immortals were particularly vulnerable to any investigation that questioned their past. Tsagaglalal hadn't left the country in decades and her American passport had lapsed. However, there was an immortal human working in New York who had once specialized in forged Renaissance masterpieces. He had a little sideline business in forged pass-ports and driver's licenses. She'd need to visit him when this was over. If she survived.

Tsagaglalal ran the tap hot, then cold, and filled the sink. Bending her head, she scooped water into her hands and washed her face with L'Occitane Shea Butter Soap, wiping away the makeup she'd put on for the gathering of immortals and Elders who'd picnicked in her backyard earlier that day.

Dying was always the hard part. There was always so much to do in the weeks and months leading up to dying: making sure all the bills were paid and the life insurance was up to date, canceling any newspaper and magazine subscrip-tions and, of course, making a will leaving everything to a "relative." Male immortals usually bequeathed everything to a nephew, female immortals to a niece. Others, like Dr. John Dee, willed everything to a series of corporations, and Tsaga-glalal knew that Machiavelli had left all his worldly goods to his "son." The Flamels willed everything to one another and a nephew named Perrier, whom she doubted had ever ex-isted.

Tsagaglalal looked into the mirror again. Without hair and with her face wiped clean of makeup, she thought she looked even older than usual. Leaning closer to the glass, she allowed a little of her rarely used aura to blossom deep in her chest. The faintest hint of jasmine filled the small bathroom, mingling with the rich warmth of the shea butter. Heat flowed up her body, across her neck and into her face. She stared at her gray eyes. The sclera—the whites of her eyes—were yel-low, threaded with veins, the right eye slightly milky with the hint of a cataract. She'd always thought that was a really nice touch.

The scent of jasmine strengthened. Heat flowed into Tsagaglalal's throat and mouth, up across her cheeks and into her eyes: and the sclera turned white.

The woman breathed in, filling her lungs, then holding her breath. The skin of her face rippled and smoothed, soft plump flesh flowing along the hard bony lines of her cheeks, filling out her nose, rounding out her chin. Lines vanished, crow's-feet filled in, the deep bruise-colored shadows beneath her eyes disappeared.

Tsagaglalal was immortal, but she was not human. She was clay. She had been born in the Nameless City on the edge of the world when Prometheus's fiery aura had imbued ancient clay statues with life and consciousness. Deep within her she carried a tiny portion of the Elder's aura: it kept her alive. She and her brother, Gilgamesh, were the first of the First People to be born or achieve a consciousness. Every time she renewed herself, she could remember with absolute clarity the moment she had opened her eyes and drawn her first breath.

She laughed. It began as the cracked cough of an elderly woman and ended with the high pure sound of a much younger person.

Powered by her aura, the transformation continued. Flesh tightened, bones straightened, teeth whitened, hearing and sight grew sharp once more. A thin fuzz of jet-black hair pushed through her scalp, then thickened and streamed past her shoulders. She opened and closed her hands, wriggled her fingers and rotated her wrists. Placing her hands on her hips, she twisted her body from side to side, then bent at the waist and touched the floor with the palms of her hands.

Standing before the mirror, Tsagaglalal watched age fall away from her body, saw herself grow young and beautiful again. She had forgotten what it was like to be young, and it had been a long time since she'd been beautiful. The last time she looked like this was the day when Danu Talis had fallen ten thousand years ago.

And if the world was going to end today, she was determined not to spend her last few hours on earth as an old woman.

Tsagaglalal made her way down the hall to the tiny spare bedroom at the back of the house on Scott Street. She strode swiftly and easily, delighting in her new freedom of movement. She twirled in the center of the landing purely for the joy of being able to spin.

Almost from the moment she'd bought the house, the spare bedroom had been used for storage. It was stuffed with a hundred years of clutter: suitcases, books, magazines, bits of furniture, a cracked leather chair, an ornamental writing desk and a dozen black plastic sacks stuffed with old clothes that she'd once thought about dumping until she'd realized they'd become fashionable again. There was an antique American flag with a circle of stars on it alongside a framed original *King Kong* movie poster signed by Edgar Wallace. At the back of the room, tucked away in a corner, half buried behind a stack of yellow-spined National Geographic magazines, was a hideous eighteenth-century Louis XV cherrywood armoire.

Tsagaglalal pushed her way through the room and heaved stacks of magazines aside to get to the wardrobe. The armoire's door was locked and there was no key in the scrolled metal keyhole. Standing on her toes, Tsagaglalal reached over the door behind an ornamental curl of wood and her questing fingers found the large brass key hung on a bent nail. Lifting the key off the nail, she experienced a sudden wash of memories: the last time she'd opened this armoire was when she'd returned from Berlin at the end of the Second World War. There was a sudden prickle of tears at the backs of her eyes, a burning in her throat. On the way back to New York, she had stopped in London and met with her brother, Gilgamesh. He'd had no idea who she was, didn't even remember that he had a sister, though he had recognized that he should know her. She had sat with him in the ruins of a bombed-out house in the East End of London and gone through the tens of thousands of papers he was storing there. They had spent the afternoon working backward, going from paper to parchment, then vellum, and finally on to bark and wafer-thin sheets of almost transparent gold, until she was able to point out her name written in a script and language still undiscovered by the humans. They had wept together as she reminded him of all they had once been. "I will never forget you," he said as she'd stood to leave. She watched him scribble her name on his scraps of paper but knew that he would not be able to recall her face or name within the hour. Tsagaglalal was cursed with a memory that forgot nothing; Gilgamesh was doomed never to remember.

Fitting the key in the lock, she opened the armoire door.

There was a wash of musty stale air, a hint of old leather, bitter spices, the whiff of long-withered mothballs and the merest suggestion of jasmine.

A nurse's uniform was on a hanger facing Tsagaglalal and she reached out to touch it, running her fingers across the thin cloth. The memories it evoked left her shaking. She'd been a nurse in both of the great wars, and in just about every war for the previous hundred years. She was one of the thirty-eight volunteers who had nursed with Florence Nightingale in the Scutari barracks in the Crimea. Tsagaglalal had seen—and caused—so much death over the centuries; serving as a nurse had been her small way of trying to repair all the hurt she had done.

Behind the uniform were the clothes of half a dozen centuries: costumes in leather and linen, silk and synthetics, fur and wool. Here were the shoes given to her by Marie Antoinette, the pearl-strewn dress she'd sewn for Catherine the Great of Russia, the bodice Anne Boleyn had worn the day she'd married Henry. Lifetimes of memories. Tsagaglalal smiled, showing perfect teeth. Museums and collectors would pay a fortune for these clothes.

At the back of the wardrobe was a thick burlap bag.

Effortlessly Tsagaglalal hauled out the sack and dragged it from the spare room into her own bedroom. She heaved it up onto the bed and tugged at the leather drawstring. It resisted for a moment; then the ancient leather snapped and crumbled to dust and the bag fell open.

Reaching in, Tsagaglalal lifted out a suit of white ceramic armor and laid it on the bed. Elegant yet unadorned, it had been designed to fit her body like a second skin. She ran her fingers across the smooth breastplate. The armor was pristine, gleaming as if it were new. The last time she'd worn it, it had been slashed and scored by metal and claws, but the armor could heal and repair itself. "Magic?" she'd asked her husband, Abraham.

"Earthlord technology," he'd explained. "We will not see its like again for millennia, or hopefully, never."

At the bottom of the bag, she found two ornate wood and leather scabbards. They each held a metal kopesh, the curved sickle-like sword favored by the Egyptians, though its origins were much older. She pulled one of the kopesh from its sheath. The blade was so sharp it whistled as she moved it through the air.

Tsagaglalal ran smooth white-nailed fingers across the featureless armor. Ten thousand years ago, her husband, Abraham the Mage, had presented her with the weapons and armor. "To keep you safe," he said, his speech a slurred mumble. "Now and always. When you wear it, think of me."

"I'll think of you even when I'm not wearing it," she promised, and never a day went by when she did not think of the man who had worked so hard and sacrificed so much to make and save the world.

The memory of him was vivid.

Abraham stood tall and slender in a darkened room at the top of the crystal tower, the Tor Ri. He was wrapped in shadow, turned away from her so she wouldn't see the Change that had almost completely claimed his flesh, transforming it to solid gold. She remembered turning him to the light so she could look at him for what she knew might be the very last time. Then she had held him, pressing his flesh and metal against her skin, and wept against his shoulder. And when she looked into his face, a single tear, a solid bead of gold, rolled down his cheek. Rising up on her toes, she had kissed the tear off his face, swallowing it. Tsagaglalal pressed her hands to her stomach. It nestled within her still.

She Who Watches had worn the white armor on the last day of Danu Talis. It was time to wear it again.

CHAPTER TEN

*E*vening fell and fog crept into San Francisco.

A few coiling wisps drifted in off the bay. They rolled along the surface of the water like threads of steam, then vanished. A few minutes later the fog reappeared, denser now, semitransparent gray-white bands rippling across the water.

The fog thickened.

A foghorn bellowed.

An opaque cloud bank gathered out over the Pacific, dark—almost black—at the bottom, then visibly raced toward land in a solid wall of mist. The thick advection fog boiled over the land, flowed under the Golden Gate Bridge, then blossomed to swallow it, rising higher and higher, until the amber lights along the towers faded to tiny spots of color. The flashing red beacons atop the towers, almost seven hundred and fifty feet above the water, briefly lit up the fog with

71

bloodred splashes, but they too faded to dull smudges. And as the fog coalesced, the lights completely disappeared.

Street and house lights came on. For a short while, the red and white lights of cars illuminated the fog and the buildings seemed to pulse and glow. The fog continued to grow and darken, dulling the lights, blanketing them, robbing them of all luster. It took less than thirty minutes—from the time the first wisps swirled across the bay to the arrival of the impenetrable fog bank—for visibility to drop from tens of yards to little more than a few feet.

Sounds grew muffled, and slowly, the entire city fell silent. Only the moan of the foghorn remained, and it was a forlorn, lonely voice.

The fog did not smell of sea and salt—it stank with the odor of something long dead and rotting.

CHAPTER ELEVEN

Sophie screamed.

A stocky, dark-skinned man in a filthy white robe darted out of an alleyway and grabbed a handful of hair, jerking her backward, almost pulling her off her feet. Sophie's Tae Kwan Do training took over. She grabbed the hand, gripping it tighter, locking it in place, then shifted her weight, spun her body ninety degrees and snapped out her right leg in a *yeop chagi*—a thrusting side kick. The heel of her heavy hiking boot caught her assailant on the kneecap with devastating force.

The attacker's eyes bulged; his wide mouth opened and closed, revealing rotten teeth, but before he could draw breath to scream, Josh darted in, punching hard with a four-knuckle strike. He caught the man in the center of the chest and, as the man folded forward, brought a hammer fist down on the back of his head, driving him to the ground.

"Okay, that's impressive," Virginia Dare murmured. "I'm not sure you two need my protection."

Josh looked at Sophie. "Are you okay?"

Gingerly, she ran a shaking hand across the top of her head where she'd been grabbed. Strands of blond hair came away on her fingers. "Looks like all those years of martial arts training weren't entirely wasted." She smiled shyly. "Thank you for . . . well, you know, rescuing me."

Josh waved a hand. "You didn't need it. The kick was enough, but I wasn't going to let anyone lay a finger on my sister."

"Thank you," she said again.

"Always said I'd protect you," he said, a touch of color on his cheeks.

"Yes, you did. But the last time I saw you . . ."

His color darkened and he shrugged uncomfortably. "I know." The last time he'd seen his sister, he'd watched her savagely attack the beautiful Coatlicue. He'd turned and run from her in horror. He shook his head. "I still don't know what to think. . . ."

Sophie let out a deep breath. "I know. Neither do I."

"But here—in this place—it's just you and me, Sis."

"It's always been just you and me," she reminded him. "Even growing up on Earth . . . back home . . . wherever that is, it was always you and me against the world."

"I know." Then Josh suddenly grinned and Sophie was reminded of the brother she'd always known. "And now it's literally you and me against the world."

She nodded. "It's good to see you again, Josh."

"You too," he said.

"I've been so worried about you."

"Things have been . . ." He paused, hunting for the right word.

"Crazy?" Sophie suggested.

He nodded. "There has to be a better word, though. Crazy doesn't even come close."

"This is all very heartwarming," Virginia said. "But can I suggest we have this conversation later?" She nudged the fallen man with the toe of her boot. He groaned. "It's clear these people are no fans of your parents. And this sorry fellow is sure to have friends."

Sophie looked at her brother. "Are they our parents?" she asked.

"I know. They look like Mom and Dad . . . but . . ."

She nodded. "But they're not Mom and Dad."

"Then who are they?" her brother asked.

Sophie shook her head. "I think the more important question is: who are we?"

"And as Osiris said: that remains to be seen," Josh said.

CHAPTER TWELVE

Virginia Dare and the twins hurried through the streets of Danu Talis. White robes taken from washing lines covered their clothes, and their heads were concealed beneath conical straw hats they'd snatched from a stall in the market. They kept to the back alleys and side streets, moving slowly toward the spire with the flapping pennant.

"You know," Josh said, "for what's supposed to be the most powerful and beautiful city in the world, it looks a bit shabby."

Sophie nodded. "When we were flying over it, it looked amazing, though."

"Distance makes everything beautiful," Virginia murmured. She stopped at the mouth of a narrow alley and stared at the rooftops, trying to orient herself, straining to find the flag over the tops of buildings.

Sophie turned and looked back down the alleyway to see if they were being followed. The only movement was a rail-thin dog rooting in a pile of refuse. It pulled out what might have been a hunk of meat and looked up at her, eyes winking red in the gloom, then turned and slunk away.

Since leaving the market square, they had run through a dozen alleys identical to the one where they stood. Flanked on either side by tall featureless walls, it was narrow and dark, strewn with rotting fruit and buzzing with flies. Sophie spotted a long-tailed rat scurrying in the gutter and watched it disappear into a hole in the wall. There would always be rats and flies, she guessed. She and Josh had traveled the world with their parents, visiting wherever Richard and Sarah Newman were working. She had seen alleys like this in South America and the Middle East, in southern Europe and across Asia—though unlike those, this alley had no paper or plastic rubbish, no scraps of wood or discarded aluminum cans.

Sophie turned and looked over her brother's shoulder. The contrast was startling. Behind her was dirt and poverty; before her lay wealth and the magical Danu Talis of legend. The alleyway opened onto a broad tree-lined boulevard. On the other side of the street was one of the canals she'd spotted from the air. Across the canal were more tree- and flower-lined streets, inset with fountains, dotted with statues of men and beasts and creatures that were neither one nor the other. Ornate buildings painted gold and silver sat behind spike-tipped walls and carved stone gates. Each building was a different architectural style, and she caught glimpses of flat-topped pyramids and windowless squares, delicate twisting spirals and crystal-wrapped circles.

"Recognize them?" Josh asked.

And she did. She suddenly realized that the buildings resembled ruins she'd visited with her parents: here were echoes of Egypt, Chaco Canyon, Angkor Wat and Scotland.

He saw recognition in her eyes. "I'm guessing these are the originals. Humans copied the designs."

"Why the different shapes?" Sophie asked.

"Different clans?" Josh suggested.

"When Elders age, they Change," Virginia said. "Sometimes in odd and unusual ways. They need odd and unusual buildings to live in."

Some of the buildings bore carvings or murals; others were daubed with paint or hung with pennants and flags. A few—mainly the flat-topped pyramid shapes—were unadorned.

"I think we're looking at the better part of town," Virginia said with a grim smile. "And like rich communities everywhere, it's full of gates and guards. Some things never change."

"Guards? Where?" Sophie asked.

Josh pointed. "Just inside the gates . . ."

She nodded, suddenly spotting them. There were little guard posts inside the gates of the mansions and palaces. Within the guardhouses figures moved in the shadows, keeping out of the blistering sun. "I think there are more guardhouses on the other side of the bridge," she said.

"I believe they are," Virginia said. "And I have a theory."

She stepped out of the alleyway and strode across the empty boulevard toward the nearest bridge. "Let us test it."

The twins looked at one another and hurried after her.

"A theory?" Josh asked.

"It is clear that this Danu Talis is just like every other civilization I've encountered." The immortal's thin lips twisted when she said *civilization,* as if she found the word distasteful.

There was a sudden flurry of movement in the narrow huts on either side of the bridge, and shapes appeared. Sunlight winked off metal.

"I was right," Sophie said. "Guardhouses."

"With guards," Josh added nervously.

"I was born in a simpler time," Virginia continued. "I ran free in the forest, living off nature, killing only what I needed, sharing what I left with the other forest dwellers. I had no money, and my only possessions were the clothes I wore on my back. I lived in treetops and caves. And I was happy, truly happy. I wanted for nothing. And then I came to civilization."

The immortal walked along the edge of the curved canal toward the bridge. The guards kept pace with her across the glassy water; others gathered at the bridge, and it was clear now that they were not human. They had the heads of jackals and were clad in semitransparent black armor. When they looked across the canal, their eyes were a solid bloodred.

"Anpu," Sophie breathed.

Virginia stopped at the edge of the bridge. "And what lessons had civilization for me?" she continued. "I learned that it ruled by creating classes and dividing people, by making some better than others."

"Hasn't it always been that way?" Josh asked. "Every civilization is divided. . . ."

"Not every civilization," Virginia snapped. "Only the so-called advanced ones." She stepped onto the bridge and the anpu took up position at the far end.

One was bigger than the rest. He wore black armor polished to mirror brightness. He stepped forward and held out his right hand. It took the three humans a moment to realize that the creature wasn't actually wearing a metal glove. His hand had been replaced by a construction of metal and gears. A kopesh dangled loosely in his left hand.

"And here we have this great civilization of Danu Talis," Virginia continued bitterly, "ruled by a collection of immortal Great Elders and Elders . . . and what do we find?" Without waiting for an answer, she continued. "We find that nothing is different. The poor live beyond the outer canals, the rich live safe within the inner circles, protected by bridges guarded by dog-headed monsters. The poor cannot even walk these streets. I guess they must be paved with gold."

"Actually, I think they are," Josh murmured. The flagstones and pavements on the other side of the canal shimmered with liquid golden light.

Virginia Dare ignored him. She walked down the center of the bridge and all the guards pulled out their curved swords. "Is it any wonder that the world we lived in was such a mess?" She spread her arms wide. "This is what it came from. The humani modeled more than their buildings on this place. The human world was doomed from the very beginning. When I have my world to rule, things will be very different, I promise you."

"They've got swords, Virginia," Josh said.

"So they have," she answered lightly.

Guards were streaming left and right along the canal banks, racing in to support those already in position on the bridge.

"So how many guards do you need to protect the precious streets of gold from a woman and two teenagers?" Virginia asked.

Josh did a quick head count. "Thirty."

"Thirty-two," Sophie said.

Virginia had reached the midpoint. The anpu were spread out, all with weapons drawn. Muzzles gaped, revealing ragged teeth, making it appear as if the creatures were grinning. The leader tapped his kopesh against his metal claw. The sound rang like a bell.

Virginia continued marching straight ahead. "And do you know what I despise more than anything else?" she snapped. "Bullies. Especially bullies who think a fancy sword and a suit of armor make them invulnerable." Reaching under the billowing white robe, Virginia lifted her flute off her back. She shook it out of its cloth case and pressed it to her lips.

She blew a single note. The sound started high and climbed until even Sophie and Josh with their enhanced hearing could no longer make it out. The effect on the anpu was immediate. They stiffened, jerked upright as if they were pulled on strings, arms wide on either side, fingers spread. Kopesh dropped rattling to the stones.

Virginia's delicate fingers moved swiftly across the flute and the anpu danced. The creatures rose up on their toes and staggered left and right, crashing into each other, armor clashing and ringing. The immortal laughed, the sound high-pitched, uncomfortably close to hysterical. "I think I will dance them all right into the canal."

"Virginia," Sophie snapped. "No!"

With the flute still pressed to her lips, the immortal turned to look at the girl.

"No!"

"No? It's what I usually do."

"It's not necessary," Sophie said. "Kill them and you become just like them. And you aren't like them, are you?"

"You have no idea what I am," Virginia whispered, but she lifted her fingers off the flute.

The anpu fell as if they had been struck, crashing to the bridge in a clatter of armor and metal. The huge leader's metal hand scraped and twitched against the stones, scoring deep grooves in the soft rock, then stiffened and fell still.

Virginia picked her way through the fallen anpu, taking care not to touch any of them. Sophie and Josh followed her example. Close up the creatures were terrifying. Their jet-black bodies were human, corded with muscle, but from the neck up, they had the pointy-eared heads of jackals. Their hands were human, though tipped with curved claws, and their feet were dogs' paws. Some had bushy tails curling from the backs of their armor, and most had tiny green and gold scarabs or what looked like cowry shells woven into their fur.

"This way, I believe," Virginia said, pointing with her flute to an enormous circular building topped by a spire flying a narrow pennant with an eye on it. The flapping eye looked like it was winking. The outer windowless walls were sheeted in gold and decorated with constellations picked out in precious stones. The building was protected by a narrow moat filled with bubbling grass-green liquid, and a pair of enormous albino anpu carrying spears taller than they were stood on either side of the drawbridge.

Virginia smiled at the creatures and twirled her flute, leaving a shimmering note hanging in the air. The creatures dropped their spears, lowered the bridge and then turned and scampered on all fours into a low hutch hidden in the undergrowth. Bloodred eyes regarded the immortal with something like awe as she passed by.

"It is better to be feared than loved," Virginia said lightly. "I believe Machiavelli said that."

CHAPTER THIRTEEN

"*O*h man, I am never—and I mean *never*—eating meat again." Billy the Kid turned away from the sight of the wounded Hel ripping into the enormous boar's carcass.

"Humans were never meant to be vegetarian," Hel bubbled, her face and fangs black with fluids.

"You're not human," Billy said, still facing the other direction.

"It is good for me. It will restore my aura. It will help me heal." There was a snap like breaking wood, followed by a sucking sound.

Billy looked up at Machiavelli. "Whatever you do, do not tell me what she's doing right now."

The Italian immortal shook his head. "She has a healthy appetite, I'll give her that," he said, then added with a sly grin, "and the marrow is particularly nutritious!"

Billy stepped away from the stink of the butchered hog and breathed great gulps of the cold night air. A thick fog had started to roll in, flowing over the prison walls like smoke, and the temperature was falling fast.

"I did not think you would be so squeamish," Machiavelli said, joining him. "I thought you were a great American hero, fearless and brave."

Billy rolled his eyes. "You've been watching too many of my movies. Always felt I should have earned royalties from them. Didn't seem fair that they were using my name and not paying me."

"Billy, you're supposed to be dead."

"I know." Something liquid popped behind him and he jumped and pressed both hands to his mouth. "I'm not squeamish." Billy's every word plumed on the air like smoke. "I've hunted buffalo, butchered my share of steers, and killed chickens and hogs for the table. I've caught and gutted fish. But I liked to *cook* my meat before I eat it!" He glanced back over his shoulder to where Hel lay on the steps of the exercise yard feasting off the remains of the Hus Krommyon. Odin sat beside her, feeding her tidbits.

Mars Ultor had taken up a position at the ruined doorway, driving away any creatures that came too close. From within the prison something that had never been human giggled with the voice of a little girl.

Hel saw Billy looking, and her smile was appalling. She offered him something glistening wet. "I saved this for you. A special treat," she lisped.

"I'll pass. Thanks. I ate something just before we came out. And besides, I'm on a diet. And I'm vegetarian. Vegan, even."

Machiavelli caught Billy's arm and eased him out into the center of the exercise yard. He pointed to the tracery of lines on the flagstones. "What do you smell?" he asked.

"You mean besides the butchered—"

"Focus, Billy."

The American immortal breathed in. "Salt air . . ."

"More."

"Oranges, vanilla, sulfur and . . ." He took another deep breath. "And sage. That's my girl, Virginia," he added.

"The sulfur is Dee." Machiavelli traced the outline of a rectangle with the toe of his scuffed boot. "And the twins of legend were here also."

"Where are they now?"

"Gone."

"Gone?"

"I believe Dee activated the four ancient Swords of Power to create a leygate to go back in time."

"How far back?" Billy wondered aloud.

"All the way," the Italian said grimly. "If I were a gambling man, which I am not, I'd say he's gone back to Danu Talis."

Billy wrapped his arms around his body and shivered. "I'm guessing that's not good."

Machiavelli shook his head. "No. No doubt he has some master plan to take over Danu Talis and rule the world. The doctor was always coming up with mad schemes like that. He always played by his own rules."

"I figured."

"And he's usually been wrong. Dee has an overinflated impression of his own importance. The doctor *is* intelligent, but he's survived because he was cunning rather than clever. And he's always been lucky."

"You can't be lucky all the time," Billy said. "Sooner or later your luck runs out." He jerked his thumb over his shoulder, toward the monster-filled jailhouse. "Maybe ours has. We're trapped on a island filled with monsters and"—he lowered his voice and nodded toward Hel and Odin—"until a few hours ago, they were our enemies."

"The enemy of my enemy is my friend," Machiavelli reminded him.

"Yes, and the enemy of my enemy can still be my enemy. And I should remind you that most people are killed by someone they know. I learned that the hard way—I knew Pat Garrett."

The Italian put his hands on Billy's shoulders and looked into his eyes. The roiling milky fog turned his gray eyes to alabaster, making him look blind. "Did we make the right decision to try to prevent Dee from loosing the monsters onto the city?" he demanded.

"Absolutely," Billy said without hesitation.

"Did we make the right decision to stand and fight with these Elders against the monsters?"

"Yes, without a doubt," Billy said again.

"Consider this." Machiavelli smiled. "What would have happened if you and I had chosen to stand with Dee and the monsters?"

Billy's expression went blank. "I don't really know."

"Dee and Dare would still be gone, and we would have been left on the island to face Mars, Odin and Hel. And while you may be a good fighter, Billy, I am not. How long do you think we would have survived against any of those three?"

"Well, I think I could have taken the one-eyed guy. . . ."

Machiavelli sighed. "The one-eyed guy is Odin."

Billy looked at him blankly.

"You must have had a dog when you were growing up?" the Italian asked.

"Sure."

"What did you call it?"

"Kid."

"You called your dog Kid?"

Billy grinned. "That was before I got my nickname."

Machiavelli nodded. "Odin—the one-eyed guy—keeps two wolves. Geri and Freki."

"Good names. Strong."

"The words mean 'ravenous' and 'greedy'—and their names are perfect descriptions for them. They are as big as small donkeys. He walks them on a single leash."

Billy turned to look at the man with the patch over his right eye. "Did he lose the eye in a fight?"

Machiavelli shook his head. "No. He plucked it out himself. Used it to pay off a giant. Do you still think you could take him?"

"Maybe not."

The Italian pointed toward the doorway with his chin. "And how long do you think you could stand against the ultimate warrior, Mars Ultor?"

Billy flattened his right hand, palm down, and rocked it from side to side.

"Or Hel, who rules a kingdom of the dead?"

"Not long," Billy admitted.

"Not long," Machiavelli agreed. He leaned forward and pressed his mouth close to the American's ear. "And remember, Hel isn't fussy about the type of meat she eats."

Billy swallowed hard. His eyes flickered toward the remains of the hog.

"That could just as easily be you," Machiavelli said.

"You really like telling me all this stuff, don't you?"

"It's educational."

"Okay then, mister educator, master strategist. Tell me how we're going to get off this island."

Machiavelli started to shake his head once again, when abruptly the fog shifted and swirled between the two men as if blown by a strong wind. But there was no breeze in the prison yard. Water droplets hung suspended in the air. They coalesced, running together to form larger beads of moisture.

And suddenly the outline of a head formed in midair.

A face appeared: it was long and narrow and had once been handsome. There were two holes where the eyes should have been, another in place of the mouth. Then the fog thickened and the water droplets turned white and became hair, and the face took on form and substance. The hint of clothing appeared: a loose white linen shirt tucked into knee-length trousers. The legs disappeared just below the knee, and there were no visible feet.

"Ghost . . . ," Billy squeaked.

The ghost's mouth moved, opening and closing, and then the voice became audible. It was a thread, a series of bursting bubbles of water splashes. *"I am Juan Manuel de Ayala. I discovered Alcatraz."*

"An honor to meet you." Machiavelli bowed and tapped Billy with his foot.

Billy nodded quickly. "An honor. Sure."

"You fight with the Sorceress, Perenelle Flamel?" the ghost asked.

"We fight the same enemy," Machiavelli said carefully.

"Then we have a common cause," the ghost said. *"Follow me."*

CHAPTER FOURTEEN

*P*rometheus raised a metal-gloved hand. "Hang on. We're just about to reach the zenith of our glide."

The crippled Rukma vimana hung suspended in the air for a single moment. There was a sudden lurch. Simultaneously, all the darkened screens cracked and shattered, metal floor plates shivered loose, screws and bolts ricocheting off the walls, and a tiny fire began in the controls under Prometheus's feet. He stamped it out.

"And now we fall."

The Rukma vimana plunged downward. William Shakespeare turned a surprisingly high-pitched scream into a cough.

The dark-skinned Saracen Knight reached out to pat his arm. "I am sure that the man who wrote so much about death must have thought about it a lot. You've written about dying, Will," Palamedes said.

"Lots," Shakespeare said, his voice a little uneven. "But

not so much about falling, tumbling and crashing in a ball of fire."

"I doubt there'll be fire," Prometheus said.

"That's comforting. So just the falling, tumbling and crashing bit."

Joan of Arc leaned forward. "I have always liked your line *For in that sleep of death what dreams may come* . . . Very poetic. It's a very French sentiment. I'm surprised it was written by an Englishman," she added with a little smile.

"*Hamlet,*" Will said, smiling weakly. "One of my favorites."

Palamedes grinned, teeth white against his dark face. "But what about: *Woe, destruction, ruin, and decay; the worst is death, and death will have his day.*"

"From *Richard II,*" Shakespeare said. "Trust you to think of that one. A great line, even if I did write it myself."

Saint-Germain crossed his legs. "I must admit I have always been partial to *King John: Death, death; O amiable, lovely death! . . . Come, grin on me, and I will think thou smilest.*" He glanced over at his wife. "Another very French sentiment, don't you think?"

"Very. Will, you must have French blood in you somewhere," she insisted.

The Bard folded his hands in his lap and nodded affably. Like most writers, he loved talking about his work, and he'd perked up noticeably at the subject. "Well, I did live with a family of French Huguenots in Cripplegate in London for a while."

"A French influence. I knew it!" Joan said, clapping her hands.

"Have you all quite finished with the death quotes?" Scathach snapped.

"Oh, I've got more," Shakespeare offered.

"Enough already!" Scathach closed her eyes and breathed deeply. She'd once been told she was going to die in an exotic location, and she guessed it didn't get much more exotic than in a vimana above the legendary isle of Danu Talis.

Dying did not frighten her—she'd spent her entire life as a warrior. There was always the expectation of death, and over the millennia, she'd come close on more than one occasion. Her only regret was that she would not be able to see her sister again. Aoife had sacrificed her life to keep the appalling Coatlicue from this Shadowrealm and from Scathach. And now Aoife was trapped in Coatlicue's lightless world, doomed to an eternity of suffering unless she was rescued. Yet who would rescue her? Who would be foolhardy—or brave—enough to venture into Coatlicue's realm? Scathach had sworn that she would rescue her sister, and now it looked like she would not be able to keep that promise.

"Uncle, you don't seem too concerned about our imminent death," she said to Prometheus.

"For the final time, girl, I am not your uncle," the red-haired Elder snapped.

"Not yet," the Shadow snapped back. "But for the hundredth time, you will be. Now—are we going to crash and die?"

"Crash, yes. Die? Maybe. It depends on whether my calculations were correct."

Scathach pushed herself from her seat and staggered to a cracked porthole.

They were racing directly toward a forest. Scathach shook her head. That was not possible. They had risen too high, and hadn't fallen far enough or long enough—how could there be trees so close?

Not trees, she suddenly realized. *A tree*—just one. They were falling into the side of a single tree.

Scathach flung herself across the cabin, bouncing off the walls, to peer through another and then another porthole. The tree was massive. Huge and twisting, it loomed before them like a vast green wall. She craned her neck, looking up and down. The trunk disappeared into the forest canopy far below, and the top of the tree soared up through the clouds, reaching high into the heavens. She was only looking at a tiny section of it, but that portion was enormous.

"Yggdrasill," she breathed.

"The One Tree," Prometheus confirmed.

"The original Yggdrasill of Danu Talis," Scathach said in awe.

"The original? It is the only one of its kind."

Scathach opened her mouth to respond but then closed it again and said nothing. She had seen Yggdrasill before. But the tree she had seen in a Shadowrealm bordering Mill Valley—though it was massive—had been puny compared to this. And then Dee had destroyed it.

"You should sit," Prometheus commanded. "Now!"

The Shadow fell back into her seat and held on to the damaged armrests. Everyone could see the tree approaching. The light filtering in through the portholes of the Rukma vimana had turned dark and green, and it looked as if the craft was falling into a forest, but they were actually descending at an angle into the side of the Yggdrasill.

"Brace yourselves!" Prometheus shouted as branches started to scrape and tear along the side of the craft.

And then they hit the massive trunk of the World Tree.

The vimana split in two.

A huge crack ripped through the craft, and the front half of the ship with Prometheus and Scathach pitched forward and lodged safely in a network of thick vines and enormous branches. Leaves rained down on top of them. The back half of the craft, holding Joan, Saint-Germain, Will and Palamedes caught on a series of branches, which bent beneath its weight, then broke and dropped the ship onto a street-sized branch twenty feet below. The ship tottered there for a moment; then the branch cracked and dipped. A second crack sent splinters shooting upward. Beneath the branch there was nothing but an endless fall into clouds far below.

Scathach crawled out of the craft, grabbed a length of vine and quickly fashioned a long rope. Tying the rope around the branch she was lying on, she lowered it into the body of the craft beneath her.

Prometheus tugged off his metal gloves with his teeth, wrapped a second length of the vine around his waist and dropped it into the back half of the craft directly below, almost into the Saracen Knight's hands.

"Quickly, quickly!" Scathach screamed. She could see that the branch the vimana was balanced on was about to snap.

Bruised and bloodied from a cut high on his forehead, Saint-Germain lifted an unconscious Joan out of her seat and slipped her over his shoulder. Gripping Scathach's vine in one hand, then entwining it around his feet, he hauled himself upward with a grunt. Scathach dug in her feet and pulled, teeth gritted, muscles straining.

Palamedes lifted a trembling Will Shakespeare and held him while he wrapped Prometheus's vine around him, tying it off in a knot under his arms. He looked up at the red-haired Elder and nodded. "Haul away."

Prometheus's massive arms bulged and he started to pull Shakespeare up to safety.

The branch creaked again, then cracked. It broke.

Palamedes leaped, and just as the branch ripped away from the trunk of the tree, he caught hold of Will's right foot and dangled, swaying slightly from side to side.

Prometheus grunted with the extra strain. The vine slipped in his hands, tearing his flesh, scraping it raw; then it began to unravel. The Elder roared his frustration.

"Will," Palamedes said, looking upward. "I've got to let go. . . ."

"No!" The Bard's eyes brimmed with tears. "No, please . . ."

"Will, if I don't, then we both die. And there is no need for that."

"Wait . . . ," Shakespeare breathed. "Wait. . . ."

96

"I have been honored by the centuries of our friendship. . . ."

"No!"

"When all this is over, you might think about writing again. Write me a good part, make me truly immortal. Goodbye, Will." The Saracen Knight's fingers loosened.

There was a hiss, and suddenly a lasso of vine wrapped around Palamedes's chest just as he let go. Abruptly, scores of threads and streamers of vines rained down and wound around Joan and Saint-Germain and Will and Palamedes like a vast spider's web, catching them, holding them. The vines retracted, pulling them up to the safety of the broad branch, where they were unceremoniously deposited. The vines slithered away, disappearing back into the tree, leaving the group shaken but alive.

Two figures appeared at the end of the branch.

"Now we're in trouble," Prometheus murmured. "She's not going to be happy." He concentrated on his torn palms, picking splinters of wood from the hard flesh.

In the green light, it was hard to make out details, but one of the figures was tall and broad, completely clad in black glass and metal armor, bright blue eyes blazing beneath an ornate helmet. The second figure was a middle-aged woman with skin the color of jet and ice-white hair tumbling to her shoulders. She was wearing a shimmering robe that flickered green and gold with every step.

Marching up to Prometheus, she put her hands on her hips and stamped her foot in annoyance. "You crashed into my tree. Again."

"I am sorry, mistress. We were in a lot of trouble."

"You damaged my tree. It will take ages to heal." Her voice dropped to a conspiratorial whisper. "You even broke some branches this time. It is not going to like that."

"I will apologize. Profusely," he added. "I'll make an offering to the roots."

"That might do. Make it a good offering. Something big. Make sure there are bones; it loves bones." The woman looked around. "So, they're here at last. Abraham was right, one more time. Though he didn't mention anything about crashing into my tree." She glared at each in turn. "They look a shifty lot. Especially this one." She jerked a finger at Scathach. Then she leaned forward and sniffed. "Don't I know you?"

"Not yet. But you will."

The woman sniffed again. "I know your mother." She sniffed again. "And your no-good brother."

Joan stepped between the two women. "Prometheus, you are forgetting your manners. Why don't you introduce us?" she suggested.

"Of course," Prometheus said. "Ladies and gentlemen, allow me to introduce the Elder Hekate, the Goddess with Three Faces." The woman bowed graciously, her dress flaring emerald. "And of course, the Champion, Huitzilopochtli."

"Mars," Scathach breathed in awe.

"I don't know that name," the warrior rumbled.

"You will," she muttered.

CHAPTER FIFTEEN

*N*icholas and Perenelle sat side by side on the metal seats outside the Hard Rock Cafe at the entrance to Pier 39. Although it was only a little after seven o'clock in the evening and the sun wouldn't set for another hour and a half, the fog had ensured that night had arrived prematurely. A cold, damp gray gloom covered everything, and visibility was down to a few feet. Traffic was light, and already the streets were starting to empty. Some of the restaurants and shops along Pier 39 had even closed.

Nicholas breathed in. "Well, I never thought I'd be spending my last night alive sitting outside a restaurant on a foggy night in San Francisco. I always wanted to die in Paris."

Perenelle reached out to squeeze his fingers. "Think of the alternatives," she said, reverting to the ancient French of their youth.

"True," he said gently. "I could be sitting here alone."

"Or I could," she said. "After all these years—I'm glad we are still together."

"Only because of you," the Alchemyst said. He turned to look at his wife, and his hand touched the antique scarab he wore around his neck under his shirt. So much had happened in the past few hours that it seemed like a lifetime ago, but it had only been earlier that day that Perenelle had used the power of Tsagaglalal's and Sophie's auras to transfer a little of her own aura into the scarab and then into Nicholas. She had given him an extra twenty-four hours of life. In return, she had shortened her own life by the same amount. Neither of them needed a watch to know that they had little more than nineteen hours left to live. They had no plans to sleep that night.

Perenelle reached out and rested the palm of her hand flat against Nicholas's cheek. "I told you: I do not want to live in a world without you."

"Nor I without you," he said softly. Nicholas knew that the transfer of aura had been at a terrible cost to his wife. He could see it etched in the new lines at the corners of her eyes and around her mouth.

Centuries of watching him allowed her to read his expression as easily as if he had spoken. "Yes, I've grown old," she said. "My hair gets grayer with every hour." She touched her long hair, brushing it back off her face. "I always said you would give me gray hairs." She ran her hand across his close-cropped skull. A thin fuzz of black hair covered his head, and the whiskers on his cheeks and chin were dark. "Whereas you . . . my aura obviously agreed with you. You look young."

"Not that young," he teased.

"Not that young," she agreed. "But young enough. No one would ever guess you will be six hundred and seventy-seven years old in a few months' time."

He squeezed her hand. "That's a birthday I am never going to have. But still," he said with a smile, "six hundred and seventy-six isn't too bad."

"Remember, every time you use your aura, you are draining the little that remains in the scarab." She touched the stone he wore around his neck. A white spark leapt from her fingers, sizzling through the cloth.

"I understand. I'll try to hoard it until I need it."

"You're going to need it soon. That stunt with the parrot could have cost you a couple of hours of life."

Nicholas shook his head. "Thirty minutes, maybe. And it was worth it. I had forgotten what a joy it was to fly. Besides, we learned a lot from my stunt. We discovered that Machiavelli and Billy are now our allies."

"I don't trust him."

"Which one?"

"Either of them. But especially Machiavelli. With Dee you always knew where you stood."

"I always felt a little sorry for the English Magician," Nicholas admitted. "And I've had a grudging admiration for the Italian. I think in different circumstances, we might have been friends."

The Sorceress made a face. "Remember Mount Etna," she said.

"You defeated him. You hurt him too."

"He poisoned you. And made the volcano erupt!"

"In fairness, I don't think that was entirely his fault. That was a by-product of your aura, which brought it to life. But look—these are strange times. There's a lot happening that we've no idea about. Let's take our allies wherever we can find them. Anyway," he added with a grin, "we'll be dead by morning and it won't be our problem!"

"You're impossible!" Perenelle pulled her hand away and folded her arms. "Don't say that."

"It's the truth."

Perenelle turned in her seat to look down the street, peering into the fog. "Where are the boys?" she wondered.

"You're deliberately changing the subject, aren't you?"

"Yes."

Even as she was speaking, two shapes—one large, the other slender—loomed out of the dense, swirling fog. It was Niten and Prometheus. The large Elder was carrying a cardboard tray with three big white paper cups. Niten was carrying a smaller cup and nibbling on a pastry sticking out the top of a brown paper bag.

The Elder crouched beside the couple and handed Nicholas and Perenelle steaming cups of coffee. "We decided that since you're both French you'd prefer coffee to tea." He glanced up at Niten. "Actually, it was Niten's idea."

"I got tea," Niten said.

"And I left the coffee black. There's some sugar in the bag"

"Thank you." Perenelle wrapped her hands around the white cup and sipped cautiously, then dipped her head so he would not see the look of disgust on her face. "Needs sugar," she murmured.

"What did you find out?" Nicholas asked. He sipped. "Not bad. Needs sugar." He lined up three brown packages and tore them open, spilling crystals into the coffee.

"The city is closing down," Prometheus said. He ran his hand through his hair. Yesterday it had been red; now it was a dirty gray-white, speckled with water droplets. "Look around you: it's June and we're on Pier Thirty-Nine. This place should be bright with lights and teeming with people. It's practically deserted. There was a TV on in the restaurant. There have been dozens of crashes on the roads, the airport is closed and all sea traffic has been halted. There's talk of closing both the Bay and the Golden Gate Bridges. The news anchor was calling it the worst fog in a century."

Nicholas breathed in. "And it is no ordinary sea fog. What—or should that be *who*—are we smelling?" he asked.

Niten shook his head. "Something dead and rotten."

Nicholas glanced at his wife. "Do you recognize it?"

She shook her head. She moved the cup away from her face so she could take a deep breath. "Rotting meat." She quickly brought the cup back to her face to banish the scent with the clean odor of coffee. "That could be any one of half a dozen Elders. Some of them smell very odd indeed, and a lot of them seem to prefer a meat odor." She smiled at Prometheus. "No offense."

"None taken. I was never that fond of it myself." Prometheus finished his coffee in a single swallow, then crumpled the cup and pitched it into a trash can. "There are two possibilities on the West Coast," he said quietly. "It could be Quetzalcoatl, or, worse, it could be Bastet. Both prefer the perfume of spoiled meat."

"Who do you think it is?" Perenelle asked.

Prometheus shook his head. "Earlier, I thought it might be Quetzalcoatl. I caught a slightly exotic, spicy tang in the air."

Niten breathed deeply. "I don't get that. All I can smell is rancid meat and maybe—just maybe—the hint of cat. Though that might be from a real cat close by," he added.

"Or it could be both Elders," Perenelle suggested.

Prometheus shook his head firmly. "No, that's not going to happen. They were always bitter enemies."

"Why?" Niten asked.

"Something that happened a long time ago, before Danu Talis fell. There is no way they will join forces."

A foghorn sounded and they stopped to listen to the long slow bellow. "Something wicked this way comes," Nicholas whispered. He put his cup on the ground and rubbed his hands quickly together. "Did you manage to contact anyone?"

Prometheus shook his head slightly. "Some. But not enough. Those loyal to the humani are already aware of the disturbance here and I'm hoping are on the way. Of course, that also applies to those loyal to the Dark Elders. However, I spoke to Barbarossa . . ."

"The emperor or the pirate?"

"The emperor," the Elder clarified. "He's in Chicago, but will come in on the first flight in the morning. If there are flights. He's already put the word out to immortals and Elders living on the East Coast. He'll bring as many as he can."

"They'll be too late," Perenelle said. "We need them here now."

"He did say that the immortal Zenobia and the Elder Pyrgomache are on the way here. They're coming in on a Greyhound bus."

"Not in this fog, they aren't," Perenelle said. "And I don't trust Zenobia. Never did."

"I spoke to Khutulun," Niten said. "She breeds horses in Kentucky."

The Flamels shook their heads simultaneously. "Who is she?" Nicholas asked.

Niten smiled. "Probably the most famous warrior you've never heard of. She was the niece of Kublai Khan, and so directly related to Genghis Khan. She was trained first by Scathach and then later by Aoife. Aoife called her Shining Moon and said she was the daughter she always wanted. Khutulun said she'd leave within the hour."

"She's driving?" Perenelle asked.

"Khutulun does not fly."

"Even if she doesn't stop to sleep, that's at least a two-day drive across country," Perenelle said. "It'll be all over by the time she arrives."

"She knows that. She said she would avenge us."

"That's very comforting."

"She was going to stop off in Wyoming and pick up the Elders Ynaguinid and Macanduc."

Prometheus nodded. "Tremendous warriors," he said. "The bravest of the brave."

". . . who are in Wyoming," Perenelle said. "Which is no use to us."

"Davy Crockett's driving down from Seattle," Niten said. "But that is at least a day away. Even with the way he drives."

Nicholas finished his coffee and carefully replaced the empty cup in the cardboard holder. "So what you are saying is that a lot of help is coming, but none of it is going to arrive in time."

The Elder and the immortal nodded simultaneously.

"Meanwhile," Perenelle added, "we already know several Dark Elders live in and around the city. Eris lives just down the road in Haight-Ashbury. . . ."

Prometheus waved his hand dismissively. "We can ignore her. She's been quiet for centuries. Nowadays she spends her time crocheting."

"Is this the same Eris who caused the Trojan War because she didn't get a wedding invitation?" Perenelle asked in disbelief. "Do you think she'll sit quietly by and crochet while the rest of her foul clan invade the city?"

"Probably not," Prometheus agreed.

"So it's just us," Nicholas said.

"I've said it before. The island is the key," Niten said.

"I'm concerned about Odin and Hel," the Alchemyst continued. "And Mars, too. When I saw them, Hel was wounded and they were barely holding their own. And I'm particularly worried about Black Hawk. He has completely disappeared. I fear we've lost him to the Nereids."

"We need to take the battle to the heart of the enemy," Niten said decisively. "We must regain the initiative. If we delay, the Dark Elders will arrive and we will be forced to fight on two fronts. And that is a battle we cannot win. We need to get to Alcatraz."

"How?" Prometheus asked. "Nothing will venture out into the bay in this fog."

Nicholas looked at Perenelle. "Do you remember when we were on the Isle of Man and Dee turned up with his trained ghouls? Remember how we got away?"

Perenelle grinned. "I remember the look on the Magician's face." Her smile faded. "But, Nicholas, we were a lot younger then, and a lot—a whole lot—stronger."

"Okay, so we'll burn up a little aura." He shrugged. "We have nothing to lose."

Perenelle leaned in to quickly kiss her husband's cheek. "True."

"How did you get off the island?" Niten asked.

"We walked."

"On water?"

Nicholas and Perenelle Flamel nodded.

CHAPTER SIXTEEN

"*I* understand there was a little . . . unpleasantness earlier," Osiris said.

"No," Virginia said evenly. She was watching as the servants laid out a round gold and silver table in the back garden of the circular house. None of the servants were human. Both males and females had the bodies of humans, and their features were almost—though not quite—those of animals. The females appeared to have cat genes, while the males had either dog or pig. And no two were identical.

A trio of cat-girls appeared. One was lightly furred, another had a long curling tail and the third had the speckled pattern of a leopard across her face and bare shoulders. All had whiskers. They laid out baskets of fruit on the table and scampered silently away on all fours.

"Genetic manipulation?" Virginia asked.

"Something like that," Osiris said. "A combination of

Earthlord, Archon and Great Elder expertise, fired by our auras. Isis and I are creating endless Shadowrealms. We need to populate them. And the humani are not suitable for every world. The average humani struggles to survive even in this world. So we tweak them a little, give them some advantages. The cat-women, for example, will do well in a jungle world, and we'll try out the dogs and pigs as hunters and trackers. They are flexible enough to go into any number of environments."

"It is science or magic?" Virginia asked.

"Who was it who said that any sufficiently advanced technology was indistinguishable from magic? Einstein? Newton?"

"Clarke," she said quietly.

"The humani are essentially a vulnerable race. We are giving them some of the advantages nature forgot."

"Humans have spread all across the globe, in any number of environments, without your advantages," Virginia said icily. "They adapt—always have, always will. What you are doing is wrong."

"We shall have to agree to disagree."

"I hate that phrase."

Osiris and Virginia Dare were sitting on either side of a round pool in a small enclosed courtyard. Overhead, a patterned silk awning protected them from the slanting sunshine. The air was bright with flowers and heavy with perfume. Virginia had grown up in the forest and later trained as a botanist and horticulturalist, yet she recognized few of the plants. Enormous water lilies covered the surface of the pool, and almost transparent thumbnail-sized frogs moved slowly across the leaves, following the sun. The frogs hissed like cats.

Osiris had changed into a loose white linen shirt and white trousers that ended high above his ankles. His feet were bare, and the American immortal noted that his toenails were painted black.

"What happened with the anpu?" Osiris asked.

Virginia's slate-gray eyes blinked gold as she looked away from the table. "Oh, that," she said lightly. "They got in my way."

"They would have stepped out of your way if you had identified yourselves. It was a mistake." Osiris smiled, but it was nothing more than a movement of his lips, and there was no genuine emotion in it.

"Their mistake was trying to stop me."

"Do you usually deal so harshly with those who get in your way?"

"Yes." Her smile matched the Elder's. "I resent anyone—or anything—who attempts to curtail my liberty."

"I will remember that."

"Do. I grew up with nothing. No clothes, no food, no money, no possessions. All I had was my liberty. I learned to value it."

Osiris steepled his hands before his face. "You are an interesting person, Virginia Dare."

"Not really. I'm actually very simple, and my rule is equally simple: stay out of my way and I'll stay out of yours."

"I will remember that also."

Sophie's laugher rang out and they both turned toward

the sound. Through a wall of glass, they caught a glimpse of Sophie and Josh exploring the vast circular house.

"First time I've heard her laugh," the immortal remarked, then turned back to the Elder, eyeing him carefully. "Their arrival here was not a surprise. I get the impression that we are nearing the end of a plan that was laid down a long time ago."

Osiris sat back in a chair that had been carved from a block of solid gold and steepled his hands before his face again. "You are very astute."

"Underestimate me at your peril." She smiled. "My Elder master did—and you know what happened to him."

"I wonder if you would be so brave without your flute," Osiris commented. .

Virginia reached under her shirt and produced the simple wooden flute. She shook it out of its cloth bag and sunlight shivered across the spiral designs etched into the wood. Osiris stiffened, and she noted how his hand dropped to the sides of the chair. She guessed there was a weapon concealed in one of the armrests—a knife or throwing star, probably. Suddenly she tossed the flute at the Elder.

Osiris snatched the instrument out of the air—and then hissed as the flesh of his palm sizzled and smoked. He flung the flute toward the pool, but Virginia caught it, spun it once to make it sing and tucked it into its bag and back beneath her clothes in one smooth movement.

Osiris dropped to his knees and pushed his hand into the water. "You could have warned me," he said.

"If I'd told you that you wouldn't be able to hold it, would you have believed me?"

"Probably not," he admitted.

"A demonstration is worth a thousand words."

"I've come across such artifacts before," Osiris told her. "Some are Earthlord or Archon. I've never been able to work out why the Elders cannot touch them. Do you know?"

"Yes, I do," she said simply.

"But you're not going to tell me?"

"No, I'm not."

Osiris returned to the golden chair and sat down, his right hand dripping water on the white flagstones. "Miss Dare, what a revelation you are," he murmured. "I suddenly realize that for centuries I have been dealing with the wrong humani agent. Dee was a fool—a useful fool, admittedly. But we should have been dealing with you."

Virginia Dare shook her head. "You were always able to control the doctor. You would not have been able to control me."

Osiris nodded. "Maybe so. But we would have dealt with you differently."

"Honestly, you mean?"

"We were always honest with him," the Elder said sincerely. "He was rarely as honest with us; you must know that."

"Why do you need the twins?"

Osiris brought his burnt hand to his lips and licked at the wound. Brilliant blue eyes regarded her evenly. Then he suddenly grinned. "I could tell you, but then I would have to kill you," he said.

"If you don't tell me, I might kill you." Virginia matched his smile once again.

"You could try."

"I could. But you really don't want me to," Virginia said.

Sophie's and Josh's voices suddenly echoed through the house, and Osiris and Virginia turned toward the sound. The voices grew louder as the twins approached.

"Here's what I think," Virginia said quietly. "You need their auras. You need the power of Gold and Silver for something. Something spectacular. Am I right?"

"You are not wrong," Osiris conceded.

"There's only one thing troubling me," she said.

Osiris's face remained expressionless as he continued to lick his hand.

"Are you really their parents?"

"They are our children," he said after considering his answer. "We have spent a lifetime preparing them for this."

CHAPTER SEVENTEEN

*Q*uetzalcoatl detested the damp. He was wearing a heavy wool three-piece suit he'd bought in London a century ago, and had wrapped himself in a three-quarter-length black leather coat with the high collar turned up. A patterned thermal scarf encircled his neck and covered the lower part of his mouth, and he wore a black fedora with a spray of feathers from his own tail in the band. His hands were sheathed in fur-lined gloves. Yet he was still freezing. He hated this Shadowrealm.

The Feathered Serpent turned as an enormous black Cadillac with darkened windows pulled into the deserted parking lot at Vista Point Overlook. Its gleaming bodywork was speckled with millions of water droplets.

Quetzalcoatl half raised his hand, then, realizing that he was probably invisible in the gloom and fog, self-consciously dropped it again. He was beginning to regret his earlier impulsive action. He had survived this long because he was a loner; he rarely mixed with his own kind. He couldn't even remember the last time he'd encountered someone from his very distant past. It was always easier to deal with the human servants; he could control them.

A smartly suited driver wearing a peaked cap climbed out of the car. Quetzalcoatl thought there was something wrong with the way he—though it could just as easily have been a she—walked, and when the driver turned his head, the Elder thought he caught the glimpse of bulging solid black eyes. The driver removed his hat, revealing a bald head and overlong bat ears, before opening the rear door.

A figure stepped out.

She was tall and elegant, wrapped in a full-length fur coat made from the skins of animals that had not walked the earth in eons. And she had the head of a cat. This was Bastet.

Quetzalcoatl watched the Elder stride across the parking lot toward him and felt an odd emotion, something he had not experienced in millennia: fear. His tail, which had been tucked into the back of his belt, slipped free, slithered out from beneath his coat and tapped nervously against the ground. Perhaps contacting the cat-headed goddess had been a mistake.

"It has been a long time, Quetzalcoatl," she said, speaking in the ancient language of Danu Talis.

The Feathered Serpent lifted his fedora and bowed respectfully. "Too long."

Bastet tilted her feline head to one side, huge yellow slit-pupiled eyes regarding him. It was impossible to read her expression, but Quetzalcoatl got the impression she was amused.

"Thank you for coming," he said. "I was unsure that you would. . . ."

"Oh, we Elders have to stick together," Bastet said in her hissing lisp. "Especially now, in these interesting times." Boot heels clicked on the pavement as she stepped forward, towering over the shorter Elder. "I was delighted to get your call. Surprised, I'll admit. But delighted."

Quetzalcoatl wondered if the cat-headed Elder was being sarcastic; her coolness made it hard to tell. "I've been meaning to get in touch," he murmured. "But you know how time slips away."

"We should get together more often: we're practically neighbors," she purred.

He knew then that she *was* being sarcastic. She hated him for what had happened on Danu Talis ten thousand years ago.

"So, you need my help?"

"Yes, I thought you might be able to assist me," he admitted. "We are so close now, victory is almost at hand. I do not want to leave anything to chance."

"Very wise." Bastet swept out her right hand, claws shredding the fog. "Is this yours? It is a nice touch."

"Thank you. I thought you would approve."

"The humani have always feared the nights. Especially foggy nights. Deep in their genetic memories, they must remember what it was like to be hunted." The goddess showed her teeth in a feral grin.

Quetzalcoatl lifted his hand and pointed to the right. Through the billowing fog, the merest outline of metal was barely visible. He blinked and his pupils changed shape, and he suddenly saw the world in shades of red and black. "The Golden Gate Bridge is here." He pointed to the left. "I'm not sure if you can see it, but over there is Alcatraz. . . ."

"I can see it. Do you forget what I am, what I became?" she hissed bitterly.

"The Change altered all of us," Quetzalcoatl said carefully.

"Some more than others."

"Indeed." The Feathered Serpent continued. "Beyond Alcatraz is Treasure Island, and just behind the island is the Bay Bridge."

Bastet turned up the collar of her fur coat. "I did not come here for a geography lesson."

"This fog covers everything within a hundred-mile radius. Nothing is moving on land or sea. I have ensured that there have been countless accidents. The authorities are stretched to the limit. The Golden Gate and Bay Bridges are already closed." He consulted an overlarge watch on his wrist. "Soon a fuel tanker will cross the central divide on Dumbarton Bridge and burst into flames."

"How do you know?" Bastet asked.

"I don't believe in leaving anything to chance." He checked his watch again. "In five minutes, there will be a series of accidents at the tollgates on the San Mateo Bridge, which will completely seal the bridges. And in ten minutes, the Pacific Gas and Electric Company, which supplies most of the power to this side of the country, is going to suffer a devastating series of computer failures." Quetzalcoatl grinned, showing his own savage teeth. "Everything will go dark."

"Can you do that?"

"Indeed. I experimented a couple of years ago on the East Coast. The great Northeast blackout was a success."

"This is all very impressive. So, what do you want me for?" Bastet asked.

"You know we have creatures on Alcatraz?"

"I know that."

"And you know that Dee has betrayed us."

"I know he was declared *utlaga*."

"He was supposed to release the beasts from the island, but he didn't, and now he's vanished."

"Don't you have people you can use?" Bastet hissed. "I have no servants left this far north."

"I put two of my best people on the job. Billy the Kid and Black Hawk." He paused and coughed. "They were accompanied by the Italian immortal, Machiavelli."

Bastet hissed. "There are certain humani we should have butchered and eaten a long time ago. The Flamels, for example, and Dee, and certainly Machiavelli. You know I love Italian food."

Quetzalcoatl sighed. "I agree with you. Machiavelli and Billy went to the island to loose the monsters into the city."

"And?" Bastet turned toward San Francisco and tilted her head to one side, listening. "I'm not hearing any screams."

"They failed," Quetzalcoatl said quietly. "I don't know how. I did see the Lotan swim in toward the Embarcadero, but it was slain by the Flamels. I've lost touch with Billy and Machiavelli, and Black Hawk has simply disappeared. I can only assume that they are all dead." He ground his teeth in frustration. "We are so close, mistress. So very close. We have an island full of monsters less than a mile away from the city streets, and when we do manage to get one almost ashore, we are defeated by a couple of immortals."

"How many immortals?"

"A handful. Flamel, his dangerous wife, the Japanese warrior and, unfortunately, our own Prometheus."

Bastet wrapped her arms around her body and shivered. "I thought he never left his Shadowrealm."

"It is no more. Faded to shadows and dust."

"Curious. And what of the supposed twins of legend? The Flamels and Dee were convinced they had them. Again."

Quetzalcoatl's teeth flashed in a smile. "They have vanished from the city. I cannot sense them anywhere on the American continent."

"That is some consolation, at least."

"You know the Flamels must have sent for help. The longer we delay, the more time we allow for reinforcements to arrive."

"We have our kind coming too, haven't we?"

"Some. Even now, the monsters and the monstrous are gathering. But don't you know that every immortal humani hero, every god of myth and legend loyal to the Flamels, or simply opposed to us, is heading this way?"

"Then let us not delay. We must get the monsters ashore and get the party under way."

"The original plan was for Machiavelli and Billy to awaken the creatures and release them from their cells. Black Hawk was supposed to sail a modified tourist boat into the jetty, load up and bring the creatures back into the city. Then he would go back for more."

"But now this Black Hawk has vanished."

"Eaten by the Nereids, I fear."

"But you have a backup plan?"

"Always."

"I thought you might."

"Even now, there is a modified tourist boat docked off the island. The captain is gathering the biggest, ugliest, hungriest, most terrifying monsters he can find. He will take them ashore and release them into the streets. Then he will go back for a second batch."

"And you can trust this captain?"

"He is my brother."

"I never knew you had a brother."

"He left Danu Talis long before the fall. The Change was cruel to him. But when I needed someone to trust, I knew I could count on him. He was happy—even eager—to help me." His teeth flashed in a nasty smile. "After all, if you can't depend on your family, then who can you trust?"

"Then why do you need me?" Bastet asked, ignoring the jibe. Her son Aten had betrayed her. "I am hearing a 'but . . . ,'" she prodded.

"The Flamels and company will do all in their power to thwart us."

"So we need to eliminate the Flamels, Prometheus and Niten?"

"Yes, and we only have a brief period of time in which to defeat them before their reinforcements arrive."

Bastet's gaze narrowed on the Feathered Serpent. "And you're sure they have no other allies in the city?"

"Everyone else is on the island." He grinned. "Hopefully, providing a tasty snack for something hideous."

Bastet rubbed her hands together. Her nails sparked off one another. "Simple, then. We divide their forces. We send in something to engage the warriors, Prometheus and Niten. Without them, Nicholas and Perenelle are little more than immortal humans who will age with every use of power. I know their auras are waning."

"What can we send? I have no resources left."

"Ah, but I have." She reached into a pocket and produced a leather bag. It rattled as she shook it. "You remember these? Drakon's teeth?"

"The Spartoi," he said.

Bastet nodded. "Indestructible earth warriors."

"Perfect. Just perfect." Quetzalcoatl checked his watch again, the luminous dial painting his face green. "In five . . . four . . . three . . . two . . . one."

The entire city went dark.

Across the city, burglar alarms went off as their battery backups took over. In the all-enveloping fog, they sounded like mice squeaking.

CHAPTER EIGHTEEN

"Who are you?" Dr. John Dee wheezed. He was aware that he was lying on the metal floor of a vimana and that its vibration trembled through his entire body. With his faded eyesight, his surroundings were a blur, and the figure sitting at the controls before him was little more than a shadow.

"I told you, I am called Marethyu." A half circle of metal gleamed in the light before Dee's face. "I am sometimes called the hook-handed man. Though it's really more of a sickle than a hook."

The Magician found he was still wrapped in the sweatshirt Josh had put over him. He pulled it closer around his shrinking frame and attempted—but failed—to straighten up. "I feel I should know you," he whispered.

"You should. We've met often enough."

"We haven't," Dee disagreed. "I would never have forgotten the hook."

"I guess you wouldn't," Marethyu said enigmatically.

"Young man," Dee began, at which Marethyu burst into laughter. "What is so funny?"

"It's been a long time since anyone called me young."

"You look young enough to me. You sound young, and you're strong enough to carry me. I am old; almost five hundred years. How long have you lived upon the earth?" the immortal demanded.

But the hook-handed man remained silent as the vimana hummed through clear blue skies. Then, just as Dee was beginning to suspect he would get no answer, the man spoke, and his voice was unbearably sad. "Magician: I have lived upon this earth for ten thousand years. And I have spent perhaps ten times that walking the Shadowrealms. Even I do not know my true age anymore."

"Then you are Elder? . . . Great Elder? . . . Archon? You're not an Earthlord. Are you an Ancient, perhaps?"

"No. None of those," Marethyu said. "I am human. A little more than a normal human, a lot less, too. But human born and bred."

The vimana's engine whined down and the craft dipped.

"Who is your master?"

"I have no master. I serve myself."

"Then who made you immortal?" Dee asked, growing only more confused.

"Why, I suppose you did, in a manner of speaking, Dr. Dee," Marethyu laughed.

"I don't understand."

"You will. Patience, Doctor, patience. All will be revealed in time."

"I do not have much time left. Osiris saw to that."

The vimana dipped lower, its engine slowing to a dull buzz.

"Where are we going?" Dee asked.

"I'm taking you to meet someone. He's been waiting for you for a long time."

"You knew I was coming?"

"Doctor, I have always known you were coming here. I have followed your progress from the moment of your birth."

Dee was tired; a leaden exhaustion threatened to overwhelm him, but he knew that if he closed his eyes, he would probably never open them again. He found the strength to ask, "Why?"

"Because you had a role to play. In my long life, I have discovered that there are no coincidences. There is a pattern. The trick is to see the pattern, but that ability is a gift—a curse, perhaps—that is given to few."

"And you can see this pattern?"

"It is my curse."

The vimana suddenly settled on the ground. The top of the craft slid back, and Dee shivered as a wash of chill, damp air flowed over him. Even with his faded hearing, he could make out the roar of the sea, nearby breakers foaming and crashing. He saw Marethyu's arms reach down for him and feebly brushed them away.

"Wait a minute . . . ," he protested.

"As you so rightly pointed out: we do not have much time."

Dee reached up and caught Marethyu's arm. "I cannot feel your aura."

"I don't have one."

"Everyone has an aura," Dee murmured, confusion once again coming over him.

"Everyone *living*," the man answered.

"You are dead?"

"I am Death."

"But you have powers?"

"Yes, vast powers."

"Could you restore my youth?"

There was a silence, and with his short sight, Dee could just about discern Marethyu watching him. "I could," he said eventually. "But I will not."

Dee couldn't understand why this man would rescue him, yet leave him to die. "Why not?"

"Call it consequences, or maybe justice. You are not a nice man, Dr. Dee, and you should pay something for your terrible crimes. What I will do however, is restore a little of your strength and allow you your dignity." Marethyu put his hand on top of the doctor's head and pushed.

A shock, like pins and needles, rippled through Dee. He felt heat bloom in the pit of his stomach. It flowed up, across his chest and down into his arms, while simultaneously surging through his thighs, along his calves and into his feet. He immediately felt stronger.

"And my sight," he pleaded. "Give me back my sight and hearing."

"Greedy, Doctor, greedy. Always and ever your failing . . ."

"You've brought me to this wondrous place, the most amazing city in the history of Earth. And yet I cannot see or hear it. If you have followed my life, you know that I have always been driven by a thirst for knowledge, by an insatiable curiosity. Please. Let me see this place, so that I may remember it for whatever time is left to me."

Marethyu leaned forward and rested his index and little fingers against Dee's eyes, pressing lightly. Dee felt a single moment of pain—an intense stab through his skull—and then Death lifted his hand and Dee opened his eyes. The shadows were gone and everything was in sharp focus. He could see. He looked up at Marethyu. The bottom half of the figure's face was wrapped in a thick scarf, above which a pair of bright blue eyes regarded the Magician with something like curiosity or amusement. "Satisfied, Doctor?"

Dee frowned. "I *have* met you," he said slowly. "You are almost familiar to me."

"We have met many times. You simply did not know that it was me. I was the face in the mirror, the voice in the shadows, the shape in the night. I was the author of those unsigned notes you received, and later, the anonymous emails. I was the voice on your answering machine, the badly spelled texts on your phone."

Dee stared at the figure in horror. "I thought it was my Elder masters speaking to me."

"Sometimes it was. Not always."

"But you are not associated with them?"

"I have spent millennia thwarting them."

"You manipulated me," Dee accused him.

"Oh, come now, don't look so shocked. You've spent lifetimes manipulating other people."

Dee came slowly to his feet. He was still elderly. He guessed his body was probably that of a spry eighty-year-old, but his sight and hearing were those of a youth. He climbed out of the vimana and looked around.

They were standing on a broad platform close to the top of a scarred crystal tower. The ground was strewn with the remains of weapons and pieces of armor, and the stones were awash with black and green liquids, but there were no bodies.

Marethyu strode toward a doorway in the tower, his black hooded cloak flapping behind him. The frame and stones around the door were pocked and chipped, and the ground was slippery with more of the sticky green and black fluids. There were speckles of what looked like human blood spattered on the ground and splashed onto the torn white crystal walls.

"What happened here?" Dee asked.

"There was a fight. A massacre, really. Recently." Marethyu's voice was a hoarse whisper. "Don't slip," he called back over his shoulder. "It's a long way down."

Dee bent and picked up what he thought might be a broken spear. The head was missing—it looked like it had been sliced clean off. Using the length of wood as a walking stick, he followed Death through the door and into a small circular room. The chamber was empty. "Where are you?" the Magician asked, his voice echoing as he looked around. He noticed that there was more blood on the floor, and when he ran his toe across it, the liquid smudged. It was fresh.

"Up here." The answer came from a concealed stairwell.

"Where?"

"Here!" Dee followed the sound of Marethyu's voice and found the stairway. He balanced the broken spear on the first step and looked up into the gloom. "Where are we going?" he called.

"Up."

The Magician heaved himself onto the step. "Where? Why?"

Marethyu's face appeared above Dee, and even though his mouth was concealed, Dee knew that he was smiling. "Why, Doctor, we've come to see Abraham the Mage. You do know the name, of course?"

The Magician's mouth opened and closed in astonishment.

"I see you do." Death's blue eyes crinkled. "He wants his book back."

CHAPTER NINETEEN

*T*he room was enormous.

Sophie Newman sat on a bed that was bigger than her room in Aunt Agnes's house in San Francisco. In fact, she thought it might be bigger than the entire top floor of the house. She had no doubt that this room had been specially prepared for her. Everything—from the huge sunken bathtub to the deep walk-in wardrobes to the flagstones on the floor— was either silver metal, silver cloth or burnished with silver. Even the bed frame was cast from a solid hunk of metal. Three of the walls were polished to a gleaming sheen; the fourth was a sliding wall of glass opening onto an enormous courtyard. An ornate silver frame sat on top of a silver bedside table. It held one of her favorite photographs—a snapshot of the entire Newman family standing in the ruins of Machu Picchu high in the Peruvian mountains. Everyone was laughing, because Josh had stepped in a pile of llama dung and it had squirted into his shoe and sock.

Without even having to see it, she knew Josh's room was going to be decorated and outfitted in pure gold.

But what convinced her that this room had been prepared in advance for her was the ceiling. It was painted a deep, rich blue. Leaning back on the bed, she looked up. Silver stars formed the constellation of Orion, and a huge luminous half-moon filled the corner directly opposite her bed.

Her mother had painted an identical ceiling in her bedroom at Aunt Agnes's house.

Sophie walked the length of the silver room and pulled open the double doors to the enormous wardrobe. She gasped in surprise: neatly lined up on two rails topped by shelves were all the clothes she'd left in San Francisco: jeans, sweatshirts, dresses, underwear. But when she ran her fingers across a pair of jeans, she discovered that they were stiff and realized they were unworn. All the clothes were brand-new, some still with the labels attached. Stepping into the deep wardrobe, she walked between the rails, trailing her fingers across the clothes. She recognized everything: every piece of clothing she had bought or that her mother or aunt had given her as presents over the past year was here, even the green, white and gold Oakland A's sweatshirt Josh had given her. Shoes, boots and sneakers were lined up in racks on the floor. She suddenly laughed out loud: she never would have guessed that UPS delivered to Danu Talis.

"Hello?" There was a knock on the door and she turned as Isis—or was it Sara, her mother?—slid open the door and peered into the room. "There you are. I was just hoping you were finding everything okay."

"Yes . . . yes, everything's . . . fabulous," Sophie said, though her voice was less than enthusiastic. "I was just looking at the clothes."

"Your father thought it might be an easier transition if you had all your familiar stuff around you."

"Thank you. It's just a little overwhelming. Well," she added, "maybe more than a little."

"Oh, Sophie." Isis stepped into the room. She'd taken off the white ceramic armor and was wearing a simple linen shirt and pants. Her tiny feet were bare, and Sophie noticed that her toenails were painted black to match her fingernails. She'd never known her mother to paint her toenails before. "I know—truly I know—how hard this must be for you."

Sophie's laugh was shaky. She was suddenly angry. Did they expect her to just accept all this without question? "Unless you've recently discovered that your mother is a ten-thousand-year-old Elder from Danu Talis named after an Egyptian goddess, I don't think you have any idea how I'm feeling."

"Actually, I wasn't named after the Egyptian goddess; I *was* the Egyptian goddess." The woman smiled, and in that moment, with the corners of her mouth and eyes crinkling, she looked like Sara Newman. "But I am your mother, Sophie, and I want you to know that all of this was done to protect you and your brother."

"Why?" Sophie demanded.

Isis crossed the room, her bare feet leaving damp

footprints on the silver tiles, and slid open the glass wall that led outdoors. A wash of exotic perfumes flooded the room. Water tinkled, and in the distance there was the vague murmur of Osiris's voice and Virginia Dare's brittle laughter. "You have the Witch of Endor's knowledge within you?" Isis asked.

Sophie nodded slowly. Even as her mother was speaking, flickering alien images danced just at the periphery of her vision, and Sophie knew that these were not her own memories.

. . . *Isis and Osiris in white armor at the head of an army of anpu, on the backs of huge lizards, riding out of a blazing city. None of the bearlike corpses littering the road were human, and none of them were armed.*

. . . *Isis and Osiris in the costumes of ancient Egypt—though this landscape was a lush, verdant jungle rather than desert—overseeing long lines of human slaves dragging slabs of stone toward a half-finished pyramid.*

. . . *Isis and Osiris in white smocks and masks standing in a gleaming laboratory watching creatures resembling huge hairless rats crawl from bubbling vats of viscous pink liquid.*

Isis smiled, lips pressed tightly closed. "And I suppose I better warn you that Zephaniah the Witch was never our friend, so no doubt you'll learn some unpleasant truths about us. But remember, what you are experiencing—*remembering*—those are the Witch's interpretations. They're not necessarily the truth. There are two sides to every story." The woman's eyes closed and the dry hint of cinnamon seeped into the room. "Sometimes all one needs is a little perspective."

Sophie shuddered as new memories tumbled and spun through her mind.

. . . Isis and Osiris in white armor at the head of an army of anpu, riding on the back of huge lizards, protecting a village overflowing with small bearlike humans against a vast army of slavering lizardlike monsters.

. . . Isis and Osiris in the costumes of ancient Egypt overseeing long lines of laughing and singing humans as they tore down a pyramid and cast the stones into the sea.

. . . Isis and Osiris in white smocks and masks standing in a gleaming laboratory watching creatures resembling huge hairless rats crawl from bubbling vats of viscous pink liquid. The couple gently helped each creature out of the vat, wrapped it in silver foil and carried it over to a bed. Above the bed, narrow rectangular windows showed a water world where the ratlike creatures darted and swam. In the distance was the suggestion of a vast white city.

Isis opened her blue eyes. "Take the time and check through your memories—Zephaniah's memories—and see if what I am telling you is true. In this place, in this time, the twins of legend have few real friends."

Faces, some human, others bestial and a few caught in transition between the two, flickered, and Sophie knew she was seeing her enemies and that Isis was telling the truth.

"Danu Talis is ruled by the Elders and the descendants of the Great Elders. There are powerful factions in the court who would strive to kill you or control you." Isis stepped up and pressed her hands to Sophie's face.

The girl tried to pull away, but the woman's grip was too strong.

"Everything we have done has been to protect you both." The woman quickly leaned in to kiss Sophie's forehead, but the girl pulled back at the last moment and hugged her mother instead. The prickle of dry cinnamon intensified, catching at the back of the girl's throat. "So get dressed, then come and eat. Your father and I will answer all your questions, I promise you."

"All our questions?" Sophie asked.

"Everything. The time for secrets is over."

CHAPTER TWENTY

"*This tunnel runs under the prison yard,*" the ghost of Juan Manuel de Ayala said. "*It connects with another tunnel, which leads to the water tower. There are steps that will lead you upward.*"

A tiny spinning ball of white energy created by Niccolò Machiavelli illuminated the low narrow tunnel, tainting the air with the musty odor of serpent. The stained walls were coated with a thick, glutinous slime, and water dripped incessantly from the ceiling. "Man, this is so ruining my boots." Billy's voice echoed off the walls.

Machiavelli turned to glare wide-eyed at him. Water sizzled off the energy ball above his head.

"What? These are my favorite boots!"

Machiavelli shook his head in despair. "Try to keep up," he said quietly.

"We're following a ghost down a tunnel under a prison."

Billy the Kid tugged at Machiavelli's sleeve. "How do we even know we can trust him . . . it? This could be a trap."

"You're beginning to sound paranoid," Machiavelli said, glancing sidelong at the American immortal. Green water splashed onto his face and curved along his cheekbones like emerald tears.

Billy blinked. "Paranoid. Let me think about this for a minute. We're the only two humans on an island of monsters and Elders. So yes, I'm feeling a little paranoid. Did you ever watch *Star Trek*?" he suddenly asked. "The original series."

Machiavelli tilted his head to one side. "Do I look like I watch *Star Trek*?"

"It's hard to tell. You'd never think it, but Black Hawk is a serious Trekkie. Has the uniform and everything."

"Billy. I ran one of the most sophisticated secret service organizations in the world. I did not have time for *Star Trek*." He paused and then added, "I was more of a Star Wars fan. Why do you ask?"

"Well, when Captain Kirk and Mr. Spock—you do know who they are, don't you?"

Machiavelli sighed. "I have lived in the twentieth century, Billy. I know who they are."

"Well, when they beamed down to a planet, usually with Dr. McCoy and sometimes with Scotty from engineering . . ."

"*Aspetta,*" Machiavelli began in Italian. "Wait a minute. So the captain and Mr. Spock—what's he again?"

"A Vulcan."

"His rank?" Machiavelli snapped.

"The first officer."

"So, the captain, the first officer and the ship's doctor and sometimes the engineer all beam down to a planet. Together. The entire complement of the senior officers?"

Billy nodded.

"And who has command of the ship?"

"I don't know. Junior officers, I guess."

"If they worked for me I'd have them court-martialed. That sounds like a gross dereliction of duty."

"I know. I know. I always thought it was odd myself. But that's not the point."

"What is the point?"

"They're usually accompanied by a guy in a red shirt. Always a crewman you've never seen before. And as soon as you see the red shirt, you know he's going to die."

"Where is this going?" Machiavelli asked.

Billy leaned forward. "Don't you see . . ." The bobbing light threw his glittering eyes into shadows. "We're the red shirts." He jerked his thumb over his head. "The Elders up there will survive; they always have. Probably most of the monsters will survive too. Dee and Dare have hightailed it. We're the ones who are going to end up getting eaten."

The Italian sighed. "During the reign of Napoleon—whom I liked, by the way—the term *cannon fodder* was coined," he said. "I fear you may be right."

"I think I preferred the term *red shirt*," Billy muttered.

"Boo!" A wicked curve of metal snaked around the American immortal's throat and a copper-skinned, sharp-nosed face loomed out of the darkness, teeth white against thin lips. "William Bonney, do you know how many times I could have killed you? You're getting sloppy."

"Black Hawk," Billy breathed. "You scared the life out of me!"

"A herd of stampeding buffalo makes less noise that you. And more sense."

Billy spun around and pushed Black Hawk's tomahawk to one side. "Oh, it sure is good to see you, old friend."

"And you." Black Hawk nodded at Machiavelli. "You too, Italian."

"We are relieved to find you alive," Machiavelli said. "We feared the worst."

"It was a close-run thing. The mermaids—"

"Nereids," Billy interrupted.

Black Hawk glared. "Excuse me, the *Nereids* swamped my boat, and I barely scrambled ashore and into a cave before this huge thing with a man's body and octopus legs attacked me."

"Nereus," Machiavelli said. "The Old Man of the Sea. I am surprised you got away."

Black Hawk looked at him blankly, light glinting copper off his skin.

"Alive, I mean," Machiavelli clarified. "Nereus is one of the deadliest of the Elders."

"Well, now he's just plain dead." The immortal warrior tapped his tomahawk against the palm of his hand and winked at Billy. "Sometimes the red shirts survive to fight another day."

CHAPTER TWENTY-ONE

With a long razor-nailed claw, Bastet pushed what looked like small square white teeth into the soft verge where the road coming off the Golden Gate Bridge curved around to the right and into Vista Point. "Feed them," she commanded.

Quetzalcoatl looked at her blankly. "What with?"

Bastet caught the Feathered Serpent's right hand, pulled off his glove and drove her nail into the tip of his forefinger. Thick red-black blood welled in the wound. Bastet squeezed.

"Ouch. Hurts!"

"Don't be such a baby. It's just a drop. You've seen enough blood in your time, I'll wager."

"Yes, but little of it was mine."

The blood fell hissing through the swirling fog and spattered into the hole, washing over the white tooth, which immediately started to sizzle and sputter like a firework.

"Feed them. One drop should be sufficient."

"Why do you get to plant them and I have to feed them?"

"Because they're my Drakon's teeth," Bastet snapped. She strode along the soft damp verge, creating more holes with her spiked high heels, then dropped a tooth in each.

"How many have you got?"

"Thirty-two. So I'm going to need thirty-two drops of blood."

"That's very nearly an armful!"

When she had planted all the teeth, Bastet returned to her car and watched Quetzalcoatl move reluctantly from tooth to tooth, feeding each one a single drop of blood from his index finger. Halfway down the line, he stopped and changed hands, puncturing a hole in his left index finger with his teeth. When he was finished, thirty-two sizzling, sparking fireworks buzzed in an almost straight line along the side of the road. He stood for a moment, sucking his index fingers, then shoved both hands in his pockets and hurried over to the gleaming black car.

"Now what?" he asked.

"Give it a few minutes. Let nature take its course." She smiled. "These are Drakon's teeth. They grow the Spartoi, the Drakon Warriors. They are earth warriors, and like many newborns, they are programmed to obey the first person they see when they emerge from the ground." Bastet smiled, teeth white in the gloom. "Run along now. Make sure they see you. Then send them across the bridge into the city."

"But how do we let Flamel and his companions know they're coming?"

"I'll take care of it." Bastet shook her head. "You really

didn't think this through, did you? What would you have done without me?"

"Sent in a messenger?" he suggested.

"Exactly. What sort of messenger? I imagine you still use snakes and birds as your couriers."

Quetzalcoatl reached into his pocket and handed over a cell phone. "There are some Sack Men in the city watching them right now," he said, his face expressionless. "You'll find the number on speed dial. You do know how to use a cell, don't you?"

Bastet's long nails scraped grooves in the back of the plastic phone as she scrolled through the menu and found the speed dial. Her call was answered on the first ring, and she recognized the peculiar liquid breathing of the creatures known as the *Torbalan*, the Sack Men.

"You are keeping four people under observation. Here is what I want you to do. . . ."

Two swords appeared in Niten's hands even before the shape loomed silently out of the fog. Prometheus moved to stand before Nicholas and Perenelle, while the Japanese immortal faded into the night.

The fog-wrapped figure looked like a young man. He was wearing shabby green combat trousers, thick-soled biker boots without laces and a coat that might once have been green but which was now streaked and indescribably filthy. The youth's head was shaven except for an inch-thick strip that stretched from ear to ear. His skin was poor, and his eyes were hidden behind badly scratched mirrored sunglasses. He carried an ornately stitched leather knapsack flung over his right shoulder. The bag slowly rippled and pulsed, as if a nest of snakes moved within it.

"What do you want, Torbalan?" Perenelle asked.

The figure reached for his coat pocket and Niten's katana appeared out of the gloom to lie flat across the knapsack. "Move very slowly," the Japanese immortal instructed. "If I see anything that even vaguely resembles a weapon, I will slice this bag open." His second short sword came to rest on the youth's shoulder. "Then I'll take your head. And you do not want that—do you?"

With infinite care, the Torbalan lifted a cell phone from his coat and tossed it to Prometheus. The big man snatched it out of the air, glanced at the screen and then handed it back to Perenelle.

"And what are we supposed to do with this?" she asked, looking from the Torbalan to Nicholas.

The phone began to chirp the theme to Looney Tunes.

"Answer it?" Nicholas suggested.

Perenelle hit Answer and put the phone to her ear. She did not speak.

The voice on the other end of the phone was female. It was low and husky, touched by an indefinable accent, and spoke in a language that had been ancient long before the rise of Egypt. "I think it unlikely that either of the warriors would have taken this phone. They would have wanted to keep their hands free for their weapons. I know the Alchemyst is uncomfortable with technology, so I would imagine I am speaking to the Sorceress, Perenelle Delamere Flamel."

"Very impressive," Perenelle said.

"I am Bastet."

Perenelle turned to Nicholas and mouthed the creature's name, then spoke into the phone. "You have returned."

"I never really went away." The Elder's chuckle turned into a deep rumbling purr. "The end is here. You fought well, some would say bravely, but now there is little left to do . . . except die, of course."

"We will not go down without a fight."

"I would expect no less. But the outcome will be the same: you will still die."

"Sooner or later we all die, Elder. Even you."

"I do not think so."

"You've gone to a lot of trouble to talk to me," Perenelle said. "Say your piece, so I can dismiss your . . ." Her eyes flickered over the Sack Man. ". . . your messenger. This one looks almost human. The sunglasses are a nice touch."

"I assure you they are not my creatures. I have better taste. However, I've just fed some Drakon's teeth into the ground, Sorceress—and you know what that means. Even now they are gathering on the Golden Gate Bridge. The Spartoi are coming." Bastet started to laugh, and then the line clicked and went dead.

Perenelle instantly hit Call and the phone dialed the last number received. The call was answered on the first ring by a slightly surprised Bastet. "Hello?"

"When all this is over, Elder, I will come for you. And if I am not able to do it in person, I will send something to hunt you down. I am the seventh daughter of a seventh daughter,

143

and I was trained by Medea herself. . . ." The Sorceress's ice-white aura formed in a silken glove around her hand and flowed over the phone.

"You don't frighten me," Bastet began, and then a scream of pain sounded over the connection and the conversation was cut short.

"What did you do?" Nicholas asked.

Perenelle shrugged. "Perhaps the phone melted into her hand." She tossed the cell back to the Sack Man, who instantly retreated into the night. The Sorceress turned to Prometheus and Niten. "The Spartoi are coming across the Golden Gate Bridge, heading this way."

"The Swordsman and I will go and hold the bridge," Prometheus said. "We will buy you as much time as we can . . . but hurry. You know what the Spartoi are like."

Tears sparkling in her eyes, Perenelle nodded.

"How many are coming?" Niten asked.

"Thirty-two of the deadliest warriors in the known world." She looked at Niten. "And you don't have to look quite so happy about it!"

CHAPTER TWENTY-TWO

*T*he size of the Yggdrasill was almost beyond comprehension. Impossibly wide, incalculably high, it stretched from ground to sky in a single massive column. Its roots plunged underground, deep into the core of the earth. Entire ecosystems thrived on the exterior of the vast tree; birds and insects, small mammals and lizards swarmed through the branches and leaves. Those living at the top of the tree in the ever-present clouds never saw those who lived close to the roots, and none of those knew about the world in the dark earth beneath the tree, where another environment flourished, pale blind creatures winding through enormous tunnels left by the roots. Endless generations lived and died on—and in—the Yggdrasill.

The tree was hollow, and within the trunk flourished the city of Wakah-Chan, one of the hidden wonders of Danu Talis.

Joan of Arc left Saint-Germain talking to Shakespeare and Palamedes and fell into step alongside Scathach. She linked her arm with her friend's. The French immortal's slate-gray eyes danced with excitement, and the faintest miasma of her lavender aura leaked from her body in a visible cloud. "We've had a lot of great adventures over the centuries," she said in English.

"We have," the Shadow agreed.

"And we have seen wonders."

Scathach nodded again.

"But in all your travels, have you ever seen anything like this before?" Joan asked.

"I have, actually. This is the second Yggdrasill I've been in this week. There is—there was—a distant relative of the original tree just north of San Francisco. It was huge, but nothing like this. Dee destroyed it," she added bitterly.

The two women were walking along a branch at least sixty feet wide. The branch was both road and bridge and stretched, unsupported, from one side of the Yggdrasill to the other, which was so far away it was lost in a swirling green mist that curled throughout the interior of the tree. Small one- and two-story buildings were scattered along the length of the branch. Slender dark-skinned men and women offered fruit and colored drinks from brightly canopied stalls in front of the buildings.

"Do you think they live here, on the bridge?" Joan asked.

"It sure looks that way," the Shadow said. "I wonder how many have rolled out of bed in the morning, stepped out their back door and gone off the side." She nodded to where the rears of the little homes were built right up against the edge of the branch. Beyond, there was nothing but a sheer drop.

"Trust you to think of that." Joan stopped then and suddenly grinned, realizing Scatty was making one of her very rare jokes. The houses had no back doors. "Very funny."

"Thank you."

"I was being sarcastic."

"I know."

The immortal craned her neck and looked upward. The vast hollow trunk disappeared into emerald-tinged clouds far above. The air over her head was crisscrossed with branches linking one side of the tree to the other, and the trunk was speckled with countless bulbous protrusions. Lights sparkled around these growths, but it was only when she walked to the edge of the branch, looked down and saw one up close that she realized she was looking at more dwellings set onto the sides of the Yggdrasill. Far below, where it was gloomy with early night, the trunk sparkled with thousands of lights.

"Careful!" Scathach caught Joan's belt as she leaned out farther. "We didn't come all this way to have you fall off the edge."

Joan pointed. "There are people flying."

The Shadow nodded. "I noticed that. They're strapped into gliders. I imagine this is the perfect environment for gliding, with thermals rising up from below."

"And did you notice also that they all look human?" Joan added. She lowered her voice and slipped into the provincial accent of eastern France, the first language she and the

Shadow had spoken together. "There are no dog-headed monsters here."

"I noticed," Scathach replied in the same language. "I'm not surprised, though; Hekate was always considered one of the great benefactors of humankind."

Still smiling, pointing at the gliders, Joan continued. "You also noticed that Huitzilopochtli was dressed in full armor."

"I saw that. And you saw the troops mustering on the branches below us?" Scathach asked.

"I did not." Joan wandered back over to the edge of the limb and peered down. Fifty feet below, on an equally wide branch, men and women were assembling in ranks. She assessed them with a soldier's eye. "That looks like a whole company . . . two hundred and fifty, maybe three hundred men and women," she said quietly. "They're all armed with simple weapons: plain armor, round shields, spears and bows." There was a crackle of leather and wood and a swarm of gliders detached from the sides of the Yggdrasill to drop down and join the rest of the soldiers. "Hmmm . . . and all the fliers are women and girls."

"Lighter than men," Scathach said.

"Their uniforms match the undersides of their gliders. Blue and white," Joan noted.

The Shadow nodded. "Camouflage. Anyone on the ground looking up is not going to easily spot them against the sky."

Joan examined the aerial troops more closely as they landed. Some had short throwing spears, but all had two or more quivers of arrows and at least one spare bow. Joan knew from years of battle that the spare was in case a string broke. The soldier would simply drop his bow and grab the backup. "I see no banners," she said quietly.

"Probably because they're not going to need them," Scathach said. "A banner is only useful on the battlefield to distinguish friend from foe. When you were fighting the English, the weapons and armor were very similar, but your men knew to flock to your white banner. A banner in a fight like this will only get in the way. I bet whoever they are fighting will be radically different—different race, different color, different species." She smiled at her friend. "These rules are a lot simpler. Anyone who doesn't look like you is your enemy."

"So they're preparing for battle," Joan murmured, almost to herself.

"I think they're already prepared." Scathach's green eyes danced. "We've arrived just in time for the war."

Joan of Arc pinched her friend's arm. "You don't have to look quite so happy about it!"

CHAPTER TWENTY-THREE

*O*siris and Virginia Dare came to their feet as Sophie and Josh approached. The twins were dressed in fresh jeans and T-shirts. Josh had tied a cream-colored Giants sweatshirt around his waist, and Sophie was wearing a black cardigan over her white T-shirt.

Virginia nodded to Sophie and smiled at Josh. "You're looking none the worse for your adventures." She glanced sideways at Osiris. "You must be very proud of your children. They've been through a lot in the last few days. It would have destroyed lesser people."

"Isis and I have always been very proud of the twins," Osiris answered evenly.

"This has been a really long day," Sophie said, acknowledging the adults. She felt a yawn swelling her chest and swallowed hard. "I'm exhausted."

"I'm famished," Josh said.

Sophie rolled her eyes at her twin. "You're always hungry."

He grinned. "I'm a growing boy. I've got a healthy appetite."

Even as he was speaking a door slid open and a series of tiny bells pinged. Everyone turned as Isis appeared. She had changed into a simple white linen robe similar to those worn by the queens of ancient Egypt. There was a narrow gold band wrapped around her head, and matching gold bracelets encircled her upper arms and wrists. Gold rings winked on every finger. Two of the cat-faced girls followed her, the bells on their toes tinkling with every movement.

Osiris bowed. He turned his head to look at the twins. "You should bow, children."

"To our own mother?" Josh demanded. "Why? We've never bowed before."

"That was then. This is now," Osiris said simply. "Everything has changed."

"I'm not bowing. That's just too weird," Josh said firmly. Sophie nodded in agreement.

The Elder looked at Virginia Dare and opened his mouth to speak.

The immortal met his gaze and held up her hand. "Don't even think about asking me to bow," she said.

Isis had crossed the courtyard and stopped before them. She acknowledged Osiris's bow with the merest nod and then looked the children up and down. The faintest moue of disappointment curled her lips. "Jeans and T-shirts? You could have chosen something more appropriate to this place and time," she murmured. "Remember when you accompanied us on our travels on the earth we always tried to dress respectfully in local costume. There are linen shirts and robes in the wardrobe. I am sure you would be more comfortable in them."

"I'm comfortable like this," Josh said, his voice hard. He looked at his sister. "What about you?"

She nodded. "I'm good."

There was an awkward moment of silence while Isis looked at Osiris as if she was expecting him to say something. "This has been a very difficult week for Sophie and Josh," he said eventually. "No doubt they are more comfortable wearing their own clothes; it is, after all, why we filled the wardrobes for them."

Sophie and Josh looked at one another. They both realized that in that moment something significant had altered in their relationship with their parents. Only a week ago, they would have returned to their rooms and changed with no questions.

"We will eat," Isis said firmly.

"Then you'll excuse me," Virginia said. "I don't want to intrude on this happy family moment. I'm sure you have a lot of catching up to do."

Without turning to look at the immortal, her gaze still trained on the twins, Isis waved a hand dismissively. "The servants have prepared a room for you at the other end of the house," she said. She sniffed quickly. "There is hot water if you wish to bathe, and I'll see to it that fresh clothes are laid out for you."

"We will send some food to your room," Osiris added, in a more pleasant voice. He smiled, trying to take the sting out of his wife's words and manner.

Virginia's smile was icy. "There's no need. I think I'm going to rest for a while. I've had quite the day too. Maybe you'll ask your people not to disturb me. No servants in or out, no food, no clothes, thank you. I'm fine with these. I just need my beauty sleep."

"None of the servants will intrude on your rest," Isis said. "If you'd like we could even post a guard on the door to ensure your privacy."

Virginia's laugher trailed behind her as she turned and walked away. "Oh, that won't be necessary. Why, it might even make me think I was a prisoner. And I wouldn't like that idea."

CHAPTER TWENTY-FOUR

$\mathcal{T}$sagaglalal moved easily through the stinking fog-locked streets.

Although it was still relatively early in the evening, San Francisco was almost completely deserted. The power outage had shut down the already quiet city. The initial surge of security alarms clanging dully across the city was starting to fade as batteries died. The whoop of emergency sirens sounded very small and distant, and Tsagaglalal's enhanced senses caught the tang of burnt rubber and gas on the air. There had been an accident. A big one. Maybe more than one. The Dark Elders were closing off the city.

It was uphill all the way to Jackson Street; then the street dipped and rose again. She turned right off Scott Street onto Broadway, where all the trees dripped water.

The streetlights on each corner were out, and traffic lights on Gough blinked a muted red. The only illumination came from the few cars still attempting to move through the streets. On Van Ness, taxis and busses crawled by in shimmering globes of light and SFPD cruisers crept slowly down the streets, hazard lights flashing. The police used their loud-speakers to advise people to get off the streets and remain indoors until the fog cleared.

Tsagaglalal's armor adapted to the surroundings, changing color, rendering her almost invisible against the night. She could smell the meaty foulness in the air and recognized both Quetzalcoatl's and Bastet's auras. The Feathered Serpent was dangerous enough, but the Elder goddess's return was a real concern: it meant that events were coming to a head. And Bastet, like Dee, did not know the meaning of subtlety. She also had nothing but contempt for humankind.

Turning left onto Hyde Street, Tsagaglalal raced toward Russian Hill Park. Less than a week ago, Bastet, the Morrigan and Dee had been involved in an attack on Hekate's new Yggdrasill in the Mill Valley Shadowrealm. In the brief and bitter battle, the ancient tree, grown from seeds salvaged during the fall of Danu Talis, was destroyed by John Dee wielding Excalibur. The Goddess with Three Faces had fallen with the tree, and her vast knowledge died with her. Dee and the Morrigan had continued to chase the twins, but Bastet had vanished. Tsagaglalal knew she had a house in Bel Air.

"When this is all over," Tsagaglalal whispered into the damp air, "and if I survive, I will make it my duty to hunt you down."

She was passing the tennis courts when a trio of badly dressed shaven-headed figures appeared in the gloom directly

155

ahead of her, rubber-soled combat boots silent on the pavement as they approached. They were chittering with excitement, the sound almost too high to hear, and threads of their gray auras, shot through with bruise-colored streaks, leaked from their flesh. Two hadn't even bothered to hide their tails. They were cucubuths on their way to feast.

"I hate cucubuths," Tsagaglalal breathed. "Nasty, foul, smelly . . ."

She Who Watches unsheathed her kopesh and sliced through them without a sound, leaving their bodies to dissolve to gritty powder.

Tsagaglalal knew that the only reason the cat-headed goddess had returned to the city was because she wanted to be around for the Elders' victory.

On more than one occasion, Tsagaglalal's husband, Abraham, had told her that he considered Bastet to be one of the most dangerous creatures he had ever met. "Her ambition will destroy the world," he warned.

At the top of the hill Tsagaglalal paused. "Right or straight on?" she wondered aloud, trying to work out the shortest route.

To the right lay Lombard Street, famous for its eight sharp curves. She could turn here, but she knew if she continued straight, she could make a right onto Jefferson, which would bring her directly to Fisherman's Wharf.

"Straight on." She jogged past the curvy road.

Bastet had always been both ambitious and greedy. Along with her husband, Amenhotep, she had ruled Danu Talis for centuries. When the Change began to work its way first through Amenhotep and later through Bastet, the Lord of Danu Talis had stepped aside and vested power in his son, Aten. Bastet had been furious: she'd spent decades working behind the scenes to ensure that her other son, her favorite, Anubis, would rule the island empire. She could control him; she had no control over Aten.

"Got any spare change, miss?"

Shimmering with moisture, two men, one unnaturally skinny, with a spiderweb tattooed across his ear, the other bigger, with a bodybuilder's broad chest and narrow waist, stepped out of the night. They had obviously been lounging against a wall on the corner of Lombard and Hyde. As she jogged nearer, she noted that the big man's face was bruised and scratched.

"Not a good night for jogging," the skinny one said.

"This fog—not healthy," the big one laughed.

"You could slip. You could fall. You could hurt yourself." The skinny one emphasized the word *hurt*.

Tsagaglalal's grip tightened on the kopesh, but she could smell that these were human. She kept her pace and saw something like alarm flicker in the bigger man's dirty eyes. "Oh no, not again . . . ," he breathed.

Her right shoulder hit the smaller man in the center of his chest. She heard something crack as he went sailing out across the road and onto the steep incline of Lombard Street. He squealed as he started to roll down the most crooked street in the world. Her left leg struck the bigger man just as he was scrambling to get out of her way. Something popped in his hip and he hit the ground hard enough to break something else.

Tsagaglalal kept going without giving them a second thought.

Aten was not without his flaws. She'd met him when he'd come to visit Abraham. The Lord of Danu Talis was arrogant—dangerously so—and impulsive, but unlike many of the other Elders, he recognized that the world was changing and that if Danu Talis—and indeed, the Elders themselves—were to survive, it had to change also. The world belonged to the new races, especially the humans. Aten worked with Abraham, Prometheus, Huitzilopochtli and Hekate to prepare a future in which the Elders and the humans could live together. Chronos had shown them many terrible versions of the future, but he had been able to show them wonders, too.

Tsagaglalal vividly recalled one particular possibility. In that time line, an incredibly advanced civilization of humans and Elders had rediscovered and then surpassed the Earthlords' knowledge. They had gone beyond this planet and begun to colonize the worlds around them. The empire of Danu Talis stretched over not a single planet, but entire galaxies. And at the heart of this huge galactic empire was the circular city of Danu Talis on a tiny blue-green planet at the edge of the Milky Way.

"A golden age," Abraham had said, unconsciously tapping his skin, which was even then beginning to thread with hard gold.

"Sadly, it will never come to pass," Chronos had gargled. "This is simply a shade of what might be."

"And why not?" Abraham had asked.

"Because Bastet and the others like her, those who live in the dark past, will not permit it. They believe that by empowering the humans they become weaker."

"Dark Elders," Abraham had murmured.

It was the first time Tsagaglalal had heard the term.

A shadow moved out of the park to her left and spread across the street. It rippled and flowed, water droplets shimmering on filthy black fur and long snaking tails. Tsagaglalal's mouth twisted in disgust. She had no feelings one way or another about rats, but these were obviously under the control of a Dark Elder. She waded into the middle of the heaving mass and they immediately swarmed her, scrambling over her feet, trying to crawl up her legs, but could find no purchase on her armor. Teeth screamed on her metal greaves like fingernails on a blackboard.

Tsagaglalal's aura flared, a brilliant blazing white. It pulsed out around her body in a series of concentric circles and the rats turned to red and black cinders, which spiraled up in the fog. The sudden throb of power also broke the controlling spell, and the surviving vermin disappeared squealing into the gutters.

Without breaking stride, Tsagaglalal turned right and continued down the street, heading for the water.

Danu Talis could have continued on to a golden age, but Bastet's greed overpowered all common sense. And on one terrible evening, Anubis and a troop of anpu staged a revolt and imprisoned Aten. The Lord of Danu Talis was accused of plotting to destroy the island empire.

Tsagaglalal suddenly stopped in the middle of Jefferson and threw back her head. There was a new odor on the air. Something ancient and appalling drifting over her left shoulder. She turned her head: it was coming off the Golden Gate Bridge. She smelled burnt enamel, rotting earth and blood and the unmistakable stench of a Drakon.

"Spartoi," she said, the word foul in her mouth.

She knew instinctively that this was why Bastet had returned.

"What to do?" she asked aloud.

The Flamels needed her help to contain the monsters on the island, but the threat on the bridge was the more immediate danger. If the Spartoi got into the city, there would be chaos. She had seen their work before. Each creature would kill hundreds—thousands—and those they did not eat would lurch back to a semblance of life as zombies, with an extra twenty-four hours of shambling movement before their bodies fell apart. The poor creatures were harmless, but their appearance was shocking and utterly terrifying. All would be lost.

With a heavy heart, Tsagaglalal turned back toward the Golden Gate Bridge. She could do nothing to help the Flamels. They were on their own.

CHAPTER TWENTY-FIVE

"How many more?" Dee gasped.

The immortal had started out well, but he'd managed barely fifty steps before he had to stop, lungs heaving for air, heart hammering.

Marethyu's voice echoed off the stone walls. "In total: two hundred and forty-eight from bottom to top. You have about two hundred left."

"Two forty-eight. One of the untouchable numbers. Why am I not surprised?"

"We need to press on, Doctor."

"And I need to catch my breath," Dee gasped.

"We have no time."

"Let me rest . . . unless you want me to expire here, on these steps."

"No, Doctor, we're not going to let you die just yet." Marethyu stretched out his hand. "Let me help you."

"Why?" Dee leaned on the slick crystal steps and looked up into Marethyu's blue eyes. "If you know who I am, then you know what I am, what I have done. Why are you helping me?"

"Because we all have our roles to play in saving the world."

"Even me?"

"Especially you."

Marethyu carried Dee up the remaining two hundred steps. The English immortal wrapped an arm over the man's shoulder and pressed his head against the figure's chest. He could hear no heartbeat, and as they climbed higher and higher, he became conscious that Marethyu was not breathing heavily with his exertions. He was not breathing at all.

The tall blue-eyed figure raced lightly up the steps. In places the walls were transparent, allowing Dee glimpses of a white-flecked gray ocean. Huge waves crashed against a rocky shoreline, outlining a town in foam and spray. Offshore, enormous blue-green icebergs smashed themselves against unseen rocks. As they climbed, Dee noticed that certain steps exuded odd odors or flickered with strange colors when they moved over them. Others trembled with musical notes or the temperature rose or fell sharply.

"We're passing through Shadowrealms?" Dee asked.

"Very astute."

"I would love to explore this place," Dee whispered.

"No, Doctor, you would not," Marethyu said with conviction. "This tower is built on the cusp of a dozen ley lines, in a place where at least as many Shadowrealms intersect. A couple of these steps bring us in and out of some of the worst worlds ever created. Linger too long on a step and you never know where you'll end up. Or what you might attract."

"Ah, but think of the adventure."

"There are some adventures not worth having."

Dee looked up into Marethyu's eyes. "And I take it you have had some of those?"

"I have."

"Is that where you lost your hand? Let me guess: some ravening monster bit it off and then Abraham created this hook for you."

"No, Doctor. You are so wrong." Marethyu laughed, and in that moment sounded very young. "Besides, I think if Abraham had made me a replacement, I would have asked him for something shaped a bit more . . . handlike, something a bit more useful." He ran the hook along the crystal walls and rainbow sparks cascaded over them. The semicircle of metal came to blazing light, writhing with arcane symbols. "In the beginning I hated it," he admitted.

"And now?" Dee asked.

"Now it is part of me. And I of it. Together we have changed the world."

Marethyu climbed up through a narrow rectangle in the floor and eased the elderly Dee into a sitting position on the flat roof of the crystal tower.

"From here I can see the world." Abraham the Mage stepped away from a squat cylindrical telescope, angling his body so that only one side was turned to Marethyu and Dee. "Come look."

"Give me a moment, I beg of you. Let me compose my-self." The doctor stretched out his legs and leaned back on stiffened arms. He looked up at the tall blond-haired figure wrapped in a cloak of shimmering gold foil. "In all the long years of my life, I always believed you were a legend," he breathed. "I never imagined you were real."

"Doctor, I am disappointed." Abraham's head moved in a tiny nod and he coughed a tiny laugh. "You know that at the heart of every legend is a grain of truth. You've dealt with monsters all your life. You consorted with creatures who were worshipped as gods, and fought alongside nightmares. And yet you consider me to be a legend!"

"Everyone likes to believe in a legend or two." Dee reached up and Marethyu helped him to his feet.

They were standing on a flat circular platform at the top of the crystal tower. A bitter wind whipped across the plat-form, rich with salt and sea spray and flecked with tiny sting-ing chips of ice.

"It is truly an honor to meet you." Dee stepped forward and stretched out his hand, but Marethyu gently pushed it down and shook his head slightly.

"The Mage will not shake your hand, Doctor."

Abraham stepped away from the telescope. "Come look."

The instrument was made of what looked like solid cream-colored crystal. The surface was faceted. Thin bands of silver encircled the tube, and when Dee peered into the eyepiece, he discovered it was shimmering and liquid, like mercury.

"Marethyu brought this back from one of his travels,"

Abraham said. His voice was labored, every word an effort. "He will not tell me where he found it, but I suspect it is Archon rather than Earthlord. The Earthlord artifacts tend to be almost brutal in their design. This has a certain delicacy to it."

"I can see nothing," Dee said. "Does it need to be focused?"

"Think of a person," Abraham said. "Someone you know well. I would say someone you care for, but I realize that might be difficult in your case."

Dee looked into the glass.

. . . *Sophie and Josh sitting at a circular table piled high with food. Isis and Osiris sat opposite them.*

He jerked his head back and lowered it to the eyepiece again.

. . . *Virginia Dare, in a loose white robe and straw hat, moving through streets teeming with small, dark-skinned people. Red-eyed, black-armored anpu watched from the shadows.*

"Extraordinary," Dee said, looking up. "It is similar to a scrying glass. Will it only see people in this Shadowrealm?"

"If the glass is fed with blood and pain, it will show other times, other places," Abraham whispered. "I do not feed it."

"But *you* have." Dee spun around to look at Marethyu.

"Sometimes," he admitted. Something sad and lost moved behind his gaze. "There are certain people I like to keep an eye on."

"I would have loved something like this. I can think of a thousand uses for it."

Marethyu shook his head. "It would have destroyed you, Doctor."

"I doubt it."

"Sometimes, when you look into the glass, you find something looking back at you. Something hungry."

Dee shrugged. "As you yourself said, I've seen monsters before. And there's not much they can do to you from the other side of a glass."

"They're not always on the other side of the glass," Abraham said. "Sometimes they come through." The Mage turned, allowing the immortal to see his entire body. The left side of his face from forehead to chin and from nose to ear was a solid gold mask. Only his eye remained untouched, although the white had turned a pale saffron with threads of gold twisted through the gray iris. The upper and lower teeth on the left side of his face were solid gold, and his left hand was covered in what looked like a golden glove.

"The Change," Dee breathed.

"I am impressed. Few humans in your time even know of it."

"I am not the average human."

"As arrogant as ever, Doctor, I see." Abraham turned back to the telescope and pressed his remaining eye against the eyepiece.

Dee suddenly found himself wondering who Abraham was looking at.

"The Change warps all of us sooner or later. Some—like your friend Bastet—it makes into monsters."

"Is every Change unique?"

"Yes, individual to the character. Changes may be similar, but no two are identical."

Dee limped over to stand beside Abraham and peered closely at his arm. "May I?" he asked.

The Mage's head moved a fraction.

Dee pressed his index finger against Abraham's shoulder and pushed. It was solid. Then he rapped on it with his knuckle. It rang with a dull thump.

"My aura is hardening on my skin."

"I saw something similar in a cave beneath Paris."

"Zephaniah took the idea for Mars's punishment from my Change."

"And it is not reversible?"

"No. Generations of Great Elders and Elders have attempted to reverse the process. There are occasional minor successes, but nothing permanent." Abraham stepped away from the telescope and turned slowly to face Dee. "What am I to do with you, Doctor? I have watched the human world for generations. I have seen heroes and villains. I have studied families and individuals, followed entire lineages for endless centuries. I understand humankind, I know what drives them, what motivates them. I know how and why they love and what they fear. And then there is you. . . . You are a mystery."

Dee glanced quickly at Marethyu. "Is that good or bad?"

Abraham walked to the edge of the tower and looked out at the distant city. "You have no idea how close we came to destroying you," he continued. "Chronos offered to send Marethyu back through time to kill your most distant ancestor so that we could wipe out your entire line."

167

"I'm glad you didn't," Dee muttered, nodding at Marethyu.

"Don't thank me. I wanted to do it."

Footsteps shuffled on the stairs and Dee turned as a beautiful young gray-eyed woman arrived on the platform. She ignored Dee, smiled at Marethyu and then flung a heavy hooded cloak around Abraham's shoulders. She glared at Dee. "I wanted to do it too."

"This is Tsagaglalal, my wife."

Dee bowed slightly. "I am honored."

"Don't be," she snapped. "I would push you off this platform with the greatest of pleasure." She eased her husband away from the edge of the platform and then moved around to stand in front of him so that he could look at her. "It is nearly time."

"I know. Go down. Get ready. I am almost finished with the doctor."

Tsagaglalal swept past Dee and disappeared below.

"She is going to hate you for millennia." Abraham stretched out his hand. "Give me my book, Doctor."

Dee hesitated.

The right side of Abraham's face moved in a ghastly smile. "A very foolish man would think about doing something stupid right now. Or worse—attempting to negotiate."

The doctor reached under his shirt. There was a soft leather bag on a cord around his neck. He tugged and the cord snapped free.

"Josh carries the pages he tore from the Book in a similar way," Marethyu said.

"I know. I just discovered that. I can't believe he had them with him all this time. They were so close; if only he'd given them to me, then everything would be so different." Dee sighed.

"Your life has been one of disappointments," Marethyu said.

"Are you being sarcastic?" Dee asked.

"Yes."

"I've had my share of disappointments," the Magician admitted. Reaching into the bag, he pulled out the small metalbound book. "I spent my entire life chasing this book. Over the centuries, I came close to securing it. But from the moment I finally got it into my hands, everything changed. It should have been my greatest triumph." He shook his head slightly. "Instead, everything started to go wrong."

Marethyu stepped forward and took the Book from the old man's hands. Resting it on his hook, he opened the cover. Instantly, yellow-white fire blazed across his hook, sizzling streamers dripping onto the stones, raining sparks like fireworks. "It's real," he announced.

With an almost painful effort, Abraham raised his golden hand and dropped it onto Dee's shoulder. "Doctor, did you ever pause to wonder why you never managed to catch up with the Flamels, why they always escaped just before you arrived?"

"Of course. I always thought they were lucky . . . ," he began. Then he shook his head. "No one is that lucky for that long, are they?"

Marethyu closed the Book with a snap. The fire died on

his hook. "You were never meant to find the Flamels and the Book. Until last week, of course, when you got the call giving you the address of the bookshop in San Francisco."

"And that was you?" Dee breathed, looking from Marethyu to Abraham. "I thought I was working for Isis and Osiris."

Death's blue eyes crinkled. "You are, but sometimes you—and they—are working for me."

CHAPTER TWENTY-SIX

When he'd been a very young child, Josh had suffered from a series of bizarre and terrifying nightmares.

He'd dreamt he was standing alongside his sleeping body, looking down at it. Sometimes he was sitting on the end of the bed staring at himself, but often, he was floating close to the ceiling, looking down on his body. Never once did he feel that he was in any danger, but the confusing images had still brought him awake screaming. Sleep had always been a long time coming after one of those dreams.

As Josh got older, the dreams almost completely disappeared. During periods of extreme stress—usually around finals—they returned, but time had robbed them of their power to frighten him. Now they were little more than strange images. Sometimes, when he drifted in that twilight zone between sleep and wakefulness, he caught the vaguest impression of the old dream, and would find himself for a single moment standing outside his body looking at himself, asleep. He was browsing the Internet one day when, by accident, he discovered there was a term for this—*an out-of-body-experience*.

And he felt like he was having one right now.

It was just like one of his dreams.

He was looking at himself sitting at a table with his parents and sister. Everything was normal: there was fruit on a plate in front of him, a glass of orange juice beside it. Large bowls filled with salad were in the center of the table, and there were two jugs of water—one with ice for his father and Sophie and a second without ice, which he and his mother preferred.

Everything was so familiar.

Except that it was *wrong*.

The couple sitting at the table looked like his parents, Richard and Sara Newman. They had the same eye color, identical lines on their faces, wrinkles at the corners of their mouths and eyes. This man who looked like his father even had a tiny half-moon scar on top of his shaven head, a pale semicircle standing out against his deeply tanned skin.

But these were not his parents.

The woman who looked like his mother was wearing the robes and jewelry of ancient Egypt.

There was nothing wrong with that. When they had gone to Egypt a few years before, she'd worn similar clothes on the boat they'd sailed in down the Nile.

But both the woman's and the man's nails were painted black.

That was odd—he'd never known his father to paint his

toenails, and black wasn't exactly a color his mother would ever have chosen.

When these people smiled, their teeth seemed too long, and although he hadn't had a close look, so he couldn't be certain, he thought their tongues looked dark purple instead of pink.

Nowhere had he seen *that* before.

And now that he looked at them, even the food and table itself didn't feel quite right.

The table was a circle of gold and silver, wrapped together like a yin and yang symbol. He and Osiris were sitting side by side at the gold curve, while his sister and Isis sat in front of the silver sections.

Josh?

The plates before him were gold, piled high with a spectacularly vivid selection of fruits—but, upon closer inspection, he only recognized a few of them. And the glass filled with juice was solid gold.

And his sister . . .

Josh looked across the table at Sophie. His twin was staring down at a silver plate heaped with cherries and grapes far too large to be natural. A silver cup brimmed with water, and the blunt knife and two-tined fork were also silver. She noticed him looking at her and raised her head, and in that instant he saw the same confusion in her eyes.

Josh?

Josh felt the world slip and shift again and he realized that this was no dream. His heart started to hammer painfully, and he could feel his lungs tightening. His subconscious was

173

telling him something important. He just wasn't sure what that was yet.

Josh!

Isis's voice was sharp.

He drew in a deep shuddering breath and felt the world shift and settle. Looking around, he discovered that everyone was looking at him, and he rolled his shoulders and twisted his head from side to side. Color flushed his cheeks. "Sorry, I sort of zoned out for a minute there. Might have even dozed off." He turned to look at his father. "What did you once call them?"

Osiris stared at him blankly for a long moment.

"Oh yes, I remember now: a microsleep. I must have been having a microsleep."

"Focus, Josh," Isis snapped. "This is important."

He was about to snap a response when he felt his sister's foot tap against his. He took a deep breath. "Sure. Sorry, Isi—sorry, Mom. I guess we're just exhausted by everything that's happened. I know I am."

"Me too. It's been a lot to take in," Sophie said. She speared one of the huge grapes with her fork and popped it in her mouth, then drained her glass. As soon as she placed it back on the table one of the cat-faced women silently appeared by her side and refilled it.

"Maybe we could get some sleep?" Josh suggested.

"I'm afraid that will have to wait. Our schedule has altered somewhat," Osiris said. "Eat, restore your energies. You have a long night ahead of you."

Josh looked at his sister, eyebrows moving fractionally upward in a silent question. She shook her head.

"You are aware by now that you are in the possession of extraordinary powers," Isis said. She turned to look first at Sophie, then across the table at Josh. "You don't need me to tell you that you are both remarkable people. In a week you've both been Awakened and trained in most of the Elemental Magics. In a week," she said to her husband, shaking her head. "It's truly astonishing."

"Ordinarily, it is a process that takes decades," Osiris agreed.

"Why didn't you Awaken us?" Sophie asked, and then immediately answered her own question without having to resort to the Witch's knowledge. "Because you can't."

Osiris's smile was icy. "We have other skills, Sophie, but no, we are not able to stimulate the Awakening process."

"So it's not a family trait?" Josh asked, confused.

"Not immediate family, no. But it is definitely clan related," Osiris said.

"Are we related to those Elders? The ones who Awakened us, who taught us: Hekate and Mars, Prometheus, Gilgamesh, Saint-Germain and the Witch?" Sophie asked.

"Distantly," Osiris muttered

"But they're not your friends, are they," Josh stated more than asked.

Isis and Osiris shook their heads simultaneously. "No, they are not."

Everything that had happened over the last several days

suddenly started to make sense to Josh. "Since no one knew you were related to us, you somehow got your enemies to Awaken and then train us because they thought we'd be working against you," Josh murmured, almost to himself.

"Yes, and we're quite proud of that strategy." Isis smiled at her husband.

"That's just great," Josh muttered.

"Thank you," Osiris said. "I see all those chess lessons weren't entirely wasted on you."

Josh dipped his head and concentrated on pushing the fruit around on his plate. He was thinking furiously, remembering a thousand tiny details from the past. Suddenly they took on a new meaning. He finally speared a segment of orange and popped it in his mouth. "So everything that's happened over the past week—"

"Don't speak with your mouth full!" Isis snapped.

"Sorry, Mom. Sorry, Isis," he deliberately amended. He swallowed hard. "So you've been behind everything that's happened over the past week?"

"Not just the past week," Osiris said. "Over the past fifteen years of your lives, and the ten thousand years leading up to that. From the first moments of your birth, we have been training both of you for this, your destiny. We taught you history and mythology so that when you did discover the truth, it would not be such a terrifying revelation, and so you would have some familiarity with the characters and creatures you'd encounter. We even insisted that you take up a martial art so that you could protect yourselves."

The twins nodded. Neither of them had ever wanted to

do Tae Kwon Do, but their parents had insisted, and no matter what city they lived in or school they attended, they had always been enrolled in a dojang to continue their training.

"We showed you the world," Isis said. "Exposed you to other cultures so that when you came here it would not be such a shock."

Osiris leaned forward. "And then, when all was in readiness, when you were both as prepared as you could be, I suggested you go for that job in the bookshop with the Flamels."

Josh blinked in surprise, then frowned, remembering. His father had showed him an ad in the university newspaper: *Assistant Wanted, Bookshop. We don't want readers, we want workers.*

"And I didn't want to do it," Josh whispered.

"And I told you I'd worked in a bookshop when I was your age. You wrote the letter and résumé, but never sent them in."

"I did," Isis said.

"And you were called for an interview two days later."

"You knew where the Flamels were hiding?" Sophie asked.

"We've always known where they are. We've been very careful to keep a close watch on the Codex."

"And you knew that when they saw me, they'd recognize me as a Gold," Josh whispered. "And Sophie as a Silver."

Isis's smile was bitter. "Those arrogant fools, the Flamels, have been seeking Golds and Silvers across the centuries. We simply gave them what they were looking for."

Osiris nodded. "The Alchemyst and his wife came to believe that they were far more important in the grand scheme of things than they really were. They were pawns. Just like Dee, and all the other humani."

"And us?" Sophie asked. "Are we pawns too?" She looked over at her brother and saw him nod.

"You are Gold and Silver," Osiris said quietly. "And yes, we have manipulated you, but not to use you as pawns. To protect you. Everything we have done was to keep you safe," he insisted. "You are like the king and queen on the chessboard: right now, in this time and place, you are the most valuable and important people on this world."

Isis leaned forward, metal bracelets pinging off the silver table. "None of this was by chance: millennia of careful planning went into ensuring that this exact sequence of events would unfold."

"You planned everything?" Sophie asked. Every new revelation made her feel slightly more sick to her stomach. "Even the bad parts?"

"Were there bad parts?" Isis asked. She looked at her husband and he shook his head. "What are you referring to?"

"I think she means the parts where we were almost killed," Josh answered for his twin. "I was almost eaten by a Nidhogg in Paris."

Isis waved a ringed hand as if Paris meant nothing. "You were never really in that much danger, Josh," she said. "You were in the company of some of the finest warriors of any generation. They protected you."

"I fought the Disir," Sophie said. She was unwilling to let

this go so easily. "I got the impression that they were trying really hard to kill me."

"And don't forget the Awakening process," Josh added.

Isis let out a light, musical laugh that sounded strangely false and practiced. "You were never in any danger from that. You are Gold and Silver," she said. "True Gold, pure Silver. Only the impure are damaged by the Awakening."

"And what about the attack by the undead in Ojai?" Josh pressed.

Isis tried another laugh. It sounded as false as the first. "Dee was not powerful enough to sustain them for very much longer. You destroyed them minutes before they would have collapsed of their own accord."

"And Coatlicue?" Sophie asked. "She was ready to feast on Josh."

"And I barely escaped the burning building," Josh added. "And then there was that thing with horns in London."

"Enough!" Isis clapped her hands, the rings on her fingers sparking as they snapped together. "This was all planned."

"Including Dee betraying you?" Sophie asked defiantly. "Because I got the clear impression that that was not in the cards."

The table fell silent.

Josh stared at his twin closely. "Dee went out on his own, didn't he?" He hadn't known for sure until she'd said it out loud.

Sophie nodded. "He grew tired of being a servant. He wanted to be the master."

Osiris held up his hand. "No plan is entirely foolproof.

There will always be some tiny unforeseen factors. Variables. Toward the end, Dee became a variable." He flashed a smile, and like his wife's laughter, it was practiced and false. "But we should balance that with the fact that he was a true and loyal servant for centuries."

"But he was your agent on earth," Josh protested. "That's not a tiny factor. That's a fairly major error."

"Enough," Osiris snapped. "He has paid the price. As does everyone who defies us. He was not our first servant. He will not be our last. Indeed, I believe Miss Dare is already moving into a position to replace him. I have made her an offer she's really not in any position to refuse."

"And she has accepted this offer?" Josh demanded.

"She has."

Josh couldn't believe what the Elder had just said. Virginia Dare? A servant to Isis and Osiris? To *anyone*? "I think you'll find that Virginia Dare is not John Dee," he said quietly.

"I know what she is," Osiris snarled.

Isis reached over and placed a hand on her husband's arm, stopping him before he could say anything else. "Josh is right." She looked at her husband carefully. "Dare is dangerous. And the flute makes her . . . unmanageable. I think you should withdraw your offer. We can easily find another human agent."

"Of course," he agreed immediately.

"But what will you do with her?" Sophie asked.

"That depends," Isis said.

"Depends on what?" Sophie demanded. Thoughts flickered at the corner of her mind, and she had a sudden image of Virginia falling from a great height into a bubbling volcano.

"On how cooperative she is."

"And if she isn't?" Josh demanded.

The smile that curled Osiris's lips was genuine this time. "We'll feed her—as we feed all traitors and criminals—to the volcano."

A door opened, breaking the silence that had fallen across the table. A red-eyed anpu appeared. One of the cat-women padded over to the monstrous creature and stood on her toes to put her head alongside his. They did not speak audibly, but the slight creature suddenly turned and ran back toward the table, tail whipping agitatedly from side to side. Isis and Osiris stood.

Josh leaned across the table toward his sister. "I'll bet Virginia's gone."

Sophie nodded.

Osiris and Isis listened to the servant's report, and the moment she'd finished, Osiris turned and hurried away.

Isis turned. "It seems Miss Dare decided she did not need her sleep after all," she said. "But not to worry, we'll find her. A *child* could follow her stink through the city. Now, you two, go get dressed. Properly this time. In clothing appropriate to this time and place."

Josh opened his mouth to protest.

Isis held up her hand. "No arguments, Josh. You will find that there is a suit of gold armor in your room; silver in yours, Sophie. Wear it."

"Why?" Josh demanded.

"You are being presented to the Ruling Council of Danu Talis this very evening."

Sophie shot her brother a fast look. "Why the rush?" she asked.

"It seems Danu Talis is in need of a ruler. Aten, the previous ruler—well, technically the present ruler, until he is tossed into the volcano—has been removed from power. Bastet thought she could be clever and acted while we were away. She'll be presenting her son Anubis to the council, making a case for him as the rightful heir of Amenhotep and the next ruler of the island." Isis's mouth twisted in an ugly sneer. "She believes we will support her. Of course, she does not know that we have you, the rightful heirs of Danu Talis."

Sophie shook her head. "I have no idea what you're talking about."

"You—both of you, Gold and Silver—are the rightful rulers of Danu Talis." Isis leaned forward, enveloping them in her cinnamon odor. "Within the hour, the Ruling Council with recognize you. At dawn tomorrow, you will be crowned rulers of the greatest empire ever to arise on the earth."

Sophie stepped back from the woman who looked like her mother. She was shaking her head. "No, that's not right. That can't be right." She frowned as the Witch's memories danced in her head. "That's not what happened before."

"A version of it did," Isis said quickly. "I was there in that time stream and I saw it all. I watched the twins fight and I saw Danu Talis fall."

"Hang on a sec. Which twins?" Josh demanded.

"Us," Sophie said bitterly.

"Us?"

"In a different time stream we fought. There have only ever been one set of true twins: us. We are the original twins of legend."

Josh felt the world shift and spin around him. His head had started to thump. "Hang on, hang on. We're the original twins. The first Gold and Silver."

"Yes," Isis said.

"And in another time stream, we fought. What happened then?"

He desperately tried to remember the fragments he'd discovered over the past days. "What happened to us, Sophie?"

Isis answered. "In the other time stream, the twins fought on the Pyramid of the Sun. They died there on that pyramid and Danu Talis fell," she said coldly. "That is not going to happen again. This particular time stream is one of the rare Auspicious Threads, those moments in time when the future is not yet fixed. There is a window—a small window—where we can change everything. We will not repeat the mistakes we made. You are the twins of legend, the original legend, created by your father and me: one to save the world, one to destroy it."

"Who saves it, who destroys it?" Josh asked. "Don't you know?"

"It does not refer to you as individuals, it means the world," Isis explained. "Together, you will save a world: Danu Talis."

"But only by destroying another world: the earth," Sophie whispered.

"Everything has a price. Now go, get dressed. We will

leave as soon as your father returns." Isis walked away, then stopped and looked over her shoulder. "A week ago you were nothing more than ordinary teenagers. Now you are on the cusp of becoming gods. Your powers will be limitless."

"I don't want to be a god," Sophie called after her defiantly.

The door slammed, leaving the twins alone in the garden. They stood in silence for a long time, trying to make sense of everything they'd discovered. When Josh finally turned to look at his sister, she was crying, huge silent tears rolling down her cheeks.

"Hey . . . hey . . . hey," he began. "Everything is going to work out. We're going to be okay."

"We're not!" she snapped. "Josh, I'm not crying because I'm sad. I'm crying because I am so mad right now. They . . ." She pointed at the closed door. "They, whoever they are, think they've got it figured out, that we're just pieces they can move around on their big cosmic chessboard and everything will work out the just way they planned it. They think we're going to go along with everything, question nothing and just do as we're told like good little boys and girls. They think we'll destroy the earth!" She shook her head and the garden filled with the scent of vanilla. "And it's not going to happen."

"It's not?" Josh asked. He loved it when his sister got mad.

"Not if we're the twins of legend," she said firmly.

"I don't want to fight you, Sophie," Josh said quickly. He shuffled his feet. "The last few days . . . I don't know what was going on. Dee . . . well, Dee just confused me. But I missed you. I really missed you."

184

"I know." Sophie smiled through her tears. "You have no idea what I did to get back to you."

"Followed me to Alcatraz, for a start. How did you do that?"

"It's complicated. And remind me to tell you about Aunt Agnes."

Josh blinked. "I'm guessing she's not Aunt Agnes."

"Oh, I think she is. And she is more, much, much more. She taught me that all the magics are equal, none more powerful that the other."

"Virginia taught me the Magic of Air," Josh said shyly.

"You like her, don't you."

"She's okay."

"You do like her!" Sophie's smile faded. "I wish she were here now—I wish someone were here who could advise us what to do."

"We don't need anyone, Sis," Josh said. "We've never needed anyone else. We're going to do what we think is right. Not what Isis and Osiris want or think they can force us to do. We're powerful—maybe even more powerful than they know."

Sophie nodded in agreement. "What was it Osiris called us: 'in this time and place, the most valuable and important people on this world.'"

"Oh, I think we're more important than that." Josh grinned. "I think we're another of the variables they've forgotten to account for."

"Variable and uncontrollable."

CHAPTER TWENTY-SEVEN

Billy the Kid followed Machiavelli and Black Hawk down the narrow tunnel. Dirty white light from a glowing ball of energy shimmered off the wet walls and dripped off the ceiling. The air stank of dead fish and rotting seaweed.

"This is just disgusting," Billy muttered.

"I'm inclined to agree with you," Machiavelli said. "But I have been in worse places. It reminds me a little of . . ."

"Don't tell me. I really don't want to know," Billy grumbled. He took a step forward and sank up to his ankle in fetid mud. A stinking bubble burst, spattering his jeans with filth. "When this is over, I'm going to have to burn these boots. And these are my favorite boots."

"I like you, Billy," Machiavelli said. "You are always so unfailingly optimistic. You're assuming that we're going to be alive at the end of this adventure so you can buy new boots."

"Well, I don't know about you, but I'm not planning on dying, that's for sure." Billy's teeth flashed in the gloom. "Black Hawk and I have been in some serious scrapes over the years." He looked over the Italian's shoulder and raised his voice. "I was just saying—"

"I heard you, Billy," Black Hawk said quietly. "In fact, I'm sure that everything on the island just heard you."

Billy shook his head. He jerked his thumb toward the ceiling. "Over that noise? I doubt it." The roars, screams and cries of the assembled monsters overhead percolated down through the rocks. "But we should look on the bright side. At least they're still on the island."

"We should only begin to worry when it gets quiet. Real quiet," Black Hawk said. "That either means they're creeping up on us or they've left the island."

"Impressive logic. Is that some Native American tracking lore?" Machiavelli asked.

Black Hawk shook his head. "Common sense." He stopped and pointed ahead. "There."

The Italian's hand moved and the glowing ball of light drifted down the tunnel, where it illuminated a rectangular doorway. Unlike the rest of the walls, which were encrusted with seaweed, barnacles and mud, this section was scraped clean and showed the original irregular bricks used to build the tunnel.

"This is the cave I was telling you about," Black Hawk said. "When I was finished with Nereus, some of the mermaid creatures were a little upset with me."

Billy grinned and opened his mouth to comment, but Machiavelli reached over and squeezed his arm, silencing him.

"Not having been left with a whole lot of choices," Black Hawk continued, "I retreated deeper into the tunnel. The women chased me—even without legs they made good time dragging themselves forward with their hands, flapping their tails. A bit like salmon swimming upriver. They were howling and hissing until we reached the bend just there. And then they stopped as if they had run into a wall." Black Hawk raised his hand and the foul tunnel air swirled with the sharp, clean, vaguely medicinal odor of sarsaparilla. Pale green flames danced along his fingertips, then drifted up to form an amorphous emerald-colored cloud, and the walls of the tunnel blossomed with shimmering, trembling silver-green light. "I saw this," he said.

"What is it?" Billy whispered, looking at the walls.

Black Hawk reached out and ran his right hand down the wall. It was covered with a fine, glimmering coating that came away on his fingers in long gossamer threads. "Spiderweb," he said. "The walls are covered in web."

"That's a lot of spiders," Billy said nervously.

Black Hawk waved his hand and the green cloud drifted deeper into the tunnel, illuminating it. "You can see where it's torn in places, so something big moved through here." He stepped forward and scooped a length of wood from the mud. "But this is what really interests me," he said. "I had just discovered this when I heard your voices." Black Hawk held out an inch-thick length of solid black wood topped with a long flat leaf-shaped blade. Machiavelli and Billy leaned over to look at the weapon.

"It's a spear," Billy said. "An old one too. I don't know that blade pattern. It's not native to the Americas."

"Looks African to me—Zulu, perhaps," Machiavelli said.

"There are some more in the mud behind me," Black Hawk said. He brought his hand over the metal head of the spear. The green aura trembling on his fingers illuminated a square hieroglyph painted onto the blade.

"Ah," Machiavelli breathed. "What have we here?" As he reached out, his fingertips popped alight and the odor of serpent filled the tunnel.

"Man, you need a better smell," Billy said.

"I like it," Machiavelli murmured absently, dirty gray light dribbling off his fingers. "It has served me well." His gray eyes took on the green of Black Hawk's aura and the square glyph reflected in his pupils. The Italian glanced up at Black Hawk. "You know what this is?"

"I've seen similar spears before," he said. "And our legends are full of them. They're ancient and deadly. Only the most powerful of medicine men can carry them." He pointed to the glyph on the blade. "I've never seen that on a medicine man's spear, though. The pattern looks South American."

Billy looked over the Italian's shoulder at Black Hawk. "I've seen something similar in Quetzalcoatl's Shadowrealm. They're in the kitchen, over the fridge. . . ."

"Yes, there's a wall carved with these square facelike shapes. The wall looks older than the rest of the house," Black Hawk confirmed.

"It makes sense that Quetzalcoatl would know the words." Machiavelli looked around. "You said there were more?"

Black Hawk lifted another two spears from the sticky mud. The heads had been daubed with more of the square glyphs, though one of them had been partially washed away by the seawater. Billy found two more spears near the tunnel wall. One head bore only a hint of writing, and the second showed signs of a glyph that had been partially scraped away.

"You'll note how the lower third of the spear is dark and stained."

Black Hawk spun one of the weapons and plunged it butt-first into the ground. The water came up to the mark on the wood.

"There would have been at least twelve spears," Machiavelli said, "set out in a particular pattern in the mud." His hand moved, describing an outline in the air. "The pattern would have formed a matrix of power."

"A what?" Billy asked.

"Think of it as a sophisticated burglar alarm. The head of each spear would have been painted in woad, red ochre or perhaps blood." He turned the flat head of a spear to the light. "These glyphs might look South American, but they're older, far, far older. These are the Words of Power, ancient Symbols of Binding, drawn from a language that was little more than a memory even before Danu Talis rose from the waves. Legend has it that the Archons used these words to protect something incredibly valuable or guard against something extraordinarily dangerous."

Billy grinned. "And we know which one it's going to be in this case."

Machiavelli spun the spear in his left hand. It hummed and vibrated and the square symbol glowed dully. The three immortals' auras flickered. "Do you feel that?" he asked, something like awe in his voice.

Billy and Black Hawk both nodded: their mouths were suddenly numb and the air felt thick. Billy rubbed his hand over his left eyebrow at the abrupt pressure of a headache. The Italian stretched out his arm and the head of the spear brushed against the cobwebs, instantly shriveling them to nothing. "Gather as many spears as you can," Machiavelli snapped. Then he brushed past the two Americans and disappeared into the gloom.

"Hey, when did we become your porters?" Billy called after him. He looked at Black Hawk. "Can you believe these European immortals?"

Machiavelli's voice drifted back down the tunnel. "I would be quite happy to carry the spears, Billy. But then *you'd* have to investigate this interesting-looking cave."

"I was going to mention the cave," Black Hawk said before Billy could answer. "I saw it as I passed."

"But you didn't go in?" Machiavelli asked.

"Do I look stupid?"

The globe of light flared at Machiavelli's fingers, revealing a black opening in the wall. The entrance to the cave was artificial—a large rectangular doorway had been cut into the solid rock. Machiavelli waved a hand and his globe rose to the lintel. The faintest outline of shifting, shimmering symbols bloomed under the gray light, and the immortal stood on his toes to look at the topmost row. "I am guessing that the lintels and doorposts would have been completely painted with Words of Power. They've been covered with mud or washed off. Recently, too," he added, pointing to the dried streaks on the wall. "Quetzalcoatl went to a lot of trouble to trap whoever—whatever—was in the cave. This was a prison." Machiavelli disappeared into the blackness, and the interior filled with wan light. "And remember, Billy . . ." His voice echoed. "The enemy of my enemy—"

"Yeah, yeah, yeah. You need a new catchphrase," Billy mumbled.

Machiavelli reappeared at the entrance a moment later. In the reflected light from his globe and Black Hawk's green light, his skin looked pale and unhealthy, but his gray eyes glittered with excitement. "It's empty."

"That's good," Billy said. He looked at Black Hawk. "Isn't it?"

Black Hawk smiled. "I think our European friend has a plan."

"Grab the spears," Machiavelli said. "I know what was in the cave . . . and I know why it was there. And I think I know how to defeat the monsters. We need to get topside."

And then the entire island trembled.

The ground shifted, water sloshing up the tunnel walls. Dust and grit cascaded from the ceiling in a gritty rain. Bricks cracked; one exploded under the pressure, spraying powder into the air, and ice water suddenly rushed into the tunnel, rising quickly to knee level.

"What manner of beast is this?" Machiavelli demanded.

"No beast!" Billy shouted. He caught one of Machiavelli's arms, and Black Hawk grabbed the other. They dragged him down the tunnel.

"Worse," Black Hawk shouted.

"What, then?"

"It's an earthquake," Billy and Black Hawk said together. Behind them the roof of the tunnel cracked. Then it collapsed.

CHAPTER TWENTY-EIGHT

*T*he Golden Gate Bridge swayed.

"Earthquake," Prometheus said. "I wonder if that means Ruaumoko has finally sided with the Dark Elders."

"No, I'm afraid our fiery friend is trapped in a Shadowrealm," Niten said with a shy smile. "He had a little disagreement with Aoife and lost."

A second aftershock rumbled and the metal bridge hummed.

The cold salty air was touched with the bittersweet odor of anise, and in the space of a single step Prometheus flickered into gleaming red armor. An enormous broadsword was strapped across his back, and he carried a war hammer in one hand and a battle-ax in the other.

Niten was still dressed in his black suit, but now he openly carried his two swords—katana and wakizashi—strapped to his back.

Scores of cars had been abandoned on the bridge when the fog closed down the city and made it too dangerous to drive. They loomed in indistinct shapes in the fog, like slumbering animals. Prometheus and Niten checked each one as they passed, but they were all empty. One car's lights were still on. The beams bounced back off a shifting impenetrable wall.

"Two against thirty-two," Niten said. "Good odds."

"I've never fought the Spartoi before," Prometheus admitted. "I only know of them by their reputation—and it is fearsome."

"We have an equal reputation," Niten said.

"Well, you do," the Elder said. "I was never that much of a fighter. And after the fall of the island, I rarely took up weapons again."

"Fighting is a skill you never forget," Niten said, a touch of sadness in his voice. "I fought my first duel when I was thirteen. I've been fighting ever since."

"But you are more than just a swordsman," Prometheus said. "You are an artist, a sculptor and a writer."

"No man is ever just one thing," Niten answered. His shoulder dropped and his short sword appeared in his left hand, water droplets sparkling from the blade. "But first and foremost, I was always a warrior." He jabbed his sword into the fog and stirred it like liquid.

"It's getting thicker," Prometheus said.

"Which is good. We can use this to our advantage."

"We won't be able to see them," Prometheus pointed out.

"Nor will they be able to see us," the Swordsman

reminded him. "We have the advantage of knowing exactly who and what we are facing. They have no idea what they're up against. Or how many."

"A good point."

"Can I make a suggestion?" Niten said, almost shyly.

"Oh course. You are the master warrior. Here, you are the expert."

"Lose the armor."

Prometheus's green eyes blinked in surprise.

Niten breathed in. "I can smell your aura. And if I can, then so can they. Also, there is just the faintest hint of crimson around you, a smudge of red light. Against this gloom, you'll stand out like a beacon."

"Can I keep the swords?" Prometheus asked.

"One sword should be enough."

"You have two," the Elder reminded him.

"I'm fast," Niten said. "But you are strong. Keep the claymore."

The Elder nodded and his armor winked out of existence, leaving him in a shirt and jeans, with just the broadsword in his hand.

"Which side of the bridge do you want?" Niten asked.

"I'll take the right," Prometheus said.

"I thought you might." Niten nodded, moving to the left side. "We cannot let the Spartoi into the city."

"Remember, warrior, we don't even have to kill them, we simply have to hold them until sunrise," Prometheus answered. "The energy that animates them will dissipate then. I am concerned that one or two will engage us here and the

196

rest will simply flow past. We can't fight them all at the same time."

Niten nodded. "What we need is a barrier of sorts . . . ," he began.

Simultaneously the Elder and immortal looked around at the vague shapes of the abandoned cars. "So how strong are you?" Niten asked.

"Very. You're thinking of a wall of cars?"

The fog turned Niten's dark hair into a silver cap. He held up two fingers in a V. "We could create a funnel. It would close the Spartoi up, push them together, channel them in toward us and rob them of the advantage of numbers. They could only come at us one or two at a time. . . ." His voice trailed off. "Or they could climb over the cars, I suppose."

The Elder grunted a laugh. "Have you ever seen one of the Spartoi?"

Niten shook his head.

"They are grown from the Drakon's teeth. You know what a Nile crocodile looks like? Of course you do," Prometheus said, answering his own question. "The Spartoi share a lot of that reptilian DNA. They are about your height but have short, short legs, long bodies, narrow heads. They can run on two or four legs, and they are fast, fast, fast. But they're not great at climbing." He squinted into the fog. "If I turn the cars on their sides, that would make it even more difficult." He peered unsuccessfully into the gloom. "I'm not sure how many cars I'm going to need, or if there's even enough on the bridge. And it's going to take me a little while to organize them."

"Then I'll go keep our crocodile friends busy." Niten's teeth flashed in a smile. "I'll try to leave a few for you." He stepped away and faded into the night.

"Be careful," Prometheus called.

A disembodied voice drifted out of the fog. "I was born for this. What's the worst that could happen?"

"You could be killed and eaten by the Spartoi."

"Doesn't frighten me."

"It should," Prometheus warned. "They won't necessarily wait till you're dead before they start to eat you."

CHAPTER TWENTY-NINE

Suddenly the still night was broken by an odd barking—a sound that almost resembled coughing.

"Dogs?" Perenelle answered.

"Not dogs, seals," Nicholas suggested.

Abruptly, gulls wheeled overhead, ghost flashes in the fog, calling and cawing.

"Something's wrong. Gulls shouldn't cry at night," Nicholas said. Closing his eyes, he tilted his head back and breathed deeply. "Odd. I don't smell anything new."

More barking—this time it *was* dogs. The sounds were muted by the thickening fog.

"Oh no!" Nicholas suddenly reached out and caught Perenelle's hand just as the pier started to roll and vibrate. The metal chairs they were sitting on trembled and rattled against the stones.

"What was that?" Perenelle asked, when the rumbling vibration had finally subsided. "Elder? Archon?"

"Earthquake," Nicholas said, a little breathlessly. "Maybe a four on the Richter scale. And close, very, very close."

"Who do you think caused it?" Perenelle wondered. "If the Dark Elders can access that sort of power, then we're in trouble. They can destroy this city without bringing a single creature ashore." She frowned. "Why wouldn't they have used it before this?"

The Alchemyst shook his head. "It's probably natural," he said. "Remember what happened when you and Machiavelli fought on Mount Etna? I'm sure the earthquake has been triggered by all the raw energies concentrated in the city." He rubbed his hands together and green sparks shimmered in the air. "Look at that. The air is alive with auras. We know Bastet is out there somewhere. Quetzalcoatl, too. Prometheus and Niten are on their way to face the Spartoi warriors—and I'm not sure if the Drakon have auras. Mars, Odin, Hel, Billy, Machiavelli—and maybe Black Hawk—are on the island." He ran his hand across his head, rubbing his cropped hair as he thought. Static fizzled across his scalp, dripping sparks like fireworks onto his shoulders. "Another reason why the Elders never congregate in any great numbers in modern times."

Perenelle licked her lips and nodded. "I can taste the power on the air."

A ten-second shudder vibrated up through the streets. "Aftershock," Nicholas breathed. "I would imagine the last time so many auras were gathered in such close proximity was on Danu Talis."

"If anyone does arrive to support us, then their auras, added to everything else here, might bring on an even bigger earthquake. We need to get over to the island and finish this." She caught her husband's hand and pulled him along the quayside, toward the water. "As soon as we start to use our auras," she said, "we reveal our location to whoever—whatever—is out there. And we start to age. If anything delays us as we make our away across the bay, we run the risk of dying of old age before we reach it."

Perenelle and Nicholas ran past the Aquarium of the Bay. They could hear the water on their left, slapping against wooden pilings. They both knew there were scores of boats, invisible because of the fog, in the berths. They could hear hulls banging and scraping against the wood, stays pinging off metal. A mast loomed directly in front of them and they suddenly found themselves right at the edge of the pier. Fog curled off the water like steam.

"Do you remember how to do this?" Nicholas asked with a cautious grin.

"Of course." Perenelle smiled. "It's a simple transmutation spell. We used to do it for the . . ." The words died on her lips and her smile faded away.

"We used to do it to amuse the children," Nicholas finished. He wrapped his arms around his wife and held her close, her hair damp against his face. "We did what we believed was the right thing," he said quickly, "and I will never accept that what we did was wrong."

"We protected the Book," she murmured.

For centuries, Nicholas and Perenelle Flamel had sought

out the twins of legend. When they found a Gold and Silver pair, they attempted to Awaken them, but none of the few who survived had ever been truly sane afterward. Until Sophie and Josh.

"So many lives lost," she whispered.

"So many saved," he said quickly. "We protected the Book from Dee. Can you imagine what he would have done if he'd found it? And ultimately, we did find the twins of legend and Awakened them successfully. We were doing the right thing, I am convinced of that."

"I think Dr. Dee probably says exactly the same thing to justify his actions," Perenelle said bitterly.

"Perenelle." Nicholas Flamel looked deep into his wife's green eyes. "Our journey has brought us here, to this place, in this time, where we can make a difference. Together, we can save this city and prevent the Dark Elders from destroying this Shadowrealm."

The Sorceress nodded and stepped away from her husband. Standing on the very edge of the pier, she stretched out her left hand, palm upward, fingers curled. Perenelle's ice-white aura formed in a liquid puddle in the palm of her hand. Slow bubbles rose and burst, and then the liquid spilled out of her hand and dropped in long, gelatinous streamers into the sea. Nicholas reached over, and in the moment before he took his wife's hand, his own aura flowed in a green glove over his fingers and the strong odor of mint filled the air. The auras mixed—white and green—to become a sticky emerald mass that dripped through their grip, hardening the wet fog to shards of green ice where it touched, before splashing onto the waves below.

"Transmutation," Nicholas said. "One of the simplest principles of alchemy."

"Simple for you, perhaps." Perenelle smiled.

"My specialty," he agreed. "All we have to do is to change the state of water from liquid to solid."

Where the Flamels' auras touched the waves, an irregular circle turned to ice. Crackling, snapping, cracking, waves hardened, caught as they rose and broke against the side of the pier in a sheet of ice.

Nicholas helped Perenelle climb down onto the frozen circle of sea. She stamped her foot. The ice creaked but held firm. Then she jumped up and down.

"Please don't do that," Nicholas whispered.

"Come on in," she called up, "the water's frozen."

"Yes. And we need to hurry," the Alchemyst said, climbing over the side of the pier. "It's not going to stay that way for long. The sea salt will eat away at it." When he dropped onto the circle of ice, it tipped and rocked. Perenelle immediately stepped over to the other side, balancing it.

The couple stood together, side by side on the frozen patch of sea. All around them the water was still liquid. The Alchemyst rubbed his hands together, as if he was rolling a ball. The smell of mint was almost overpowering. He threw out his arm, casting his green aura in a ribbon that stretched about four feet ahead of them. The aura splashed onto the water and immediately hardened into a narrow ice bridge on the surface of the sea. Hand in hand, the Alchemyst and the Sorceress stepped onto the crackling bridge.

When they reached the end of the bridge, Perenelle flung out her arm, and a shimmering six-foot length of white smoke formed on the surface of the sea, freezing it.

The couple pushed on in silence, creating stretches of the ice bridge bit by bit before them. Behind them, the salt sea-water quickly reclaimed the frozen pathway. This close to the water, wrapped in the ever-thickening fog, they couldn't see anything, and they had no idea how close they were to the shore. They knew they had moved out into the bay, because the waves were higher, solidifying into beautiful S-shaped patterns. But the surrounding seas were rougher and the ice paths survived for only seconds, barely enough time to allow them to race from one to the next.

Perenelle suddenly squeezed her husband's hand. Without speaking, he nodded.

Something had splashed through the water off to their left. There was a second and then a third splash. And then, faintly, like the noise from tiny distant headphones, they heard what sounded like a zoo at feeding time and realized they were close to the island.

Nicholas threw down another path. They were just stepping onto it when a monster reared out of the fog.

And then a second and a third.

Nereids.

They surged out of the fog in flashes of wild green hair, ragged teeth and flashing claws, descending on the two figures on the melting strip of ice in the middle of San Francisco Bay.

CHAPTER THIRTY

The Nereid was huge.

Unlike her two green-haired companions, she was bald, and a long, ancient white scar and puckered indentations ran across one side of her face, leaving one eye a milky globe. Mouth open in a gargling scream, the scarred monster rose on her tail, arm raised, and jabbed a wickedly spiked stone trident directly toward Perenelle.

The Sorceress jerked backward and her feet went out from under her. She crashed onto the ice, which immediately split in two. Salt water poured in.

Nicholas flung a handful of green aura into the creature's face. The seawater covering the Nereid froze in crackled sheets from her head, across her chest and stomach and down to her tail, turning her into a solid block of ice. The Alchemyst wrenched the trident out of the creature's claws a moment before the weight of the ice flipped her, head over tail, dragging her beneath the choppy waves. He jabbed the trident at a Nereid scrabbling to climb onto the ice. It floundered back into the water, tail thrashing.

Still lying on her back, Perenelle kicked out at the third creature, which was trying to drag her into the water. She sprayed slivers of ice into the Nereid's eyes but it continued to crawl out of the sea, long nails digging into the ice path.

And then Nicholas splashed it with his aura. The Nereid instantly turned to a block of ice, but the weight of the creature snapped the path in two again, leaving Perenelle on a tiny rectangular section of fast-melting ice.

And the waters around them were coming alive with Nereids.

Pressing his hand to the scarab around his neck, Nicholas drew upon his reserves of strength. His splayed fingers sent thick streamers of green aura across the sea. Instantly a crystalline emerald carpet coated the surface of the water, trapping the Nereids beneath. They howled and hammered on the frozen surface.

Perenelle leapt off her tiny fragment of ice just before it melted. She landed on the green carpet and slid across the frozen sea. Nicholas stretched out the trident and she caught it, almost pulling him to the ground.

The frozen green carpet shattered and the sea around them boiled with the savage mermaids, waves frothing and foaming with green hair and fish tails.

The Sorceress pointed off to the left. "The island is this

way." She snatched the spear from her husband's hand and swung it at a razor-toothed Nereid that launched itself out of the water. The creature squealed as the stone blades sheared off a hank of green hair; then it hit the ice on its back and spun back into the waves. Perenelle jabbed at another. The creature flipped head over tail in an attempt to get away from the weapon, but Perenelle caught it a glancing blow across the side of the head. The Sorceress swung the trident again. It hummed with raw power, leaving the stench of fish in the air behind it, and she suddenly remembered where she'd seen it before: in the tunnels beneath Alcatraz in the hands of the Old Man of the Sea.

"This is Nereus's trident," she called to Nicholas. "I wonder how he came to lose it."

"Not voluntarily, I'll wager." Her husband grunted. With his hand pressed to the scarab on his chest, he focused on creating another length of the ice bridge, but he was weakening fast. The ice was thinner, cracking even as they ran across it. "I can't do this much longer."

"We're nearly there," Perenelle shouted over the thrashing creatures in the sea around them. Although she was trying to save the remainder of her aura, she knew they had little choice if they were to survive. She recalled a little spell she'd learned from Saint-Germain—something effective that wouldn't take too much power. Thick liquid leaked from her palms and soaked into the gray stone trident, turning it a deep red, then a dark, almost blackish blue. The Sorceress plunged the trident into the waves and the color leaked into the water like oil. She churned the spear, sending twists of ink out into the sea. *"Ignis,"* she whispered.

The sea popped alight, pale blue-red flames dancing across the surface of the water, illuminating a scattering of seaweed-covered rocks. Directly above the rocks was a low rust-streaked wall topped by a metal fence. Looming over the fence, surrounded by trees and bristling cacti, was a huge flaking wooden sign:

WARNING

PERSONS PROCURING OR

CONCEALING ESCAPE OF

PRISONERS ARE SUBJECT

TO PROSECUTION AND

IMPRISONMENT

With the last of his strength Nicholas threw his aura over the stones and watched it freeze into a series of crude steps. Then he held out his hand to his wife and helped her over the slippery stones. The trident's blade sheered through the fence and the couple crawled on all fours up to a damp and narrow footpath beneath the sign. They collapsed, rolled over onto their backs and looked up at the flaking sign.

"Welcome to Alcatraz," the Alchemyst said. Exhausted and shaken, they climbed to their feet and collapsed once more onto a wooden bench. In previous years, tourists would have seated themselves on the very same benches to look out across at the city and bridge. The couple sat for a moment, catching their breath, and then Nicholas turned to look at his wife. The fog gave her face an almost unearthly appearance, making it even more beautiful than usual. "I've just realized something," he said in archaic French.

Perenelle nodded. "I know."

"We're not going to get off this island alive, are we?"

"No, we're not."

CHAPTER THIRTY-ONE

*H*ekate, the Goddess with Three Faces, sat in the throne room of the living tree.

The room was surprisingly small, little more than a round antechamber scooped out of the Yggdrasill. The chamber had been waxed and polished to a mirrorlike sheen, and a stunted gnarled branch had been shaped and worked into an ornate throne. The walls were bare, and the only item in the room was a white candle as thick and as tall as an adult human, positioned to the right of the throne. The warm yellow flame was protected by an enormous crystal globe. The top was open, and an almost invisible trail of black smoke had left a perfect circle on the ceiling above.

Prometheus stood to the left of the throne, arms folded across his massive chest. Scathach had taken up a position beside the door, with her back to the wall. Palamedes mirrored her position on the opposite side of the door.

Shakespeare stood by the window, mouth agape as he looked down into the heart of the tree. He was scribbling shorthand notes on a scrap of yellowed paper with the chewed stump of a pencil. Hand in hand, Joan and Saint-Germain stood before the throne and looked at the Elder.

Hekate had aged with the day.

Her Change was unique: she was a young girl in the morning who slowly turned into a mature woman in the afternoon and rapidly aged into an old woman as the day wore on. The ancient woman was laid to sleep in a long, narrow, hollowed root of the Yggdrasill, and with the dawn she was young again. The young girl who awoke in the morning had no knowledge of the woman she had been the previous day, and the old woman she became in the evening forgot all that had transpired during the hours of sunlight. Only the mature woman, who ruled during the afternoon hours, when the sun rode high in the sky, had complete knowledge and comprehension of the other aspects of herself. She was inextricably linked to the tree, and the tree was older than the Shadowrealm, its origins long lost in the mists of history. Many believed that it was sentient.

"I have but moments, and there is much that must remain unspoken," the white-haired woman on the throne said. "I'm aging fast, and in a few minutes, I may not even know who you are." Her teeth flashed white against her dark face in a smile, but no one laughed. They knew she wasn't joking.

"Events are moving to a conclusion," she said quickly, looking from face to face. "I do not know who most of you are—though your coming was foretold by Abraham, and that is good enough for me. The Mage told me that humani from the Time to Come would arrive to stand with us, to fight for the survival of my world and the future of theirs." Rainbow colors shimmered iridescent, flowing up the length of her dress. "We live in dangerous times. I have been told, though I do not fully comprehend it, that in this particular time stream there exists an opportunity to shape the future and remake everything. It sounds remarkable, outrageous, even, but then, we live in the age of the extraordinary. It appears that others are attempting to reshape the future to their particular needs. Abraham and Chronos have assured me that if those others succeed, then untold billions of lives will simply cease." She shook her head. "I will not allow it."

"So you are preparing for war," Scathach said. "We saw the troops mustering."

"Not a war. A rescue mission. Though I fear it will not end well." The aging woman turned to look at Prometheus. "Is all in readiness?"

"Yes, my lady." The Elder nodded. "We await your command."

The first wrinkles had appeared on Hekate's face: creases on her high forehead, almost invisible against her black skin. She frowned and the lines deepened. "Do you know the greatest gift a parent can give to a child?" she asked, looking around the room.

No one answered.

"Independence. To allow them go out into the world and make their own decisions, travel their own paths. We Elders inherited a paradise from the Archons and the Great Elders.

We have not treated it well, and it is clear to everyone with eyes to see that this world is doomed if we continue as we are. And we will continue—there is no appetite for change. Do you know the greatest mistake a parent can make?" she asked.

No one moved.

The Elder looked around the room again. "Have any of you children?" she asked.

William Shakespeare stepped back from the window. "I had. Two girls and a boy," he said proudly.

"You are the storyteller, the Bard?"

Shakespeare nodded. "I was once. A long time ago."

"Tell me, then, storyteller—what is the greatest mistake a parent can make?" she asked.

"To believe that your children will be just like you."

Hekate nodded. "The world is changing. It belongs to the next generation." She reached out and rested a hand on Prometheus's arm "It belongs to humankind. But there are Elders led by Isis and Osiris or those who follow Bastet who cannot conceive of a world they do not rule. So they have schemed to remain in control. They will destroy us. All of us—Elder and humans alike. And that I will not allow." The rapidly aging woman stood. "Earlier today, just as I grew into this form, I learned that Bastet and Anubis have moved against Aten. The end must be very close indeed. It is time."

The faintest vibration trembled along the height of the Yggdrasill, a buzzing that shivered up through the thick wood. The candle flame danced. Prometheus immediately leaned over, lifted the glass globe and extinguished the flame between thumb and forefinger.

213

Hekate dipped her head and held up her right hand. "Listen," she whispered.

"Will, what's happening out there?" Palamedes called.

"The lights are going out," the Bard whispered, looking into the empty heart of the tree. "Leaves are falling like snow."

One by one, all the lights in the World Tree winked out. Voices stilled.

The creaking, cracking, and sighing of the Yggdrasill were clearly audible.

"She is in pain," Hekate whispered.

A second vibration rattled through the tree.

"Earthquake," Scathach whispered. She felt it tremble up her spine.

"They have become increasingly regular in the last few days," Prometheus said. He made no move to relight the candle. "Also in the last few days, Elders—and even some Great Elders—have returned from their Shadowrealms and congregated in the Earth Shadowrealm. It has been many centuries since so much power was gathered together in one place."

"The facts cannot be unconnected," Saint-Germain said.

"Is it unusual to have so many Elders in the city?" Joan asked.

"It is. We are . . ." Hekate paused and glanced at Prometheus. "We are solitary by nature. Especially those whom the Change has radically altered."

Prometheus leaned forward. "The Ruling Council of Danu Talis sits tonight. And now that Bastet has removed

Aten from control of the council, who knows what will transpire. She will seek to have Anubis appointed the Lord of Danu Talis. He created and controls the anpu. They will support him."

"They will sentence Aten to the volcano," Hekate said, her voice beginning to crack. Her face was now lined with deep wrinkles and her breathing had become ragged. "And that I will not allow either," she breathed.

"So we go to Aten's aid?" Prometheus asked. "To rescue him?"

The old woman looked at him, frowning. "Who?"

"Aten," he said patiently, "the rightful Lord of Danu Talis. Only you can command it." He was clearly struggling to keep the note of panic from his voice. "And if you do not give the order now, then by the time you resume your second aspect tomorrow afternoon, it will be too late."

"I fear it is already too late for Danu Talis," the old woman whispered. "Go, Prometheus, go and bring Aten home."

"And if it means war?"

"Then so be it."

CHAPTER THIRTY-TWO

*V*irginia Dare was standing in a huge market square directly in front of a spectacularly ugly pyramid-shaped building protected by high walls: she guessed it was either an army barracks or a prison. Prison, she decided, judging by the number of jackal-headed guards who were facing inward. The massive sloping walls were lined with anpu, and there were more of the red-eyed creatures guarding the solid stone gates. Behind the walls, the pyramid had a flattened top, similar to those she had seen in South America. Narrow, steeply sloped steps led up to the top of the structure. The top steps, she noted, lips curling with disgust, were dark with stains.

The immortal suddenly felt her skin start to crawl with static. The same instincts that had kept her alive and out of danger for centuries were vibrating through her, warning her that something was going to happen. Pressing her hand against her white robe, she felt the flute warm and safe in its bag against her flesh. A spark snapped from the wood through the cloth and stung her finger.

Virginia was already moving out into the middle of the courtyard, away from walls and statues and milling people, and had crouched down, both hands pressed flat against the ground, when the earthquake rumbled through the city.

The ground vibrated strongly enough to send dust spiraling upward. The crowd around her moaned aloud, a single exhalation, the sound of abject terror. Their reaction puzzled her. It was not a large earthquake—a four, perhaps—and the only damage had been the upsetting of some of the carefully built piles of fruit in the market stalls. Glancing around, she realized that everyone had turned to look toward the huge volcano that dominated the island. Thin gray-white plumes shot toward the sky, and even as she watched, a column of black smoke belched into the heavens.

There was a second rumble and gray-black smoke boiled into the skies over the volcano. The dark cloud flattened and spread across the mouth of the volcano, then quickly dissipated.

In the silence that followed, Virginia heard a high-pitched, almost hysterical laugh; then, suddenly, all the sounds of the city came rushing back. The crowd surged toward the prison gates and someone began a low chant. "Aten . . . Aten . . . Aten . . ."

Curious, Virginia moved off to one side, circling around the back of the ever-growing crowd. These seemed to be the ordinary people of Danu Talis—short, dark-skinned, dark-haired. No one showed signs of wealth. Many were barefoot, none wore jewelry or ornamentation and most were wearing the usual costume of simple white shifts and robes, though some of the stall holders wore leather aprons. Almost everyone wore a conical straw hat for protection from the blistering sun. Looking around, Virginia noticed no human-animal hybrids in with the people; however, none of the guards, she observed, were human. Most were jackal-headed anpu, while others had horns and seemed to have the heads of bulls or boars.

One of the massive prison doors opened and a dozen enormous anpu in full black armor charged out. They carried narrow bamboo canes and slashed and cut their way through the screaming crowd, driving them back.

A young man in a dirty white robe—Virginia thought he looked to be no more than thirteen—threw a handful of rotten fruit. It sailed through the air and exploded across an anpu's breastplate. The crowd erupted into cheers. A troop of guards immediately shoved through the knot of people and grabbed the young man. They lifted him off the ground and carried him, kicking and screaming, back toward the prison. A grief-stricken woman raced after them, obviously pleading with them to release the boy. An anpu turned, raised its bamboo cane and bared its fangs, and the woman shrank back, terrified.

"Oh, I don't think so," Virginia murmured. Her hand closed over the flute tingling warm against her chest and she started forward.

"You cannot fight them all."

Virginia spun around. She was facing a tall young man wrapped in a long white robe. The bottom part of the robe was thrown back across his left shoulder, concealing the lower half of his face, and he was wearing a large straw hat that threw much of his face into shadow. His eyes were a brilliant blue.

"I don't have to," she snapped. "Just those bullies."

"There are another thousand like them in the fort. Ten thousand like them scattered around the city. Will you fight them all?"

"If I have to," the immortal said, turning back to the prison. The anpu had rounded up a handful of people—indiscriminately snatching men and women, young and old—from the crowd and were hauling them to the prison. She saw the boy. He was still struggling in the arms of the huge anpu. He called out, screaming a name again and again. Virginia bit her lip, watching as his mother pressed her hands to her ears and collapsed onto the stones. The anpu guard held the boy aloft in one hand, and just before the gates slammed shut, the boy stopped struggling and called out at the top of his lungs, "Aten!" The crowd roared back the name.

"What will happen to him?" Virginia asked the mysterious man.

"If he is lucky, he will be sentenced to the mines or to join one of the slave gangs who build the Elders' pyramids."

"And if he is unlucky?" she began, and then stopped, suddenly realizing that the young man had spoken in English. She turned to face him.

"If he is unlucky, he will be sent to one of the Shadow-realms as a slave. That's a life sentence. Some would feel it is better than the alternative."

"And what is that?"

"To be fed to the volcano."

"For what?" she demanded. "For throwing a piece of fruit?"

"All the punishments are unnecessarily harsh. They are designed to keep humans under control. It is how the few control the many. With fear."

"Humankind should rise up," Virginia snapped.

"They should."

"I suppose Isis and Osiris sent you to find me?" she asked.

"They did not."

The immortal looked at the man carefully. "You know me, don't you?"

The corners of the man's eyes crinkled as he smiled. "I know you, Virginia Dare," he agreed. "And if you look over my shoulder, you'll see someone else who knows you."

Virginia shifted her gaze and looked over the figure's right shoulder. Leaning against the wall at the mouth of an alleyway, supporting himself on a tall broken stick, was Dr. John Dee. The Magician raised his own straw hat in greeting.

"Go to him, and wait. I will join you presently."

Virginia reached out to catch the man's arm, but a curved metal hook wrapped around her wrist. "It would be better if you did not touch me," he whispered icily. Slivers of yellow fire crawled across the hook and the immortal felt her flute grow almost painfully hot.

The blue-eyed man nodded and walked past her. He moved through the crowd, taking care not to touch anyone, and Virginia noticed that everyone unconsciously stepped out of his way. Uncharacteristically shaken, the flute throbbing like an extra heart against her skin, she crossed the square and slipped into the darkened alleyway alongside the aged Magician. "I thought you were dead," she greeted him.

"That's a charming hello. I almost was."

Shaking her head slightly, she looked him up and down. "I should have guessed you'd be hard to kill."

"I bet you didn't think of me once," he said with a tired smile.

"Maybe just once or twice," she admitted warmly. "I hoped you'd died quickly, and feared you had not."

"Is that something like concern I'm hearing?" he teased.

"You're looking old," she said, avoiding the question.

"Not as old as I was. And I'm still here."

Virginia Dare nodded. "I'm guessing Isis and Osiris weren't the ones to renew your youth."

"They did not."

"The blue-eyed man?" she guessed.

Dee nodded. "Marethyu, the hook-hand."

The name sent a shiver down Virginia's spine. "Death," she whispered.

"Who gave me life," Dee said, shaking his head. "What a world we live in. Once upon a time, you knew who your friends were."

"You never had any friends," she reminded him.

"True. Now all is topsy-turvy."

Virginia Dare turned to look back across the milling crowd. The blue-eyed man had vanished. She saw the woman who had lost her son. There was a young girl—no more than three or four—clinging to her skirts. "Where is Marethyu?"

"He's gone to visit someone in jail."

Dare turned back to Dee. "This jail doesn't look the type that has regular visiting hours."

"I don't think that would bother him too much." The Magician laughed. "He's gone to see Aten."

"I heard the people call his name. What is he?"

"Aten was the Lord of Danu Talis," John Dee explained simply. "An Elder, but sympathetic to the humani. Humans," the doctor corrected himself. "Now he is a prisoner and awaiting execution."

"Doctor," Virginia asked, "do you want to tell me what's going on?

"I wish I knew." Dee attempted a smile. "All I know is that I've spent centuries planning and scheming. I thought I was clever, making plans that would take years or even de-cades to bring to fruition. Little did I know I was part of something bigger, plotted by creatures who had never been human, whose plans encompassed millennia. Today I learned that everything I did was either already set or permitted. I was only allowed to do whatever fit into their plans," he fin-ished, a note of outrage in his voice.

"Shame," Virginia murmured. "Though you'll get no sympathy from me."

"Oh, but you're not exempt either. How would you feel

if I told you that you too were part of this extraordinary plan? It spans millennia."

Virginia looked closely at the stooped immortal, his eyes bright in the gloom. She'd never noticed it before, but she suddenly realized that his eyes were the same color as hers. She frowned, remembering. The same color as Machiavelli's. "Part of a plan?"

"A little while ago, I spoke to an Elder who was slowly turning into a gold statue," Dee said. He reached under his robe and pulled out a slender rectangle wrapped in a palm leaf. "He asked me to give this to you."

Virginia turned it over in her hands. "What is it?" she asked.

"He said it was a message."

"For me?"

Dee nodded. "For you."

"That's impossible. How did he know I was going to be here?"

"And how did he know I was going to be here?" Dee asked. "Because he planned it. "He and Marethyu planned everything."

"Planned what?" she demanded.

"Why, Virginia, nothing less than the destruction of the world."

CHAPTER THIRTY-THREE

"Oh, I hate trolls," Perenelle Flamel groaned.

The creature that click-clacked down the narrow stone path looked like a primitive human. Short and squat, it had flat brutish features, and its entire body was covered with greasy red hair that was almost indistinguishable from the animal skins covering it. It carried a blade carved from the shinbone of an animal that had gone extinct before dinosaurs walked the earth. The creature's eyes were the color of dirty snow, and when it smiled, its pointed teeth were appalling.

"Did that thing just lick its lips?" the Sorceress asked, disgusted.

"Dinner," the troll said, in a surprisingly pure and clear voice. There was the trace of an accent.

"They rarely travel alone . . . ," Nicholas began.

There was a clicking, like claws scrabbling, and then two more—one unmistakably female, with her wild red hair tied in two pigtails—appeared out of the swirling fog. Even over the smell of the sea and the meaty odor of the fog, the stink wafting off the creatures was overwhelming.

"Not trolls." The female's face twisted in disgust. "They're filthy beasts. We're Fir Dearg," she said proudly.

"Well, technically, we're the Fir Dearg," one of the creatures said. "We're male. You're Mna Dearg. Female."

Sighing, the Sorceress leaned on the stone trident and turned the three creatures to stone with a single gesture of her hand. "At least trolls just want to eat you and not talk you to death."

"Could have been worse," Nicholas said. He stepped toward the frozen creatures and tapped one—the female—as he moved past. Yellow eyes glared at him through a stone face. "They could have been leprechauns."

Perenelle shuddered. "You know I hate leprechauns more than almost anything."

Moving cautiously, the Alchemyst and the Sorceress followed the narrow pathway around the island to the quayside. They could hear the Nereids following their progress, splashing invisibly in the sea to their right.

"Dee is not a fool," Nicholas said. He stopped when they reached the jetty where the tourist boats once docked, and turned to look at the empty pier. "He gathered these creatures on the island. . . ."

A rat-faced boy appeared out of the night, running at the Alchemyst, hands hooked into claws. Perenelle spun around and stamped on his tail as he passed her, bringing him to a squealing halt. He rounded on the Sorceress and she repeated the spell she'd just used, turning him to stone. He was caught, one eye open, the other shut in a permanent wink.

Without turning around, Nicholas continued. "There must have been a plan in place to get the creatures ashore."

"The only way on or off the island is by boat," Perenelle said. "Perhaps the plan changed, or events moved too quickly for him to adjust to the new timescale. Remember, originally the Dark Elders were not due to come back to the Earth Shadowrealm until Litha. That's still two weeks away."

"Dee would have had contingency plans. He must have spent months getting the creatures here. But how? There are no ley lines on the island."

Perenelle nodded. "And neither of us felt any tremendous use of power. It had to be by boat."

"Which, as you said, is the only way off the island." Nicholas thought for a moment. "He sent the Lotan ashore to rampage through the streets. While that had everyone's attention, I'll wager a boatload of creatures was scheduled to come over from Alcatraz and join in the fun."

"And with Dee gone, that leaves the Feathered Serpent in charge?"

"Or Bastet," Flamel suggested. "We know Dee's worked with both."

"I would imagine Dee worked with Quetzalcoatl. The Feathered Serpent lives here—well, close, at least," Perenelle said. "And remember—when I was trapped on the island, Areop-Enap was attacked by flies. Quetzalcoatl must have sent them."

"So Quetzalcoatl is sending a boat," Nicholas began, "but we haven't see anything at sea. Nothing passed us."

"There is one other alternative," Perenelle interjected

Nicholas looked at her and then slowly nodded. "Unless it is already here," he breathed.

"But where could it be?" Perenelle asked, suddenly alarmed. "There cannot be that many places to land on Alcatraz."

Catching his wife's hand in his, Nicholas pulled Perenelle over to a stand before the bookshop showing a map of the island. The laminated surface was speckled with dew, and he ran his hands across it. A simplified map depicted the island, with all the buildings picked out in gray, then numbered in red. Above the graphic, in alternating strips of red and black, the numbers were explained.

"We are here at the wharf," he said, touching the bottom right of the map. There was a number two alongside a red circle that read YOU ARE HERE.

Perenelle traced her finger up along the shore, past the guard tower and the guardhouse and the electric shop. "What's number six?" she asked. "It looks like a substantial building."

Nicholas checked the number. "Six is the North Road. It says *Prison Industries.*"

"Look at the Quartermaster Warehouse," she said. "It's big, close to the water, alongside the Powerhouse. You could bring a boat right up to the island, and in this fog no one would be the wiser."

"How far away is it?"

"Nicholas, this is Alcatraz. It's ten minutes away."

"In this fog?" he asked dubiously.

"You're right." She rolled her eyes. "It might take us fifteen."

CHAPTER THIRTY-FOUR

Through the enveloping fog, the sound of clanging metal rang across the Golden Gate Bridge. Niten folded into a sitting position in the center of the bridge. He could feel the commotion vibrating up through the ground. He smiled at the sudden image of Prometheus tossing cars from one side of the bridge to the other to build his barrier. He heard the tiny tinkle of glass and wondered if being tossed across the Golden Gate Bridge by an Elder was covered by insurance.

The small Japanese immortal sat cross-legged, his two swords resting flat on the ground before him. He folded his hands in his lap, closed his eyes and breathed through his nose, forcing the chill night air deep into his chest. He held it for a count of five, then shaped his lips into an O and blew it out again, puncturing a tiny hole in the swirling fog before his face.

Even though he would never admit it to anyone, Niten

loved this moment. He had no affection for what was to come, but this brief time, when all preparations for battle were made and there was nothing left to do but wait, when the entire world felt still, as if it was holding its breath, was special. This moment, when he was facing death, was when he felt completely, fully alive.

He'd still been called Miyamoto Musashi and had been a teenager when he'd first discovered the genuine beauty of the quiet moment before a fight. Every breath suddenly tasted like the finest food, every sound was distinct and divine, and even on the foulest of battlefields, his eyes would be drawn to something simple and elegant: a flower, the shape of a branch, the curl of a cloud.

A hundred years ago, Aoife had given him a book as a birthday present. He hadn't had the heart to tell her that she'd missed his birthday by a month, but he had treasured the book, a first edition of *The Professor* by Charlotte Brontë. It included a line he had never forgotten: *In the midst of life we are in death.* Years later, he'd heard Gandhi take the same words and shift them around to create something that resonated deeply within him: *In the midst of death life persists.*

Niten had long since fallen out of love with battle.

There was no honor in war, less in killing and none in dying. But there was true dignity in how men comported themselves in battle. And there was always honor to be found in standing for a just cause and defending the defenseless.

Cupping his hands in his lap, Niten called up a little of his aura. It puddled in his palms, a rich royal blue liquid trembling against his dark flesh, the skin seamed and calloused from centuries of holding a sword. He blew on it and the liquid thickened. Niten rolled it like dough between the palms of his hands, creating a tiny blue sphere, before flattening it to an irregular rectangle of what looked like stiff blue paper. With infinite care, the immortal carefully creased the edges of the paper, folding and refolding to create a delicate origami *kame,* a turtle.

Placing the blue turtle on the bridge before him, Niten picked up his swords and faded into the gloom just as the first of the Spartoi appeared out of the fog.

"Minikui," Niten breathed. "Ugly."

The immortal had fought monsters before and had learned a long time ago never to judge by appearances. Concepts of beauty changed from country to country and even generation to generation, but he doubted anyone would ever find the Spartoi pretty. Not even another Spartoi.

Short and squat, it looked like a crocodile walking on two legs. It was five feet tall and thick-bodied, its skin gnarled and scaled, with the flat wedge-shaped head of a crocodile. Enormous, slit-pupiled bronze and gold eyes set wide apart on the top of its head penetrated the gloom. When it opened its mouth, it revealed rows of ragged teeth and a thick unmoving white tongue.

Niten had seen serpent folk before: they turned up in the legends of just about every country on earth, and many of the nearby Shadowrealms were populated by lizard creatures. Almost without exception, the lizards despised the mammals and the mammals feared the lizards.

Bareheaded, this creature was covered in a long knee-length

poncho that looked like it was made from its own skin. It carried a small circular shield covered in the same material, and its almost humanlike hands clutched a massive studded war club.

Niten assessed the creature with a warrior's eye.

The Spartoi was lightly armored; its head was vulnerable. It was armed only with the club, which was not as long as Niten's short sword, so he would have the advantage of being able to attack without getting too close. The immortal was vaguely disappointed: he'd been expecting something a little more formidable. Maybe Quetzalcoatl thought the sight of the Spartoi would terrify the humans into submission. But then, in Niten's experience, the Elders were often remarkably ill-informed about the race they wanted to rule and the world they needed to control.

Niten watched the creature approach the blue origami turtle. If it was intelligent—well, if it were intelligent, it would never have come near the turtle in the first place—but if it was intelligent, it would fade back into the night and wait for reinforcements. Head swiveling from side to side, the Spartoi crept closer to the blue turtle. If it was really stupid, Niten predicted, it would probably fall on all fours to sniff at the object. The immortal's grip tightened on his sword as he assessed the creature's weaknesses: he would take it under the arms, perhaps, or through the mouth.

The Spartoi dropped to all fours and moved its head over the origami.

Stupid, then.

Fog swirling around him like a cloak, Niten raced out of the night, katana raised, then lowering in a deadly whistle.

And the Spartoi moved.

Lightning fast, the lizard's shield came up and Niten's sword screamed off it in a blaze of sparks. The creature's blunt club struck the immortal hard in the center of the chest, and Niten knew instantly that ribs had cracked. The force of the blow sent him spinning, and he tumbled to the ground on the far side of the bridge.

The Spartoi ignored the fallen immortal. He scooped up the blue turtle and popped it into his mouth. "Green tea," he said in a raspy whisper. "My favorite."

Niten rolled to his feet, wincing at the pain in his chest. He breathed deeply, evaluating his wounds. Two ribs, maybe three, were broken, maybe the same number cracked. He dropped into a defensive pose and moved back toward the creature.

"You insult me, immortal," the Spartoi said. "You look at me and see a brute creature and assume that your crude trap will ensnare me."

Niten was suddenly conscious that there were other shapes in the gloom. The Spartoi had crept up on him and were standing, watching. He knew then that he had made a critical mistake: he had underestimated the enemy.

The Spartoi stood on its hind legs and moved toward Niten, shield and club weaving together in a mesmerizing pattern. The rest of the creatures closed in to form a circle around them. "In this world, are you honored as a great warrior?"

"I am Miyamoto Musashi. In these times I am called Niten and am unknown, but the man I once was is still honored."

"You must consider yourself a brave warrior to stand here alone against us."

"I consider this necessary."

"You will die," the creature croaked.

"Everyone—everything—dies," Niten said as he edged closer to the Spartoi. "And when I am gone there will be many more to stand against you."

"Many will fall."

Niten attacked as the creature was speaking. Ignoring the pain in his chest, he cut and slashed. The first move was a feint to draw the creature's shield up; the second was designed to take its head off.

The Spartoi blocked the blow with its club, and upon impact, Niten's unbreakable katana broke. Three-quarters of the blade went pinging off into the night. The edge of the Spartoi's round shield swung around to catch the immortal on the left arm. It went completely numb from shoulder to fingertip, and his short sword clattered to the ground.

"We are the Spartoi. Thirty-two in number. Always thirty-two. And we have fought better men than you, immortal. We are infinitely faster than you. I look at you and it is as if you are moving like a snail. I can see your muscles tense long before they move into action. You think you are silent, but your every breath is a rasping roar and you stomp around like an elephant in grass."

Niten's hand moved and the ragged end of the broken katana caught the crocodile in the center of the chest. Eyes wide, mouth gaping in surprise, it staggered back into the fog. "You talk too much," Niten whispered.

CHAPTER THIRTY-FIVE

$\mathcal{V}$irginia Dare moved down the darkened alley away from Dee, shredding the palm-leaf wrapping as she walked. Nestling in her hands was a flat rectangle of emerald stone. She felt a raw energy trembling through the green slab and recognized the feeling instantly: her flute exuded the same shivering when she used it.

The emerald tablet was about four inches across and eight inches long. She turned it over in her hands: both sides were covered in etchings, pictographs that vaguely resembled some of the ancient human writings from the Indus Valley. Wisps of Virginia's pale green aura leaked from her fingers across the tablet, and the scent of sage filled the shadowed alleyway. Virginia caught her breath, watching as the writing flowed over the stone, forming and re-forming, the pictures coming briefly alive: tiny ants crawling, fish swimming, birds flapping, sun wheels spinning.

She had not seen writing like this in a very long time.

The pictographs shivered, then faded to nothing, leaving just a single string of arcane symbols in the center of the tablet. Then they shifted, crawled and formed a single word in English: *CROATOAN*.

Virginia Dare collapsed against the wall as if she had been struck. Then she slowly slid to the ground.

CROATOAN.

She had been a child, no more than twenty-four or thirty months old, when she had watched her father carve that word into a wooden fence post outside their home in Roanoke.

CROATOAN.

Silently, her lips formed the word. Those letters, that single word, were the first she had ever seen. That word was the first she'd known. It was the secret she carried deep in her heart. A secret only she knew. Pale green tears ran down her cheeks.

The letters shivered and broke apart. Tiny scratchlike representations appeared on the stone: turtles and clouds, a whale, the moon in all its phases and a sun wheel flowed across the emerald tablet in narrow horizontal lines. Virginia pressed her index finger to the bottom left-hand corner and moved it slowly to the right, her lips moving as she remembered a language she had long thought she'd forgotten.

I am Abraham of Danu Talis, sometimes called the Mage, and I send greetings to you, Virginia Dare, daughter of Elenora, child of Ananias.

By this word, Croatoan, *a word whose meaning is known only to you, shall you know that everything I say to you now is the truth. So when I say to you that I have watched over you all the days of your life, you will know this to be true. When I say to you that I have protected you and cared for you, you will know this also to be true. I directed you to the cave in the Grand Canyon where you discovered your precious flute. And I allowed you to kill your Elder master and protected you from the consequences.*

I know who you are, Virginia Dare, and more importantly, I know what you are. I know what you are looking for, what you seek more than anything else in the world.

And today you can achieve your life's ambition.

Today, you can make a difference.

You will not walk the Earth Shadowrealm for more than nine millennia. And yet you receive this tablet from me this very day. You will hold it in your hands mere hours after it has left mine. When I first began to follow your time line, I never imagined it would loop back and we would both end up on the same continent in the same time stream.

You are a remarkable woman, Virginia Dare.

You survived when all around you died. And you did more than survive. You thrived. You lived alone and feral in the heart of the forest. But you were never truly alone. Did you ever wonder why the wolves never hunted you and the bears avoided you, why you never succumbed to illness or fell ill from rotten food or stagnant water? And in the depths of winter, when the snow thickened on the ground, you never developed sickness. You were never short of food, never went hungry, never even broke a bone or chipped a tooth. When the plagues devastated the native tribes, you remained unscathed. When your enemies came in search of you, they became lost in the forest. When trappers hunted you for the reward, they came to sudden and mysterious ends.

Truly, you lived a charmed life.

And while I watched over you, Marethyu, the hook-handed man, protected you. He was your shadow, your guardian. Together we kept you safe, because we knew that one day we would need you.

We need you today, Virginia Dare—just as you have always wanted to be needed.

Being abandoned and orphaned as a child, being left alone for years to run wild, should have made you selfish, greedy and perhaps even a little mad.

And yet you are none of those things.

It is a testament to your courage, to your strength of will, your integrity.

When you had food to spare, you shared it with the native tribes. Even when you had little enough for yourself, you left parcels of food hanging from the branches of trees. You ensured that their traps and nets were always filled. You cared for them in ways you yourself had never been cared for. The natives knew it and honored you for it.

238

You accepted immortality from an Elder you despised simply so that you would have more time to help those who needed it. And for centuries now, you have hidden your passion for justice behind an uncaring facade. Few know you, and those who do assume you are interested only in yourself. Even the English Magician, who thinks he knows you better than any man alive, knows nothing about you. He does not know the real Virginia Dare.

I know you.

I know you have always resented the arrogance of authority. You have always stepped forward and spoken for those who had no voice of their own. And now you find yourself in a land where an entire class is voiceless, where a handful of Elders, many of whom are so Changed that they are barely recognizable, continue to hold on to power. Worse, they have no intention of ever letting it go. They intend to destroy or enslave the humani. They are determined that the world you know, the world you grew up in, will cease to exist. The people of Danu Talis need a voice, Virginia Dare. They need someone to speak for them.

They need you.

Virginia's tears sizzled and steamed off the stone.

A white-robed shape moved in the alleyway and she quickly blinked away the tears. No man had ever seen her cry. She shoved the tablet under her shirt. The stone felt cool against her skin.

"I got one too," Marethyu said gently. "Abraham left

them for those he loved or respected. Dee didn't get one," he added, eyes crinkling.

"I don't know this Abraham," she said, eyes huge behind unshed tears.

"He knows you," Marethyu answered.

"He said you also watched over me in the forest."

"I did."

"Why?"

"To keep you safe. Abraham kept you out of trouble, made sure you were fed and clothed. I . . . well, I protected you."

"Why?"

"You were kind to me once . . . or rather, you will be kind to me in the future."

"I know you, don't I?" Virginia whispered. "I have met you before."

"Yes."

"Death was not always your name," she said.

"I have had many names."

"I will find out who you are," she promised. "I will find out your real name."

"You can try. Perhaps you will succeed."

"I'll hypnotize you with my flute," she threatened, half seriously. "You'll tell me then."

Marethyu shook his head. "None of the artifacts have any effect on me."

"Why?"

"Because of what I am," he said simply. "But I need to

know: Will you stand with us, Virginia? Will you fight for the humans of Danu Talis and the future of your world?"

"Do you have to ask?"

"I need to hear you say yes."

"Yes," she said simply.

CHAPTER THIRTY-SIX

Sophie Newman stared at her reflection in the polished-silver-framed mirror. For a moment, she didn't recognize herself.

Memories flickered and danced.

. . . of a girl in silver armor on the top of a pyramid . . .

She blinked and there was a rapid succession of images of girls and young women down through the ages, in a variety of costumes, some in battle, others in fields or classrooms, in caves and castles, in tents on windswept steppes . . .

And while the faces were different, they all had her blond hair and blue eyes.

Sophie reached out and touched the glass. She realized she was seeing the line of her ancestors across thousands of years and hundreds of generations. But was she the first . . . or the last of her line?

She'd found the silver armor when she returned to the

room. It was laid out on the bed like a three-dimensional metal jigsaw puzzle. She'd sat down on the end of the bed and looked at the armor and thought for a long time about whether she would put it on.

And finally, for reasons she did not quite understand, she began to pull on the armor, piece by piece.

The young woman who looked back at her from the mirror was dressed in semitransparent silver armor that was molded to the shape of her body. It fit her so precisely that it could have been made for no one else. The armor was unadorned and had been polished to a mirror sheen. Partially visible through the metal was the silk-soft chain-mail shirt beneath. She wore knee-high chamois-lined silver boots with wicked spiked toes, and her articulated silver gloves had been fitted with long extended nails, like claws. Sophie didn't even like the look of them. Strapped to her back were two empty silver sheaths, and although she'd searched the room and gone through the wardrobe, she hadn't been able to find weapons anywhere.

There was a tap on the door. "It's me," Josh called.

"It's open," Sophie answered.

Josh stepped into the room, wearing an almost identical suit of armor. His was gold, as was the chain-mail vest he wore beneath. He was grinning, eyes sparkling with delight. "Did you ever think we'd get suits of armor?" He opened and closed his hands, flexing his fingers. The metal whispered like silk. "It's metal, but it's also glass. Sort of a ceramic or something. It has to be really high-tech."

Sophie watched her brother in the mirror. "Does yours fit?"

243

"Like a glove," he began, and then stopped. "Do you think these were made for us?"

Sophie nodded. There was no question. "Just for us."

He turned slowly. "What do you think—fancy, right?"

She smiled. "Very fancy. Did you have any problems putting it on?" she asked.

He shook his head quickly. "You know, I was thinking about that. It was weird—I climbed into this as if I'd been wearing it all my life. I knew where each buckle and clip was, where all the straps went, how to cinch it."

Sophie nodded. "Me too." She tapped his shoulder where the empty sheaths were visible. "It looks like they don't trust us with the final part of our costumes."

"I bet these are for the four Swords of Power. Two for me, two for you."

"I wonder which two you'll get," Sophie asked lightly, though somewhere in the deepest part of her consciousness, she already knew the answer.

"Dee used the swords to create the leygate on Alcatraz." Josh stopped examining himself and looked up at his sister. "Did the swords fall through the gate with us? I don't remember seeing them."

"I do," Sophie said. "When I jumped in after you, they tumbled through. I saw them when I opened my eyes. I thought they were rusted spars of metal, but then Osiris collected them just before we took off and I realized they were important."

"What happens now?" Josh asked.

Sophie caught her brother's arm and led him over to the glass wall. Pushing it back, she stepped out into the garden. The perfumed air was touched by the rotten-egg stench of sulfur from the volcano, and tiny speckles of black grit and gray ash swirled in the air. The garden was deserted, and Sophie led Josh to a fountain where a carved mammoth shot water into the air from its upraised trunk. The tinkling sound of the water created a low musical buzz.

"What are we going to do?" she asked in an urgent whisper. "Every time I start to think about what's been going on I feel sick. These people . . ." She waved her gloved hand in the direction of the house. ". . . These people—and I'm not even sure if they're our parents—they're different."

"They *are* different," Josh agreed. "For a while there I thought Mom and Dad had been kidnapped and replaced by look-alikes, like in *Invasion of the Body Snatchers.*"

"And now?" Sophie asked.

"I think they're the same people we grew up with. They look like them, walk and talk like them, even have their little mannerisms, but they're not the people we know."

"They're not," Sophie agreed.

"And obviously now that they have us here, under their control, they've dropped whatever act they had on earth. We're seeing them as they really are." He dipped his glove into the water and watched as the water turned golden. The air suddenly smelled of citrus. "Look! It's orange juice!"

"Josh. Focus!"

"You sound just like Mom or Isis or whatever her name is.

They're different," he repeated. "But you know what: when they were at home, they were always a little strange. They weren't like normal parents."

Sophie nodded. "I'm not sure what normal parents are like," she said.

"Think about it. They didn't encourage us to have friends. We never had sleepovers, we weren't allowed to stay over at anyone's house. We never went on field trips."

"And we kept changing schools," Sophie whispered. "They isolated us."

"Exactly."

"But we *did* have friends."

"Casual friends, but not best friends. Who's your best friend?" Josh gave his sister a challenging look.

"Well, there's Elle. . . ."

"Who's in New York, and who you haven't seen in how long?"

Sophie nodded. "A long time."

"We never had a regular childhood," Josh continued. "Dad—Osiris. Oh, I'm just going to call him Osiris from now on—is right: we were trained in amazing things. And don't get me wrong. Some of it was fun. But is visiting an ancient archaeological site a normal family outing? The year I wanted to go to Disneyland, we ended up at Machu Picchu."

"Where you stepped in the . . ."

"I know. We learned about history, archaeology, we were shown ancient languages, taken to museums to look at weapons and armor." He tapped his metal fingers against his chest.

"When I first looked at this, it was so familiar to me. How many other sixteen-year-olds—"

"Fifteen and a half," Sophie corrected.

"—fifteen-and-a-half-year-olds would know that this is Gothic-style armor from the late fifteenth century?"

Sophie laughed. "I didn't know that."

"But I did."

"You are kind of a geek," she reminded him.

"What are your shoes called?" he asked.

Sophie looked down at her spike-toed metal boots. "Sabatons," she said immediately.

Josh grinned. "I'm sure every fifteen-and-a-half-year-old knows that. I bet your fashion-conscious friend Elle probably has a pair."

Sophie laughed. "She'd have found hers in a boutique in the Village."

"And she would have sent you a long email . . ."

"With photos . . ."

"With photos of the shoes, the boutique and the coffee and bagel she had afterward."

The air trembled and a vimana swept in low over the house and then dropped out of sight. They both caught a glimpse of Osiris at the controls, and their laughter faded.

"They've been preparing us," Sophie said. "Training us. So what do we do?"

"We do what we feel is right," he answered.

"But right for who? For us, for them?"

"When in doubt, we follow our hearts. Words can be

false, images and sounds can be manipulated. But this . . ." He tapped his chest, over his heart. "This is always true."

Sophie looked at him, eyes wide in surprise and admiration.

"Someone told me that," he added quickly, a touch of red on his cheeks.

"Flamel?" she guessed.

"Dee."

The sliding glass door opened and Isis and Osiris appeared. They were dressed in plain white ceramic armor and were each carrying two swords, one in each hand.

"They look like they just stepped out of *Star Wars*," Josh muttered. He began to hum the Imperial March under his breath.

His sister bit her lip and tapped him with her pointed shoe to make him stop. Something told her that laughing wouldn't go over well.

Isis and Osiris stopped before the children—Isis before Josh, Osiris in front of Sophie.

"You look magnificent," Isis said. "You will make a wonderful impression."

"You look like rulers," Osiris agreed. "And every ruler needs a sword, a symbol of authority and power. And it is only right that the twins of legend should each have two swords—twin blades."

Isis lifted the two swords she held. They were almost identical; the details on the leather-wrapped hilts differed in subtle ways. The swords were each about twenty inches long and were shaped from a single piece of glittering gray stone.

"Old these are, older than the Elders, the Archons or even the Ancients. It is said they were shaped by the Earthlords, but I doubt it: they worked in different materials. These swords have had many names down through the millennia, and have been worn by emperors and kings, carried by knights and simple warriors. But they have always been yours, Josh." She held the two stone swords high and sun shimmered off the blades. "Here is Clarent, the Sword of Fire, and this is its twin, Excalibur, the Sword of Ice." Isis moved around behind Josh as she spoke and slipped the two swords into the empty sheaths on his back: Clarent on the left, Excalibur on the right.

"And you Sophie, have Durendal, the Sword of Air, and Joyeuse, the Sword of Earth," Osiris said, slipping the weapons into the empty silver sheaths on the girl's back. "These are the weapons carried by the rulers of Danu Talis for generations. Now you have them."

Isis and Osiris stepped back. "I have dreamt of this moment for millennia," Isis whispered. "The moment when the twins of legend would stand before us in the armor of the Lords of Danu Talis."

"Come now," Osiris said, "let us go claim your birthright."

CHAPTER THIRTY-SEVEN

*H*e was Aten, Lord of Danu Talis.

Yesterday, he had ruled over the greatest empire ever to stretch across the earth.

Yesterday, he had been worshipped, honored and respected by millions of people: Great Elders, Elders, humankind and everything else, even the beasts and hybrids paid him homage. In his long life he had achieved so much, but uniting the peoples of the island empire and the world beyond had been one of his proudest achievements.

Yesterday, he had met Death.

And in that moment everything had changed.

He'd been betrayed by his mother and brother, accused of treachery, captured and cast into a cell deep below Tartarus, the fortress prison. There was a single cell on this level: a circular stone cage on a round island in the middle of a bubbling lava pool. The only way on or off the island was via a stone bridge that it took three huge anpu to lift and set in place. The furnacelike air was almost unbreathable, filled with particles of burning stone and grit. Lava frothed against the edge of the island, splashing it with long streamers of molten rock. Aten had not been burned yet, but he knew it was only a matter of time.

Under normal circumstances, no prison would have been able to hold Aten. He was incalculably powerful and, as the Lord of Danu Talis, had studied in the great libraries all across the world and into the Shadowrealms. He had the largest collection of Archon and Ancient lore in existence and had conducted experiments that would have appalled his subjects and frightened even his closest friends.

Under normal circumstances, he would have shattered the bars, turned the lava to a velvet carpet and strode to freedom.

But these were not normal circumstances, and in truth, he had allowed it to happen. When Anubis, his brother, had come for him with the anpu guards, Aten could have destroyed them all, reducing them to dust motes. But he had not. He had surrendered and allowed himself to be taken and chained.

The bracelets on his wrists and ankles and the chain wrapped around his waist were composed of iron surrounding a mercury core. Most Elders were allergic to iron, and those who had undergone the Change were especially susceptible to it. And the Change had been working on him for a long time now. Unlike his brother and mother, who had become beastlike, Aten retained mostly human features but they had altered subtly: his skull, nose and jaw had elongated, his lips had thickened and his yellow eyes now had a pronounced slant.

Aten could feel the poison leeching into his skin, and it took all his strength and aura to try to counteract the fire coursing through his body. But his strength would not last much longer, and then the iron would overwhelm him. He would die in absolute agony. A smile curled his thick lips. Of course, he would probably be cast into the volcano before then.

A massive door clanged.

On the other side of the lava pool, a rectangle of white light appeared. Two irregular shapes moved into the doorway and stepped to one side, and then three huge anpu appeared. Aten stepped up to the bars, taking care not to touch them, and squinted across the dancing waves of heat shimmering off the red-black lava. His pupils went from circles to horizontal lines.

The anpu took up their positions and maneuvered the long narrow stone walkway out across the lava. It locked into position with a shudder that vibrated through the prison cell, and two figures set out across the narrow bridge: one a short man in the leather apron of a jailer, the other taller, wrapped in a white robe and wearing a straw hat.

Aten recognized the jailer, Dagon, first. He belonged to one of the water races from a nearby Shadowrealm. He wore large leather and crystal goggles to protect his bulbous eyes from the heat. When he spoke, two rows of tiny ragged teeth were visible behind thin lips.

"Visitor for you, Lord Aten. Five minutes," he said, then stepped away and turned to walk back across the bridge, leaving the second character alone at the cell.

"I am surprised you were able to bribe Dagon," Aten said lightly. "The Fish Folk are considered incorruptible."

"I did not bribe him," Marethyu said. "I told him his future."

"At least he has one." Aten smiled without opening his lips.

"I told him that in ten thousand years' time, he would find himself in a river battling an undefeatable warrior, and that he should say my name and she would free him."

"And he believed you?" Aten asked, surprised.

"I am Death. I have no need to lie."

"And did you tell the anpu their futures too?"

"They have none," Marethyu said shortly. "But no, I did not." The curve of a metal hook appeared beneath his white cloak. "It was far easier to ensorcel them. They are primitive creatures, and the spell will leave no trace."

"Are you here to free me?" Aten asked.

"I can if you wish," Marethyu said.

"But it is not part of your plan, is it?"

"No, it is not. But I can still free you if that is what you want."

Aten ignored the question. "Tell me what is happening," he said.

"As soon as the humans of Danu Talis heard that you had

been taken, they began to gather outside the prison and the Temple of the Sun. There have been some disturbances. There will be more," he promised. "You are well loved."

"I should have done more for them," Aten muttered.

"You did enough. Your imprisonment has angered your subjects and your friends. Hekate has sent the People of the Tree to free you. They are led by Huitzilopochtli. They are not many, it is true, but they are enough, and it will encourage the people to rise up."

"And if the people don't?"

"They will," Marethyu assured him. "I have given them a voice. Someone to speak for them. The only real variables are the twins. Where will they stand?"

"During times of turmoil, it is the nature of children to side with their parents," Aten said.

"That would change if they were to discover that Isis and Osiris are not their parents," Marethyu said.

"And they are being offered an empire," Aten reminded him. "That is enough to tempt anyone."

"But they are not just anyone. They are the twins of legend."

"The boy will have the swords," Aten whispered, "and that is dangerous."

"The pyramid will dampen its powers," Marethyu said quietly, and tapped the edge of his hook against the bars, cutting a chip from the stone.

"And the boy is strong?" Aten asked. An enormous bubble of lava popped, turning the air briefly unbreathable, and the Elder coughed.

"Stronger than he thinks. Also, he will be carrying Excalibur. The two swords tend to neutralize one another."

"What happens now, Death?" Aten asked.

"The Ruling Council gathers. Every Elder that can walk or crawl is here. Bastet and Anubis are waiting, convinced that Anubis will be acknowledged as your successor. And Isis and Osiris are on the way with the twins."

Aten shook his head. "I'd love to be a fly on the wall for that meeting."

"I think you'll get your wish." Marethyu smiled. "The first order of business is your trial. It will be left to the new ruler—Anubis or the twins—to carry out your execution."

"My brother will have no problems with that." He raised a brow. "I wonder how he'll react to the appearance of the twins?"

"Not well, I would imagine. And Bastet will be livid!"

CHAPTER THIRTY-EIGHT

*M*ist swirled and the Spartoi closed in on the defenseless Niten. Lightning fast, one lashed out at him, catching him a blow on the thigh, and he fell to the bridge with a grunt of pain. He lay flat on his back, looked up at the lizardlike creatures and realized that he was going to die. The immortal felt just the vaguest pang of regret: he had always wanted to die in his beloved Japan. And he had made Aoife promise that if he fell in some foreign country or Shadowrealm, she would bring his body back to Reigando in the southwest of his country. But Aoife was gone. He would never be able to fulfill his promise to rescue her. And he would never rest in his home soil.

"We will kill you slowly," one of the creatures said, in his young boy's voice. He stepped up to the immortal and looked down, jaws gaping, ropes of evil-smelling saliva dangling from his teeth.

At that moment a Toyota Prius sailed out of the foggy night and crushed two of the creatures against the bridge. The entire metal structure shook and rang like a bell.

The Spartoi looming over Niten spun in surprise. The immortal pressed his back to the bridge and kicked upward with all his might. Both feet caught the creature beneath the chin. Its jaws closed with a click and it dropped its club, hissing in pain. Niten caught the weapon before it struck the ground and slammed it down on the creature's toes. The Spartoi screamed like a boiling kettle as it hopped on one foot. Niten brought the club down on the other foot and heard something crunch. The creature keeled over, its screams now so high-pitched, they were inaudible.

A second car, an ancient VW Bug, bounced across the bridge, spraying sparks, and crashed into two more Spartoi.

Prometheus appeared out of the night, a massive long sword held before him in a two-handed grip. Two of the crocodile creatures darted toward him and the enormous blade keened through the air. One Spartoi lifted its shield. The sword rang off it in a detonation of sparks, driving the creature to the ground. The second tried to block the blow with its club. The sword ripped the club from its hands and sent it sailing over the side of the bridge into the water far below. Weaponless, both creatures scrambled back into the fog.

The Elder took up a position over the fallen immortal. "Are you hurt?"

"Give me a moment. Let me heal." Niten climbed slowly to his feet. The air around him shimmered blue and the fog was touched with the odor of green tea. Niten's aura thickened around his waist and in the center of his chest, coating his wounds. "All I need now is a couple of days' bed rest and I'll be fine." He scooped up his fallen short sword.

"No chance of that." Prometheus grinned. "Let's get back down the bridge. I've got all the cars in place. We can't let any of the Spartoi slip through."

Niten limped after the Elder. "Thank you," he said. "You saved my life."

"And before this night is out, I have no doubt you will save mine." Prometheus smiled again.

"I thought you weren't a warrior," Niten said.

"I'm not," Prometheus answered. "But I've fought my share of battles."

"I think I killed one," Niten murmured. "And the first car you threw got two more."

"Are they dead?"

"Not sure. But a car did fall on them. The VW took out another two, and I busted another one's toes. That's if they have toes," he added.

"The two I got with the VW—did you see them get up?" Prometheus asked.

"I saw the car hit them—you wouldn't think a crocodile's face could show surprise, but you'd be wrong! They went down under it, but they were swallowed up by the fog. They're probably dead," he said.

At that moment, the distinctive hood of the VW spun out of the fog like a lethal Frisbee.

Niten's short sword flashed up and sliced through the

thin metal as if it were made of tinfoil, and the hood spun away in two pieces—one to the left and one to the right. "Maybe they're not dead," he muttered.

Prometheus had constructed a deep V of cars across the bridge. The cars had been turned on their sides and were piled two high, with the wheels facing inward. At the bottom of the V was an opening just wide enough for one man.

"This is perfect," Niten said, admiring the work.

"It was your idea."

The Japanese immortal ignored the compliment. "We can hold them here," he said. "They shall not pass. Oh, and remember what I said about not using your red armor."

Prometheus nodded.

Niten eyed his friend and changed his mind. "Forget that. Use the armor. They know we're here, and they're fast, very, very fast. We're going to need every advantage we can find."

There was the hint of anise and the Elder flickered into brutish red armor. He glanced at Niten. "Are you not going to change?"

Niten shook his head. "The effort of healing took a lot of my energy. I need some time to recharge." He spun his sword and the Spartoi's club in his hands.

"Let me take the first watch, then," Prometheus said. He positioned himself in the center of the opening and worked his head from side to side, easing stiffened muscles. "Rest awhile. Heal if you can."

"They're not going to let us rest," Niten said grimly. Even as he was speaking, there was a flicker of movement in the air and the fog swirled. "Here they come."

Six creatures raced down the narrowing tunnel. They were almost identical in appearance, and while most carried the clubs, two had short stabbing swords. All were carrying shields.

"They look unhappy," Prometheus murmured.

"They're not used to losing," Niten said, peering over the Elder's shoulder. "It will anger them, but an angry enemy makes mistakes."

The car-lined path was wide enough for four Spartoi, then three, and then only two. Finally, just one creature faced off against the Elder. It lunged at him with its club while the five behind it jostled, pushing forward, trying to get closer.

Prometheus's huge sword smashed into the Drakon warrior, crushing its shield to a twisted ruin. Its spiked club screamed as it ran along the length of the Elder's sword, and Prometheus lashed out with his metal-clad foot, stamping down hard on the creature's bare toes.

The Spartoi hissed, golden eyes bulging in shock, and Prometheus stepped forward, reversed the sword and brought the heavy pommel down hard on its head. It slumped back on top of the others, blocking them. The other creatures clawed at it, dragging it out of the way, allowing another to push through.

"You will pay for that . . . ," the Spartoi began, and then Prometheus's metal-gloved hand shot out, grabbed it by the snout and rapped it over the skull with the pommel of his sword. He flung the lizard back into its companions and all six went sprawling. "This isn't too bad," the Elder laughed. "I'm starting to enjoy myself."

The foggy air curled and suddenly four spears arced out of the night. Prometheus's huge sword flashed and twisted. He managed to chop two of the wickedly barbed spears out of the air, sending their broken halves spinning off into the night. But the second two struck his breastplate, shattering it.

The Elder fell without a sound.

CHAPTER THIRTY-NINE

"*M*other! Stop fussing." Anubis realized his mistake even as the words were leaving his lips.

Bastet turned and stalked away, her black metal foil cloak scraping across the floor with the sound that set his overlong teeth on edge. "Fussing," she hissed. "Is that what I was doing? Fussing? Well, excuse me for trying to make my son the ruler of an empire!"

"Mother . . . ," Anubis sighed.

The cat-headed Elder turned her back on him, leaned her furry forearms on the window ledge and stared out over the city. Her ragged claws dug gouges in the stone. "Do you know how long I have schemed to bring us to this particular moment in time?"

"Mother."

"The sacrifices I've made?"

Anubis knew when to admit defeat. "Yes, Mother."

The huge Elder went to stand alongside Bastet. He pressed his back against the wall and folded his arms across his chest. When she was in this sort of mood, it was easier—and safer—not to argue. And although he commanded one of the largest armies in the world, and had created the anpu—which he was now starting to resemble as the Change took him—he was still in awe of his mother. "I'm just nervous," he admitted, his teeth pressing against his chin.

Bastet relented. "You have nothing to be nervous about. You are of the house of Amenhotep. I ruled with your father, your brother ruled, it is only right that you should rule. Very few of the Elders will oppose you. Why, even Isis and Osiris are coming tonight. They will support us," she said confidently.

Anubis looked around. He had grown up with his brothers in this palace, and they'd spent more time in this room than in any other part of the house. It was their father's library, the long stone shelves overflowing with books, piled high with the treasures of a hundred Shadowrealms, while tables and drawers were stacked with fragments, scraps and hints of the earth's distant history. It was in this room that his brother Aten had discovered his fascination with the past.

"Will I really have to kill him?" he asked suddenly.

"Who?"

"My brother."

Bastet moved back from the window. She could hear the distant braying of a mob, and it was starting to annoy her. Where were the guards? Why was she not hearing screams as the humani were dispersed?

"No, you will not have to kill Aten yourself," she said. "You will simply sign his death warrant. Someone else will push him into the volcano." She looked her son up and down and nodded approvingly. "The black armor is a nice touch."

Anubis was wearing ornate black armor etched with red on every joint and seam. The rivets looked like drops of blood.

"I wasn't sure about the color," he said. "It was either this or the purple, and with my skin beginning to change, I though the red and black would look more dramatic."

"The purple would have clashed," Bastet agreed.

The texture and hue of Anubis's copper-colored skin was undergoing the Change. In some places it was coal black, lined with tiny red veins; one hand had begun to stiffen into a claw, and the cartilage of both ears was beginning to thicken and extend upward

"What will I say at the council meeting?" he asked.

"As little as possible," Bastet directed. "You will be the strong silent type. I will speak for you."

There was a swell in sound and the streets and alleyways on the other side of the canal suddenly boiled with a humani mob. They were all howling Aten's name. Some were carrying sticks or brooms; a few carried long knives. Most were unarmed.

"They want their leader," Anubis said, joining his mother at the window. The crowd was about a hundred strong, and there were at least twice that many heavily armed guards on the bridges.

"Your brother was weak," Bastet snapped. "He began to

see the humani as our equals. They are little better than animals. Just because he abolished servitude, they think he is their savior. Now look at what his weakness has spawned. They are burning the city in protest." She shook her head in astonishment. "Do they honestly think this display will force us to release him?"

Smoke curled from scores of fires across the city.

"My officers tell me that hundreds are streaming toward the jail," Anubis said. "There are even wild reports that anpu were attacked, and I've heard stories of rioting in the humani slums. A rumor raced through the marketplace today that a humani defeated a dozen guards and crossed the canal."

"Ridiculous!"

"What will the humani do if we do execute Aten?" Anubis asked.

"Run wild for a few days. Let them burn their wooden houses and the grain stores. When they get cold and start to grow hungry, they'll begin to come to their senses. And when you are the ruler here, I expect you to deal harshly with this disconnected, lazy rabble."

"I hope I'll be a good ruler," Anubis said sincerely.

"Of course you will," Bastet snapped. "You'll do exactly as I say."

"Yes, Mother."

CHAPTER FORTY

*M*ars, Odin and Hel prepared to make their final stand in the corridors of Alcatraz.

"There are just too many of them!" Mars shouted. The Elder was standing in a corridor facing down a host of gray Moss People. Short and stunted, their skin the texture of tree bark, they were covered in thick moss, and although they were armed only with wooden swords and spears, their weapons were deadly. Mars's armor was scratched and torn, and he was bleeding from a score of minor wounds.

Behind and to his left, he heard Odin grunt and knew the one-eyed Elder had sustained another wound. He was facing off with a dozen filthy vetala.

"There is no shame in running away to live and fight another day," Odin grunted in the lost language of Danu Talis.

Behind them, propped against a wall, lay Hel. She had

managed to drive back a hairy minotaur with her long metal whip, but not before its horns had opened a deep gash in her side and along her left arm. "Running would be good," she grunted, "if we had somewhere to run to."

Realizing that if they remained in the exercise yard they would eventually be overwhelmed, the three Elders had fought their way through the prison corridors. Attacked on all sides by nightmarish creatures, they had defeated scores, but for every one they killed, another three appeared. Each creature was different: some fought with weapons, others with teeth and claws, but curiously, they did not fight with one another. They were focused solely on attacking the three Elders.

"They're hungry," Hel said. "Look at them: most are skin and bones. They've probably been in these cells for months in a deep sleep. And now, like animals coming out of hibernation, they need to eat. Unfortunately, we're the only things here they can eat."

"I wonder why they don't turn on one another," Mars said.

"They have to be under some sort of binding spell," Odin said.

"I think it is simpler than that," Hel lisped. "I don't think they can see one another. They can only see us."

"Of course!" Odin answered. "They're under a glamour."

Mars hacked at a pair of Moss Men—or they could have been women; it was hard to tell under the moss and hair—and they staggered back, unperturbed by the slashes across their woody skin. "If we could lift the spell . . . ," he began.

". . . they would attack one another," Hel said. "That would make our job easier."

As the Elders fought their way down a corridor lined with stacks of cells, they were cut, stabbed and bitten, their flesh scraped and torn. It was difficult for them to use their auras to heal the wounds as they ran and fought. And now they were tiring, their auras were fading and they were starting to discover that some of the wounds had been infected by the monsters' poisonous teeth and claws.

A howling cucubuth dropped from one of the upper cells and landed on top of Mars. Long teeth snapped at the Elder's head, biting into his ears. Odin caught the creature by the tail, spun it once, twice, then sent it sailing the entire length of the corridor. It hit the wall hard enough to crack the stonework.

Hel was swarmed by a dozen horned Domovi. Each creature was about the size of a small child, completely covered in hair, except for circles around the eyes. They bit and snapped, bending their heads to gore her with their short, razor-sharp horns. Mars grabbed two by the legs and used them as clubs to beat the others away from her. The two he held wriggled and twisted, screaming and scratching at his hands, jabbering in a language that set his teeth on edge.

Odin faced the vetala. Their faces were those of beautiful young men and women; their bodies were skeletal, and they walked on talons that were a cross between human feet and birds' claws. They fought with leathery bats' wings, which were tipped with one long hooked finger. The vetala were blood drinkers and had the enormous savage teeth of their kind.

"Wish I had my wolves with me now," Odin muttered. "They'd make short work of these filthy things." He hissed in pain as a spike-tipped wing ripped his arm open from wrist to elbow.

And then Mars's sword sliced apart the attacking vetala's wings as if they were paper, and Hel's whip punctured holes through another.

Odin called up his aura. The air buzzed with ozone, and gray smoke shimmered over his flesh. He focused on the wound in his arm. The blood stopped pumping out, but the wound didn't heal. "My aura is almost completely depleted," he muttered. The Elder slumped back against a wall, exhausted.

Hel pressed her claws to her uncle's torn arm and squeezed. Her bloodred aura flickered once, then faded to pink smoke. "Nothing. Something is draining us," she said.

A shiver ran through the assembled monsters, but instead of crowding in, they started to pull back. The minotaur pointed to Hel and deliberately licked his thick lips. She bared her fangs and stuck out her tongue at him.

"They're backing away," Odin said. He tried to raise his aura again, but only the merest veil of gray danced over his skin.

"I'll wager that is not good news," Mars said. A shadow danced along the wall. "Something's coming," he said.

The monsters parted and a sphinx stepped forward. The

body was that of an enormous lion with the wings of an eagle. The head belonged to a young woman who was beautiful until she opened her mouth to reveal her sharp teeth and serpent's tongue. The sphinx smiled and tilted her head to one side. Her long black forked tongue flickered, tasting the air. "Oh, I can taste all your auras. They are very sweet." She licked her lips as she approached, her claws digging into the stones at her feet. "I've waited my entire lifetime to eat an Elder's memories and suddenly three Elders come along together. What wonders will you reveal to me?"

"I knew something was draining our auras," Hel muttered. The sphinx had the ability to drink any aura and drain its energy.

"So you are Mars, Odin and Hel. My mother sometimes spoke of you. She did not like any of you. But you," she said to Hel. "She especially disliked you: she said you were ugly."

The Elder laughed. "You think *I* look ugly . . ." She moved her mouth, and the fangs jutting up from beneath her bottom lip made her look astonishingly like the boar she had just eaten. "I knew your mother both before and after the Change took her. She was ugly before and, let me tell you, there was little difference afterward. Your mother was so ugly that even the magic mirrors would not talk to her. Your mother was so ugly, she—" Hel was about to continue, but Odin leaned a hand on her arm and shook his head.

"Enough!"

"But, it's true," Hel protested. "Her mother was so ugly—"

"You are a daughter of Echidna," Mars said evenly. He

planted his sword point-first in the ground and rested his arms across the pommel. "We knew her. She was kin to us. Which makes you kin to us also." He spread one arm. "I wonder if you are not fighting on the wrong side?"

The sphinx shook her beautiful human head. "I am on the right side. The winning side."

"Dee is gone," Mars said.

"I do not work for Dee," the sphinx said quickly. "Dee is a fool, a dangerous fool. He attempted to betray us and was declared *utlaga*. No, I am working with Quetzalcoatl."

"Be careful of him," Odin advised. "He is not to be trusted."

"Oh, I don't know. He told me he could give me a proper human body." She took a step forward, lion's claws scratching on the stone. "Could he do that?"

"Probably," Mars said.

"Could you?"

Mars shook his head.

"What about you, Odin, or you, Hel? Could you give me a human body?"

Hel shook her head, but the one-eyed Elder said, "I could not, but I know some people who could. I could take you to a Shadowrealm where we could grow you the most perfect body and implant your consciousness and memories into it."

"Quetzalcoatl said he can morph this body to a new shape. Can he?" she demanded.

"Probably," Odin said. "Who knows what that monster can do?"

"So why are you here?" Mars asked.

"I came here to guard our grotesque guests, and then stand watch over Perenelle Flamel. I was promised her memories as my fee."

"Did she not escape?" Mars said with a savage grin.

"She eluded me. When I reach the mainland, I will make it my special duty to seek her out. I am hoping she will still be alive so I can kill her. I am also hoping she has enough of her aura left to resurrect herself, so that I can kill her again."

"Better creatures than you have tried to kill her and failed," Mars said.

"She is humani. And all humani are weak. She escaped last time because she was lucky." The sphinx threw back her head and breathed deeply. "I will drain your auras and drink your memories," she announced. "It will be a banquet indeed."

"I'm going to make sure I think my foulest thoughts when you are draining me," Hel promised. "I'm going to give you indigestion."

As the sphinx stepped forward, the three Elders felt a sudden rush of warmth, and then all energy left them. All their minor wounds flared to agony, and more serious wounds reopened.

Mars stood in front of the other two and attempted to lift his sword, but it was a solid leaden weight. The air filled with the stink of burnt meat, and a shimmering purple-red mist started to steam off his flesh. Behind him, Odin's gray aura gathered around him, and a bloodred miasma coiled off Hel's mottled flesh. Ozone mingled with rotting fish and the stench of burnt meat.

"Smells like a barbecue," the sphinx purred. "I've been on this island for months." Her nails clicked as she continued toward them. "I came here because I was promised a feast. The memories and aura of the Sorceress were denied me. But you three—you more than make up for that disappointment."

Mars fell to his knees, sword clattering across the stones, and Odin collapsed beside him, sprawled on the ground. Only Hel remained on her feet, and that was because she had dug her long nails deep into the wall to hold herself up. She was willing the sphinx to come a few steps closer so she could try to launch herself at the creature. Although the sphinx's body was that of a lion, the head was a small fragile human being.

The sphinx stopped and cocked her head to one side. "Do you think you can do it, Elder? Do you think you have the strength to throw yourself at me? I don't. I think I will take you first." Delicate nostrils flared as she breathed deeply, and her long black snakelike tongue flickered in the air. "Your defiance will add a certain spice to the meal."

Hel tried to lash out with her whip, but she could barely raise it off the ground; she knew she didn't have the strength to send it cracking through the air.

"Brave," the sphinx said. "But foolish, too. You are doomed, Elder. Only a miracle will save you now."

"You know," came a new voice, filling the hallway, "I've been called many things in my life. But I've never been called a miracle before."

The sphinx spun around, hissing.

273

Standing alone in the center of the corridor was the American immortal Billy the Kid.

The sphinx took a step toward Billy. "It seems I was mistaken when I said I would take Hel first. It looks like I'll be starting with an American first course. An appetizer." Without warning, her hind legs bunched underneath her and she leapt the length of the corridor, claws extended, mouth gaping.

CHAPTER FORTY-ONE

*I*n a windowless chamber, deep beneath the Yggdrasill, Hekate, now an ancient and withered woman, lay down in a long coffinlike network of tree roots and folded her arms across her chest, left hand on right shoulder, right palm on left shoulder. The entire tree shuddered and sighed; then the roots coiled around her, embracing her.

"Weary with toil, I haste me to my bed," William Shakespeare murmured, "the dear repose for limbs with travel tired."

"She is the tree," Scathach said. "Indivisible from it, inextricable, entwined with it. If one dies, the other goes too."

"That will never happen," Huitzilopochtli said confidently, urging his companions out of the windowless circular sleep chamber. "The Yggdrasill has endured for millennia. It will always survive. And so too will the goddess."

Scathach's pointed teeth bit her lip. Less than a week ago

she had watched the Yggdrasill—admittedly a smaller version—fall. She had seen the death of Hekate. But that would not happen for ten thousand years.

Prometheus was waiting outside the door. He was dressed from head to foot in ornate red armor, and a massive red-bladed sword was strapped to his back, the hilt projecting above his left shoulder. Behind him stood a troop of Torc Allta, the wereboars created by Hekate. Two of the huge creatures took up positions outside Hekate's bedchamber. Their bodies were those of enormous muscular humans, but their faces were porcine, with flattened noses and jutting tusks. Their eyes—bright blue—were human.

"The Torc Allta will watch over her while she sleeps. None will get close," Prometheus said.

"Will they fight with us?" Scathach asked. "They would be more than a match for the anpu."

"No, the Torc Allta are loyal only to Hekate," Prometheus said. "And it is better that humankind stand together for the final battle." He turned to Huitzilopochtli. "It's time."

Without another word, the two Elders set off down the long twisting corridor.

"Wait!" Scathach called. She raced after them, leaving Shakespeare, Palamedes, Joan and Saint-Germain to bring up the rear.

More heavily armored Torc Allta appeared out of the shadows and crowded around the root-covered entrance to the inner cave. The creatures did not speak, but suddenly weapons were visible in the dull green light.

"I think they want us to move on," Palamedes muttered.

"I didn't know you spoke Torc Allta," William Shakespeare said, a touch of awe in his voice.

Palamedes shook his head. "For a bright man, you can be very stupid sometimes. When someone—man or beast—bares his teeth and produces a dagger as long as his arm, that's a clue."

"I'll make a note of that," Will muttered.

Palamedes raised his voice. "We need to get out of here now. The two people who know us and can vouch for us—Huitzilopochtli and Prometheus—have left, and our red-furred friends are looking a little agitated. And with those tusks, I doubt they're vegetarian."

The four immortals hurried to catch up to the others.

"What's the plan?" Scathach asked, falling into step with the two Elders.

"Plan? We will lead the People of the Tree into Danu Talis," Prometheus said. "We will free Aten and overthrow the Elders."

"Just like that?" she asked in astonishment. "I thought you two were great warriors."

"It is simple and effective," Huitzilopochtli said.

"And we have the advantage that it's a new stratagem," Prometheus continued. "The humans have never risen up before."

The wooden corridor opened onto an enormous staircase leading up into the body of the tree. The steps were shaped out of gnarled roots, polished smooth and glassy by the passage of centuries, and each one was a different height, width and length.

Prometheus took the stairs at a run, and Huitzilopochtli and Scathach jogged along, staying one step below. "If humankind have never risen up before, then how can you be sure they will do it now?" Scathach demanded.

"They worship Aten," Huitzilopochtli answered. "For generations, the humans were enslaved by the Elders. When Aten came to power, he formally recognized them as an intelligent species and granted them the rights of citizens of Danu Talis."

"Many of the Elders resisted, but none dared move against Aten," Prometheus added. "Until now, that is. Bastet must have been planning this for centuries."

"But are you sure humankind will rise when you appear?" Scathach insisted.

"I have been told that they will," Prometheus said coolly.

"Who told you . . . ," she began, and then shook her head. "No, don't tell me. Let me guess: a hooded man with a hook for a left hand."

"So he is known in your time also?"

"I know of him. And I know that the Elders will not give up without a fight," she added.

"We know," Prometheus said. "We want peace, but we are prepared for war."

"In my experience, when you turn up at someone's gate with an army behind you, there is always war," Scathach said grimly.

Huitzilopochtli glanced over at her. "But if we do not move now, then we doom the humans to an eternity of servitude. Or worse. My sister, Bastet, has been advocating the eradication of the entire human race and replacing it with the anpu or some other Were clan. If she can put Anubis in power, then nothing will stand in her way. She will control Danu Talis."

"Why are you doing this, Huitzilopochtli?" Scathach asked.

"Because it is the right thing to do." He shook his head slowly. "Abraham and Marethyu showed us the future," he added, "and the world without humankind is not a pretty one. Not all Elders are monsters. We are not many, but we are powerful, and we will do whatever we can to save the world."

"And if you cannot save the world?" Scathach asked.

"Then we will save as much of the human race as we can."

"And we are here to help you," the Shadow said.

"Why?" Huitzilopochtli demanded. "This is not your fight."

"You are mistaken. This is more than just our fight. This is our future."

"You would think," William Shakespeare wheezed, pressing his left hand to his side, "that a place as sophisticated as this would have an escalator." He slowed to a stop and leaned forward, arms and hands straight on the wooden steps in front of him.

Palamedes waved Joan and Saint-Germain on and

stopped. He sat down on the step and waited for the Bard to catch his breath. "We're nearly there."

"This place will be the death of me," Shakespeare muttered.

The Saracen Knight reached out a hand. Shakespeare took it and Palamedes hauled him upright. "But this is wonderful research, Will. I've seen you making notes. Think of the play you'll get out of it!"

"No one would believe me. I am serious, old friend, I fear I will die here." He climbed up a step.

The Knight stopped and looked at the Bard, who was one step above him. Their faces were level. "Death comes to all of us. And you and I, we've lived way beyond our allotted span of years. We should have few regrets."

"What's done is done," Shakespeare agreed.

"And we are here for a reason," Palamedes added.

"You know this for certain?"

"Marethyu would not have brought us back here if we did not have roles to play." Something shifted behind the knight's dark eyes and the Bard reached out to take hold of his friend's arm.

"What are you not telling me?"

"You are as observant as ever," the knight said.

"Tell me," Will insisted.

"The emerald tablet Tsagaglalal gave me earlier . . ." He stopped and shook his head. "Was it only earlier today? It seems so long ago."

The Bard nodded. At the impromptu garden party in San Francisco, Tsagaglalal had presented everyone with an emerald tablet. Each tablet contained a personal message from Abraham the Mage.

"What did it say?" Shakespeare asked urgently.

"It showed me scenes from my past, of battles fought, some won, some lost. It showed me the last battle, when the Once and Future King fell and I briefly claimed Excalibur. And it showed me standing over you," he finished in a rush.

"Tell me!"

"I saw the death of us, Bard. The death of all of us." He glanced up to where Saint-Germain and Joan were patiently waiting at the top of the steps. "I saw Scathach and Joan of Arc, bloodied and filthy, standing back to back on the steps of a pyramid surrounded by huge dog-headed monsters. I saw Saint-Germain raining fire down from the skies. I saw Prometheus and Tsagaglalal facing off against a swarming army of monsters. . . ."

"And us?" Will asked. "What of us?"

"We were on the steps of a huge pyramid, overrun by monsters. You were lying at my feet and I was holding a lion-headed eagle at arm's length."

The Bard's bright blue eyes twinkled. "Well, then it ends well."

The Saracen Knight blinked in surprise. "Which part of what I've just described suggests a good ending? There is death and destruction in our immediate future."

"But we are all together. And if we die—you or I, Scathach, Joan or Saint-Germain—then we will not die alone. We will die in the company of our friends, our family."

Palamedes nodded slowly. "I always imagined I would die alone, on some foreign battlefield, my body unmourned and unclaimed."

"And we're not dead yet," Shakespeare said. "You did not see me dead, did you?"

"No. But your eyes were closed."

"Maybe I was sleeping," Shakespeare said, turning away and running up the steps. He stopped and glanced back at the Saracen Knight. "But you should know this, Palamedes— I would not wish any companion in the world but you."

"It will be an honor to die with you, William Shakespeare," the Saracen Knight said very softly. He hurried up the irregular steps after the immortal Bard.

"There is a chess term that I believe is applicable now," Saint-Germain said to Joan as they waited at the top of the stairs ahead of Shakespeare and Palamedes.

Joan nodded. "The endgame."

"And we have reached it."

The stairs opened into the very heart of the tree. On a vast wooden plane an army had gathered, men and women standing in long uneven lines, green light running off metal and armor, giving everything an underwater appearance. The air above was dark with whirling gliders, and somewhere a drummer was beating an irregular tattoo. A bagpipe joined in, the sound lost and lonely.

Saint-Germain and Joan watched as dozens of vimana were wheeled out of hangars. Most were patched with wood and leather; others were bound together with rope or had leaves over portholes instead of glass. Humans in thick wool and leather flying suits swarmed around the craft, checking them over, while others loaded spears and crates stacked with crystal globes into the holds.

"I am reminded of the young men who flew over the battlefields of Europe in the First World War in wood and fabric planes," Joan said quietly. "How many survived?"

"Very few," Saint-Germain said.

"And how many of these will return?" she asked.

Saint-Germain looked at the ancient vimana with their patchwork of repairs. "None."

The tiny French immortal breathed deeply. "I seem to have spent most of my long life on battlefields watching young men and women die."

"And you spent as many years as a nurse saving lives," Saint-Germain reminded her.

"After the last war, I swore I would never end up on a battlefield again," she said.

"We do not always get what we want. Sometimes life presents us with surprises."

"Well, this adventure certainly counts as a surprise." She smiled. "And while I really do love surprises, I'm not sure I'm loving this. But here we are, and here we will do what we must do."

"You know," Saint-Germain said, looking around, "I think I'm getting an idea for a new album." His hands moved through the air, tapping time with the drum and bagpipe. "It's going to be a big concept album, with an orchestra and choir. . . ." He started to whistle.

Joan held up her hand, silencing him. "Why don't you just surprise me." A sudden thought struck her and she turned back to her husband. "Do you have a title for this album?"

"Armageddon!"

CHAPTER FORTY-TWO

The ground floor of the Alcatraz Powerhouse pulsed with a dull gray glow.

Moving cautiously through the ever-thickening fog, Nicholas and Perenelle crept toward the light. The Alchemyst's right hand trailed against a metal railing. Beyond the railing, they could hear—but not see—the sea lapping against the shore.

Perenelle breathed deeply. Above the salt and rotten-meat stink of the fog, she caught the hint of another smell: the dry musty odor of wet feathers. She placed her mouth close to Nicholas's ear and whispered. "I think I know what is going on here."

"So do I," he said, surprising her. Then he hissed in pain as his toe smacked into a piece of broken masonry. This section of the island was in a state of disrepair. The salt erosion and the weather were gradually reclaiming Alcatraz, slowly wiping away signs of man.

They could just about make out the steeply slanting roof of the Quartermaster Warehouse and the Powerhouse. Behind them was a tall chimney stack. And docked alongside the Powerhouse was the vague outline of a battered and rusty tourist boat, similar to the type that had brought tourists to the island before Dee's company bought it and closed it down. Most of the boat was concealed behind the Powerhouse and the shifting fog, but they caught a glimpse of a series of lights stretching from the back of the ruined building out to the boat.

"Tell me," Perenelle whispered.

"Think about the monsters you saw in the cells. . . ."

He felt her hair brush his face as she nodded.

"And you said that some cells held more than one type of creature."

The Sorceress nodded again. "Some held two or three."

"But these are small cells, Perenelle. Five feet by nine feet . . ."

"The bigger monsters," she said immediately. "Of course! There were no big creatures in the cellblocks." She turned to look at the vague shapes of the two buildings. "I did see a minotaur, but it was relatively small—a baby. The sphinx was the biggest creature there, and she was walking free."

"It makes sense that Dee and his masters would not have confined themselves to just the regular-sized creatures. If they really wanted to make an impact on the city, they would need some of the great monsters."

286

"So what's in there?"

"Full-sized minotaur," Nicholas guessed. "Probably an ogre or two. You know Dee likes his ogres."

"A dragon?" Perenelle wondered. Then she shook her head. "No, if he had a dragon he would have unleashed it already. But something with scales, a wyrm or a wyvern, perhaps. And a smok. Remember when he raised the smok in Poland?"

They crept closer, moving across rubble and broken stones, barking their shins and scraping their arms on jutting concrete and metal. They were close enough to the warehouse now to peer in through the tall rectangular windows. Grotesque shadows danced across the walls, and they caught glimpses of fur and scales. This close to the house the smell was overwhelming: the stink of wet fur, warm dung and filthy hair, of too many serpents and mammals crowded close together. The reek of wyrm and smok was distinct now: the fire-breathers exuded a nauseating sulfurous miasma every time they opened their mouths.

The Flamels heard shouts within—a thin high voice speaking in a guttural language. " 'One more.' " Perenelle translated the arcane language. " 'We can take one more this trip. Bring something big.' "

Nicholas nodded in admiration. "I'd forgotten you spoke it." He suddenly squeezed her hand. "Even after all these years, there is so much I still do not know about you."

"Medea taught me the lost language of Danu Talis," she said. "And you know enough about me. You know that I love you."

The Alchemyst touched the scarab he wore around his neck. It throbbed beneath his hand. "I do," he said.

Nicholas and Perenelle rounded the end of the building just as a door slammed open. "Anpu," the Sorceress whispered.

Two of the jackal-headed warriors appeared, each tugging on a long iron chain. A second pair of anpu hurried out of the building. They were holding smoking tridents, which they used to jab at the long green-skinned two-legged serpent that slithered from the building, attached to the iron chain. The creature was at least twenty feet long. Another pair of anpu followed behind the creature. They had wrapped more chains around its spiked tail.

"Lindworm," Nicholas said. "Front claws, but no rear feet. But don't think for a moment that it is slow. Its bite is deadly and its tail is a lethal weapon."

The anpu dragged and prodded the lindworm toward the boat.

"We cannot let the boat leave the dock," Nicholas said.

"How do we stop it?"

"These creatures—all of them, monsters and anpu—are under the control of a single person. If we can defeat that person, the beasts will turn upon one another. They'll rip the boat apart for us. So the question is, who is controlling them?"

"I think I know. . . ." Perenelle's lips twisted in disappointment. "I thought she had changed. . . ."

"Who?"

"She helped me escape. I was hoping she might remain neutral, but it seems I was wrong. I smelled her earlier."

"Perenelle . . . ," Nicholas said.

But before she could respond, fog swirled upward in two concentric coils and a dark figure dropped to the ground directly in front of Nicholas and Perenelle. The Alchemyst and the Sorceress both held out their hands, the first hints of their auras appearing on their fingertips.

The figure was dressed from head to foot in gleaming black leather, moisture running off the shining silver bolts that studded her jerkin in a spiral design. Draped over her shoulders, its full hood pulled up around her face, and sweeping to the ground behind her was a cloak made entirely of ravens' feathers. Most of her face was hidden by the hood, but her black lips curled away from overlong incisors.

"We meet again, Sorceress."

"Nicholas," Perenelle said, "let me introduce you to the Morrigan."

CHAPTER FORTY-THREE

*B*illy the Kid threw himself forward and down, curling into a tight ball and rolling smoothly back to his feet.

The sphinx sailed over his head and crashed to the ground, claws slipping and scrabbling for purchase on the stone floor. "You are just delaying the inevitable," she snarled, spinning around, expecting to see Billy racing down the corridor away from her.

The immortal stood facing her, arms hanging loose by his sides. He was close enough to her now that his own aura, a deep reddish purple, had begun to rise in a thin mist off his flesh. The air smelled of red pepper, and the sphinx sneezed. Billy tilted his head to one side and smiled. "Remember me?"

"Oh good," she answered. "My first course is already seasoned." She leapt into the air, claws extended.

Billy's hands moved.

Two ancient leaf-shaped spearheads were tucked into his

belt on the left and right, just above his hips. In one fluid movement, he scooped them out and flung them through the air.

The sphinx screamed a defiant laugh that rose to a screeching wail.

And then the spears struck her.

And time slowed.

And stopped.

The sphinx hung suspended in the air. The spearheads had penetrated deep into the lion's skin. They pulsed, once, twice and then again, throbbing blue, then red and finally white-hot.

Directly around each wound the sphinx's flesh changed color, darkening to a deep blue, then paling to white and turning transparent. The transformation flowed through the creature, racing across her body, flesh turning to glass, revealing the bones beneath the skin. The sphinx managed a single gasped breath, but the skin on her face had begun to turn to glass, revealing the white bone skull beneath. Gradually the skull and all the bones in the glass sphinx transformed from bone to crystal.

And then the sphinx fell and shattered to a million pieces on the floor.

Billy the Kid bent and carefully plucked the two leaf-shaped blades from the shards of glass on the ground. He spun them on his fingers and stuck them back in his belt. He turned and winked at Mars, Odin and Hel. "Some things you just don't forget." He grinned.

CHAPTER FORTY-FOUR

*T*he flat-topped stepped pyramid was enormous.

It sat in the precise center of the island of Danu Talis, surrounded by a vast golden plane, which was in turn encircled by a ring of water. Canals radiated from the circle like spokes on a wheel.

"The Pyramid of the Sun," Osiris said. "The heart of Danu Talis." He banked the vimana so the twins could look out over the extraordinary building.

Josh tried to gauge its size. "What is it—ten blocks, twelve?"

"Remember when we took you to see the Great Pyramid at Giza?" Isis asked.

The twins nodded.

Isis turned to look out the vimana's porthole, admiring the massive structure. "That is a puny seven hundred and fifty-six feet long. The Pyramid of the Sun is ten times that length."

Josh frowned, trying to do the calculation, converting

feet into miles. "Nearly one and a half miles," Sophie said with a smile, putting him out of his misery.

"And it rises almost a mile high," Isis continued.

"Who built it?" Josh asked. "You?"

"No," Osiris said. "Those who came before us, the Great Elders, raised the island from the seabed and created the first pyramid. The original was bigger. Much of the rest of the island is of our creation, though."

Sophie, who was sitting behind Osiris, leaned forward. "So just how old are you, really?"

"That's hard to tell," Osiris said. "We have wandered the Shadowrealms for thousands of years; time flows differently here. We've lived here for millennia and of course, we spent fifteen years on earth, raising you."

"So when you said you were going off on digs, you were really slipping off to some Shadowrealm?" Josh asked.

"Sometimes," Isis said. "Not always. Sometimes we really did go on digs. History is our passion."

"And Aunt Agnes—Tsagaglalal—you knew who she was?" Sophie asked.

Josh looked at his sister. "Aunt Agnes?" he mouthed.

The couple's laughs were identical. "Of course we knew," Isis said. "Did you think we would abandon you to some perfect stranger? We've always been aware of She Who Watches. She moves in and out of human history, but only as a neutral observer. She never takes sides. When she offered to care for you, we were quite surprised. And she was the perfect choice: neither Elder nor Next Generation. And not really humani, either."

293

"Aunt Agnes?" Josh mouthed again, looking at Sophie. She shook her head at her twin. "Later," she mouthed.

The vimana curled away from the pyramid, banked sharply and flew low over an enormous blocky building that lay in the shadow of the pyramid. The roof was laid out in a spectacular garden with seven distinct circles, each one bright with flowers. At the edge of the roof, vines and trailing roses flowed over the walls. "The ziggurat is the Palace of the Sun, home of the rulers of Danu Talis," Isis said. "And beginning today, your home."

"I hope we have gardeners," Josh muttered.

"Josh, you will have everything," Isis said sincerely. "On this island, you will both be the absolute rulers. The humani will worship you as gods." She swiveled around in her seat to look at the twins. "You have been Awakened; you have a hint of the extent of your powers. Those powers will expand in the months to come. We will find the finest teachers to train you." She smiled and her black tongue wriggled like a worm in her mouth. "Soon you will be able to create your own Shadowrealms. Think of that: you could make a world and populate it with anything you desire."

Josh grinned. "That'd be cool. I'm having no snakes in my worlds."

"Once you become the rulers of Danu Talis, you can have anything—everything—you want," Osiris added.

"You've never really explained what we have to do to become rulers," Sophie said hesitantly.

Isis swiveled in her seat. "Why, you do nothing. We will simply present you as the Gold and Silver."

"And we do nothing?" Sophie persisted. It just didn't sound right.

"Nothing," Isis said, turning away.

The twins glanced at one another. Neither believed her.

"The assembled Elders will know you to be the true rulers of the island," Osiris said. "For the last few millennia, a single family has ruled Danu Talis, but it was not always thus. In the beginning, even before it was first raised from the sea, the Elders, and the Great Elders too, were ruled by Gold and Silver—individuals with extraordinary auras."

"Individuals?" Sophie said, looking quickly at her brother, wondering if he realized the implications of what their father—Osiris, she corrected herself—was saying. "Not twins?"

"Usually individuals," Osiris said. "And rarely, very, very rarely, twins. In the entire history of the island, there has only been a handful of Gold and Silver twins. Their powers were almost beyond comprehension. It is said that the original twins created the first Shadowrealms, that they could move through time itself. There's even a story," he laughed, "that this world is a Shadowrealm created by them. But Gold and Silver twins have always been the true rulers of the island."

"So you see," Isis said, "the Elders of Danu Talis will have to accept you as their rulers."

Sophie sat back in the chair. "There has to be someone who will object."

"Of course," Isis said very softly, "and we will deal with those objections when the time comes." Although her voice was just as light and unemotional as it had been since they'd arrived, there was a clear threat in her words.

"Is it normal for so many people to be out in the streets?" Josh asked. He was leaning to his right, looking over the side of the craft to the city and canals below.

Sophie saw Isis and Osiris glance at one another, but they said nothing. She looked across Danu Talis. Plumes of smoke spiraled up in the still evening air and her pulse quickened. "Look! There are fires! It looks like burning buildings."

"There is some unrest," Osiris snapped, voice rising in outrage. Then he took a deep shuddering breath and continued in a more even tone. "There is a *little* civil unrest. In every city, in every time, there will always be the discontented."

"They too will be dealt with," Isis said flatly. "But not today and not tonight. This is a time for celebration!"

The vimana swung around and dipped toward the pyramid, its circular shadow skimming across the canals and golden streets.

Sophie noticed that all the canals leading to the pyramid were guarded by anpu. There were crowds of white-robed humans on the opposite side of the water. They seemed to be shouting and waving their fists, and Sophie thought she saw fruit and other missiles sailing over the canals and into the massed ranks of the anpu.

"I thought we'd be landing on top of the pyramid," Josh said.

"Not landing on it, landing in front. It's hollow," Isis said. "We're going into it."

Osiris tipped the nose of the craft and a huge golden square in front of the pyramid came into view. As they moved closer, the twins could see that the square was crowded with people and carriages. Half a dozen vimana, in various states of disrepair, were scattered about. They sat alongside carriages and wagons, none of which were pulled by horses. The area swarmed with dog-, jackal-, bull- and pig-headed warriors, all dressed in full armor. There were a few cat warriors, but they kept apart from the others—especially the dog soldiers.

"They're expecting trouble," Sophie said.

"Oh, it's purely ceremonial," Isis said quickly. "This is a rare occasion: I don't remember the last time all the Elders gathered in council." She swiveled in her chair again, and Josh was suddenly reminded of endless summer road trips across America, with his father driving and his mother turning to give them instructions or point out some local landmark, or more often just to separate a fight. "This is probably the last time we're going to see all the Elders of Danu Talis gathered in one place. The Change has taken many of them and made them . . ." She paused, hunting for the word.

"Hideous," Sophie said.

"Hideous," Isis agreed.

"But you haven't Changed," Josh said. "Have you?"

"No, we haven't," Isis said with a tight-lipped smile.

"Though not all changes are external," Sophie murmured.

The craft dropped alarmingly, then rocked to a gentle halt on the square before the towering pyramid. Anpu in black and red ceramic armor fell into a formation of two lines outside the craft. "Now, just say nothing and do as you're told," Isis said firmly.

Josh dipped his head to hide a smile. It was just like a Sunday road trip.

297

CHAPTER FORTY-FIVE

*N*iten stood over the fallen Prometheus.

More spears appeared out of the fog, but the Japanese immortal was fast, and he had trained against swords and arrows in his youth, learning to chop them out of the air. It was a useful skill for a warrior, and in his youth he'd done it blindfolded, listening to the faint keen as the blade came nearer. He used the same trick now, standing with his head bent, his left side—his good ear—turned to the fog. He could hear the faintest whistle of the spearhead, the hiss of parting air, even the slight creaking as the wooden spear shaft flexed. The hardest part was knowing when to move. Too soon and he'd miss the spear, too late and the blade would have already struck him.

Two spears, each sounding slightly different, curled out of the fog.

Niten relaxed, eyes half closed, tracing the path of the

spears by sound. Then he moved. The Spartoi club in his left hand knocked one spear aside; the wakizashi in his right sliced the second in two. The ground before him was littered with broken and shattered lengths of wood.

Niten caught glimpses of Spartoi as vague shapes in the gloom, but none approached. He hoped they hadn't managed to find a way around the barrier of cars, but he knew he couldn't move from his present position to investigate.

Long and bitter experience had taught the Swordsman to focus exclusively on the battle. A moment's distraction could prove fatal. A warrior needed to be single-minded. He wasted no time thinking about the Flamels, wondering how they were faring: they were beyond his help.

A trio of barbed spears whistled out of the night, trailing tendrils of fog like smoke. He smashed one aside and sliced the other in two, but the third caught him high on the left shoulder, piercing his flesh and numbing his entire arm. The club fell from his fingers and rattled to the ground.

Niten grimaced in pain and then allowed a little of his royal blue aura to wrap around his arm, sealing the wound. But he could feel himself age as he healed, could feel the heaviness in his legs, the tightness in his lungs, and he knew it would take time for feeling to return to his arm. He would have to finish this battle one-handed.

Still facing out into the night, he crouched beside Prometheus and put a finger on the side of his neck, feeling for a pulse. There was none, but he felt the Elder stir under him. "You're alive," Niten said, relieved.

"Did you think I was sleeping?" Prometheus grumbled.

He dug his heels in and pushed himself up into a sitting position. "Takes more than a little spear to kill me."

"For the record: it was two spears, and they were not little. How do you feel?"

"Like I've just been stabbed by two spears." The front of Prometheus's armor had been staved in, marred by two holes. He pressed both hands to his chest and his entire body glowed red. The smell of anise briefly covered the odors of salt and meat.

Metal scraped in the fog, the sound high-pitched and grating.

The Elder visibly aged before the Japanese immortal's eyes as he healed, his hair turning snow-white, lines etching into his forehead, deep grooves forming alongside his nose and at the corners of his mouth.

Out in the night, glass cracked and the bridge vibrated as more metal clanged.

Niten held out his hand and helped the Elder to his feet. Prometheus rubbed his hand over his armor, repairing the holes, filling out the metal. "I doubt I can do that again. What about you?" he asked, squinting at Niten.

"I have a little aura left. Not much. Perhaps enough for one more healing if the wound is not too bad."

"At least your hair has not turned gray."

"Oh, I think mine will be black till the day I die. And by the way, your hair is not gray anymore," Niten said. "It's white."

"I've always been fond of red."

Metal screamed again.

Niten reached out to rest his hand against the nearest car. It was vibrating. "They're pulling the barricade apart," he said.

"That's what I would do." Prometheus nodded. "I wonder if they will fight or bypass us and swarm into the city?"

"They'll fight," Niten said confidently. "We have offended them."

"Offended them—how?"

"By not dying quickly. These are professional warriors; I have fought their like all my life. They believe they are invincible. It makes them arrogant, and stupid, too. And I have found that stupid people make mistakes. A sensible commander would leave a few here to engage us and move the rest of his forces into the city. But pride will keep them here. Now they have to kill us. And there will be great honor given to the one who brings us down." He stopped. "Why are you smiling, Elder?"

"I'll wager that somewhere out in the fog is a Spartoi commander telling his Drakon troops almost exactly the same thing."

"He would be mistaken," Niten said. "We are far more deadly than the Spartoi."

Prometheus's smile turned rueful. "I'm not sure I agree."

"Oh, but we are. We have a reason to be here. We have a cause. In my experience, a warrior with a cause is the most dangerous soldier of all. We must make a choice now. We can stand here and fight . . ."

". . . or we can take the fight to them." The Elder looked up into the sky, trying to gauge the time, but the stars were invisible behind the fog. "I only regret that we didn't manage to delay them longer."

"They are still here, aren't they? Every moment we keep them from the city is a victory for us. If we stand here, they will pull the barricades apart and flank us. But if we move now, we have the element of surprise on our side: in their arrogance, they would never believe we might attack," Niten said. Pins and needles tingled in the fingertips of his left hand and he shook it to get the circulation going again.

"Agreed: we'll attack. But we have to stick together," Prometheus said quickly. "If we separate, they will easily overwhelm us. We'll try and cut right through them to the other side of the bridge. That will make them turn away from the city. We'll see if we can hold them till the dawn."

Niten flashed a bright smile in the gloom as they began to walk the length of the bridge.

"You seem cheerful for a man heading for sure and certain doom," Prometheus remarked.

"The last few years have been uneventful," the Swordsman admitted. "Boring, even. Aoife's reputation was so fearsome that no one dared challenge her. Most sensible people simply avoided us. Even when we went into the deadliest Shadowrealms we were usually left alone."

"What did you do to pass the time?"

"I spent a lot of time painting a houseboat in Sausalito."

"What color?"

"Green, always green. I could never find just the right

green, though. Apparently there are more than forty shades of green."

"Green's a good color," Prometheus said, his broadsword resting lightly on his right shoulder. "Don't get me wrong: I like red. But I've always been partial to green."

They walked on in silence, watching shapes flicker and move through the fog around them.

"Have you any regrets?" Prometheus suddenly asked.

Niten smiled shyly and a touch of color bloomed on his cheeks.

"You're blushing," Prometheus said, astonished.

"One regret. One regret only. I am sorry Aoife is not with us now. How she would have relished this battle."

Prometheus nodded in agreement. "And she'd have defeated the Spartoi too."

"They would have run from her," Niten agreed. "I should have asked her to marry me."

Prometheus looked at him. "You loved her?"

"Yes," he said simply. "Over the centuries I came to love her."

"Did you ever tell her?"

Niten shook his head. "No. I came close on a couple of occasions, but somehow, at the very last moment, my nerve always failed me."

Prometheus sighed. "So you didn't do it. In my experience, we only ever regret the things we have not done."

Niten nodded. "You know that I have faced and fought centuries of monsters, both human and inhuman, and there is no one alive who could call me a coward. But I was afraid to ask Aoife to marry me." The immortal looked over at the Elder. "What would I have done if she'd said no? Could we have remained together as friends if she'd rejected me?"

"You should have asked her," Prometheus said.

Niten's shoulders fell. "I know."

"Do you think she loved you?" Prometheus pressed.

"It was hard to say with Aoife."

"And yet she stayed with you for how long?"

"About four hundred years."

"I'd say she loved you," the Elder said confidently.

"And now she is gone," Niten added. "Trapped in a Shadowrealm with a savage Archon, and no one to rescue her."

"I feel sorry for the Archon," Prometheus said.

"True." Niten smiled, then froze and sniffed the air. "I am smelling . . . ," he began, then turned, breathing in deeply. The smell was all around them, a putrid stench that suddenly intensified as the Spartoi flowed out of the fog, spears and swords jabbing, mouths wide, claws outstretched.

"It has been an honor to know you," Prometheus said, sword blazing red in a semicircle about him, sparks screaming and exploding off shields and swords.

"And it is an honor to die with you," Niten answered. He dodged a spear, caught the head of another and wrenched it from a Spartoi's hand, then deftly flipped it and plunged it into the surprised monster.

The Drakon attacked.

CHAPTER FORTY-SIX

The twins followed Isis and Osiris across a path of golden stones toward the entrance to the impossibly tall Pyramid of the Sun. Their boots clicked on the gilded walkway, the only sound in a cone of silence that gradually spread around them as everyone turned to look.

Josh leaned close to his sister. "We're attracting a lot of attention," he said quietly.

"I get the feeling that was the plan," Sophie whispered back. She saw her brother's blank look and continued. "I have a feeling we could have landed a lot closer to the entrance, but we didn't. Isis and Osiris wanted us to go the long way so everyone would see us. I bet this is one of the reasons they made us wear the armor." Sophie nodded to the people who had started to crowd around. "Look—who else is wearing armor?"

"Well, the guards—" Josh started.

Sophie cut him off before he could finish. "Besides the guards—who are all wearing black, I might add."

"Just us, I guess," he conceded. "I hate it when you're right."

"And this gold and silver armor is not exactly discreet, is it?"

"They're showing us off," he said softly. Then he frowned. "Actually, I'm not sure I like that. It's kind of like we're animals in a zoo."

Sophie nodded. "Exactly—like prize attractions. They want everyone to know we're here."

"I wish I'd brought my sunglasses," Josh said suddenly. "Though it would probably ruin the look," he added with a grin.

"Armor and sunglasses." Sophie smiled. "It would be an interesting image, that's for sure."

"Wish I'd brought a camera, too," Josh said, craning his neck to get a better view of the towering structure directly ahead of them. "The pyramid is pretty awesome. Look at the size of that door!"

Directly ahead of them was a massive entrance into the heart of the Pyramid of the Sun. One hundred anpu stood shoulder to shoulder across the opening, all of them armed with spears that leaked a pale blue light. On either side of the door countless steps stretched to the sky, where the evening sun ran bloodred and golden off the polished stones.

"Is it made out of real gold, do you think?" Josh asked.

"Everything else is," Sophie said. "Do you really think it's paint?"

As the twins approached, the crowd moved closer, forming into two long lines at their sides.

"These must be the Elders of Danu Talis," Sophie murmured.

None of the figures were entirely human, and most were half hidden by hooded leather cloaks or swaths of cloth. There were occasional glimpses of fur or leathery flesh, a ragged claw, an animal's bloodshot eye or a horn. But there were a few who chose to proudly display the Changes that had overtaken them—the frightening alterations and bizarre additions to their bodies.

"Don't look now," Josh said suddenly, "but there's a woman on my side who's got wings. And bird's feet," he added, in awe.

"That's Inanna." Sophie turned to look, and then nodded. "Inanna. One of the most respected of the Elders. Powerful, deadly, but not an enemy of the humani. The Witch's memories," she told her brother quickly, before he could ask her how she knew.

"So I guess you'll know about everyone here. That could come in real handy."

"I'll know most, I guess. I've been trying to push back the Witch's thoughts—Joan of Arc showed me how. But sometimes bits and pieces trickle through, like names. Or I'll remember the trivia that stuck in the Witch's head." She tilted her head slightly. "Inanna keeps lions, so she always smells like big cats, damp straw and dung. The Witch hated that smell. And she was allergic to cats—they made her sneeze."

Josh laughed out loud at the thought of the Witch of Endor being allergic to anything.

"They make her break out in hives, too," Sophie added with a grin, and then laughed with him.

"Will all the Elders look like monsters?" Josh asked as they stepped out of the sunshine and into the shadow of the pyramid. The temperature immediately fell, and their clattering footsteps were dulled and absorbed by the enormous gold pyramid.

Sophie nodded. "Mostly. There aren't many Elders that the Change hasn't . . . uh . . . changed in some way . . . ," she began, and then stopped, realizing what her brother was suggesting.

Josh nodded at Isis and Osiris, who were up ahead, dwarfed by the enormous doorway, waiting patiently for the twins to catch up. "So what does that make this pair?" he asked. "They don't look Changed."

Sophie shook her head. "No. They're Changed," she said confidently. "We're just not seeing how."

CHAPTER FORTY-SEVEN

Wrapped in a hooded leather cloak, Marethyu moved easily through the Elders crowding around Sophie and Josh Newman before the Pyramid of the Sun. Tucked in his shirt, bundled up in an oiled leather bag, the hook that took the place of his left hand burned and buzzed against his chest.

He should not be here.

Not now.

Especially not now.

He was in a crowd of Elders. If he brushed against any of them, even by accident, the consequences would be catastrophic. But it had been a long time since he had taken risks, and there were some risks worth taking.

When he was younger, first coming into his powers, he had been a daredevil. What had he to fear? He was invulnerable and immortal. He could be wounded and injured, and unless he lost his head or shattered his spine, he would heal.

But once he had begun to conceive the plan to save the world, he had taught himself to be cautious, trained himself to be a little fearful. Without him, the plan would not succeed. He had lived so long and led so many lives that he did not fear death, but he knew that one slip, one tiny mistake, could bring it all crashing down.

Yet here he was, risking everything by coming here today.

When he had returned to Danu Talis to set in motion all that needed to happen, he had known deep down that he wanted to witness the arrival of the twins. It would be one of the defining moments in the extraordinary history of the island empire. He wanted to see the brother and sister, the fabled twins of the ancient prophecy—one to save the world, one to destroy it.

He felt it was worth the risk.

Isis and Osiris had timed their arrival perfectly.

Marethyu was standing in the shadows, watching as their crystal vimana swept down out of the sky. Osiris had waited until most of the council had arrived at the pyramid, a handful riding in decrepit vimana, the rest in carriages ranging from the hideously ornate to the grotesque. Then Osiris had deliberately taken a long curling loop before landing so that the dipping sun would splash across the craft, lighting it up like a shooting star.

They had landed in one of the farther parking bays, usually occupied by the carriages of minor Elders. By rights Isis and Osiris could have landed almost on the steps of the pyramid and none would have objected. But they wanted the twins to make the ten-minute walk across the courtyard to the entrance of the pyramid. Osiris had also cleverly turned the craft so that when the sides opened and Sophie and Josh emerged, their armor lit up like beacons in the sinking sun's light, blazing silver and gold.

The council always waited until the last minute before going into the pyramid, because its slanting gold walls would drain their auras. They were all witness to the arrival of the mysterious couple in the gold and silver armor.

Isis and Osiris strode quickly ahead, leaving the twins to follow. The hook-handed man knew what they were doing—keeping the focus completely on the teenagers.

By the time Sophie and Josh were halfway across the square, Marethyu had heard the first whispers ripple through the crowd. . . .

. . . *gold and silver* . . .

. . . *twins of legend* . . .

. . . *sun and moon* . . .

Marethyu had to give it to Isis and Osiris—it was a masterly move. If the two Elders had simply brought Sophie and Josh to the Council Chamber and announced them as the twins of legend, many of the Elders would have laughed in disbelief. But with an entrance like this, the council were already convincing themselves that these were the twins of prophecy, even before they'd stepped into the pyramid.

It was genius.

Marethyu moved quickly to the back of the line, keeping pace with the twins. He watched them chat quietly with each other, all the while knowing every word they said. He saw

311

Josh spot Inanna and saw the moment his eyes widened with awe when he noticed her bird's feet. The hook-handed man saw Sophie's blue eyes flicker toward the winged Elder, and his own lips formed the words as she said them: "That's Inanna."

Marethyu had chosen this particular moment from all the moments that were available to him because the twins looked happy. He watched Sophie's lips, and although he could not hear her, he knew she was telling Josh about the Witch of Endor being allergic to cats and sneezing. The twins laughed together, the sound pure and high, carefree and full of life.

That was what he had come to hear.

Marethyu's age was now beyond reckoning. He had traveled back and forth across endless streams of time. He had lived for centuries in Shadowrealms where the rules of time were different or nonexistent. He had seen much and experienced even more and had forgotten nothing. That was part of his curse.

And he knew that this was the last time Sophie and Josh would laugh together.

CHAPTER FORTY-EIGHT

*D*ressed in full ceremonial armor, Anubis stood outside a beautifully carved metal door and took a deep breath. He found his left hand going toward his mouth and then stopped himself. He'd given up chewing his nails when the Change began to alter his skull, making it beastlike, elongating his teeth, thinning his lips. On a couple of occasions when he'd absentmindedly put his nail in his mouth, he'd almost bitten his finger off.

"Why don't you come in," a voice snarled from inside the room. "I know you're out there."

Fixing his lips into a semblance of a smile, Anubis pushed open the door to Bastet's private chambers and stepped inside, quickly pulling the door shut behind him to prevent anything within from escaping into the corridors. The room was in almost total darkness, and he stood with his back to the wall as he allowed his eyes to adjust to the gloom. The

313

smell in the room was appalling, and he tried his best to breathe only through his mouth. "How did you know I was outside?" he asked.

"I could hear you breathing." Bastet's voice came from his right and he turned toward the sound. He could just about make out the shape of her huge cat head against a darkened window. It was thrown back, and she was in the process of swallowing something still wriggling. "What news?"

"Isis and Osiris have just arrived," Anubis announced.

Bastet swallowed her meal, wiped her mouth with her arm, then coughed and hacked like a cat. "Good," she gasped finally. "I told you they would be here for your inauguration. They hold huge sway with the rest of the council. Once they endorse you, you are guaranteed the leadership."

"They came in that amazing vimana of theirs," he said quietly. "I want one. It hardly seems fair that they have a ship like that and I don't." Taking a deep breath, he tiptoed across the floor toward his mother. He winced with every step as tiny bones crunched and cracked beneath his feet. Before the Change, his mother had only eaten peeled fruit on crystal plates. Now she ate raw—and often live—meat, and the marble and gold floor was littered with the cast-off bones of her recent meals. The room, older than most civilizations and once beautiful, now stank of waste and rotting food.

"When you are ruler, you can have anything you want," Bastet answered. "You should ask them for the vimana. They'll hardly refuse."

"They didn't come alone," he added casually.

314

"Oh. Who have they brought? Anyone we know?"

Anubis crouched before his mother, and even though she was sitting, their faces were on the same level. He'd often wondered at the quirk of fate that had made her Change into a cat while he became a dog. The Change was more pronounced with her: she had a tail, razor-sharp teeth, retractable claws and a taste for live rodents and birds.

"It's a couple. A girl and a boy. I don't know them. I've never seen them before," he said quietly.

"I wonder who they are." She turned to appraise herself in a mirror only she could see. Anubis smelled powder and the slightly sour perfume his mother preferred as she sprayed it over her fur

"They look like humani, to be honest," he said, coming slowly to his feet and stepping back.

"How odd," Bastet said mildly.

"They're wearing gold and silver semitransparent ceramic armor. And I think they might be twins," he finished in a rush. He ducked as Bastet screamed and flung a perfume jar at his head. Only his extraordinarily fast reflexes saved him. "I'll wait outside," he called as he left the room.

Anubis stood in the corridor, arms folded across his massive chest. Through the thick gold-plated walls, he could hear his mother rage around her room. Glass shattered. Furniture crashed. The last time she'd been in one of her rages, she'd punched a hole through a six-inch-thick solid-gold door and pulled the antique chandelier out of the ceiling. He heard the tinkle of expensive crystal, and then the door vibrated as something heavy—he guessed it was the chandelier again—shattered against the other side.

Occasionally, animal-headed servants would appear at the end of the hallway, spot him outside Bastet's door and slowly back away. The Elder's rages were legendary, and deadly to anyone who got in her way.

Anubis closed his eyes and sighed. When he ruled Danu Talis, he wondered if it would be possible—or wise, even—to think about removing his mother to one of the outer Shadow-realms and then sealing off the leygates, trapping her there. She had many allies on the council, but very few friends. He might be able to find a small group willing to assist him—maybe even the mysterious Isis and Osiris.

Isis and Osiris were unlike any of the Elders he knew. In a council chamber where most of the Elders were showing some aspect of the Change, Isis and Osiris seemed untouched. He'd heard a rumor that they were Great Elders or maybe even Ancients, but he didn't believe that, and he knew they couldn't be Archons. They didn't spend a lot of time on Danu Talis, and he could probably count on the claws of one hand the number of times he'd seen them at the council meetings over the last fifteen years.

And now they had turned up with twins in gold and silver armor.

Anubis was not particularly bright—his brother Aten was the brains of the family—but even he knew this was not a good sign. Everyone knew the legend of the Gold and Silver twins who had first ruled the island. Danu Talis was built around the twin symbols of sun and moon, opposite and equal. The city was even laid out like a sun and crescent moon. So for Isis and Osiris to turn up on this day with a couple in gold and silver armor could not be a coincidence.

The big Elder's face fixed into a grim mask. He would rule Danu Talis today—one way or another. He had an army of ten thousand anpu, and the new bull-headed Asterion hybrids encamped in the squares and streets nearby. His latest experiments in boar, bear, cat and bull hybrids were waiting in the sub-basements deep below the pyramid. He had put them in place so that when he was declared the Lord of Danu Talis, he could parade them as symbols of his power. But they were all armed and in full armor—and had been bred to be loyal only to him.

Bastet's rages were like a summer storm: furious and dramatic but quick to pass. When the door opened a little while later, the Elder was calm and composed, her fur neatly combed, dressed from head to foot in a black and red leather robe and a black cloak lined with crimson.

"That looks rather like my armor . . . ," Anubis began, and then stopped.

"Why do you think I chose it?" She linked her arm with his, and together they walked down the long corridor lined with enormous slabs of polished crystal. Their reflections, broken and distorted, kept pace with them, and each mirror showed the Elder couple against a different moving background.

"Now, tell me everything you can about this couple in gold and silver."

"I've told you all I know," Anubis answered. "My spies informed me that Isis and Osiris had arrived and I went out on the balcony to take a look at the craft. I really want it, it is fabulous," he added.

"Anubis . . . ," Bastet warned.

"And that's when I spotted the twins."

"You don't know they're twins," she snapped. "Stop saying that."

"I know you think I'm stupid . . . ," Anubis began. He saw the look on his mother's face and hurried on. "I saw a young man and woman who looked humani to me, in expensive- and ancient-looking gold and silver armor."

"Who was wearing what?" she asked.

"The boy was in gold and the girl in silver, of course."

"Describe them."

"I just have—a boy and a girl."

"Hair color, eyes," Bastet said, and her grip tightened painfully on his arm.

"Their hair was blond. I didn't see their eyes; I was too far away. I did note that the boy was taller than the girl. It's hard to tell humani ages, but they were fifteen or sixteen summers, perhaps."

"How do you know they were humani?"

"Because there are no Elder children," he reminded her, and then braced himself, preparing for her grip on his arm to tighten again in response to his disrespect.

"What are Isis and Osiris up to?" she asked, almost as if speaking to herself. "The gold and silver armor is a deliberate insult. A reminder that our family did not always rule the council."

"I thought you said Isis and Osiris would support my claim," he said.

"Well, who else were they going to support?"

"Unless they have their own candidates," Anubis suggested.

Bastet started to shake her head, then stopped. "You know, you might not be as stupid as you look."

Anubis said nothing, not sure that was a compliment.

At the end of the corridor, a pair of black-armored anpu snapped to attention and hauled opened two massive white quartz crystal doors. Trapped within the glass, a tentacled creature lazily opened a single eye, then closed it again.

Bastet and Anubis stepped through the doorway and out into a golden-sanded courtyard. It had once housed a spectacular garden, but Bastet in her rages had ripped up the flowers and rare blooms so often that Anubis had instructed the gardeners to plant only cacti and spiny succulents, plants she would not be so keen to tear from the ground. A carriage was waiting, an enormous shimmering globe carved from a single pearl Anubis had brought back from a watery Shadowrealm. A pair of albino saber-toothed cats, their incisors curled up like elephant tusks, were harnessed to the carriage. They were a new hybrid Anubis was breeding.

Anubis opened the door and held out his hand. Bastet ignored it and stepped into the carriage unaided.

"Maybe they are the twins of legend," Anubis suggested innocently as he climbed in after his mother.

"Don't be ridiculous!" she snapped. "Where would Isis and Osiris find twins? Your father and I wiped out that blood-line a thousand years ago."

Shocked, Anubis spun to look his mother in the face just as the tigers surged forward, jerking him back in his seat. They needed no driver; the big cats had been programmed to find their way to the Pyramid of the Sun. "I never knew that," he said.

"Few do. And I don't want you repeating it." She turned her head, resting her chin on her left claw. Her pupils shrank to pinpoints at the slanting evening sunlight streaming through the translucent walls of the pearl coach. She sat quietly, the razor claws on her other hand absently tearing through the supposedly indestructible hide covering her seat. Every time she rode in the carriage, she ripped apart the upholstery; Anubis decided that the next seat was going to be carved from stone.

"If Isis and Osiris have found other claimants," Bastet said quietly, "then why reveal them to us so early? That doesn't make sense. They could have smuggled them into the Council Chamber and introduced them as a huge surprise later."

"They obviously want us to know," Anubis said, resting his great head on his fist and staring out across the city. There was smoke in the skies, and he could smell its stink on the air. The humani were burning their hovels again.

Eight huge anpu were waiting at the gates. They split into

two groups of four and fell in alongside the carriage. Their role was more ceremonial than protective. All the principal houses and palaces of the rulers of Danu Talis were protected within the rings of canals, and the only access to the inner circle around the pyramid was across the closely guarded bridges. No humani had ever walked the golden stones around the great pyramid.

Anubis realized his mother had stopped speaking and turned to look at her.

"What did you say?" she asked.

Anubis frowned, trying to remember. "I said that they obviously wanted us to see the twins—the couple in gold and silver armor. When you are fighting a battle"—he leaned forward—"you can conceal the size of your troops and surprise the enemy. Sometimes that strategy works, but often if the enemy does not know how many warriors they are up against, they will keep fighting. The other option is to reveal yourself to the enemy: show them that they are outnumbered, demoralize them. Often you can get a quick bloodless victory."

Bastet was nodding. "You know, we really need to spend more time together. You're full of surprises."

Was this a second compliment in one day? Anubis wondered if the world really was coming to an end.

"I've spent my entire life fighting. I know battles," he said quickly.

"Where are they now?" Bastet asked.

Anubis gave his mother a blank look, then shrugged. "In the Pyramid of the Sun, I suppose. Maybe even in the Council Chamber."

"No, I doubt it. It's too early. Isis and Osiris will want to make a grand entrance into the Council Chamber." She was confident. "It's what I would do. However, I have no doubts they are meeting the other Elders, planting seeds, dropping hints about the couple in gold and silver. They'll have stashed the couple somewhere quiet and out of the way, saving them for the big reveal."

"But you said they can't have the real twins. So they found a couple of children and dressed them up in fancy gold and silver armor. What's that going to prove? The council will laugh at them."

"Isis and Osiris are cunning. I guarantee you that they have not arrived with just any children dressed in armor. This pair will have some skills. Maybe enough to fool the council." She shook her head. "Isis and Osiris must have been plotting this for centuries. Maybe longer. When you are ruler," she added, "I want you to have that pair killed."

"Which pair?" Anubis frowned. "The children?"

Bastet shook her head and yowled. "No, not the children. Well, yes, you can have them killed too, if you wish. I want Isis and Osiris taken care of."

"The last people who tried to assassinate them ended up as jewelry," he reminded his mother. "Isis wore that necklace of tiny people for months afterward. And most of them were still alive," he added in a whisper.

Bastet suddenly sat forward and put her hand on Anubis's knee. A razor claw pierced his flesh, though he bit his lip and said nothing. "But you're right, of course. . . ."

"I am?" he asked, the surprise of his mother agreeing with

something he'd said briefly wiping away the pain. "What am I right about?"

"Kill the children."

"Kill them?" He regarded her evenly, then tipped his head to one side. "That's easy enough. They can have a little accident in the next few days."

All of Bastet's claws punctured his flesh and he gasped. "Sometimes you can be very stupid!"

When he was ruler, he was definitely banishing her to a Shadowrealm. Someplace with lots of dogs.

"Kill them now. Kill them before Isis and Osiris can present them to the council." She squeezed his knee for extra emphasis. "Are you listening to me?"

"Yes, Mother," he said through gritted teeth.

"And have it done properly."

"Yes, Mother," Anubis repeated. "I know just the creatures for the job. They have never failed me."

CHAPTER FORTY-NINE

Strapped into a flimsy wood and paper glider, Scathach flew past the window and waved.

Within the rattling vimana, Joan of Arc waved back. "She's enjoying herself," she said.

"What?" Saint-Germain asked. He had drawn a staff of five lines in his Moleskine notebook and was rapidly filling it with notes and rests, humming along as he wrote.

"Scathach. I just saw her glide past the window. She looked like she was enjoying herself," she said, shouting to be heard over the noise in the vimana.

"Who is?" Saint-Germain clambered to his feet and peered through the window. He saw Scathach rise and cut right, wheeling down on an invisible wind current, just above the canopy of trees. "Well, that's nice for her," he said absently. "Now, just give me a sec, I want to get this melody down." He slumped to the floor and bent his head back over the notebook.

"I think she may be safer out there than she would be in here," William Shakespeare muttered. He was sitting to the right of Prometheus, watching nervously as the big Elder struggled to control the ancient craft.

Palamedes stood behind the Bard, and even his usually impassive face was creased with concern.

"It was the last vimana available," Prometheus explained. He pulled down on the throttle and it snapped off in his hand. He tossed the broken stick aside and gripped the end with his fingertips. "No one else wanted it."

"I can see why," Will said.

"You didn't have to come," the Elder snapped. "You did have a choice."

Will looked up at Palamedes and grinned. "We didn't, really. It all ends today."

"Nothing will happen today," Prometheus said confidently. "There'll be a lot of shouting and banging on tables. It will take humankind days to get organized. Aten was the closest thing they had to a leader, and he's gone now. They have no one to lead them."

Scathach leaned to the right and felt the glider shift beneath her. Then she banked left and right in a series of quick zigzags. She had never flown in a glider before, but she was an accomplished horsewoman and a world-class surfer. And gliding, she discovered, was just like surfing, except she was riding air instead of water.

She'd learned to ride the waves in the bitterly cold waters that pounded her island fort of Skye millennia before surfing became a sport. Centuries later she'd even led a band of Maori warriors on a raid from one island to another to rescue some captured children. The lookouts had been watching for sails to signal the arrival of the enemy—the Maori had evaded them by surfing in on long boards.

She whooped a war cry. She was loving this and had only one tiny regret—that she'd discovered it so late in life.

Scathach the Shadow adjusted her weight, bringing the front end of the glider up, forcing air under the wings. The glider rose in slow spirals, and when she thought she was high enough in the sky, she swung around and looked down.

Directly below her the forest spread out in a vast unbroken carpet of green. In the distance, shimmering on the horizon, were the blue of the sea and the gold of Danu Talis, with the great Pyramid of the Sun dominating the skyline.

There were three thousand gliders in the air below her, and though they had been designed to carry only one person, most carried a second strapped precariously beneath the first. Paper and leather crackled as they flew, the sound like distant thunder.

Almost forty vimana sped through the air below the gliders. Most had been scavenged and bolted together from bits of other craft. There were a few of the rare triangular shapes, a scattering of the big Rukma warships, but the vast majority were the small circular craft designed to hold two people but jammed with five and six warriors. None of the craft were new, and a couple—including the one carrying Joan and the others—were ancient, with glassless portholes, their metal shells held together by knotted vines, pocked with holes that had been patched with leaves and wood. All of the craft were dangerously overloaded. Before they'd taken flight, Huitzilopochtli had told Scathach he was committing the Yggdrasill's entire defenses—almost ten thousand warriors—to the battle. Four thousand would descend from the air, while six would march through the jungle. It would still take them two days to reach Danu Talis. And no one knew what they would find when they arrived.

Scathach had refused to join the others in the battered circular vimana. There was something she had to do—and she couldn't afford to be trapped onboard the ship. She had insisted on strapping on the pair of glider wings and launching herself from a branch out into the sky, knowing with absolute confidence that she would be able to master the required skill. She had learned to swim the same way—by jumping into the icy depths off Skye and flapping about in the water until she started to float.

Scathach circled the vimana and waved again. Joan waved back. Prometheus was too busy struggling with the controls to notice; Will and Palamedes watched him anxiously. Only Saint-Germain seemed completely relaxed, hunched on the floor, writing in his notebook. Scathach hoped he survived to finish his symphony: she had a feeling it would be epic.

The Warrior took one last look at her friends, and then she allowed the wind to take her, pulling her higher and higher. When she knew the others would not be able to see her, she banked to the right and descended, falling through the sky, toward the outskirts of the city.

CHAPTER FIFTY

$\mathcal{N}$icholas Flamel's hand flared into a green glove, and a solid ball of energy buzzed and spat in the palm of his hand. He drew back his arm and was about to throw the ball at the Morrigan when Perenelle suddenly grabbed his forearm. "Wait!"

"Wait?" Nicholas looked at his wife, confused.

The Sorceress was gazing intently at the black-cloaked figure. "You're not the Morrigan, are you?"

"This is the Morrigan, the Crow Goddess," Nicholas insisted. The ball of energy spinning in his hand was starting to shrink.

The hooded figure standing before them raised her head. Her pale face was framed by the hood, and when she spoke, traces of an Irish or Scottish accent were clearly audible. Her eyes were closed. "The Morrigan is still sleeping," she said, and opened her eyes. They were bloodred. "At this moment, I am the Badb."

The creature's eyes slowly closed, then blinked open. Now they were a bright yellow. "And now I am Macha." The Celtic accent was even stronger, and deeper, harsher.

The creature's eyes closed once more, and when they opened, one was a lustrous red, the other a brilliant yellow. Two voices rolled from the same mouth, the sounds buzzing slightly out of sync with one another.

"And we are the Morrigan's sisters. We are the Crow Goddess."

Nicholas looked from the creature to his wife, eyebrows arching in a question.

"They are three in one," she explained. "Like the three aspects of Hekate, but the Morrigan, Macha and the Badb are three separate personalities existing within the same flesh. Centuries ago, the Morrigan took over the other two, trapped them within her." She smiled. "I released them, and now it is the Morrigan who is trapped within."

The Crow Goddess smiled, sharp white teeth pressing against her black lips. "You should hope that she never escapes, Sorceress. She is not very happy with you."

Nicholas closed his hand into a fist and his green aura sank back into his flesh, emerald fluid running down his arm like ink.

"Thank you for saving me," Perenelle said.

"Thank you for freeing us," the Crow Goddess said quickly.

"To be truthful, I never thought I'd see you again"—the Sorceress spread her arms— "especially not back here."

"We had not planned for it either," the Crow Goddess said. She turned toward the Powerhouse, her feathered cloak whispering along the ground. "This is . . . *wrong.*"

Nicholas and Perenelle looked at one another. "Wrong?"

"We are Next Generation," the creature said. "We grew up in the terrible days after the Fall of Danu Talis. It was clear to us then—and it should have been clear to our sister—that the Elders were the architects of their own destruction. They had grown lazy and arrogant, and that helped destroy their world. They believed the people worshipped them as gods, but in reality, humankind despised and feared them. We weren't there, but we heard the stories of the human uprising often enough." A black-nailed claw pointed back toward the Powerhouse. "If these beasts get ashore, the Elders will re-turn to this earth and the cycle of destruction will begin again." She smiled, exposing her razor teeth, white against her black lips. "And despite our crowlike appearance, we were never the enemies of the humans. Many nations held us in honor. It seems we are allies once again, Sorceress."

The immortal Frenchwoman nodded. "Thank you. And thank you for returning; your presence here makes all the dif-ference. It gives us a chance." She stretched out her hand.

The Crow Goddess looked at it and then slowly, almost tentatively, reached out and shook it. "Do you know," she said, "we do not believe a human has ever voluntarily offered us their hand."

"Why not?" Nicholas asked.

"Oh . . ." The Elder let out a gentle laugh. "I suppose sometimes we really do bite the hand that feeds us."

"So what do we do now?" Nicholas asked. "Are the three of us strong enough to attack whatever is inside either building?"

The Crow Goddess shook her head and her feathered cloak rasped as it settled back in place. "We have seen what is within. Every great beast of human legend, every monster imaginable, and a host of anpu. They're under the command of Xolotl," she added significantly.

Nicholas and Perenelle shook their heads, not recognizing the name.

"Quetzalcoatl's twin brother," the Crow Goddess explained. "The evil twin." She smiled. "They were once identical, but the Change has been particularly unkind to Xolotl: there is no flesh on his skeleton—his bones are bare, and he now has the head of a dog. Quite an ugly dog too. The anpu worship him as one of their own. We are powerful, but we are Next Generation and we could not defeat him. Only an enormously powerful Elder might stand a chance. And we do not know where to find one."

"But I do," Perenelle said answered quickly. "Areop-Enap is here. If we could awaken the Old Spider, she would stand with us."

"But while we're doing that, the boat will sail," Nicholas protested.

"You are the Alchemyst," the Crow Goddess said. "Master

of the arcane arts. And you"—she nodded at Perenelle—"are a sorceress. Surely there is something you can do?"

"We're already weakened . . . ," Nicholas began.

Perenelle laid a hand on her husband's arm. "Think simple, Nicholas. Keep it simple."

"And fast," the Crow Goddess added. "The boat is getting ready to cast off for shore."

Nicholas looked around desperately. "If I had more time I could alter the structure of the metal and turn it porous, or magnetize the hull and pull every piece of metal toward it."

"We don't have time for something so complex," Perenelle said.

The Crow Goddess gathered her cloak about her as she turned to look toward the shore. "As a last resort, we could drop onto the boat and kill a few of the guards, maybe the captain or the wheelman."

"You wouldn't stand a chance," Perenelle said. Despite her ferocious appearance, the Crow Goddess had a bird's brittle bones; she might get one or two anpu before she was overwhelmed. The Sorceress looked back at her husband. "Could we try freezing the sea again?"

"I doubt I have the strength for it, and besides, you saw how quickly it melted earlier."

"We could toss a few fireballs onto the boat. That would cause some chaos, maybe panic the creatures aboard. If they stampeded it might tilt the boat—upend it."

"Let's keep that as a last resort," Nicholas said. And then his eyes lit up and he smiled. "Simple. You're right—sometimes simple is best." Nicholas crouched down and scooped up a handful of pebbles. He rubbed them between his hands, grinding them to dust; then he brought his palms to his lips and tasted the powder with the tip of his tongue.

"Ugh. That's disgusting," the Crow Goddess said.

"Not enough cement," he observed. "The buildings here are old. Eaten with salt, ravaged by the weather." He bent to lift a piece of a brick off the ground and held it at arm's length in the palm of his hand. "The structure of the bricks is already falling apart. The molecular bonds holding them together are parting. A long time ago, whenever Perenelle and I needed some money, we would take a lump of coal and transform it into a piece of gold."

"You're going to turn the ship into gold?" the Crow Goddess asked in astonishment. "That would be spectacular!" She frowned. "It would sink, wouldn't it?"

The Alchemyst shook his head. "No, I'm not going to turn the ship into gold. I doubt that even at the height of my power I could have done that. Besides, I have always preferred to work small. . . ."

The Alchemyst's words trailed off and the air was touched with the scent of mint. Slowly the edges of the brick in the palm of his hand started to crumble, dissolving into gritty powder.

"Put your hand on my right shoulder, Perenelle; lend me some strength. You too, Crow Goddess," he instructed. "Come stand behind me."

"I really prefer not to touch humankind . . . ," the goddess grumbled, but took a step closer.

"And I prefer not to be touched by something older than

humanity, but these are strange and unusual times," Nicholas answered.

The Crow Goddess and Perenelle positioned themselves behind the Alchemyst and allowed a little of their auras to flow into him. The smell of mint intensified, but it was slightly sour and bitter.

"Hurry, Nicholas," Perenelle urged. "Someone—or something—is sure to notice."

"First, one has to focus. . . ." The Alchemyst gazed intently at the powdered brick in his hand. Slowly the dust began to dribble off his hand, flowing like water. "Once the desired result is achieved, then one must simply project the creative or destructive energy. Observation, then application."

Somewhere in the night, something cracked, the sound like a gunshot.

Stones ground together, grating and squealing.

"Is it another earthquake?" Perenelle asked.

The ground vibrated as a new series of popping crunches echoed through the night. Onboard the heavily laden ship and within the Powerhouse and the nearby Quartermaster Warehouse, beasts roared and screamed.

The fog cleared momentarily to reveal the tall smokestack jutting up behind the Powerhouse. The hulking chimney shuddered and swayed as all around the base of the tower, bricks exploded, spraying grit in all directions.

Nicholas brought his hand to his face and blew gently, scattering the rest of the dust on his palm into the night air.

The trio watched as the tower folded in two and, almost slowly, trailing fog like smoke, crashed down onto the back of the docked boat, driving it deep below the water and sending the bow shooting up into the air. Metal screeched and the boat snapped in two. A cascade of water washed over the docks and walkways, sweeping a handful of anpu onto the rocks and out to sea. The front end of the broken boat crashed back into the water, sending another wave washing over the docks. The two halves of the shattered craft immediately listed to one side, and the air was filled with the sound of metal grating against the island's stones as the pieces sank.

Nicholas brushed off his hands. "And all I had to do was crush half a dozen bricks. The weight of the chimney did the rest."

Perenelle leaned in and kissed her husband's cheek. *"Magnifique,"* she whispered.

"A triumph," the Crow Goddess agreed. "You'll pardon us if we do not kiss you."

"And you will pardon me if I tell you that I'd prefer you did not."

"We are about to have some very irritated company," Perenelle said.

A blaze of light cut into the fog as the doors to the Quartermaster Warehouse were flung open. Anpu poured out into the night and took up positions around the door, snouts raised to the air, sniffing. The figure that then stepped into the opening bore only the vaguest resemblance to anything human. A multicolored hooded and feathered cloak was wrapped around a skeleton. A gust of wind blew back the robe to reveal polished white bones encasing the vital organs of a man. Unlike the rest of the body, the head was covered in flesh and fur and was that of a long-snouted pointy-eared dog. Its skin was speckled with mange, and one of its ears looked torn. The creature moved awkwardly, and as it approached it became clear that its feet were reversed, heels to the front, long black-nailed toes facing away.

Throwing its head back, the creature sniffed the air like the anpu. Its jaws worked, and when it spoke, its speech was a liquid gargle. "What is this I smell?" it growled. "Ah, mint, the stench of the infamous Alchemyst. My brother told me he would ensure that you never made it to the island. But I told him you would be here. I am Xolotl, brother of Quetzalcoatl, son of Coatlicue, and I have come to claim this city for the Elders."

When there was no reply, he shuffled closer, one skeletal hand clutching the cloak around his neck, his other hand held high, each bony finger tipped with a dancing yellow flame like a candle. When he peered out into the gloom, his eyes burned red and round, reflecting the flames. He barked like a dog, then reverted to English. "Where are you, Nicholas Flamel? Let me see you before you die."

The Alchemyst stepped forward and allowed his green aura to illuminate him. "What will you do, monster, with no boat to bring your beasts ashore? It seems you are trapped on the island with me."

Xolotl waved his burning hand vaguely toward the city of

San Francisco, scattering flame. "There are more boats, Alchemyst. Dee purchased a small fleet of the tourist boats for this eventuality. Even as we speak, they are making their way toward us, or they will when the fog clears." He shook his head. "I did tell my brother that the fog was a mistake. But until the boats arrive, how shall we amuse ourselves?" The dog's jaw gaped in a grin. "Why, by hunting you down." He pointed toward the Alchemyst with his burning hand and a dozen silent anpu raced to his side. "Bring them to me. Alive! I will have the pleasure of killing you myself, Alchemyst," Xolotl promised.

Nicholas clapped his hands together and a wall of green flame sprang up on the hard earth directly in front of him. The intense heat drove the jackal-headed warriors back, their fur singed and smoking.

"This is an island, Alchemyst, there is no place to hide," Xolotl howled.

"I am not hiding," Nicholas said, stepping away from the flame. "I am coming for you, monster."

"You will die on this island!"

"And you will die with me."

Nicholas turned back to Perenelle and the Crow Goddess. "We need to awaken Areop-Enap now. She is our only hope."

"And what if we cannot?" the Crow Goddess asked.

Perenelle and Nicholas looked at her, saying nothing. Finally Perenelle spoke. "We will awaken her," she said shortly. "Or we will die trying."

"And probably be eaten," Nicholas added with a smile.

"Is it always this exciting around you two?" the Crow Goddess asked.

"Even for us, this last week has been . . . exceptional," Nicholas said.

CHAPTER FIFTY-ONE

"Stay here. Do not leave the room," Isis ordered.

"Touch nothing," Osiris added. "The age of most of the artifacts here can be measured in tens of millennia."

"Do not leave the room," Isis repeated. "When we leave, lock the door behind us. Do not open it for anyone."

"What about you?" Josh asked.

Isis frowned. "What do you mean?"

"You said not to open it for anyone—does that include you?"

She sighed. "Josh, you're being deliberately stupid now. Of course you'll open it for us. We'll be back in less than an hour to take you up to be presented to the council."

Osiris rubbed his hands together eagerly, and in that moment resembled the man the twins had called Dad. "We were able to speak to some Elders already, so everyone knows you're here. There will be huge excitement when you arrive."

"Yes. Everyone is talking about you," Isis added. "Now, remember . . ."

"Lock the door," Josh finished.

"Don't leave the room," Sophie added.

Isis nodded, but there was no smile on her face. She clearly didn't find the twins' attitude funny. She pulled the heavy door behind her as she left and it closed with an echoing boom. Josh struggled to turn the massive circular key the Elders had left in the lock. It finally clicked into place, leaving the twins alone in one of the largest rooms they had ever seen.

"It's enormous," Josh breathed. "You could fit a football field in here."

Sophie walked toward the center of the floor. "More than one," she said, looking left, then right. The twins stood in a windowless room so big that they couldn't see the walls to their left or their right through the gloomy shadows. The wall directly in front of them slanted inward at an angle.

Sophie pointed toward it. "That must be the outer wall of the pyramid."

"It looks like this room runs the entire length of the building," Josh said.

"That would make it about a mile and a half long."

"Now, that's a big room," he said. "I'm surprised it's not divided up into smaller rooms. It would make more sense."

"Josh, these people make worlds, they create entire Shadowrealms. They are never going to divide up a room just to be practical." She paused for a moment, then said, "I wonder what it's used for, though. It sort of looks like a gallery." She pointed to a wall where faded rectangles were visible against the stones. "See? Something used to hang there." She turned in a complete circle. "No windows, only one door . . ."

"So where's the light coming from?" Josh asked. He couldn't find any source.

"I think it's coming from the walls themselves," Sophie said in wonder.

Josh walked over to the wall and placed his hand flat against the gold stones, but they were cool to the touch.

"There's something here." Sophie pointed to the floor, where the remains of an ancient pattern were barely visible. Josh came back from the wall, dropped to the ground and blew hard. Dust swirled away to reveal a series of perfect circles, one within the other, made from thousands of tiny gold and silver tiles. The inner circle was filled with yellow and gold squares, and silver tiles had been used to create a long C shape, like a moon.

Sophie traced the outline of the silver crescent with the toe of her boot. Then she tapped the innermost circle. "Sun and moon." She stepped back and looked closely at the design. "It looks like this section of the floor is older than the rest. See? The stones are completely different." She knelt and ran her hand across it, tracing the outline of the moon with her finger. The merest wisp of her silver aura dribbled from her fingertip and seeped through the glove of her armor to puddle in the crescent, running like mercury. "I wonder where it came from. . . ."

. . . a wall . . .

. . . impossibly long, incredibly high . . .

. . . in a scarred desert where the sky and earth were brown, and the sun was a distant dot . . .

She shuddered as the images filled her mind, then faded. She looked over at her brother. "It's older than the pyramid. Much older. I don't even think it's from this world."

Josh circled the pattern, studying it. "This world is such a crazy mixture of magic and technology. They've got this amazing mile-high pyramid with lighted walls, and yet they can't even fix the vimana. They can create Shadowrealms and make human-animal hybrids, but they wear armor and everyone carries swords. There are no cars, no phones, and nothing that even *looks* like a TV!"

"I think we're seeing a dying world, Josh," Sophie said slowly. "Whoever created the original technology and built the pyramids is either gone or Changing. Sure, there are people like Isis and Osiris who have amazing abilities. But what do they do: instead of using those powers to do something useful, they've spent thousands of years working to make sure that we'll rule Danu Talis."

"For them," Josh said suddenly. He crouched down and looked at his sister. "They've gone to all this trouble to make sure that we'll rule Danu Talis *for them*." He emphasized the last two words as he looked into Sophie's blue eyes.

"I guess they just expect us to do whatever they want."

"I guess they're going to be disappointed."

"And then what happens?" she asked.

He shook his head. "I have no idea. Well, I do, actually, but I don't want to even think about it yet." Josh straightened and rolled his shoulders. "It's kind of creepy in here, don't you think?"

"Creepy? What do you have to be scared about?" Sophie stood, dusting off her gloves, and stepped away from the ancient tiled pattern. "Josh, did you get a good look at some of the people we just walked past? I guess they weren't really people, but just think of all we've seen and done over the past few days."

Josh nodded.

"You should never be scared again," Sophie concluded.

Her twin shrugged. "I'm a little scared now," he admitted.

"Don't be," she said firmly.

Josh rolled his eyes. "You're always bossing me around. I can be scared if I want to."

They both grinned, and then Sophie leaned in and lowered her voice. "Maybe it's my enhanced senses, but I think we're being watched."

Josh nodded again. He rubbed the back of his neck casually. "My neck is tingling—you know that feeling you get when someone is staring at you?"

"Isis and Osiris?" she suggested.

"I don't think so. What reason would they have to spy on us? They're used to us doing what we're told, like good little boys and girls. They trained us to be obedient, just like they trained their servants."

"Let's walk," she said very softly. "Our boots will echo off the walls in here and it'll be harder to listen to us." She clasped her hands behind her back and started down the center of the

343

room, eyes seeking out the dark corners, watching for movement in the shadows.

Josh fell into step beside her. Their metal boots pinged off the floor, then echoed and reechoed off the stone.

"Maybe this was a library. It looks like there were shelves on the walls here," Sophie said loudly, pointing. "You can see the marks." Then she frowned. "Osiris said not to touch anything"—she looked at her twin and lowered her voice—"but there's really nothing here to touch."

"So whatever *was* here was removed," Josh said, rubbing his hand across his mouth as he spoke.

"And Isis and Osiris don't know about it yet," Sophie added.

"I get the impression they don't spend a lot of time here," he said.

Sophie nodded in agreement. "I wonder why."

The twins moved back to the center of the floor, as far away from the walls as possible. They spoke loudly about the size of the room, its height, the light. Josh even whistled and clapped his hands to hear the echo.

After they'd been walking for quite some time, they reached one of the end walls. Horizontal lines etched into the gold stone clearly marked the outlines of shelves, and tiny punctures in the brickwork showed where they'd been fixed in place. But the shelves themselves were missing, and along with them, whatever they'd held.

Josh ran his finger along the wall and it came away clean. "This happened recently. Dust hasn't even had time to gather."

Sophie looked at her brother, impressed. "That was smart. I wouldn't have thought to check that."

"I saw it in an old Sherlock Holmes movie," he admitted with a grin.

The twins started back toward where Isis and Osiris had left them. Sophie hesitated for a moment, then reached over to touch her brother's arm. Her metal glove scraped against his armor. "They're not our parents, are they?"

Josh continued walking. He had taken almost a dozen steps before he answered. "I've been thinking about that almost from the first moment they told us who they were."

"So have I," Sophie admitted.

"On earth, for all these years, they sure acted like our parents. They were good parents to us too, and they did everything the right way. But . . ."

"But they were always a little cold," Sophie said, nodding. "Even before all this happened, there were times when I'd wonder if they'd read instructions out of a book on how to be parents. There was something weird about it. Everyone else's mom and dad were more . . ." She paused, looking for the word.

"Natural?" Josh said.

"Yeah. Natural. It seemed easy for them, and I don't think that was ever the case with our parents. I even said something to Mom—Isis—about it once; right after we settled in Austin. She just laughed and said that of course we were different, and of course we'd feel weird about it. We were twins, and new to the school, of course we were going to feel out of place."

"And remember what they said?" Josh added. "That they were educating us . . ."

"Preparing us."

"Training us,"

"They just didn't say it was for this role," Sophie finished.

"But if they're not our parents, then what are we?" Josh slowed and stopped. "I was thinking about this earlier. You know the Flamels spent all their lives looking for Gold and Silver twins. . . ."

Sophie started to nod; then her eyes widened in shock, realizing what he was suggesting.

"Maybe Isis and Osiris did the same thing. Only they found us first."

Sophie's jaw dropped. "But then who does that make us, Josh? Where do we come from? Are we adopted?" Her hands flew to her mouth. "Are we even twins?"

Josh rested his hand on her shoulder and brought his forehead down to rest against hers, strands of their blond hair mingling. "I will always be your brother, Sophie. I will always look after you."

She blinked away tears. "I know that. I just wish I knew who we are."

"Would the Witch know?" Josh wondered. "Would it be in her memories?"

"I'm not sure . . . ," Sophie began, but even as she was speaking, a tumble of images sent her staggering. Josh grabbed her arm, holding her upright. The girl shuddered, then gasped for breath. She opened her eyes, swaying in place.

"What did you see?" he asked.

346

"The Witch's memories . . ."

"Of what?"

"You and me on top of this pyramid. Fighting."

He shook his head firmly. "That's not going to happen."

"Yes, it is," she said simply. "It will happen today. Soon."

"No, you're seeing one of those probable futures. One that will never happen," he said fiercely.

A single silver tear leaked from the corner of Sophie's eye.

"Did you learn anything about us?" he asked.

"No," she lied. She didn't want to tell him what else she had seen. That she had seen him alone and lost on the pyramid, abandoned, while she fled. . . .

"But I did see Scathach. I saw Joan and Saint-Germain, Shakespeare and Palamedes. They were all here."

"Where?" he demanded.

"Here, on the steps of this pyramid," she insisted.

"That's impossible."

They heard a scuffle of footsteps outside the door and a brief hurried knock.

"About time," Josh muttered. "I was starting to feel like a prisoner."

The ornate door handle, a gold circle showing a snake swallowing its own tail, turned and the door rattled on its hinges.

"Hang on, hang on." Josh hurried over to the door and turned the key in the lock. He glanced over his shoulder at his sister. "How would they all get here?" he asked.

And then the door slammed open, sending Josh skidding into the room on his back. He tumbled over and over, his golden armor striking sparks from the stone floor. Sophie raced to her brother's side.

A hooded shape moved through the doorway and stepped into the room. Two more followed, and the last one to enter closed the door and turned the key in the lock once more.

The figures were tall and muscular, and even before they had shrugged off the hooded cloaks, it was clear that they were not entirely human. Although their bodies were those of men, they had the heads, claws and feet of black bears. Their clothing hung in rags about their bodies, and they wore thick bearskin belts around their waists.

"Bear-sarks," Sophie whispered. "Berserkers."

The three creatures produced short-handled battle-axes and black obsidian glass knives.

Josh scrambled to his feet and pulled his two swords free. Sophie took up a position to his left and balled her hands into fists. "Do you have any idea who we are?" Josh demanded.

"No." The berserker's voice was a brutal grunt. "Nor do we care. We have been sent to kill you," he said. "It will not take long unless you fight. We hope you fight," he added.

"Oh, we'll fight," Josh promised grimly.

"Good. More sport for us."

CHAPTER FIFTY-TWO

"Virginia," Dr. John Dee began, "I really do not think this is a good idea."

Virginia Dare ignored him.

Dee fell into step beside the American immortal and caught her arm, forcing her to slow down. "Hang on, hang on, I'm not as young as I used to be." He was red-faced and gasping. "I'm going to have a heart attack."

Virginia's face remained expressionless.

"I could die. Right here, right now," he said.

Virginia's lips turned up in a feral grin. She dropped a heavy hand on his shoulder. "Is that a threat or a promise?"

"Oh, you're harsh. You weren't always like this," he grumbled.

"Like what?" she demanded. They were standing in the center of a fruit market and her raised voice attracted attention. Some of the stallholders and customers glanced at her curiously. Although she was wearing the white robe and conical hat of the humani of Danu Talis, it was clear that this young woman was different. It showed in the way she held herself, in the way she walked and especially in the way she dealt with the older man standing before her.

Virginia poked Dee in the shoulder with a stiffened finger. "Never once, not even once, in all the years of our association did you ever bother to try and find out any information about me. You know nothing about me."

He glanced around nervously. "Lower your voice; people are starting to stare."

"I don't care."

"I know you killed your Elder Master."

"And that is all you know," Virginia spat. "In fact, that is all anyone knows about me. The first thing everyone says to me is 'Oh, you're the immortal who killed her master.'"

"Well, it is an impressive fact," Dee said. "There are probably a handful of people who can claim it, and of those, you're the only one I'd believe."

"What is going on here?" An Asterion, one of the huge, bull-headed guards, pushed through the gathering crowds and stepped in close—too close to Virginia—enveloping them in a strong farmyard odor of meat and manure.

Virginia didn't turn to look at the creature. "You. Get away from me," she ordered.

The Asterion's huge mouth opened and closed in shock. No humani had ever spoken to him like that before.

Virginia ignored him and glared at the English Magician. "Am I married, do I have children? Siblings, perhaps?

Parents? What is my favorite tea? Which ice cream gives me a rash?"

"Virginia?" Dee murmured, looking around. People had started to gather in a semicircle.

"You know nothing about me because you've never even asked. And that's because you . . . simply . . . never . . . cared." She emphasized the last three words by poking him in the chest.

The Asterion stepped in, hand falling to the whip attached to his side. "Let's break this up. You are causing a disturbance."

Virginia finally glanced sidelong at the bull-headed creature. "If you try to use that whip," she said, "you will regret it."

The beast rumbled a laugh. "Threatened by a humani girl. What is the world coming to?"

With a flick of her wrist Virginia turned him to stone.

A low moan ran around the market square and Virginia focused once more on Dee. "It doesn't bother you that these people are enslaved?"

Dee looked at the people milling about. "No."

"And why not?"

"They're not my people, for a start," The doctor grinned. He watched as an orderly line began to form, people coming up to tap on the stone statue that moments ago had been a soldier, first with their fingers, and then with coins or blades, testing it. They marveled at the level of detail on the statue, the creases in his leather uniform, the stone beads of perspiration on his forehead. They were awed by the huge brown eyes still moving in the statue's face.

The circle around Virginia and Dee grew larger as the story of what had just happened raced through the marketplace.

"Look at them," Virginia snapped. "These *are* your people. They are humans. Not Elders, not Next Generation, nor some hybrid monsters or Changelings. They are human. Just like you. And if you tell me that they are not just like you, then I am going to smack you or turn you to stone. Or both."

Dee closed his mouth without a word.

"I was an orphan, living wild and alone in a primeval forest. I had no one. No friends, no family, nothing. But I was free. And I learned to value and treasure freedom. All through my long immortal life I have fought for freedom."

"So when you wanted a world from me . . ."

"It was not what you imagined. I did not want a place where I would rule as a dictator. I wanted to create a place that was truly free."

"You should have told me," Dee suggested.

"You would have laughed at me—and you'd have regretted that," Virginia promised.

A troop of Asterion led by a scarred anpu jogged into the square, drawn by the crowd. They carried whips and clubs and started pushing their way through, roughly shoving the people aside. Since the civil unrest had begun, Anubis had banned all humani gatherings.

The anpu leader spotted the people gathered before the Asterion statue and, puzzled, slowed to look at it. He'd been through this square on patrol less than an hour ago, and there hadn't been a statue there. Also, he'd never seen a carving of one of the bull-headed warriors: why would someone create a statue of a beast? It wasn't until he was within a few feet of the gray stone that he suddenly recognized the brutal features. It was one of his own men. He looked into his face . . . and huge terrified bovine eyes moved, silently pleading.

Shaken, the anpu commander staggered back and raised his closed fist. The Asterion troop fell into battle formation around him in a tight circle, spears and swords facing outward. The anpu's fingers trembled as he scrabbled to lift a horn off his belt. He put the horn to his lips and blew to summon help.

Nothing happened.

Puzzled, he shook the horn and tried again. No sound came out.

He turned as a slender female humani stepped forward, lifted her hat and handed it to the old man at her side. She held a wooden flute pressed to her pursed lips, but the anpu could hear nothing. He dropped the horn and reached for his kopesh. But the metal turned to dust beneath his fingers, and then, abruptly, all the metal on his uniform, the buckles and hooks, the knife in his belt, was flaking, crumbling to dust and blowing away. Finally, his metal boots crumbled to dust around his feet.

The Asterion's battle formation began to fall apart as their weapons, armor and finally, their clothing, cracked, snapped and dried to dribbling dust.

Someone in the crowd started to laugh. And then a

second, and a third. A wave of laughter ran around the market square, growing and swelling into a roar of derision.

"Not quite the bully now without the leather and metal, are you?"

The anpu looked at the humani, unsure whether to attack or flee. There had been rumors in the barracks about a humani who'd crossed the canals, leaving at least two troops of anpu unconscious on the stones. He hadn't believed the stories, of course. They were patently ridiculous.

"Tell your masters we're coming," the humani said. Her right hand spread out to encompass the crowd. "All of us."

The anpu, his clothing in shreds, turned and fled, followed by the Asterion. The wave of mocking, jeering laugher went on for a very long time.

The people crowded in around Virginia and Dee, roaring their delight. "See," Virginia laughed, "that is how you get the people on your side. You just make them laugh at the enemy. And we didn't have to kill anyone."

"What about the statue?"

"Oh, he's not dead. It'll wear off soon enough. Now let's go talk to these people about freedom." She climbed onto a fruit stall and reached out to help Dee stand beside her.

"So having the argument with me was just a ruse to draw attention to us?" he asked. "It was a trick?"

Virginia said nothing.

"Wasn't it?"

The American immortal looked out over a sea of faces and spread her arms. Her mane of jet-black hair rose behind her like wings. The crowd rippled with murmurs and then fell into awed silence.

"What do you know about me?" she asked Dee quietly. "Besides the fact that I killed my Elder Master?"

He thought for a moment. "Nothing," he admitted.

"And how long have we known one another?"

"A long time," he said. "Four hundred years, perhaps more."

Virginia looked at him and said nothing.

Dee shrugged. "You're right. I should have asked. What can I say, I was selfish. But that was a different person in a different time. People can change. I've changed," he said quickly. "I'm no longer immortal, for a start; that gives me a different perspective."

"Humans of Danu Talis," Virginia said loudly, her voice echoing across the still square. "I am Virginia Dare. . . ."

"Virginiadare . . . Virginiadare . . . Virginiadare . . ." The crowd murmured her name as one word.

"And this is John Dee . . ."

"Johndee . . . Johndee . . . Johndee . . ."

"And we have come to set you free!"

The crowd howled, a long bellowing roar like the crash of a breaker on the shore.

"Cookie-dough ice cream," she said suddenly, raising her voice above the shouts, "makes me break out in a rash."

"Oh good."

"Good?"

"It's my favorite. It means all the more for me."

CHAPTER FIFTY-THREE

With the destruction of the sphinx, all the monsters gathered on Alcatraz had suddenly become aware that they were not alone on the island. Most had turned on one another behind the metal bars of the prison cells, and the stone walls echoed with screams and howls. A new smell filled the air: the rich copper of blood.

Black Hawk led Billy and Machiavelli down a long cell-lined corridor called Michigan Avenue. Odin helped the injured Hel and Mars bring up the rear, protecting them from the creatures that darted from darkened corners.

Bill the Kid laughed. "They're so busy eating one another, they couldn't care less about us."

"No," Hel whispered, licking her lips. "Many of these creatures"—her whip sliced a trio of human-headed vampire bats out of the air—"many of these creatures are man hunters and blood drinkers. You three," she said, jabbing the butt of the whip at Billy, Machiavelli and Black Hawk, "smell like a banquet to them. They will keep coming."

"Are you saying I smell?" Billy demanded.

Hel's nostrils flared as she breathed deeply. "Like roast chicken. With just a touch of rosemary."

"What about you?" Billy demanded, turning to look at the three Elders. "You're saying they won't touch you?"

Odin shrugged. "None of us is safe," he said. "While we are not human, we *are* still meat, and these poor things are hungry."

"You feel sympathy for them?" Machiavelli asked. The Italian immortal had been bleeding from a shallow cut on the top of his head; he looked like he was wearing a red mask.

"They are not here by choice," Odin answered. "They are as much prisoners as the humans who were incarcerated here in times past."

"They will still kill and eat us," Mars said grimly. He spun to one side as a three-headed serpent reared out of a darkened cell, spitting streamers of thick yellow ichor at him. His sword rose and fell and two of the heads dropped to the ground. "And if they escape into the city, they will feast for weeks or even months before they are captured."

"None are getting off this island," Black Hawk said grimly. He had reattached two of the leaf-shaped spearheads to wooden shafts and he tapped them, butt-first, into the ground. "We will stand and fight."

"Then you will die," Hel said.

"People have been telling me that all my life," Black Hawk said, shaking his head. "And I am still here, while they are not."

An undersized minotaur appeared out of a cell and dropped heavy cloven hooves onto Billy the Kid's shoulder, driving him to his knees. Machiavelli's hand moved, trailing the rancid odor of snake. The minotaur suddenly howled, tossing its head from side to side as it began to scratch furiously, tearing grooves in its own flesh. Black Hawk swung the shaft of one of the spears, catching the beast's legs, tugging them out from beneath it. It went down with a crash and rolled along the floor, shrieking and scratching furiously.

"Earwigs and fleas," Machiavelli said with a smile. "I have always found them to be hugely underrated insects. Especially when inserted into the ears."

"You put earwigs in his ears," Billy said with a shudder. "That's gross."

"You are perfectly correct. Maybe you would have preferred that I let him take a bite out of you."

Before Billy could answer, two satyrs stepped into an open doorway at the end of the corridor. They had the stunted torsos of men but the horns and legs of goats. Both were armed with short bone bows. They bleated with delight as they nocked black-headed arrows and pulled back their bowstrings.

Machiavelli made a half circle in the air with his hand, fingers opening and closing in a lightning-quick pattern.

The satyrs' bleats turned to shrieks of alarm as their

bowstrings twisted into writhing serpents and coiled up their arms. They flung the bows to the ground and raced out into the night.

"Illusion," Machiavelli said. "Always my specialty."

"You're just full of surprises," Billy said, impressed.

The Italian arched an eyebrow. "You have no idea."

The group of Elders and immortals raced down the corridor, then through a narrow doorway. Beyond lay a series of glass-walled rooms that led outside into the stinking fog. The goat-men had vanished, but the darkness was alive with sounds, and none of them were pleasant. Hideous shapes moved in the gloom, and Mars and Odin slashed at any that came too close.

"Wait a moment." Machiavelli stopped in the doorway, trying to orient himself. "We need to work out where we are on the island."

"We've just come out of the Administration Building," Black Hawk said immediately.

"How do you know?" the Italian demanded.

The American immortal caught Machiavelli's arm and turned him slightly. Directly over the door they had just exited was an ornate carving of an eagle, wings spread, above an American flag in the shape of a shield. Below the carving, the flaking words ADMINISTRATION BUILDING were clearly visible.

"The lighthouse should be almost directly ahead of us," Black Hawk said, pointing through the fog.

"But where is Areop-Enap?" Mars asked. "Flamel used the parrot to tell us that the Old Spider was on the island."

The fog coalesced and the ghost of Juan Manuel de Ayala appeared out of the damp. Everyone—even Mars—jumped with fright.

"You nearly gave me a heart attack," Hel muttered.

Billy grinned. "I didn't know you *had* a heart."

"To your left," the ghost whispered, its voice filled with the sound of popping bubbles, *"are the ruins of the Warden's House. Areop-Enap is within."*

"Let's go," Billy said, turning to leave.

"Billy—wait!" Machiavelli and Black Hawk called together.

The American ignored them. As he moved cautiously through the fog, he began to make out the tall pillar of the lighthouse tower to his right and then the vague outline of gray walls and empty windows to his left. Suddenly he saw a figure—tall, misshapen, shrouded in fog—move past one of the openings. Billy caught a glimpse of the creature and thought he saw a white mane flowing down its back. Was it a centaur or another satyr? He watched as it stopped, then turned toward him, the white oval of a face peering at him. Claw-tipped fingers rose at its sides, pointing at him, and Billy's hands fell to his waist as he pulled the spearheads from his belt and sent them whistling through the air . . .

. . . just as Perenelle Flamel, white hair glistening in the damp, stepped forward, hand raised in greeting.

CHAPTER FIFTY-FOUR

On the wild northeast shore of Danu Talis, the crystal tower rising out of the pounding waters began to glow and pulse with a pale golden light. Then it began to vibrate, a deep subsonic disturbance that trembled deep into the earth, thrashing the water to white foam.

"I'm here," Tsagaglalal said. She was wearing the white ceramic armor her husband had given her, the matched kopesh in sheaths across her back.

Abraham the Mage stood tall and slender in a darkened room at the top of the Tor Ri. He was wrapped in shadow, facing away from her, so that she would not see the Change that had almost completely claimed his flesh, transforming it to solid gold.

"Let me look at you," she whispered, turning him to the light. "Let me see you, and remember this moment."

"I would rather you remember me as I was."

"I carry that image within me always," she said. She pressed the palm of her hand against his chest. "But this is you also, and I will never forget this. I will never forget you, Abraham."

She held him, pressing his flesh and metal against her skin, and wept on his shoulder. She looked up into his face and saw a single tear, a solid bead of gold, rolling down his cheek. Raising up on her toes, she kissed the tear off his face, swallowing it. Tsagaglalal pressed her hands to her stomach. "I will carry it within me always."

"You are about to begin a journey that will last ten thousand years, Tsagaglalal." Every one of Abraham's breaths was a labored effort now. "I have seen your future, I know what lies ahead for you."

"Don't tell me," she said quickly. "I don't want to know."

Abraham pressed on. "Like any life, there is both sorrow and joy in it. Entire tribes and nations will rise and honor you. You will be known by a thousand names, and many songs will be sung and stories told about you. Your legend will endure."

The tower was vibrating harder now, the top swaying from side of side, tiny featherlike cracks appearing in the crystal.

"If I have a wish for you, it is for you to have a companion, someone to share your life with," he continued. "I do not want you to be lonely. But in all the years of your life to come, I do not see you with anyone."

"There will never be anyone," she said firmly. "By rights we should never have met: I was a statue of mud, brought to life by Prometheus's aura. You are one of the Elders of Danu Talis. And yet the moment I saw you, I knew—with absolute conviction—that we would be together for the rest of our lives. I can say now, with the same conviction, that there will never be another."

Abraham drew in a shuddering breath. "Do you have any regrets?" he asked.

"I would have liked to have had children," she said.

"In your years to come, Tsagaglalal, you will be a mother to many children. You will foster and adopt thousands of humans. Untold numbers of children will call you mother and aunt and grandmother, and they will be as dear to you as if they were your own. And toward the end, in ten thousand years' time, when you watch over the twins and protect and guide them, there will be much joy. This I have seen: though you will exasperate and often infuriate them, they will love you with all their hearts, because they will instinctively understand that you love them unconditionally."

"Ten thousand years," she breathed. "Do I really have to live that long?"

"Yes. You must," he rasped. "There are no unimportant players in this extraordinary plan Marethyu and I have constructed. Everyone—Elders, Next Generation and humankind—has their role to play. But Tsagaglalal, yours is the most critical role of all. Without you, everything falls apart."

"And if I fail . . . ?" she whispered. She staggered as the tower shifted. The vibrations were becoming more intense.

"You will not fail. You are Tsagaglalal, She Who Watches. You know what you have to do."

"I know. I don't like it," Tsagaglalal said fiercely, "but I know."

"Yes. So do it," he said with difficulty. "You have the Book?"

"Yes."

"Go, then," the Elder said, his breath the merest whisper. "Count down one hundred and thirty-two steps and wait there."

The tower swayed and suddenly a huge chunk of the ancient crystal shattered. The sea below started to boil and foam.

"I love you, Tsagaglalal," Abraham sighed. "The moment you came into my life, I realized I wanted for nothing."

"I have loved you and I will continue to love you all the days of my life," she said, and then turned and ran.

"I know," he whispered.

Abraham listened to his wife running down the stairs, her metal heels pinging off the crystal. He counted her steps.

The tower groaned and lurched, glass shattering, enormous slabs breaking off to explode into the sea far below.

Fifty steps . . .

Abraham turned his eyes to the horizon. Even now, with death—the true death—just a few moments away, he found he was still curious. He could just about make out the faintest line of the polar ice cap in the distance, and the ragged tops of the Mountains of Madness. He had always planned to mount an expedition there, but there had never been time. He'd even spoken to Marethyu about his fascination with the arctic whiteness. The hook-handed man told him he had been there and had seen wonders.

One hundred steps . . .

Abraham had lived perhaps ten thousand years, and there was still so much more he wanted to do.

One hundred and ten . . .

So much more he wanted to see. He was going to miss the joy of discovery.

One hundred and twenty . . .

But more than anything else . . .

One hundred and thirty . . .

. . . he was going to miss Tsagaglalal.

One hundred and thirty-two.

The footsteps stopped.

"I love you," he breathed.

Tsagaglalal stood on the step and waited.

Abraham had always instructed her never to linger on the steps. At least twelve ley lines radiated from the staircase, and they intersected with at least as many Shadowrealms.

She felt the tower shiver and a sudden wash of heat flowed up through her body. She looked down and saw a pattern on the stair she stood on, something she had never noticed before: a sun and moon picked out in thousands of gold and silver tiles.

Tsagaglalal's aura flared and the air was filled with jasmine.

✧ ✧ ✧

The volcano erupted directly beneath the base of the Tor Ri. The tower was simultaneously ripped apart and swallowed into the boiling lava. Within the space of a dozen heartbeats, the crystal tower and all it contained were gone.

CHAPTER FIFTY-FIVE

*O*ne hundred people had followed Virginia Dare out of the marketplace. By the time she reached the square outside the prison, the crowd had swelled to ten times that number, with more and more arriving every minute. They were chanting Aten's name, sending it rumbling and vibrating across the stones.

"Ah, your first big test," Dr. John Dee said, almost gleefully. "In a few minutes the prison gates will open, and the anpu and Asterion will appear. If your people scatter, then you have lost. And believe me, Virginia, as soon as they see blood, they will run. They have been running all their lives."

"Thank you for your words of encouragement," Virginia muttered. But deep in her heart she knew the Magician was correct: when a troop of heavily armed warriors raced into the crowd, the humans' newfound courage would instantly evaporate.

"These are farmers, shopkeepers and slaves," Dee said. "What do they know of war?"

"Some of them are bringing weapons," Virginia noted.

The square before the prison was filling with people, and the new arrivals were indeed carrying makeshift weapons: shovels, spades and sticks. She saw a baker with a rolling pin, and many others were carrying flaming torches.

"Oh yes, and I can see these 'weapons' being very effective against swords, spears and bows." Dee stood beside her and looked up at the high prison walls. There were guards everywhere now, and he could clearly hear mocking laughter drifting down from above. "You didn't think this through, did you? Marethyu spoke to you and suddenly you were off raising a revolution."

"No," she admitted. "Everything happened so fast."

"Are you regretting it?" he asked.

"Absolutely not!" she snapped. "When the English, the French and the Spanish invaded my country, I could have—I *should* have—stood against them. But I didn't. I might have made a difference."

Dee frowned. "What are you talking about? You're English."

"I'm an American," she said proudly. "I am the first European born on American soil." Virginia's hair began to rise in a crackling sheet as her anger buzzed through her. "Look around you, Doctor: what do you see?"

He shrugged. "The people of Danu Talis. The ordinary people," he added.

"Who are enslaved by the Elders, who use monsters to

enforce their laws. I've seen this before, on this world and many other worlds, and not all monsters wear the shapes of beasts. I watched it happen in my homeland. I will not allow it to happen again," she said fiercely.

"You could die here," he said quietly.

"I could."

"For people you do not know . . ."

"I know them. I have seen people like them all my long life. And now fate has brought me here."

"Well, actually, *I* did. Though the hook-handed man had a lot to do with it."

A moan ran through the crowd as the prison gates creaked open and troops started to pour out and form into long straight lines. The evening sunlight ran bloodred off their armor and weapons.

"And I have to believe that I am here to make a difference." She poked the Magician in the chest, hard enough to make him stagger. "So what are you here for, Dr. Dee?"

She had asked him the question that had been troubling him from the moment Marethyu had restored his health, if not his youth. Why was he here? The day had been one of such extraordinary mixed emotions. He'd gone from triumph to despair in a matter of moments; he'd been dying, then been revived. And for what? His long life had equipped him with extraordinary skills. How should he use them?

The old man sighed as he looked around. The crowd in the square had doubled to around two thousand people. They were shouting and chanting Aten's name, but none dared approach the prison's sloping walls too closely. In a moment, the animal-headed monsters would attack, and Dee had no doubt there would be a terrible slaughter in the square. There was a time when that would not have bothered him. But he'd been immortal then, more than human. Now he was just a man again. And that gave him a different perspective.

"Well," Dee said finally. "I did spend a good portion of my mortal life advising England's greatest queen. I helped defeat the Spanish Armada. So it seems that at the end of my life, I return, full circle, to my original role: as advisor to a queen."

Virginia blinked in surprise. "I'm not a queen."

"Oh, you will be," he said confidently. "So here's what I suggest."

CHAPTER FIFTY-SIX

Scathach wandered the outskirts of Danu Talis wrapped in a white robe, her blazing red spiky hair hidden under a conical straw hat.

The streets were almost deserted. A few elderly men and women sat in darkened doorways and watched her hurry past. Tiny children in rags played on the unpaved streets and looked at her with wide curious eyes.

Scathach paused by a crumbling fountain and allowed a handful of the brackish water to dribble into her hand. She sipped cautiously; it tasted vaguely of salt and bitter soil. Looking around, she tried to get her bearings. Here, at the very edge of the city, neighborhoods that were little better than slums gradually gave way to bigger homes, and then, farther in, closer to the center of the city, she could see the pyramids, ziggurats and palaces of the nobility rising into the sky. Beyond them, dominating everything, lay the Pyramid of the Sun.

Turning, shielding her eyes against the dipping sun, she looked into the west. The slanting light was blinding—Huitzilopochtli had deliberately timed the attack so that the sinking sun would help to conceal the arrival of the vimanas and fliers. But she saw them, vague dots against the sky. They would arrive soon.

A scratch of movement made her spin, hands falling to the weapons concealed beneath her white robe. A young girl with huge brown eyes that seemed far too big for her head was standing beside the fountain. She had a younger child firmly by the hand. They were barefoot and dressed in scraps of clothes that had probably never been white. The two children stared up at the Shadow. "Are you lost?" the girl asked.

Scathach looked down at the child. It was hard to tell her age—four or five, perhaps and the younger child was probably two. Crouching down, she looked at the girl, green eyes sparkling. "You know, I think I am. Maybe you can help."

"Everyone has gone to the prison," the girl said.

"Aten," the boy added. He was sucking noisily on his thumb.

The girl nodded solemnly. "Everyone has gone to rescue Aten. He is in prison."

"Bad men," the boy said.

"The bad men put him there," the girl said.

"Do you know which of these big buildings is the prison?" Scathach asked gently.

The girl nodded. Rising up on her toes, she pointed high into the sky. "Can't see," she said.

"Maybe if I lifted you . . . ," Scathach suggested.

"And my brother, too," the girl said immediately.

"Of course." Curling her arms under both children, the Shadow lifted them. The girl immediately put her arm around Scathach's shoulder and brought her face close to her cheek. She pointed toward a sloping flat-roofed pyramid. "There. That's the bad house."

"Bad house," her little brother said.

"Mama says if you're bad, you're taken to the bad house. Is that true?"

"Sometimes," Scathach said. She bent, placing both children back on the ground, and then knelt before them. She ran her fingers through the girl's hair. She wished she had something to give the child, but all she had—all she ever had—were the clothes on her back and the weapons at her side. "Would you like to tell me your names?" she asked.

"I'm Brigid and this is my brother Cermait. Mama calls him Milbel," she added with a giggle.

"Honey mouth," Scathach whispered. She recognized the names from her time in ancient Ireland and Scotland; she knew who the children were and knew also that they would survive the Fall of Danu Talis.

"Are you going to the bad house?" Brigid asked.

"Yes." Scathach nodded. "There's someone I have to see."

"A bad person?"

"I don't know yet. I am going to find out."

Cermait tugged on Scathach's robe and rattled off an incomprehensible sentence. "He wants to know if you are a bad person," his sister translated.

"Sometimes," she whispered. "But only to bad people."

"Who are you?" Brigid asked.

"I am Scathach the Shadow."

CHAPTER FIFTY-SEVEN

"*No!*" Billy screamed, the sound high-pitched and anguished.

The leaf-shaped blades came to glowing life as they spun through the air, slicing through the fog, trailing spirals of moisture in their wake.

The American saw Perenelle's eyes widen in shock, and in that moment they both knew she could not escape the blades.

Time slowed.

Hel's whip lashed out, but she was too far away and it missed.

Machiavelli shouted and flung a wave of gray-white aura after the spearheads, but it stopped short.

Nicholas Flamel roared, green light blazing from his hands, singeing the edges of the spears as they tumbled past.

Juan Manuel de Ayala reached for them, but they cut through him in an explosion of water droplets.

"No . . ." Billy the Kid staggered and would have fallen if Black Hawk had not caught him. "What have I done?" he gasped.

Time stopped.

And then a figure darted in front of the Sorceress, wrapping arms around her, enfolding her, protecting her.

The spearheads sliced through the cloak of black feathers in an explosion of cold fire. The force of the blow pushed the Crow Goddess into Perenelle's arms, knocking her off balance and toward Nicholas. The Alchemyst grabbed both women, keeping them upright.

The Sorceress looked into the Crow Goddess's red and yellow eyes. "Why?" she whispered. She wrapped her arms around the creature, holding her tight, feeling her start to shake. "Why?"

The Crow Goddess rested her chin on Perenelle's shoulder. "You freed us," she whispered, teeth chattering. "You released us from an eternity of suffering. In all the years of our long lives, that was the only kindness ever shown to us by a human. That is a gift worth repaying."

"You saved me," Perenelle said, voice thick with emotion. "You didn't have to."

"Yes, we did. It was the right thing to do."

"And you have always done the right thing," Perenelle realized with a start.

"We have . . . though the Morrigan, not so much." The Elder's voice grew weaker as she spoke. "Now, Sorceress, you have work to do. Do not let our sacrifice be in vain."

The Sorceress stroked the creature's short hair. "If we succeed here tonight, it will be because of you."

The Crow Goddess was shaking so violently now that Perenelle could barely hold her. The Elder's voice was changing, flickering between Macha's and the Badb's. "And do not think too badly of our younger sister. She was led astray." She suddenly lifted her chin and looked into Perenelle's eyes and the Sorceress saw that the once red and yellow eyes had turned solid black. The Morrigan had awakened. Her mouth opened, savage teeth inches from Perenelle's throat.

Every instinct in the Sorceress told her to pull away, but she continued to hold the shivering creature.

And then the Morrigan's mouth closed and her black eyes softened. "I hated you for what you did to me," she breathed, "but no more. Thank you, Sorceress, for reuniting me with my sisters." Her eyes started to flicker, black and red and yellow, but the colors were fading.

"I will remember you," Perenelle promised. "All three of you: Macha, the Morrigan and the Badb."

And then the Crow Goddess crumpled to black dust in the Sorceress's arms. The only sound in the night was the noise of the metal spearheads clanging onto the stones.

Perenelle Flamel took Billy the Kid by the hands and pulled him up off the ground. The young immortal was shaking and his face was damp. She ran her palms across his cheeks, leaving black streaks of what was left of the Crow Goddess on his white flesh, then caught his chin in one hand and used the edge of her shirt to wipe his cheeks. "Billy, do not reproach yourself. You did nothing wrong."

"I could have killed you."

"But you did not."

"But I killed the Morrigan. . . ."

"That was not just the Morrigan. That was Macha and the Badb, her sisters. They sacrificed themselves willingly. And at the end, the Morrigan awoke: I do not think she was unhappy. They died together, as one."

"I reacted," he whispered.

Perenelle's fingers tightened on his chin, forcing him to look up. "We will grieve for the Crow Goddess later. Now we should honor her memory and destroy the monsters on the island." She pressed the two spearheads back into his hand. "You're going to need these. Come now, let us awaken Areop-Enap."

Billy's hand shot out and he grabbed the Sorceress's arm. Wisps of his reddish aura coiled around his fingertips. "I swear I will protect you for all the days of your life," he said sincerely.

"Thank you, Billy," she said. "But my life is now measured in hours, not days."

"I'll still look after you," he said quickly

Perenelle Flamel smiled. "I know you will."

378

CHAPTER FIFTY-EIGHT

"$\mathcal{I}$t shouldn't be on fire, should it?" William Shakespeare asked, leaning away from the curl of smoke leaking from the control panel.

"No, it should not." Prometheus grunted. "So why don't you do something useful and put it out?"

"How?" Shakespeare demanded. He started patting his body. "Do I look like I carry a fire extinguisher with me?"

Palamedes leaned between the Elder and the immortal to rip away a smoking panel, and a tongue of fire shot out, singeing off his eyebrows. "Glad I've got no hair," he said lightly. The flames died down and he peered inside as best he could. "It's a mess," he announced. The air filled with the scent of cloves, and a cloud of olive green dripped from his hand and washed over the fire, extinguishing it.

The vimana's humming engine slowed to a whine.

Shakespeare looked up in alarm, and even Saint-Germain raised his head from his book.

"We're fine," Prometheus said as the engine resumed its high-pitched buzzing. "Some of these early vimanas can repair themselves."

Joan peered through the empty porthole. The city was much closer now, a brown smear of slums and narrow streets giving way to broad avenues and golden terraces, the sparkling circles of canals and the spectacular profusion of assorted buildings. Directly ahead, rising like a solid gold mountain at the precise center of the vast city, was the Pyramid of the Sun. "Where will we land?" she asked.

"I'm going to bring us down on the square, as close to the pyramid as possible," Prometheus answered. "We need to take up positions on the pyramid to defend the steps."

Palamedes joined Joan by the window. "Lot of activity down there," he murmured. "Lots of armor and weapons. We'll be dropping right into a war zone."

Joan nodded. "Prometheus, what about landing on top of the pyramid?" she suggested. "It's flat."

Palamedes's teeth flashed in a white grin. "It's also very sneaky. I like it."

"Can you do it?" Joan asked.

"I'll try."

"What about defenses?" Will asked.

"There will be a handful of vimanas. Whatever survived the attack on the Tor Ri," Palamedes said, "and some of the wealthier or older Elders will have their personal vimanas, but they're not armed. Most of Huitzilopochtli's fliers are going

380

to try to land in the square before the pyramid. If they can defeat the anpu guards, that will open up the bridges and allow the rest of the people to swarm across the canals. A few of our vimanas and fliers will land on the opposite side of the canals to support the population and engage any anpu there."

"And what about Aten?" Palamedes asked. "Why aren't we attacking the prison and freeing him?"

Prometheus shook his head. "Marethyu was very clear about that. He said that the prison could only be attacked by the people of Danu Talis. It had to be their victory or their defeat."

"I know what he means," Joan said. "If they can take the prison, it will show the rest of the population what they can achieve. A victory like that will ignite the entire city."

A series of scattered sparks danced across the control panel. Shakespeare rubbed them out with his sleeve. "How soon before we land?"

"Soon," Palamedes said. There was a crack and suddenly a rectangular panel fell out of the floor, allowing them to see into the outskirts of the city below. Bitter air whipped into the cabin.

"Not soon enough," Shakespeare said, just loud enough for everyone to hear.

CHAPTER FIFTY-NINE

*J*osh rotated his wrists and the edges of Excalibur and Clarent keened as they moved through the air.

"There is an easier way." Sophie's hand opened and closed and a ball of silver fire bloomed in her palm. "You really don't have any idea who we are," she said to the bear-headed men.

The silver ball sizzled, then fizzed and shrank before popping like a burst balloon.

"And you have no idea where you are," the huge berserker said, grunting the words with effort. He pointed to the ceiling with the blade of his battle-ax. It was glowing a little brighter than before. "No aura power in the pyramid. The walls drink it."

"How good are you with those?" Sophie asked Josh, nodding to the swords.

"Not great," he confessed. "Usually, Clarent does all the

work for me." He shook the sword in his left hand, but nothing happened.

"Whatever is absorbing our auric power must be draining the swords, too," she said. Sophie pulled her two swords free. She was carrying Durendal, the Sword of Air and Joyeuse, the Sword of Earth. They just felt like heavy lumps of stone in her hands.

"Pretty toys," the berserker said. "Four swords. Three of us. I will take two. My brothers will have one apiece." He pointed to Josh with the black glass knife. "I will take yours."

The big berserker standing immediately to the warrior's left suddenly punched him in the shoulder. "I want that one." He pointed to Clarent.

A dozen strategies flickered through Josh's head and he knew he was accessing some of the knowledge Mars Ultor had filled him with. He risked a quick glance at his sister. "We need to play for time," he whispered. "Isis and Osiris have to be back soon." Then, loudly, he announced, "Clarent is a sword fit only for a leader. So, really, whoever's the leader among you should have it."

"That's me," all three said simultaneously.

Josh stepped backward and the three berserkers automatically moved forward. "If I could lure them farther down the room, do you think you'd be able to get past them to the door and open it?" he wondered.

"Not a chance," Sophie said.

"Try it anyway."

"Give me the sword," the biggest of the three berserkers said.

Josh looked at the other two. "Should I?"

"No," they both grunted.

He looked back to the biggest warrior and shrugged. "Sorry. They said no."

The three bear warriors started arguing amongst themselves in savage growling voices.

"If they attack, do we split up or stay together?" Sophie asked.

"Split up," Josh said immediately. "We'll race halfway down the room, then I'll turn and engage them. You double back and get to the door as fast as you can. If you can get out into the corridor and raise the alarm, we'll be fine."

"We've decided," the biggest berserker announced. "We're going to kill you both and take the swords. We'll draw lots for them later."

"I bet you're hoping to win this one," Josh said, holding up Clarent casually. He looked at the other two bears. "You know that if he does win it, then he's been cheating."

The largest bear growled, the sound echoing around the empty room. "I've never cheated in my life. That is an insult to my good name."

"Do berserkers have good names?" Sophie asked.

The creature's jaws opened, showing his massive teeth. "Bad names are better."

"Before you kill us," Josh said, "who sent you here? I think we have a right to know who ordered our deaths."

The three berserkers looked at one another and then nodded. "Anubis," one grunted. "Jackal-headed Elder. Ugly," he added. "Real ugly."

"Though not as ugly as his mother," another said.

The berserkers nodded in agreement. "Very ugly. She probably put him up to it," the biggest warrior said, his eyes narrowing on the twins. "Now, enough chitchat!" With that he launched himself forward, knife and ax whirling in a deadly blur before him.

Josh shouted in alarm and brought both swords up in an X in front of his face. More by accident than design, he caught the descending ax. It screamed off the swords in a shower of sparks. But the berserker ducked and with his left hand plunged his knife straight toward Josh's chest.

Sophie screamed.

And the obsidian knife crumbled to dust on contact with the ceramic armor.

Josh lashed out with Clarent. It scored a shallow scrape across the berserker's torso, and instantly the sword pulsed. Josh felt it with his entire body—a single heartbeat—and in that moment he knew that if he could feed it blood, the blade would know what to do.

The other two berserkers circled Sophie.

Drawing a deep breath into her lungs, she screamed.

The sound ricocheted across the walls, echoing along the chamber, and both berserkers staggered back, shocked by the noise. She darted between the two creatures, left and right swords lashing out. She missed one of her attackers but caught the other on his meaty rump and he bellowed, a mixture of surprise and pain.

Josh attacked the creature standing before him, blindly hacking and slashing with both swords. Sweat was already pouring down his back, and his shoulders were starting to ache. Surprised, the berserker backed away, leaving Josh to join his sister.

"Not so tough now," Josh panted.

"You were lucky," the bear grunted.

"Oh, I don't know. You're chest is pretty cut up, and your friend there won't be sitting down for a week. We're unscathed."

"Un-skat-ed?" the bear asked, shooting a confused look at his companions. "What's skating got to do with it?" The two berserkers shook their heads.

"Unharmed," Josh explained.

The three berserkers spread out. "We were going to kill you quickly," one said. "But not now. Now you will have to—" He stopped.

Sophie and Josh looked at one another. "Have to?" Sophie prompted.

"What will we have to do?" Josh asked, and then he realized that the three berserkers were no longer looking at the twins, but behind them.

Sophie and Josh turned together.

A woman stood in the center of the room on the circle of gold and silver sun and moon tiles. Slender, in white ceramic armor, she held the metal-bound Codex in her left hand and a golden kopesh in her right. She raised her head and looked at the children with slate-gray eyes, and they both experienced the same shock of recognition. She was somehow familiar.

The woman walked out of the circle and handed Josh the

Codex. "A gift from Abraham the Mage," she said. "You have the pages needed to complete it, I believe." Then she slipped the second kopesh from its sheath and faced the three berserkers. The beast-men were suddenly looking unsure.

"Which of you wants to die first?" she asked. "You?" She pointed to the biggest berserker. "Or you? . . . Or you?"

"Our quarrel is not with you. We were sent to kill the humani."

"Then your quarrel *is* with me," she answered. "They are in my charge. I watch over them."

"Who are you?" Josh and the berserker asked simultaneously.

"I am She Who Watches. I am Tsagaglalal. . . ."

And even as she was speaking, Sophie realized who she was. "Aunt Agnes," she breathed.

CHAPTER SIXTY

$\mathcal{T}$he Council Chamber at the heart of the Pyramid of the Sun took up the entire 314th floor, at the precise midpoint of the building. Rows of tiered seats were arranged in squares and dropped down to a circle at the heart of the room. The chamber was acoustically perfect: conversations on the opposite side of the room, even at its farthest point, more than one thousand feet away, were clearly audible, as if they were taking place at one's side.

The room, like the rest of the pyramid, also absorbed all auric energies.

When the Great Elders had created the even larger original Pyramid of the Sun, they had recognized that they needed a secure environment in which to conduct their business. One where no Elder could influence another by force of aura. A combination of mathematics and crystal with sheets of gold and silver lining the walls swallowed any auras. Any energies that leaked from this unique security system were channeled into lighting the vast rooms. Within the Pyramid of the Sun, all the immensely powerful Great Elders and the Elders who came after them were equals.

And most of the modern Elders who ruled over the island empire hated the pyramid for exactly that reason.

"Look at them," Bastet hissed.

"Who?" Anubis asked, searching the room to see where his mother's gaze had fallen.

"Isis and Osiris—who else!"

Bastet and Anubis were standing in one of the highest tiers of the chamber. As prominent Elders, they were always positioned in the front row in the square of gilded seats before the circle. But Bastet had insisted that they hang back so they could look down over the huge crowd now filing in.

Most of the figures were still vaguely human, but the rest had grown hideous as age and the cumulative use of their auras had damaged them. Furry animal heads and limbs were commonplace; some figures had wings. Others had begun to warp into creatures of stone or wood, while a few had become tentacled monstrosities.

"Only a handful have not turned up," Anubis noted. "I don't see Chronos."

"Good."

"Black Annis is missing."

"Pity, she is a good ally," Bastet said absently, leaning forward to follow Isis and Osiris's progress through the crowd. They were easy to track—they stood out, dressed in white ceremonial armor. She watched them nodding and smiling. "They will do nothing at this time. They've created this excitement and will promise to reveal all very soon."

"How do you know?" Anubis asked his mother.

"It's what I would do." She glanced quickly at her son. "The children: are they dead?"

He nodded confidently. "I sent three berserkers." He grinned.

"Three for two children. That's overkill, don't you think?"

Anubis shrugged. "I wanted to be sure."

Bastet nodded happily. "Good. Keep thinking like that and you'll make a great ruler. And Aten?"

"On the way. Ard-Greimne said there were humani protesting outside the prison. He just needs to clear them away first."

"I like him. He is brutal and efficient," Bastet said. "I'm sure we will find a role for him in the days to come."

Anubis noted her use of the word *we* but said nothing. He had plans to rule Danu Talis his way . . . and they did not include his mother.

Tiny Janus strode to the center of the circle. The Change had altered the Elder terribly, and he now had four completely different faces, each one capable of moving and talking independently of the other. Usually he kept them covered under a black glass helmet and revealed only one face at a time to the world, but today he had left off the covering. While horrible to behold, his particular Change meant he could face all four sides of the chamber at once. Raising a miniature silver triangle, he struck it with a gold hammer. The pure sound cut through the room, instantly silencing all conversations.

"Elders of Danu Talis," he announced. "Please be seated for this, the first Grand Session in lo these many years."

There was a hum of movement as everyone began to move into their rows. In some places seats had been removed to accommodate the Elders' mutated forms.

Janus struck the triangle again. "This is a great and terrible day. A day when we come to choose the next ruler of this city, and a day when we stand in judgment over one of our own."

Elders continued to wind through the aisles, making their way to their seats. Anubis followed Bastet down through the rows, nodding and smiling as he went. He had many friends here—well, not so much friends, more like allies, really. And in the entire room, there were probably no more than a handful who supported Aten and the humani, but they were powerful Elders and not to be lightly dismissed.

Janus struck the triangle for a third time. "However, I believe this may be the greatest day in the history of Danu Talis."

Bastet twisted her head at an unnatural angle to look back at her son. "I bet Isis and Osiris paid him to say that." She smiled nastily at the four-faced Elder and slid into her seat in the front row.

Anubis took up a position beside her. He nudged his mother. The two seats directly opposite belonged to Isis and

Osiris, but only Isis sat there. "Where's Osiris?" he asked, completely forgetting that his voice carried clearly across the room.

"He has gone to bring us the twins of legend," Isis said loudly, her voice ringing through the room.

All the gathered Elders sat forward at her words and the vast chamber grew deathly silent.

"Yes, they are here. The rightful rulers of Danu Talis have come home." Isis was turning to face the doors when suddenly they burst open and a wild-eyed Osiris appeared. "They're gone!" he shouted, his voice thundering. "There's blood everywhere!"

"Oh, shame," Bastet purred.

"Sad," Anubis agreed. "A tragic loss."

"There are three dead berserkers in the old museum."

Bastet gripped her son's arm again and her nails punctured deep enough to scrape bone as the room erupted with shouts and questions.

A grizzled and scarred anpu ran through the open doors and pushed past Osiris. The room fell deathly silent. None of the beasts or hybrids were allowed inside the Council Chamber. And this one had touched an Elder.

"Defend yourselves," the anpu barked. "We are under attack! Humani from the skies."

As the room dissolved into chaos, Bastet turned to Anubis. "I did not know they could talk," she said.

"Neither did I," he muttered. "They never spoke to me."

And then the entire pyramid began to tremble.

"Earthquake," Bastet breathed. "Oh, can this day get any worse?"

From across the room, Isis and Osiris both turned and looked at her, and their smiles were identical. "Oh yes," they breathed. "Much worse."

CHAPTER SIXTY-ONE

*O*n a tiny island surrounded by bubbling lava, Aten, the Lord of Danu Talis, sat in a cage, waiting to be called to execution.

He was exhausted, burnt and scarred from splashing lava, his robes dotted with singe holes. He was also conscious that the lava was rising, the bubbles getting larger and more regular. The air, already thick with sulfur, was becoming less breathable by the moment. If they didn't come to kill him soon, they'd find him dead of asphyxiation. And he was guessing that neither his mother nor brother would be too pleased about that.

On the other side of the lava pool, a rectangle of white light appeared as a door opened. Three huge anpu pushed the bridge into place, and then Dagon, the jailer, hurried forward, the protective goggles he wore making his face even more fishlike. Two of the huge guards accompanied him, while the third remained at the door. Even if a prisoner did manage to overpower the guards, he would never get back across the bridge before the guard at the door had slipped through it and locked it from the other side.

Dagon refused to look him in the eye as he fiddled with the complicated lock. "It is time, Lord Aten."

"I know."

"The guards have instructions to kill you if you try to escape."

"I will not try, Dagon. Where would I go? What would I do? I am where I am supposed to be."

The jailer bubbled a grim laugh. "Why, Lord Aten, anyone would think you allowed yourself to be caught." He looked up suddenly. "Oh," he whispered, as realization dawned. Dagon stepped closer to the bars and lowered his voice. "The humani call for you, Lord Aten. They are protesting outside the jail. There have been disturbances all across the city." He lowered his voice even more to a breathy whisper. "There are rumors that even now a great army is marching to rescue you."

"Whose army?" the Elder asked lightly.

"The Goddess with Three Faces has sent Huitzilopochtli to save you."

"And where did you hear that?"

"From Ard-Greimne himself. You know he has spies everywhere."

Aten dipped his head, as if deep in thought, but both he and Dagon knew the gesture was meant to thank the jailer for the information.

Ard-Greimne ran the huge prison and was responsible for

keeping order in the city and the country beyond. The ancient Elder controlled a force of anpu and Asterion constables, as well as some of the new hybrids—the boars, bears and cats coming out of Anubis's laboratories. One of his proudest boasts was that no humani would ever patrol the streets of Danu Talis and that none would ever set foot on the gilded cobbles of the inner circles around the Elders' homes.

The cell door clicked open and Aten stepped out.

"Follow me," Dagon said. "And be careful; some of the slats on the bridge are broken. I've been meaning to replace them, but I haven't gotten around to it."

Aten fell into step behind Dagon. "I am about to be tossed into a volcano—a little singeing is nothing."

Dagon was unsure whether Aten was mocking him. "Ard-Greimne wants to see you before you leave."

"Oh, I'm sure he wants to gloat." Aten's voice was still light. "He never liked me, and the feeling was entirely mutual. It was no secret that I've been looking for his replacement."

Dagon led the ruler across the bridge and then waited at his side while the anpu lifted it away from the searing lava. If the bridge was left in place too long, it would burn.

The guard opened the door and Aten followed Dagon through. Aten blinked as he stepped into the light, the pupils in his flat yellow eyes shifting into horizontal lines.

"There are many stairs," Dagon apologized, looking up.

Aten followed his gaze and saw hundreds of narrow shallow steps soaring into the gloom.

"If this is to be my last walk, then I will enjoy every one,"

Aten answered, and the two—jailer and prisoner—started the long climb from beneath the prison to the jailhouse above.

"Halfway," Dagon said a little while later.

Dagon seemed to be unaffected by the climb, but Aten could feel his heart pounding in his chest. He was also conscious of a low rumbling noise. At first he thought it was the lava, and then he realized it was coming from above. "What is that?" the Elder asked.

"It is the humani protesting outside," Dagon said. "When I entered, the numbers had been swelling every moment. There were a thousand there earlier; now it might be eight thousand or maybe even ten thousand. The people are demanding your freedom."

"And what does Ard-Greimne say?" Aten asked.

"He is prepared to send everything he has out to crush them. I believe he has instructed the guards to be brutal. He said he is going to teach the humani a lesson they will never forget."

"I see." It was clear to Aten what was happening. "He needs to get the protesters away from here so that the guards can take me to the pyramid."

Dagon's face showed no reaction. He pushed his goggles up onto his head, making it look as if he had two sets of eyes. "I understand Bastet and Anubis are awaiting your arrival there."

Aten nodded "And I'm sure they do not want me to be late for my own funeral."

Ard-Greimne waited at the top of the stairs.

He was a short, slender, rather ordinary-looking Elder. He bore only the vaguest marks of the Change—the hair on his head had fallen out, and his skull had elongated and stretched in a way that pulled all his features back along the sides of his face. Two threads of a red mustache hung below his nose and curled past the edges of his mouth, and his eyes were a startling green. He was dressed, as always, in an archaic rectangular robe that stretched from his neck to his feet but left his arms free. The style had gone out of fashion centuries ago.

"How the mighty have fallen," he said, looking down on Aten. Ard-Greimne was short and incredibly sensitive about his height. He always wore shoes with lifts in them. When Aten didn't respond, he tried again. "I said, how the mighty—"

"It wasn't funny or even clever the first time you said it," Aten said. "Nor is it original."

The little man's pale face squeezed into a semblance of a smile. "Brave words for a man about to die."

"I am not dead yet," Aten said.

"Oh, but you will be."

Aten reached the top of the staircase and stepped past the Elder, emerging from the prison of Tartarus into a vast courtyard.

The shouts from outside the prison walls were a storm of sound, thrumming against the stones. "Aten . . . Aten . . . Aten . . ."

"Your people call for you," Ard-Greimne mocked.

Directly in front of Aten were four long lines of

Ard-Greimne's constables. Most were anpu or Asterion, but there were bulls and boars among their ranks as well. All wore black leather armor embossed with Ard-Greimne's personal symbol, the ever-open always-watching eye. They were carrying clubs and whips, and a few had spears. There were even bowmen scattered among the group.

"I know you respect these humani . . . ," Ard-Greimne began.

"I do," Aten answered before the short Elder could finish.

Ard-Greimne's thin lips curled. "And that you consider them the successors of the Elders."

"I do."

"If you have that much respect for them, I want you to go up onto the walls and tell them to disperse peacefully."

"Why would I do that?" Aten asked.

"Because if they do not, I will release the constables on them. I'll put one hundred—no, two hundred archers on the walls and have them fire into the crowd. There will be panic. Then I will send out my men.

"It would be a slaughter," Aten whispered.

"Only a few hundred would die. We'll not kill them all. We do want some to return home and spread the word. And it is always bad for business to kill all the slaves."

"You want me to talk to the people?" Aten confirmed.

"Yes."

"I'll do it," Aten said without hesitation.

"I thought you would refuse," Ard-Greimne said, surprised.

Aten shook his head. "I will tell them what they must do."

CHAPTER SIXTY-TWO

"*B*race yourselves!" Prometheus shouted.

"I am never getting into a vimana again," Shakespeare vowed. "If they don't crash, they're on fire. I can see why they went out of fashion."

Rattling and banging, the vimana fell from the sky straight toward the great Pyramid of the Sun.

"We have to move quickly before they realize what we're going to do," Prometheus said. "So once we land, get out and take up positions on the steps. Let no one up onto the roof. Is that clear? No one."

"Why?" Joan asked.

"I have no idea. But Abraham gave me very clear instructions about that."

Joan nudged her husband with her foot. "Put the book away. I think you're about to do some practical research for the finale of this musical piece."

"What sort of research?" he asked.

"The crashing, screaming kind, I believe," she answered.

"Armageddon," Saint-Germain said as he climbed to his feet, bright blue eyes sparkling with excitement. "I'm going to call this work 'Armageddon,' or maybe 'Armageddon Rocks!' With an exclamation point."

"I didn't need to be reminded of that just now," Joan said gently.

"Not a good time?"

Joan pointed out the window, and Saint-Germain moved to look. He stood beside her, watching as the massive pyramid raced toward them. He put his arm around his wife and held her as the craft began to rattle apart. The engines were shrieking, the sound painfully loud, and every surface was vibrating.

Windows popped and shattered and a long strip of metal peeled away right under William Shakespeare's seat, leaving his feet dangling in midair. Palamedes caught him and hauled him back just as his chair was torn off and sucked through the opening.

"Don't say a word!" Palamedes warned.

The entire control panel in front of Prometheus began to crumble and crack, then melt into globules of liquid.

"It's so noisy!" Will shouted, pressing both hands to his ears.

The engines stopped, and suddenly the only sound was the air whipping through the openings.

Will pulled his hands from his head and looked around. "I preferred it when it was noisy."

Then the vimana hit the top of the pyramid in a scream of metal. It skidded across the structure's polished flat surface, spinning in circles.

"We're going to go over the edge at this rate," Saint-Germain said calmly. He reached out through the shattered window and moved his fingers. *"Ignis,"* he whispered, and the air was touched with the odor of burnt leaves as a spiral of butterflies curled from his sleeve.

Intense white-hot flame washed over the surface of the pyramid, melting the gold surface, turning it sticky and tacky. The sliding, spinning vimana instantly slowed in a shower of gold droplets. Saint-Germain snapped his fingers and the gold turned solid once again, bringing the craft to a shuddering, creaking halt about three feet from the edge of the roof.

Will Shakespeare broke the long silence that followed. "Very impressive, Musician," he said shakily. "I'll make sure to thank you in my next play. In fact, I might even have to write you in."

Saint-Germain grinned. "A hero?"

"Don't you think villains are much more interesting?" Will asked. "They get all the best lines."

Prometheus and Palamedes kicked out the sides of the craft and hopped out. The Saracen Knight held out his hand and helped Joan out, followed by Shakespeare and finally Saint-Germain. Prometheus put his shoulder to the ruined vimana and heaved. It resisted for a moment, and then, pulling chunks of solidified gold from the top of the pyramid, it went over the side. It sailed out in a shallow arc and hit the steps in an explosion of wood, metal and glass.

"That'll be a surprise for someone down there," Joan said as she peered after it. The steps stretched on forever, and the people far below were little more than specks.

"I doubt there'll be anything left by the time it hits the bottom." Saint-Germain smiled. "Dust, probably."

Below them the rest of the vimana and the fliers were dropping out of the sky into the square, and faintly—very, very faintly—came the first sounds of battle.

"Go down a few steps and take your positions," Prometheus instructed. "Let no one onto the roof. Will and Palamedes, you take the north side. Saint-Germain, can you take the west? Joan, the east is yours. I'll guard the south."

"How come you get the dangerous side?" Saint-Germain asked.

The big Elder smiled. "They're all dangerous sides."

The small group hugged one another quickly. Although nothing was said, they knew this could be the last time they ever saw one another again.

Saint-Germain kissed Joan before they parted. "I love you," he said softly.

She nodded, slate-grey eyes shimmering behind tears.

"When all this is over, I suggest we go on a second honeymoon," he said.

"I'd like that," Joan smiled. "Hawaii is always nice at this time of year, and you do know I love it there."

Saint-Germain shook his head. "We're not going anywhere that has a volcano."

"I love you," she whispered, and turned away before they could see each other cry.

"Am I in your new play?" Palamedes asked Shakespeare as they began to descend the steps on the north side of the pyramid.

"Of course. I'm going to make you the hero."

"I thought you said the villains have all the best lines," the knight complained.

"They do." Shakespeare winked. "But the heroes have the longest speeches."

"Do you have a title yet?"

"A Midsummer Nightmare."

Palamedes laughed. "It's not a comedy, then?"

CHAPTER SIXTY-THREE

*N*ot touching anyone, Scathach moved easily through the enormous chanting crowd gathered before the prison. She ran a practiced eye over the throng, gauging the numbers: ten thousand, perhaps, maybe even more. And not all were young, either. There were men and women of all ages gathered before the prison's walls.

She listened to them talk nervously, excitedly.

They knew the dangers, but they were aware that this was the only chance they would ever have for freedom. If Aten died, then all hopes of a better future would die with him.

And they had a champion—a voice.

The stories had raced through the slums and backstreets of a raven-haired human who had mocked and chased off ten guards, or a hundred, or perhaps it was a thousand. She had turned a man into stone, or a beast, or she had shrunk him and then squashed him underfoot. The people of Danu Talis had flocked to see the woman who had the powers of an Elder.

Scathach slipped to the front of the crowd and stopped as if she had run into a brick wall. She hadn't known what—or who—was now leading the humans. But she would never, in all her ten thousand years, have expected to find herself facing Virginia Dare . . . and Dr. John Dee.

The two were standing in front of and a little apart from the crowd, heads bent close, deep in conversation, and Scathach could see the woman jabbing the English Magician in the chest with her finger as she made a point.

Beyond the two immortals, on the other side of the square, standing still and silent before the prison walls, was row upon row of anpu and Asterion warriors, all armored and heavily armed, as if they were going up against troops rather than unarmed humans. Scathach's long teeth bared in a vampire smile. This would be a battle worth fighting.

Lights flared all along the top of the prison's massive walls, illuminating the long lines of archers taking up position. She estimated a hundred, then two hundred. Scathach knew from experience that a good archer could fire up to fifteen arrows in a minute. The moment the first arrow left the bow, the next arrow would fly.

A sigh ran through the crowd. No one moved, but the chanting grew louder.

More lights flared and a figure appeared on the prison's front wall. He was short and pale, with a slightly elongated face and a wisp of a long red mustache over his lips, dressed in a black robe that shimmered with oily light. He raised two pale arms and waited until silence gradually fell over the massive crowd. Then his voice boomed.

"Humani of Danu Talis."

A murmur ran though the crowd. No one liked the term *humani;* it was an insult.

"Humani of Danu Talis," he repeated. "You know me. I am Ard-Greimne, and my word is law. You have placed yourselves in grave danger today. But there is still a chance to save yourselves. Go now, return to your homes, and you may live out the night. But if you stay here, your futures are not so certain. I do not have the power of foresight, but stand here before these walls and I can promise you pain and death. Is that what you want?"

Someone in the crowd shouted, but was quickly silenced by those around him.

"You may think you are many, but you are facing the finest warriors in the known world. Here are anpu and Asterion, here are berserkers and all the new hybrids who will one day replace you, doing those tasks you are incapable of doing."

Ard-Greimne fell silent, waiting for the crowd to disperse.

"If you will not listen to me, perhaps you will listen to the one whose name you chant."

Ard-Greimne stepped to the side and a tall thin figure in a scorched white robe appeared. Even from a distance, his features were distinctive.

The crowd howled his name. "Aten! Aten! Aten!" Their voices pulsed like a solid heartbeat, rolling on and on, showing no sign of stopping.

✧ ✧ ✧

Dr. John Dee turned to look at the crowd and found himself gazing directly into Scathach the Shadow's grass-green eyes. In a day filled with surprises, this was just another to add to the growing list.

She saw him notice her and stepped out of the crowd, tossing the hat aside, shrugging off the white robe, revealing her black shirt, black combat pants and steel-toed boots. She wore two short swords on her back, matching long knives slung low on her hips and a pair of nunchaku tucked into her belt.

The people around her saw the transformation and howled, and word of her appearance flowed through the throng.

"Have you come to kill me, Shadow?" Dee asked

"Another time, perhaps," Scathach answered coolly.

The Magician extended a hand to Dare. "Virginia Dare, allow me to introduce to you the legendary Scathach the Shadow."

The two women eyed at one another and nodded. Then Virginia smiled. "I was expecting someone taller."

"I get that a lot."

"Are you here to rescue Aten?" Dee asked.

Scathach shook her head. "I am here to see Ard-Greimne, the Elder."

"Why?" Dee asked.

"I wanted to see for myself if he was as bad as people said he was."

Virginia looked at Scathach and then squinted up at the

figure standing on the wall. "There is a resemblance in the cheekbones and chin," she said. "He is related to you?"

Scathach nodded.

"Your brother?"

"He is my father," she whispered.

And then the earthquake shook the entire island.

CHAPTER SIXTY-FOUR

_X_olotl's backward-facing feet made walking difficult and often impossible. His bare bones scraped the stones as he hobbled toward the mixed auras of the gathered Elders and immortal humani.

He was looking forward to killing the Alchemyst. And even more exciting, Xolotl knew that if the Alchemyst was on Alcatraz, then his wife was around also. The Elder's stomach rumbled at the thought. It would be a feast.

Xolotl breathed deeply again, mangy dog's head turned to the skies, black nostrils opening and closing. He thought he could distinguish at least seven—or possibly eight— different auras in the air tonight. The meaty-smelling fog blanketed all other odors, so there might have been another up there, but it did not matter. He would kill them all, eat his fill and leave the rest to the monsters now trailing behind him.

And it didn't really matter if Flamel had ten companions

or ten times ten; he could not escape what was now crawling, slithering and staggering toward him.

In the corner of the ruined Warden's House was an enormous mudlike shell. Nicholas tapped on it. It was solid.

Niccolò Machiavelli folded his arms across his chest and looked at the Alchemyst. "I always knew we would meet again," he said in French. "Though I never imagined it would be in these circumstances," he added with a smile. "I was certain I'd get you in Paris last Saturday." He bowed, an old-fashioned courtly gesture, as Perenelle joined her husband. "Mistress Perenelle, it seems we are forever destined to meet on islands."

"The last time we met you had poisoned my husband and attempted to kill me," Perenelle reminded him, speaking in Italian.

Over three hundred years previously, the Sorceress and the Italian had fought at the foot of Mount Etna in Sicily. Although Perenelle had defeated Machiavelli, the energies they unleashed caused the ancient volcano to erupt. Lava flowed for five weeks after the battle and destroyed ten villages.

"Forgive me; I was younger then, and foolish. And you emerged the victor of the encounter. I carry the scars to this day."

"Let us try and not blow up this island," she said with a smile. Then she stretched out her hand. "I saw you try to save me earlier. There is no longer any enmity between us."

Machiavelli took her fingers in his and bent over them. "Thank you. That pleases me."

Mars and Odin moved outside into positions guarding one of the paths to the house, while Billy and Black Hawk went to watch the other path. Hel leaned against the doorway of the Warden's House, favoring her injured leg. She was the last line of defense.

Nicholas, Perenelle and Machiavelli stood around the hardened ball of mud. "You're sure Areop-Enap is within?" the Italian asked, rapping his knuckles on it.

"I saw her climb in and wrap it around herself," Perenelle said.

"How do we open it?" Machiavelli asked.

"I'm not sure we should even try," Nicholas said. "It could be dangerous to Areop-Enap, and more likely dangerous to us. Areop-Enap is unpredictable." He looked at his wife. "Do I need to remind you about the last time we met the Old Spider?"

Machiavelli grinned. "Let me guess—you fought."

"We did," Perenelle said. "And it was on an island, too: Pohnpei."

"What is it with you people and islands?" the Italian asked. "Japan, Ireland, Pohnpei, the Aleutians. You leave chaos, death and destruction in your wake."

"You're well informed," Perenelle said.

"It was—still is, I suppose—my job."

"And usually it was your friend Dee who caused the chaos, death and destruction," Perenelle added. "We were always running."

"Dee is no friend of mine," Machiavelli said shortly. He laid his palm on the mud ball and his dirty gray-white aura flowed over the rough surface. It sizzled and bubbled, but the aura dribbled away to nothing, running off the clay like water. He bent his head, pressing his ear to the stone. "Silence," he said finally.

The three immortals placed their hands on the ball and brought their auras to fizzling life. The smells of mint and serpent mingled on the foggy air, ice-white, green and dirty-white misty energies flowing over the hard shell.

Nicholas was the first to break away. He was gasping for breath and there were new wrinkles lining his forehead and the sides of his nose. "A moment, if you will. Let me recharge a little. What made you change your mind?" he asked, tilting his head to look at the Italian. "Why did you side with us?"

Machiavelli shrugged. He leaned against a stone wall and brushed at his ruined and filthy black suit. "I have been troubled by my association with the Dark Elders for a long time," he said quietly. "But coming here and working with Billy and Black Hawk brought up a lot of old memories. I was reminded of something my dear wife, Marietta, once said. She accused me of being an uncaring monster. She told me that I would die lonely and alone because I did not care for anyone." He smiled sadly. "I realized that she was probably right on both accounts. And then Black Hawk asked me a question. He wanted to know if I had ever done anything purely for the thrill of it. I told him I had not, not for a very long time, at least. And then he told me that he pitied me, and that I was wasting my immortality. He said I was not living, that I was just surviving. And you know something—he was right."

"I sometimes think the immortal do not truly appreciate the wonderful gift of immortality," Nicholas said.

"It is not always a gift," Perenelle said very quietly.

"And then I fell in with Billy," the Italian continued. "He is young, exuberant—irritating, yes, but he has a big heart. He reminded me what it is to be human. To enjoy life and living. And when it came right down to it, we decided—he and I—that we did not want monsters in the streets of San Francisco, we did not want the deaths of many thousands on our hands or consciences. Not when we could do something about it." The immortal stopped suddenly. "Do you know: I believe that is the longest speech I've given in a century. Maybe two."

There was a whistle followed by the scrape and clatter of approaching hooves on stone.

"Quetzalcoatl's twin brother, Xolotl, controls the monsters on the island," Nicholas quickly explained to Machiavelli. "He is a little upset because we sank a boat of his monsters. He swore revenge."

"You mean there are more creatures?" the Italian asked, a note of despair in his voice.

"Many more," Perenelle answered with a grim smile. "The cell blocks only housed the smaller monsters. The really big ones were kept in the Powerhouse and the Quartermaster Warehouse by the shore."

"We'd best get this open, then," the Italian said.

The three immortals turned back to the mud ball and placed their hands on its shell, pouring their energies into it.

The room came to life with their auras, green and white sparks hissing and snapping from every metal surface.

Nicholas slumped first, then Machiavelli. Both men collapsed with their backs to the ball. Perenelle looked down at them. "We will try one more time," she said. "If we fail, then we'll leave it: we cannot afford to expend any more energy." She knelt beside Nicholas and traced the new lines on her husband's face. "Already we are dangerously weakened."

Black Hawk suddenly raced through the open door. "We have incoming," he said breathlessly. "A hundred anpu and some real ugly unicorns are heading this way."

"What color are their horns?" Perenelle asked quickly.

Black Hawk shook his head. "I didn't hang around to find out."

"Think! You saw them!"

"White . . . black . . . red at the tip," he blurted.

"Monokerata. Their horns are poisonous, avoid them at all cost."

Red-faced and panting, Billy the Kid ran into the room. The two spearheads in his hands were black with blood. "Forget the anpu and the unicorns," he gasped. "We've got a bigger problem. There's a giant crab out there."

"How big?" Machiavelli asked.

"Real big!" Billy snapped. "Like as-big-as-a-house big. One of those bull-headed guys got in its way and it snapped him clean in half. Well, not quite so clean, actually."

"Karkinos," Flamel and Machiavelli said simultaneously.

"Does that mean a big crab?" Billy asked.

"No. It means a giant crab," Machiavelli said.

"And . . ." Billy drew in a deep breath. "And they're being led by a skeleton with a dog's head," he finished dramatically. "A real mangy, ugly-looking dog."

"Oh, we've already met him." Perenelle smiled. "We chatted earlier."

"That is Quetzalcoatl's twin brother," Machiavelli said.

Billy blinked in surprise. "That old monster has a brother!" Then he grinned. "I'm guessing they're not identical."

"They were once," Hel said, from her position by the doorway. "This is Xolotl. This is the evil twin."

Mars and Odin hurried in through the empty doorway. "Decision time," Mars announced. "We can either make our last stand here," he said, looking around at the space, "or we can run, maybe try to find another place to hole up in."

"We stay here," Flamel said firmly. He tapped the mud ball. "You must keep them at bay while we try to awaken Areop-Enap. She is our only chance now."

"Maybe we can hold the windows and doors," Mars said doubtfully. The ruined building was little more than a shell, with no roof and gaping empty rectangles for windows. "But if they charge us . . ."

"They're charging!" Hel shouted.

CHAPTER SIXTY-FIVE

Sophie and Josh followed Tsagaglalal down a corridor.

They were still shaken by what had happened in the long room. One moment, the young-looking woman in the white armor had been standing in front of the three monstrous berserkers, and the next she was standing behind them, her curved swords dripping black blood. The three bear men had folded to their knees with looks of absolute surprise on their faces.

"Questions later," Tsagaglalal said as they raced outside, "but let me give you some answers first."

An unlucky anpu guard spotted them and made the mistake of reaching for Sophie. Josh hit him hard enough to send him cracking back into the wall.

"We need to get out of this building so you can use your powers," Tsagaglalal said.

Suddenly the entire building shook, a deep shuddering vibration running up through the floor.

417

"Earthquake," Sophie breathed.

"My husband created it," Tsagaglalal told them. "Even now the shock wave is racing here. He made it for one of you to use. But you need to be in a place where you can use it."

Josh stopped so suddenly that Sophie ran into him. Their armor clanged together. "I'm starting to get sick and tired of people telling us what to do and expecting us just to do it. If it's not you, it's Isis and Osiris."

Tsagaglalal's gray eyes were huge in her head. "Oh, believe me, Josh, I am not telling you what to do. You will make—you *must* make that decision yourself." She pointed down a corridor and the twins saw Isis and Osiris emerge around a corner.

The couple spotted the children at the same time, raised their hands and started to run toward them.

"You may believe that they trained you for one thing," Tsagaglalal said, "so that they could rule this land through you. But my husband has always believed that there was more behind it. They are powerful enough to put anyone on the throne—so why spend millennia plotting and planning to make sure it was a Gold and a Silver? They want to use you for something more than just ruling the island empire. You two are powerful—incredibly powerful. Abraham believed it was your power they were trying to access. But that very training they gave you will allow you to take control and make your own decisions." She spread her arms. "It's your choice."

Sophie put her hand in her brother's. "Let's get out of here—we've already chosen."

"I know," Tsagaglalal said.

"How do you know?" Sophie asked.

"Because I trusted you to make the right decision."

The twins turned their backs on Isis and Osiris and raced down the long hallway, toward the opening and the light.

Behind them, the two Elders screamed their names. It was not a pleasant sound.

"Kill them. Kill them all!" Bastet screamed. "No survivors."

She stood in front of the pyramid and watched the vimana circling and the gliders dropping out of the sky.

The air was starting to buzz with arrows, and a few of the anpu had tonbogiri rifles and were firing at the attackers.

The ground continued to tremble with minor earthquakes, and cracks were starting to appear in the stones.

The Elders began to stream out of the pyramid. They looked around in shock, stunned at the sight of the vimana and gliders in the air. Arrows and spears began to rain down. An Elder, his face caught somewhere between man and monkey, staggered and fell, and that was all it took to galvanize the Elders. One creature, a figure wrapped in stinking wet cloths, raised his arm to expose a three-fingered hand, and immediately a vimana overhead burst into flames and spiraled down to explode across the square.

The Elders howled, screamed, squawked and cackled in delight.

"Kill them all!" Bastet shouted again. "Death to all the humani!"

The cry was taken up by the majority of the Elders. "Death to the humani!"

"No survivors!" Bastet howled.

"No survivors!" the Elders chanted. Their mixed auras flared into a rainbow of colors as they began to pull down the vimanas with their powers. A handful of the bigger craft burst into flames and streaked across the city like burning comets.

"No!" Inanna the Elder strode out of the pyramid, claws scratching on the ground. "No!"

"Yes!" a rat-faced Elder shouted. "After this night, the humani will be no more. It is time to end this mistake."

Inanna leapt, her claws and wings carrying her twenty feet into the air. When she landed on the rat-faced Elder, his brittle bones snapped and he was dead before he hit the ground.

"I said no," Inanna repeated. "We cannot exterminate an entire race."

"Oh yes we can," Bastet screamed. "We should have done it a long time ago."

Hands and talons dragged Inanna to her feet, but she turned on them, scratching and clawing, and suddenly one of the Elders to her right erupted into a ball of fire, and one on the left crumbled into a pillar of salt.

The courtyard in front of the pyramid dissolved into chaos as Elder fought Elder and the hybrid guards fought the humans. But those Elders who supported the human cause were vastly outnumbered by those who called for their annihilation. And thousands more of the hybrids were streaming from the pyramid.

And in the midst of all the confusion, Tsagaglalal led

Sophie and Josh out the entrance and started the long climb up the steps of the pyramid. Their gold and silver armor took the evening sunlight and they blazed brightly, reflecting streaks of light across the golden stones.

Bastet grabbed Anubis's arm, squeezing hard enough to leave a bruise. "Kill them!" she screamed. With surprising strength, she spun her son around her. "Kill them, and Danu Talis is ours. Yours." She lowered her voice and put her head close to his. "Let the humani kill as many Elders as possible and you will be able to rule as an absolute emperor, with no one to oppose you. Think of that a moment."

Anubis shook off his mother's arm and fought and kicked his way through the milling humani to grab the nearest anpu commander. He pointed to the three armored shapes—white, gold and silver—scrambling up the side of the pyramid. "Leave the humani to the Elders. Take everyone, take every single beast, monster and hybrid under your command, and chase down those three. Kill them and bring me their heads and their armor as proof."

The anpu looked around and pointed left and right, a question clear on his jackal face. A small group of humani archers were picking off the anpu guarding one of the bridges over a canal. Another group had crashed a vimana into a troop of Asterion, decimating them. With the bridge breached, humani were starting to pour into the square.

Anubis shook his head. "Those are all minor irritations. Kill the children."

The anpu grunted, raised a hunting horn to his lips and blew hard, three short blasts. Suddenly all the anpu, followed by the rest of the hybrids, retreated toward the pyramid, leaving the cheering humani to have the bridges and the square.

Another short blast sent every creature racing up the pyramid after Tsagaglalal, Sophie and Josh.

And on the opposite side of the square, moving low and fast, avoiding the conflict, Isis and Osiris ran toward their vimana.

CHAPTER SIXTY-SIX

"People of Danu Talis," Aten called.

Everyone screamed aloud his name, but he held up his manacled hands for silence and a hush fell over the crowd.

"Humans of Danu Talis. Ard-Greimne wants me to tell you what to do."

The crowd moaned.

"He wants me to tell you to go home . . ."

The crowd groaned even louder.

". . . and leave this place."

"No!" someone shouted.

"But I am not going to tell you to do that," Aten said loudly. The flickering torchlight painted his features in flame and shadow, making him seem even taller than he was. "If I had remained in power, you would have become the equals of the Elders. But now the Elders are determined that you will never be more than you are. And if some have their way, you will cease to exist altogether."

"Get ready," Scathach said suddenly. She'd been watching Ard-Greimne, noting the way his muscles were bunching, seeing the line twitching in his jaw.

She'd never known the person her father had been before the Fall. The family never spoke about it. He'd always had a temper, and there were hints here and there that he had been a monster—worse, that he had killed hundreds, maybe even thousands of humans—but she'd never believed it.

And yet, here he was, prepared to order archers to fire into an unarmed crowd before loosing troops on them.

"Ard-Greimne wants me to tell you what to do," Aten continued. "I want you to look toward the Pyramid of the Sun and tell me what you see."

As one, the crowd turned. Outlined in the setting sun against the clear evening sky, they could see streaks of light as vimanas fell to the earth. The sky was filled with fliers.

The shiver of excitement that ran through the crowd was a physical thing. They started to shout and scream.

"The People of the Tree have risen up," Aten said. "Human people. They are led by Hekate and commanded by Huitzilopochtli. Prometheus protects and guides them. Abraham the Mage watches over them. Elder and human together. Equal, as one."

The crowd roared.

424

Scathach watched Ard-Greimne step up to Aten. Immediately she started to run, flying across the ground directly toward the massed anpu ranks.

Dee shot out his hand and gripped Virginia's arm. He too had seen Ard-Greimne move and knew what he was going to do. "Take my aura, Virginia, and do what you have to do."

Virginia Dare carefully lifted his hand off her arm and then wrapped her fingers around his. "Thank you, John."

"John," he breathed.

She looked at him quizzically.

"In all the years we have known one another, you have never called me by my name," he said.

"Of course I have. Many times."

"But never with affection . . ."

"That's because for all the years I've known you, you have been an arrogant immortal called Dee."

Ard-Greimne stepped up to Aten and sighed loudly. The two Elders looked down over the cheering, screaming crowd. And then Ard-Greimne looked to the Pyramid of the Sun. "I am guessing they will not be needing you tonight?"

"I guess not," Aten answered.

Ard-Greimne put his hand on Aten's shoulder. "But you should see this first," he said, then shouted, "Fire at will!" to the line of archers.

Two hundred bowstrings sang and the arrows loosed, again and again and again. The arrows each had a tiny hole cut into the head so that they screamed as they flew through

425

the air. They arched high into the night and fell in a shrieking, deadly rain into the crowd.

And then the salty evening air of Danu Talis suddenly smelled of sage and sulfur.

A pale green fire outlined Virginia Dare, while the faintest nimbus of yellow steamed off the English Magician.

"Give it everything you have," Dee had advised her when he'd outlined the plan earlier. "You will only get this one chance."

"I've never done anything like this before," she had answered.

"This is as good a time as any to start."

Virginia Dare was a mistress of Air magic. She had learned her skills in the woods on the East Coast of North America and perfected them in the wild forests of the Pacific Northwest. She knew how to make and shape clouds, how to use air as a tool . . . and a weapon.

The immortal called upon every iota of her aura and gathered it for one massive outpouring. She could feel the Magician's heat flooding into her hand, seeping through her flesh, strengthening her. His was a dark, bitter power, but it complemented hers.

The arrows rose.

Virginia Dare closed her eyes

The arrows screamed down.

The American immortal's aura burned brighter and brighter, until she was a blazing green beacon. Dee's aura burned a bright sickly yellow, sending grotesque shadows dancing across the ground. Virginia's eyes snapped open and she felt John squeeze her hand.

"Now," he whispered.

Virginia exhaled in a great bellowing breath.

And the arrows stopped, hanging suspended over the stricken crowd, caught by an invisible wall of air.

Everyone in the crowd and along the walls fell utterly silent.

Then the wind shifted, and the hundreds of arrows turned in the air to face the opposite direction. With another burst of wind, they screamed into the massed ranks of armored warriors standing before the prison walls, mowing them down in a clatter of metal and armor.

On top of the walls, watching the guards fall beneath him, Aten nodded. "I am glad you made me wait to see that. What will you do now, Ard-Greimne?" he asked. "It looks like about three-quarters of your troops are dead, and I'm not sure how keen the rest will be to fight. And do you know, I believe it was a human who did that to you." He nodded toward the Pyramid of the Sun, which was now speckled with fires. "Where will you go?"

"I will survive," the Elder snapped, "which is more than can be said for you." Placing his hand in the small of Aten's back, he pushed hard, sending him sailing out over the edge of the wall.

Running as she had never run before, Scathach raced across the square toward the wall. She saw the anpu directly in front of her stiffen and reach for their weapons, obviously unsure of what they were seeing—a single girl charging them.

The Shadow heard the bowstrings above her head twang and twang and twang again and listened to the arrows scream down, and then felt the wash of the sage- and sulfur-scented auras. The screaming suddenly stopped, as if the sound had been muted. Scathach dropped to the ground and rolled as the arrows began shrieking again. They hissed over her head in a horizontal black rain, and then she was back on her feet even as the lines of anpu and the other hybrids were falling under the deadly onslaught.

Overhead she saw Aten fall. She knew that her father had pushed him, and she knew that everything she had heard about him was true.

And then, as they did in every battle, her acute senses took over, and it was as if the world around her slowed but she continued moving at a normal pace.

Aten fell . . .

. . . and fell . . .

. . . and fell . . .

His eyes were closed, she noticed, and he looked serene.

Scathach surged over fallen anpu, climbing on them, her feet barely touching the ground, and then she leapt into the air, twisting, turning in a half circle.

And she caught him.

CHAPTER SIXTY-SEVEN

Xolotl perched on a low wall and watched the anpu race toward the ruined building. The jackal-headed monsters were silent until the last moment before they went into battle, and then they howled. The sound was so appalling it often shocked their enemies into immobility or made them turn and run. Xolotl doubted it would have that effect on the Flamels and their companions. His dog mouth opened in a grin: besides, they had nowhere to run.

The anpu were followed by the monokerata unicorns.

He'd chosen these himself. Xolotl loved unicorns, but these were not the delicate white unicorns beloved by the humani. These hailed from India, and while they *did* have white bodies, they had bloodred heads, with deadly four-foot-long tricolored horns spiraling from the center of their foreheads. Monokerata would impale their victims, then tilt their heads back and allow them to slide down the horn so that they could eat them.

The skeletal Elder turned and squinted back down the path. He could just about make out the shape of the giant crab through the fog. It was having difficulty finding purchase on the slick stones with its spindly legs, but it managed to pull itself along with its enormous front claws, gripping walls and heaving itself forward.

Xolotl rubbed his hands together, bones clicking and rattling—he wished he had something to eat while he watched the entertainment. He hopped off the wall and wandered around the path, hoping to find something to snack on while he waited for the main event.

Odin took up a position beside Hel in the doorway of the Warden's House. "I remember the last time I faced anpu," he said.

Hel nodded. "On Danu Talis. What a day that was." Her black eyes sparkled at the memory. "I was almost beautiful then."

"You are still beautiful," he said quietly. "Step back now, Niece."

"Why?" she asked.

Odin's hand brushed the metal patch he wore over his right eye. "The anpu will pour through these walls," he said, slipping into a guttural language never before spoken on earth. "The immortal humans will fall before they can awaken the Old Spider and all this will have been for naught." Wispy gray ozone-scented aura drifted off his fingertips. "But I can buy them some time."

The anpu were nearer now, close enough that the Elders could see the saliva glistening on their fangs and the beads of moisture from the fog gathering and running off their metal and ceramic armor.

"They will scream in a moment," Odin said softly. "Billy and Black Hawk and probably Machiavelli and Nicholas will be stunned by the sound and will fall."

"The woman will not fall, nor will Mars," Hel said. "And we will not fall."

"No. We will not fall. Nor will we be able to stop them. Not with weapons . . ."

Hel stretched out her clawlike hand. Odin looked at it, then turned to stare into her leaking black eyes. "Are you sure?" he asked.

"My world is gone. The Yggdrasill—your Yggdrasill too—is no more. Where will I go, what would I do?" she asked.

Odin nodded in understanding. "I came to this world to avenge my dear Hekate. I swore vengeance on Dee, but perhaps we can have a greater victory." He took Hel's hand in his, locking their fingers together.

The clean scent of ozone was touched with the rancid odor of rotting fish. "I always meant to change that smell," Hel murmured. "But over time, I rather grew to like it."

Odin's hands were smoking, and suddenly the others in the room became aware that the Elder's aura was coming alive.

"Brother Odin," Mars said in alarm. "No . . ."

"Yes," Odin whispered.

The anpu opened their mouths to scream.

"Down," Mars shouted. "Everyone down! Cover your eyes."

Odin squeezed his niece's hand. "Why don't you tell the jackals just who I am."

Hel nodded. Straightening, she threw back her head and began to exude her bloodred aura. The stench of rotting fish became overwhelming, and, deep and powerful, her voice echoed off the stones. "You stand in the presence of Odin, Lord of the Aesir, the Mighty and Wise, the Aged and the Merciful. . . ."

Odin's right hand was a solid gray glove. "We don't have time for all two hundred names," he muttered. He reached for the patch that covered his right eye.

"You stand before Yggr, the Terror."

Odin peeled back the metal eye patch.

"Who is also known as Baleyg the Flaming Eye."

A focused beam of solid yellow-white light shot from the Elder's eye and splashed across the front line of the anpu and the monokerata. They crisped to spiraling cinders. The Anpu in the second line screamed as their armor melted in the intense heat, and more were caught, crushed or impaled on the unicorns' horns as the beasts fled. But the beam of light was unrelenting. Stones at their feet cracked and shattered, bubbling like thick liquid.

Odin turned his head slowly, the yellow-white light washing over everything. Nothing escaped his gaze.

A few surviving monokerata scattered in terror, leaving the anpu to face the blazing lance of fire. In grim silence, the anpu pressed on, desperately trying to get close to the two Elders. They flung spears and even swords, but Odin rendered them into pools of sizzling metal as he turned his eye upon them.

The air filled with black soot and cinders. It was rank with rotting fish and ozone, but the smells quickly grew bitter and sour as Hel's strength weakened. Odin's gray aura began to fade, then turned pink as Hel poured the last of her strength into her uncle. Her red aura flickered and spat like a guttering candle, and another dozen anpu raced toward the house.

Odin's gaze flared brighter than before, slicing right through them, flames reaching high onto the walls of the Administration Building, bathing it in flames, washing along the length of the lighthouse before it. Odin staggered, his head jerked back and a curl of flame shot into the sky, then arced down to splash before Xolotl, who desperately scrambled to escape. A thread of sticky fire caught his multicolored cloak, setting it alight, and he flung it away, dancing in fury as he watched more of the anpu rendered into ash.

Hel's red aura paled even more, then faded to white. Her legs buckled under her, but she still held on to her uncle's hand. The beam of light lancing from Odin's right eye flickered and then winked out. He slumped in the doorway next to his niece, smoke and gossamer-thin threads of his gray aura curling off his flesh. The once tall Elder had shrunk and was now bent over and wizened.

Almost incoherent with rage, Xolotl sent the last of the

anpu, his personal bodyguard of a dozen scarred warriors, up toward the house. "Kill everything within," he commanded. "Everything!"

The twelve creatures, bigger and broader than any of the others, spread out into a broad semicircle and approached the two small figures in the doorway. On an unseen command, they raced forward as one, mouths stretched wide to howl their victory.

Odin raised his head for a final time. "I am Odin," he shouted, light blazing from his eye once more—only brighter, more intense than ever before. He looked at each of the anpu in turn, incinerating them. He fell to his knees, but the blazing light never wavered. He raised his niece's arm. "And this is Hel. Today we are your doom." The light faded from his eye. He turned to look at Hel and saw her as she had once been: tall, elegant and very, very beautiful, with eyes the color of a morning sky and hair like storm clouds. A tiny pink tongue moved against her full lips and white teeth. "How many did we get, Uncle?" she asked.

"All of them," he whispered.

Suddenly a scorched wild-eyed anpu appeared out of the smoking night. It reared over them both, a huge kopesh raised high, jaws gaping.

"All of them!" Mars's huge sword hammered the creature into the ground. The warrior dropped to his knees beside Odin and Hel and gently lifted Odin's eye patch back into place. Mars took both of his hands in his; they looked childlike and were tiny against his calloused skin. Odin, who had

434

been as tall and as broad as Mars, was now half his size. "It has been an honor to fight alongside you today," he said.

"It is an honor to die in your company," Odin said, and breathed his last. His skin was the color of ancient yellowed parchment. It cracked and flaked away, then crumbled to dust that collected in the cracks in the stone beneath him and disintegrated.

A colorless liquid coated Hel, who was still beautiful, and then, suddenly, like a bursting bubble, she dissolved, soaking into the same stones that had swallowed her uncle's dust.

CHAPTER SIXTY-EIGHT

Scathach and Virginia Dare knelt on either side of John Dee. Aten crouched by his feet. They were surrounded by a protective band of humans, all carrying weapons they'd lifted off the dead warriors.

Most of the rest of crowd were rampaging through the prison, tearing it apart, freeing the prisoners. Smoke was starting to curl from the upper windows, and already people were calling for the pyramid to be torn down. Others had raced off to spread the word through the city. Any anpu or other hybrid survivors had slunk off into the night.

Dee was dying. He had used the final shreds of his aura to supplement Virginia's as she created the massive shield of air to protect the people and then sent the arrows into the guards. He had been old earlier; now he was ancient, his features lost in a shriveled mass of wrinkles.

Virginia took his hand in hers. It nestled, tiny and delicate, in her palm, almost like a newborn child's.

Dee's eyes cracked open and he peered shortsightedly at Virginia and Scathach. "I never thought I'd breathe my last with you two looking down on me." He shifted his head toward Scathach. "Though I always had the suspicion that you would be the one to kill me. You came close enough on far too many occasions."

"I'm glad I didn't," Scathach said. "We would never have been able to do what we did tonight without you."

"It is good of you to say that. But it is not true. Virginia did all the work."

Virginia Dare shook her head. "Scathach is right. I didn't have the strength to do it alone. And remember, it was your idea in the first place."

"I could heal you," Aten said quietly. "I could restore a measure of your health, your sight and hearing, too. Your body would always be as it is now, though."

Dee shook his head slightly. "Thank you, but no. I've been old and healed enough times already today. And, as Mr. Shakespeare would say, my hour is almost come. Let me die in peace. It is the one great adventure left for me to experience; death holds no fears for me."

"John," Virginia Dare said softly, "don't go yet. Stay awhile."

"No, Virginia. You have much to do in the weeks and months to come. You are a symbol for the humani . . . for the *humans* here," he corrected himself. "The people will make many demands on you. You do not need to be distracted by looking out for a tired old man." He turned to look at Scathach. "Why did you come here, Shadow?"

"Obviously to rescue Aten," she said lightly.

"Why did you really come here?" he asked.

"To see Ard-Greimne," she said softly.

"Your father."

Scathach nodded. "My father."

Aten shook his head and looked confused. "But he does not have a daughter."

"Not yet. But he will," Scathach said simply. "Two, in fact. Growing up, my sister and I knew little about our parents. We heard occasional snatches of stories about our father, however. They painted him as a monstrous beast."

"Oh, he is," Aten said. "Make no mistake about that."

"And when my sister and I were bad, my mother—who favored our brother and never had much time for us—would tell us that we were just like our father. I grew up wondering if I was a monster like him." She bared her vampire teeth in a brief smile. "And when these grew and I realized my true nature, I came to believe that it might be true and that I *was* a monster. The moment I ended up here, in this place, at this time, I knew I needed to see him, to look at him just once so I could know what he was like."

"And did you find what you were looking for?" Aten asked.

Scathach nodded. "I discovered that I am not now nor have I ever been like him. Neither was my sister, Aoife. And for that, I am truly grateful."

"Help me stand," Dee said suddenly, and Scathach and Virginia gently lifted him to his feet. There was moisture on the Magician's face, and when Virginia gently brushed it away, she asked, "Why do you weep? Do you regret what you have done?"

"Not really," he said. "I more regret what I did not do." He looked at Scathach. "What news of the Flamels?"

She shook her head. "I have no idea where they are or what has happened."

"If you ever see them again, tell them . . . tell them what I did here today."

"I will do that."

"I want them to know that, at the end, I did the right thing. Maybe, just maybe, it will make up for some of the other things I've done." He raised his hand and looked at it. His skin was starting to disintegrate into powder, blowing away in fine trails.

"You helped free a people and save a world," Virginia said. "That counts."

"Thank you." Dee raised his head for a final time and looked at Aten. "Your world ends tonight."

"Danu Talis ends. . . . The modern world begins." Aten looked into the distance and they all followed his gaze to the Pyramid of the Sun. "Now it is up to the twins."

"Josh will do the right thing," John Dee said. "He has a good heart."

And the remains of the Magician swirled away and scattered on the wind.

CHAPTER SIXTY-NINE

Clicking, scratching, scrabbling on the stones, the bright orange Karkinos approached.

The crab was huge.

"Oh man," Billy whispered. "I am never having crab legs again. And you know I love crab legs with a little lemon and butter."

"We are in so much trouble here," Black Hawk said, "and all you can think of is your stomach."

"Well, I'm hungry. And besides, we're only in trouble if it catches us," he added.

"We *are* hard to catch," Black Hawk agreed.

The two American immortals stood in the open doorway of the Warden's House and watched the huge crab draw nearer. "Is it ten feet tall?" Billy asked.

"More like twelve; maybe fifteen."

"It's not too steady on its legs," Billy pointed out.

Black Hawk nodded. "I noticed that."

The crab's eight walking legs ended in sharp, armored points. They clattered and scraped along on the slick stone, seeking holes to dig into to gain purchase. Plate-sized gray eyes inset with a vertical black pupil fixed on the two figures ahead. The crab's shell was knobbed and speckled with irregular spines.

"And how big do you reckon those claws are?" Billy wondered.

"I think the chelipeds look around twelve feet," Black Hawk said.

"Chely-whats?"

"Chelipeds. The two front claws are called chelipeds."

"You don't say? Are you in training for a quiz show or something?"

"Everyone knows they're called chelipeds," Black Hawk said.

"I didn't. When I go into the store I get a bucket of claws, not a pound of chelipeds." He stopped and watched the huge crab tip-tapping its way closer, carefully placing each leg, balancing gingerly. "Reminds me of a newborn colt," he said quietly, "trying to find its footing."

"Once it gets to the flat section here, it's going to be steady enough," the big copper-skinned man said. "It'll plant itself sure and solid and then chip away at the house with those huge claws. Who knows, might be able to reach right in and pluck us out." He grinned. "All those crab claws you ate; just try not to end up being eaten by one in turn."

"You don't have to sound so cheerful about it." Billy

441

looked at the approaching monster. "It seems to me that we should try to prevent it from getting to the flat section." He looked at Black Hawk, who nodded almost imperceptibly. "Give me a minute," Billy said. He crossed to Mars and spoke quietly to him, then went over to where the Flamels and Machiavelli were still pouring their auras into the massive ball of clay. The effort had aged all of them, Nicholas and Perenelle especially. The Sorceress's hair had turned almost completely white, and the veins across the backs of her hands were prominent.

The three immortals standing around the sleeping Areop-Enap turned to look at Billy and he jerked his thumb toward the door. "The big crab is almost here. Black Hawk and I are going to step outside and see if we can delay it some. Give you folks more time to do what you have to do." He lifted the two spearheads from his belt and placed them on top of the hardened mud. "I thought you might hold on to these for me just in case . . . well, just in case," he finished.

"Don't go, Billy," Machiavelli said quietly.

The American shook his head. "We've got to. Black Hawk and I can stand in the door and wait for the monster to come right up and pluck us out, or we can go out and see if we can cause some mischief."

"You have no idea what else is out there," Perenelle warned.

"Not a lot is left, actually. Odin and Hel took care of most of the anpu, and the ugly unicorns they didn't kill ran off into the night. Anything out there with an iota of sense is staying well away from us. Except for the big crab and Quetzalcoatl's skeleton brother. He seems pretty riled up." He rapped the hardened mud with his knuckles. "How are you getting on with Old Spider?"

"We're working on it," Machiavelli said.

"People usually say that to me when nothing's working," Billy said.

Perenelle smiled. "Good luck, Billy."

"Don't do anything stupid," Machiavelli advised.

Billy tossed them a quick salute and hurried back over to the door. "I've been thinking . . . ," he said to Black Hawk, "what we really need is some rope to make a lasso."

Black Hawk held up his tomahawk. Its long shaft was wrapped in strips of sweat-stained leather. Half of the leather had been peeled off to expose the white wood beneath. "Start tying these together," he said, unraveling what was left and handing Billy a dozen long strips of brown leather.

"You're always prepared. You should have been a Boy Scout," Billy muttered.

"I was a Scout Master for a while. Had one of the best troops in the West."

"You never told me," Billy said, quickly knotting the leather pieces together.

"You never asked."

"I think I'd have made a great Boy Scout."

"I think you would too." Black Hawk peeled off the last leather strip and handed it to Billy. The outlaw added it to the end of the knotted leather rope, then expertly twisted the rope into a lasso.

"Just like old times." Billy grinned.

"This is nothing like old times," Black Hawk said. He spun the tomahawk in his hand. "When was the last time we went hunting crab?"

Perenelle, Nicholas and Machiavelli watched the two Americans slip out into the night. They all knew that the chances of seeing either of them alive again were slim. Perenelle turned back to the mud ball and went to lift the two spearheads Billy had left behind.

The leaf-shaped blades had sunk into the mud.

Perenelle picked one up and pressed a fingertip to the blade. She expected to find it sizzling hot, but it was cool to the touch. "Nicholas," she breathed.

The Alchemyst snatched up the other spearhead and plunged it deep into the hardened mud. It penetrated easily. Then, gripping it in both hands, he dragged it up across and down again in a long rectangle. Perenelle dug her fingers into the edge of the hardened mud and pulled the giant piece out of the ball. It crashed to the floor and broke in half.

Machiavelli grabbed the second spearhead and began to cut another hole in the hardened mud. "Get Billy and Black Hawk back in here," he called to Mars. "We need their spearheads."

"Too late," the big Elder said. "They've gone hunting the Karkinos."

CHAPTER SEVENTY

Sophie and Josh scrambled after Tsagaglalal up the steps of the Pyramid of the Sun.

And the monsters raced after them.

The dog-footed anpu scampered easily up the side of the pyramid, but the bulls, bears and boars moved more slowly, finding it difficult to mount the high narrow steps—they were so steep it was almost like climbing a ladder. Hissing and spitting cat-headed hybrids scurried on all fours, bouncing from step to step. They would be the first to reach the twins.

Arrows started to fall on the stones, and a tonbogiri ball screamed off the step by Sophie's hand, showering her in golden flecks that pinged off her armor.

"How many steps to the top?" Josh asked.

"A lot," Tsagaglalal said grimly. "Too many. We're never going to make it."

"And why do we have to get to the top?" Sophie demanded. She risked a quick glance down and immediately wished she hadn't. There were hundreds of creatures—maybe even a thousand—flowing up the stairs after them. She saw movement from the corner of her eye and guessed that there were more running up the other sides. The beasts would come at them from all directions and they would be overwhelmed.

"Power," Tsagaglalal said simply. She waited for the twins to catch up. "This pyramid is more than just a building. Think of it as a huge battery. It was built using very special materials to very precise specifications and mathematical angles. At one time, a handful of Great Elders controlled the entire world from the top of this pyramid. They created the first Shadowrealms. When a rogue planet threatened to crash into this one, they used the power of this place to capture it and put it into orbit as the moon. But over time those skills have been forgotten, and the Great Elders are no more—dead, Changed or gone to Shadowrealms of their own creation. Yet the power remains: from the top of this pyramid you can control the entire world."

"Slow down," Josh gasped. He was breathing hard, and his heart was thumping solidly against his chest, hammering against the armor.

"Josh," Sophie said. "We don't have time. They're close."

"Keep going," he panted. "I'll hold them." He lifted his hand and his aura started to rise in gold smoke.

"No!" Tsagaglalal cried. "You shouldn't waste it. You will need every ounce of strength for . . . for later."

"But if we don't use our auras, we're never going to get to later," Josh said urgently.

The earth shook again, tremors rattling up through every step. Two of the huge bull creatures screamed and bellowed as they lost their footing and fell, tumbling down the steps, crashing into a dozen others and dragging them down with them.

"How about if only one of us uses their aura?" he asked.

Tsagaglalal watched the rapidly approaching anpu. There were thousands of the beasts now moving up the pyramid. "You, Josh. Only you. Sophie, you keep your strength."

Sophie opened her mouth to protest, but Tsagaglalal shook her head and waved her index finger at her, and the girl broke out into a huge grin. "In ten thousand years you'll still be shaking your finger like that."

Josh turned and sat on the steps, placing his gloved hands on his kneecaps.

"Josh, I really don't think this is the time—" Sophie began.

Josh whistled. Five notes ringing out pure and clear in the air. All the anpu pricked up their ears.

"Josh?" Sophie asked.

"You know your trigger tattoo?" he called back to her.

She nodded. A thick black band encircled her right wrist like a bracelet. On the underside was a perfect gold circle with a red dot in the center. Whenever she needed to call up the Magic of Fire, she simply pressed the dot.

"I've got a trigger whistle." He whistled the five notes again.

"That's the tune from . . ." It was so familiar, yet she struggled to remember the name of the movie.

"Close Encounters of the Third Kind," he said, whistling it again. "Virginia Dare taught me the Magic of Air when we were on Alcatraz." He stopped and frowned. "Was that today—or was it yesterday?"

A snarling cat-headed creature launched itself up the last ten steps toward Josh. Tsagaglalal's kopesh sliced through the air, close enough to cut off its whiskers. It tried to twist midleap but hit the steps and started to slide down.

"Josh, if you're going to do something . . . ," Sophie urged.

"Sit beside me," he said. "You too, Aunt Agnes . . . Tsagaglalal."

"This is hardly the time for sitting," Tsagaglalal protested.

"Trust me," he said with a wicked grin.

Sophie sat on the step to Josh's right, while Tsagaglalal settled nervously to his left. "Even the beasts look surprised," Tsagaglalal muttered.

"Put your arms through mine and hang on."

Josh whistled again.

Tsagaglalal grunted as the ground shifted again. The earthquakes were becoming more frequent. And then she realized that it wasn't the stones beneath her than were shifting. She wasn't even sitting on the stones anymore. She was rising slowly into the air.

Josh was grinning widely. "Isn't this the coolest thing?" he asked. "Virginia showed me how to do it." He straightened his legs and allowed them to dangle, and Sophie followed him. "Sure beats walking." The three were spinning slowly around one another as they rose skyward.

"I'm standing on air," Sophie said, stamping her feet.

"Solidified air—it's the same principle as a hovercraft." He turned to Tsagaglalal. "What do you think?"

She smiled. "You should have seen the looks on the anpu's faces."

They rose faster and faster, the air streaming cold around them now, the steps blurring beneath them. The city grew small; the many battles diminished to dots of flame.

As they neared the top, Sophie looked down between her feet and watched a shadow flowing up the steps and realized it was the anpu and the other hybrids. "They're still coming. There are thousands of them."

"They will never stop until they are called off," Tsagaglalal said. "And neither Bastet nor Anubis will do it. They need you dead."

Sophie looked up. "How close are we . . . Oh, there's someone on the steps above," she said in alarm. "It looks like . . ." She stopped, suddenly speechless.

In burnished red armor, Prometheus sat on the steps close to the top of the pyramid, arms resting on his thighs, fingers clasped together. "Ah, there you are," he said pleasantly. "We've been waiting for you."

"We?" Josh asked weakly. He was beginning to tire out.

"Why don't you take a spin around the pyramid," Prometheus suggested lightly.

With a tremendous effort of will, Josh brought the cushion of air clockwise around the sides of pyramid, finding

Saint-Germain lying stretched out on a step, busy with his notebook. He waved up to them. "Wonderful evening, isn't it?" he called. "Just look at that sunset—it's positively musical."

Palamedes and William Shakespeare were on the north side of the great pyramid. The Bard looked at the Saracen Knight and pointed as the three people floated slowly past. "Now, that is something you do not see every day."

And finally they floated to the east side, which was already deep in shadow. Joan of Arc sat crossed-legged on a step, eyes closed, upturned palms resting in her lap. She opened her eyes, smiled brightly and inclined her head. "Very nice armor, Sophie." As she was speaking, she spread her arms, the air suddenly filling with lavender as her own silver armor flowed over her body.

"What are they doing here?" Sophie asked.

"They are here to guard you and protect you," Tsagaglalal explained as they floated higher, creeping closer to the top of the pyramid. "They will keep the anpu at bay for as long as possible. But don't delay too long."

"What are you talking about?" Josh demanded. He was starting to shiver with the strain of holding the cushion of air together. "How close are we? I can't keep this up much longer."

"Take us in to the steps," Tsagaglalal commanded. "Now!"

They had barely reached the stone steps before Josh slumped. Sophie and Tsagaglalal helped him stagger the last half-dozen stairs to the top of the pyramid . . .

. . . just as Isis and Osiris's crystal vimana dropped out of the sky and landed on the flat roof.

"So now it ends," Tsagaglalal murmured. "Now the fate of the world—this world and all the other worlds and Shadow-realms—is yours to decide." Reaching into her armor, she pulled out a small rectangle of emerald and pressed it into Josh's hands. "But before you make your final decision, you should probably read this."

"What is it?"

"It is a parting gift from Abraham the Mage. It is the last message he ever wrote," she said. She stopped at the edge of the steps, turned back and took both twins' hands in hers. She smiled sadly, large gray eyes shimmering in the fading light. "I would hope to see you again in ten thousand years' time. Be nice to your old Aunt Agnes, and know that she loves you very much." Then she kissed each one on the cheek and turned away, walking down to stand beside Prometheus, leaving the twins alone on the roof with Isis and Osiris.

Josh looked at Sophie. "Just you and me," he said.

"As always."

Then, together, they walked toward the vimana.

CHAPTER SEVENTY-ONE

*T*sagaglalal ran onto the bridge.

Her aura blazed cold white against the fog, searing it away, creating a hole in the swirling damp around her. She raced through the opening between the two lines of cars and knew immediately what Niten and Prometheus had tried to do. She saw the broken spears on the ground and then spotted the blood: they had fought here and been injured. She caught the scent of their auras on the night air where they had healed themselves, but the auras were slightly soured and bitter—a sure sign that they were desperately weakened.

A Spartoi warrior lurched out of the fog to her left. "What's this?" he asked with a giggle. "Fresh meat . . ."

Tsagaglalal's wicked kopesh flashed and he fell without ever finishing the sentence.

Shapes moved ahead of her: two Spartoi racing down the

bridge toward her, swords and spears jabbing. The Spartoi were fast, inhumanly fast, but Tsagaglalal cut them down without breaking stride. A long time ago, when the world had been a very different place, and before the Fall of Danu Talis, she had been trained by some of the finest warriors in all creation. Later, when she had been called Myrina and commanded the most fearsome warriors on any of the Shadowrealms, she had passed those skills on to two girls under her command: Scathach and Aoife.

Tsagaglalal ran past the last of the cars. There were deep grooves in the bridge where the metal wall had been pulled apart. She guessed that when Niten and Prometheus had realized the creatures were disassembling the barrier, the Elder and immortal had taken the battle to the enemy rather than standing and allowing themselves to be overrun.

There was the hint of green tea in the air, the suggestion of anise, and then, directly ahead of her, the merest touches of blue and red on the blanketing fog. Tsagaglalal raced toward it. A wounded Spartoi staggered toward her, a look of absolute surprise on his face, obviously astonished that he'd been injured. Her kopesh rose and fell and the creature died with the same shocked expression on his face.

Tsagaglalal could hear weapons clashing ahead of her, metal ringing off metal, the meaty slap of wood against flesh, the hissing of the Spartoi and the grunts of the two men. She burst out of the fog to see the Elder and the immortal standing back to back against almost ten times their number. The Elder's armor was a blaze of red light, but it was fading fast, and the immortal shimmered with gossamer tendrils of his blue aura. Both men were badly wounded, but half a dozen of the creatures lay still at their feet.

Abruptly, at some unheard command, all the Spartoi swarmed forward, spears and swords jabbing.

Tsagaglalal saw Niten go down beneath a dozen blows. Prometheus stepped back to stand over the immortal's body, guarding it, sword blurring, but the Spartoi were just too many, and they were too fast. Prometheus fell, stabbed in the back by those afraid to face him.

She Who Watches screamed.

The sound was ancient and primal, a raw ululation that should never have come from a human throat. But Tsagaglalal was not, and had never been, human. The sound cut into the fog and lanced through the night, stopping all movement. The Spartoi turned toward the howl and began to move in the direction of the figure in white ceramic armor.

The air abruptly filled with the rich, thick scent of jasmine.

"The Elemental Magics," Tsagaglalal snarled, hammering a creature to the ground without even looking at it. "Equal and identical. None greater than the other. Water . . ."

An entire section of the bridge turned to dirty liquid. Six of the Spartoi were immediately swallowed up, falling through the aqueous bridge to tumble into the sea far below.

"Air . . ."

Another portion of the bridge vaporized. Three of the creatures barely had time to scream before they too disappeared to fall through the suddenly empty space into the unforgiving waters of the bay.

"Fire . . ."

A six-foot stretch of the metal structure turned white-hot, blazing to incandescence. Three unlucky warriors were crisped to cinders in a heartbeat.

A handful of the Spartoi remained. Hissing nervously, they backed away from the small woman in white.

"And Earth."

The section of bridge where the Spartoi stood turned to quicksand. The warriors did not even have time to scream before it swallowed them. Then it instantly hardened and re-formed, leaving vague impressions of their bodies in the rippled surface.

Tsagaglalal dusted off her hands. She unceremoniously tossed aside the bodies of the fallen lizards to get at the two men and kneel beside them. "Do you know," she said, "I was telling Sophie only earlier today that there is no magic greater than the other. They are all the same and equal. . . ." She stopped. Neither man was moving. "Oh, no," she breathed.

When she pulled away the last of the Spartoi, she discovered that both men were crisscrossed with wounds. Prometheus's armor was a ruin, and Niten's black suit hung in shreds about his thin body. Delicately she pressed her fingertips to Niten's throat, but there was no pulse. There was no point in feeling for Prometheus's pulse, because he had never had one, but she peeled back his eyelids and saw nothing but white.

"No," she said fiercely.

The Elder and the immortal had given their lives defending the city.

"No," Tsagaglalal said firmly. "I will not allow it." Then she threw back her head and howled aloud her anguish.

Up on the ridge looking down over the Golden Gate Bridge, Bastet and Quetzalcoatl suddenly smelled jasmine on the air and saw the globe of white flare in the fog below.

And then the sound pierced the night, and although it had been ten thousand years since they'd last heard the noise, they recognized it immediately.

The two Elders turned to look at one another, then ran toward their cars. Seconds later, Bastet's limousine peeled out of the parking lot, tires slipping and spinning on the wet pavement. Quetzalcoatl followed, wondering if he would make it back to the safety of his Shadowrealm in time.

Neither of them wanted to face the wrath of She Who Watches.

CHAPTER SEVENTY-TWO

"*J*ust what do you two think you're doing?" Osiris demanded, face flushed with anger.

"Why did you run from us?" Isis snapped. "We told you—"

Sophie clapped her metal-gloved hands together, the sound cracking off the pyramid's top like a gunshot, silencing them. "Who are you?" she said quietly.

"*What* are you?" Josh asked.

Shocked, Isis and Osiris stood at the foot of their vimana, exchanged a glance and then turned to stare at the twins. "That's no way to speak to your parents—" Isis began.

"You're right," Sophie interrupted. "But you're not our parents, are you?"

Isis and Osiris remained silent, but something subtle happened to their faces. Shadows bloomed beneath their eyes; color touched their cheeks.

"You know I have within me the Witch of Endor's memories," Sophie said, closing her hands into fists. Smoking silver aura began to mist off them and the evening breeze whipped away the scent of vanilla. "She never liked you."

"She was a—" Isis protested.

"She spent centuries trying to find out just who you were," Sophie continued. "She didn't believe you were Elders. And she knew you weren't Great Elders or Ancients." Even as she was speaking, images were tumbling through her mind, snatches of the Witch's experiences. Sophie gasped as the images grew sharper, crisper. "She never quite figured it out. She came close, though. And as she began to suspect what you might be, she set out destroying millennia of ancient knowledge. Just to keep it from you."

A deep shudder rumbled through the pyramid.

"The Witch was, is and will be a fool," Isis said petulantly. "And you are a fool for listening to her or believing her."

Osiris wandered over to the edge of the pyramid and peered down. The tireless anpu were closing in fast. "It is still not too late," he said.

"Too late for what?" Josh spread his arms. "Look around. The Elders are finished. The people of Danu Talis have risen up."

"So what? You could wipe them out with a word," Osiris retorted.

Isis looked at Sophie. "Do you have any idea of the power you wield?"

"No," Josh said truthfully. "Do you?"

458

Osiris blinked at him, and in that moment, Josh knew that he didn't.

Another spasm shook the pyramid, and off to the right, Huracan, the volcano, began to heave black smoke. Bright red cinders spiraled upward into the darkening sky like fireworks.

"You are not our parents, are you?" Sophie demanded.

"We have raised you as our own," Isis offered.

There was a terrifying noise from below as the anpu howled their war cry and closed on the six individuals protecting the top of the pyramid.

"That's not the question I asked," Sophie snapped. "Are you our parents?"

"No," Isis said, unable to conceal the twist of disgust that curled her lips. "We did not birth you."

The twins looked at one another. Although they had already guessed the answer, it was still a shock. "Good," Josh said shakily. "I don't think we want you as our parents."

Sophie's face was a white mask, ghastly against her silver armor. Memories of the Witch's search for the truth began to fall together.

"And Sophie and I . . . are we related?" Josh asked the question he didn't really want the answer to.

Isis and Osiris remained silent, looking at them, eyes mocking.

"Are we!" he shouted suddenly, and they both jumped.

"Not by blood, no, but you are Gold and Silver," Osiris said. "It is an ancient bloodline. There is a kinship there."

"Who are we?" Sophie screamed. She'd started

to tremble, a combination of fear and anger and a feeling of terrible loss burning through her. She was unaware of the silver tears streaming down her face.

Isis shrugged. "Oh, who knows?" she said casually. "We've hunted Gold and Silver across the centuries and through the Shadowrealms. We picked up Josh in a Neanderthal encampment more than thirty thousand years before we found you. We discovered you somewhere on the steppes of what would now be Russia in the middle of the tenth century . . . or was it the ninth?"

"Tenth, I think," Osiris said.

"We kept you both safe, isolated and cocooned in a Shadowrealm where time does not run, and then, when all was in readiness, brought you out together into twentieth-century Earth."

Sophie felt as if she might faint, or collapse, at least, but Josh stepped over and caught her.

"Why?" he whispered.

"You were Gold and Silver," Osiris said lightly. "The purest auras we had ever encountered in millennia of searching. We could not let you rot in some primitive hut."

"You kidnapped us," he murmured.

Isis and Osiris laughed. "Well, kidnapped is a bit harsh," Osiris said. "Compared to what you would have had, we gave you a life of unimaginable luxury. In fact, we are more parents to you than your real parents would have been. Do you know the life expectancy for a newborn Neanderthal baby or a child on the frozen steppes of Russia? We may not be your birth parents, but we gave you life."

"And for that you owe us a debt of gratitude and respect," Isis added.

"We owe you nothing!" Sophie said.

Almost directly below they could hear the clash of weapons, the howling of anpu and the hissing of cats.

Trembling with rage and fear, sick to his stomach, with a stabbing headache almost blinding him, Josh turned his back on Isis and Osiris and walked to the edge of the roof. He couldn't look at them anymore. His hands were opening and closing spasmodically as he tried to take in the terrible revelations.

Directly below he saw Palamedes and William Shakespeare. The Bard's hands were moving and he was conjuring serpents and lizards out of the air, laughing as he rained them down on the beasts gathered below, driving them back.

Josh saw one anpu raise a long riflelike weapon and fire. Shakespeare fell without a sound, and the stinging lizards and coiling snakes instantly disappeared. The attackers surged forward, and a lion-headed eagle darted out of the throng to peck at the fallen immortal. Palamedes grabbed it, holding it at arm's length; then he tossed it into the sea of beasts below. But the anpu closed in.

Josh threw back his head and screamed his fear and frustration. He pressed his thumb into the palm of his hand, igniting the Fire magic Prometheus had taught him, and sent a blade of flame roaring down onto the steps. It foamed and splashed, washing away the monsters.

He staggered to the right, where a grim-faced Saint-Germain was plucking fireballs from the air and tossing them into the midst of the savage monsters. The gold stone steps were melting.

Hands still blazing, Josh looked down on Prometheus and Tsagaglalal: the Elder was standing tall and unmoving, hands outstretched, while cold white fire flowed down the steps like water.

Josh finally made it over to the east side of the pyramid to Joan.

Her torn armor was blazing like a silver torch, blinding the beasts that howled and snarled and gibbered in the gloom. She was surrounded on all sides by the jackal-headed anpu; some were creeping up behind her. Josh raised his hand, a spear of flame forming, but then he stopped—the creatures were too close. The fire would catch Joan, too.

And then a shape formed out of the night air.

A rider spiraling in on a glider.

And the light from Joan's blazing armor lit up a white face and bright red hair and savage vampire teeth.

Josh watched as Scathach unhooked herself from the glider at the last moment and dropped screaming with delight onto the startled anpu. She stood back to back with Joan; the Shadow's weapons blurred and the beasts fell in waves.

But the monsters continued to climb the pyramid on all sides.

"No more," Josh pleaded, turning back to Isis and Osiris. "Let this end now."

"Only you can end it," Isis said. "Only you have the power." She smiled. "Think of this: you could wipe away the anpu and the humani, and the Elders, too. This world, and all the Shadowrealms, could be yours to command."

"Look around you!" Osiris shouted, spreading his arms wide. "Look at what could be yours. The greatest empire ever seen. It is yours for the taking."

"But we don't want it," Sophie said, speaking for both of them. "You do."

"And we don't want to give it to you," Josh added.

Isis and Osiris looked at them blankly.

"You will do as you are told," Isis insisted.

"No!" The twins spoke as one.

"Then you are useless to us," Isis hissed. She looked at Osiris. "Kill them."

CHAPTER SEVENTY-THREE

"*M*an, that is one ugly crustacean," Black Hawk said. The two American immortals were creeping through the fog toward the giant crab, crawling on their bellies across the stones.

"Good eating in those claws, though," Billy said with a grin. "At least two weeks' worth of eating."

"Now, don't get stupid, Billy," Black Hawk muttered. "Remember what happened last time." The last time the two men had gone hunting, Billy had almost been trampled to death in a buffalo stampede.

"There were about a million buffalo that time," Billy said. "All we have here is one crab. Admittedly, a giant crab."

"There will be a moment when it comes around by the Administration Building," Black Hawk said. "It should be off balance, hind legs lower than its forelegs. If you can hook a leg, you can pull it back." The copper-skinned man carried two spears strapped to his back. He shrugged them free and handed one to Billy. "If you get a chance, take it. And, Billy," he added, "remember, there are other creatures out there. Make sure they don't sneak up and take a bite out of you. Don't be creative. Don't be stupid."

"That's what Machiavelli said. You guys really have a lot of faith in me, don't you?"

"Neither of us wants to lose you. Just be careful, Billy."

"Careful is my middle name."

Black Hawk rolled his eyes. "You told me it was Henry."

Using the spearheads, Nicholas, Perenelle and Machiavelli had carved a huge hole in the shell encasing Areop-Enap. In places the mud was several feet thick, speckled and encrusted with the corpses of some of the millions of flies that had poisoned the creature earlier in the week.

Perenelle stuck her head into the opening, then pulled it out again, tears streaming down her cheeks. "Stinks," she gasped. Turning away, she inhaled in a deep breath, then used her aura to bring her index finger alight. She pushed her arm into the opening and watched as the flame danced, flaring as it burned through the noxious gases. With Nicholas holding on to her belt, she shoved her head into the opening again and looked around. When she jerked it out, her eyes were bright with excitement. "I saw Areop-Enap."

"Is she alive?"

"That's hard to tell. But she looks healthy; the horrible blisters and wounds are gone from her flesh."

"So all we have to do is to wake her," Nicholas said. He

looked at the Italian. "Have you any idea how to wake a hibernating Elder?"

Machiavelli shook his head.

"Mars, what about you? Any advice?"

"Yes. Don't."

Vegetarian, Billy decided. When all this excitement was over and done with, he was turning vegetarian. Vegan, actually. Nothing that crawled, walked, slithered or swam was going into his mouth ever again. Especially nothing with legs. Alcatraz was littered with monsters—or rather, parts of monsters. None were alive, and most of them he couldn't even recognize.

Billy had seen the results of buffalo kills, had walked battlefields and witnessed the aftermath of natural disasters of all kinds, but nothing could have prepared him for the carnage he now saw. He'd never had any doubt that releasing the monsters into the city was wrong. But seeing what they had done to one another made him shudder to think of the havoc they would have wrought on humans. The death toll would have been terrifying.

The American immortal pressed his back against the side of the Administration Building and focused on his breathing. On the plus side, he realized, when they killed one another, they left one less creature for him or Black Hawk to deal with.

He smelled the rich and familiar brine of the sea just as he heard claws scratching on the stones. He risked a quick glance around the corner. Through the billowing fog, he could see the Karkinos making its way up the incline toward the

Warden's House, using its huge claws—chelipeds, Billy reminded himself—to pull itself forward.

And sitting on the back of the giant crab was Quetzalcoatl's dog-headed twin brother. Xolotl was hammering on the crab's head with his bony hand, kicking with his backwards feet, trying to make it go faster. But he was kicking with his toes rather than his heels, and it had absolutely no effect on the crab through its armored carapace.

Billy started to twirl the lasso above his head. Black Hawk had told him to be careful—Black Hawk *always* told him to be careful—but the immortal had also said that if he saw a chance he should take it. And here was a chance. Billy eyed the makeshift lasso, wondering if it was long enough and deciding that even if it wasn't, he was going to make the throw.

Six feet away, Black Hawk slipped into position. He could just about make out Billy through the shifting bands of mist. He saw the fog curl in a circle as Billy started to twirl the lasso. All the outlaw had to do was to hook a leg and pull. If the Karkinos was off balance, he should be able to pull its legs out from under it. Then, while it floundered and scrambled to get back on its feet, Black Hawk was going to jump onto its back and hammer the spearhead into its body. He wasn't sure whether his attack would have any effect, but it would certainly irritate the monster and maybe give those in the ruined house a few more minutes to awaken the Old Spider. He wasn't as convinced as they were about the spider, though. In a battle between a spider and crab, he was betting on the hard-shelled big-pincered crab over the soft hairy spider.

Black Hawk watched Billy move and immediately knew something was wrong. "Please, Billy, don't do anything stupid," he begged under his breath.

Billy stepped right out in front of the giant crab.

"Something like that," Black Hawk muttered. Scrambling to his feet, all pretense at concealment forgotten, he ran toward his friend, tomahawk in one hand, spear in the other.

Billy the Kid twirled the makeshift lasso, the leather whipping and snapping in the air, and stepped closer to the giant crab.

"The leg, Billy! Catch the leg! Pull the leg!"

But Black Hawk knew Billy was not going to catch the leg.

The Karkinos's eyes were fixed dead ahead, and Billy was only five foot eight. The crab was so tall that it hadn't seen him. Black Hawk spotted Xolotl on top of the crab at the precise moment the skeletal Elder discovered Billy below.

"Oh, Billy," Black Hawk said in despair.

Xolotl pounded on the crab's head, trying to make it look down, but one of its forelegs slipped sideways and it crashed forward at an angle onto the ground, leaving its enormous eyes and gaping jaws directly in front of Billy. The immortal ignored the monster in his face. He was concentrating on the Elder on its back. Twirling the rope one final time, he released it.

"He shoots . . . ," Billy called.

The lasso dropped directly on top of Xolotl, slipping over the dog head and tangling in his bony ribs.

"He scores!"

Billy dug the heels of his boots into the earth and

tugged hard. With a yelp, the Elder sailed off the top of the Karkinos.

The huge crab caught a glimpse of movement, and its enormous right claw rose, opened and closed in a snap around the Elder and caught him in midair. It would have snapped a normal human in half, but it had caught the Elder around the waist, where there was no flesh, only bones, which fit neatly into the space between the crab's claws.

Enraged, Xolotl shrieked, demanding to be let down. He hammered and kicked at the creature, and the Karkinos opened its claw. The Elder crashed to the ground in a rattle of bones.

The claw had also cut through the lasso. Billy tried to maintain his balance, but he tumbled and fell, and the remains of the leather rope encircled him like a writhing serpent.

The giant crab's gaze followed the movement of the rope, saw it drop onto the struggling immortal and snapped at him with its huge claw. Billy rolled to one side and the claw screamed across the ground.

"Missed me!" he laughed.

And then the Karkinos impaled the outlaw through the chest with its spiny armored foreleg, pinning him to the stones.

Howling a savage war cry, Black Hawk flung himself at the Karkinos. His tomahawk screamed off its leg, and he jabbed again and again with the spear. The crab jerked its leg up, actually lifting the impaled Billy off the ground, and Black Hawk grabbed his friend and pulled him free, then bundled him in his arms and raced back toward the Warden's House. "What did I tell you!" he shouted. "Be careful, I said. But did you listen? Oh no!"

"I was careful," Billy whispered. He was deathly pale and there was blood on his lips. "I was watching the claw. I didn't know he was going to stand on me in some sort of crab-ninja move."

"Use your aura," Black Hawk said. "Heal yourself quickly. You're losing a lot of blood."

"Can't," Billy gasped. "Not enough aura left for a big wound like this. Shouldn't have wasted it healing those scratches earlier."

"Let me heal you."

"No, you can't. This isn't some scratch. Besides, you have about as much of your aura as I do. Save it."

Something with massive teeth and wings hopped out of the night, attracted by the scent of Billy's blood. Black Hawk ran right over it.

"I got the skeleton guy, though, didn't I?"

"You did."

"Guess I can't go back to working for Quetzalcoatl, eh?"

"When this is over, Billy," Black Hawk said, "I think maybe you and I should go and visit the Feathered Serpent. Hand in our resignations. I'll bring a box of matches."

"You going to toast some marshmallows with him?"

"I'll toast something," Black Hawk promised. The house coalesced out of the fog and the immortal shouted, announcing their presence. "Mars, we're back." He didn't want to be struck down by the Elder guarding the door.

Mars stopped them at the entrance to the building and assessed Billy with a professional soldier's eye. Then he resumed his position.

"That's not good, is it?" Billy asked. "It's never good when they say nothing."

Black Hawk laid Billy on the ground inside. He ripped the outlaw's sodden shirt apart to examine the wound beneath.

"How bad is it? Will I ever play the piano again?" Billy joked.

Machiavelli appeared and dropped to the floor beside the two Americans. Without a word, he pressed his palm to Billy's chest, and his dirty-gray aura bloomed over his hand. It dripped onto the open wound like sour milk.

"Smells like snake," Billy mumbled, eyes unfocusing as he slumped into unconsciousness

"I like snake," the Italian muttered. Desperately, Machiavelli forced his aura through his hand into Billy's wound. As he did, he visibly aged. Attempting to awaken Areop-Enap had exhausted him, etching new lines into his forehead, carving bags under his eyes. But with the strain of healing, now he actually grew old. His fuzz of hair turned the same color as his gray eyes and then drifted off his head like dust, leaving him totally bald. His spine curved, and deep wrinkles appeared on his forehead and at the corners of his nose, while his thin lips almost completely disappeared and brown spots suddenly speckled the backs of his hands.

"Enough," Black Hawk said. "You will burn yourself out."

"Let me give him just a little bit more," he pleaded.

"No!"

"I have a little left. I can give it to him," Machiavelli gasped.

"No," Black Hawk insisted. "If you use any more, there will be nothing left for you." He gently lifted Machiavelli's hand. "Enough. Or you will burst into flames. You have done more than anyone could, more than I could. It is out of our hands now. Now he will live or die: it is up to him. And he is Billy the Kid. He will survive." The immortal suddenly reached out and caught Machiavelli's hand. He squeezed tightly. "Whatever happens: you have made a lifelong friend here tonight, Italian. Two, if Billy lives."

"Three," Mars said from the doorway, saluting Machiavelli with his sword. He smiled. "This is what I have always loved about you humans. You are essentially good."

"Not everyone," Machiavelli said tiredly.

"No. Not everyone. But enough." Mars turned back to the doorway and settled into his battle stance. "The Karkinos is back," he announced. "And I do believe it is growing!" He suddenly threw himself back into the room. "Down!" he shouted.

An enormous claw ripped a chunk out of the side of the building. A second claw tore out the steel girders that supported the walls, snipping them apart as if they were made of straw. The Karkinos loomed over the open roof and peered down. It had doubled in size, and then doubled again in the few minutes since Black Hawk had snatched Billy from its claws.

"It's eaten Xolotl," Mars said. "That's why it's grown." He rolled to one side as another section of the wall was pulled down. "I've seen this happen before. Elder flesh works wonders on their systems, making them huge. And once they get a taste for Elder flesh, nothing else will satisfy them. It's probably after me now." Then, when the creature ignored him, he added, "Or not . . ." Two huge claws reached over the top of the building and punched into the hardened mud surrounding Areop-Enap. They found the hole the Flamels and Machiavelli had carved and went straight for it, snipping at the opening, enlarging it, ripping it apart.

"It's after Areop-Enap!" Perenelle screamed.

"We have to protect the Old Spider. If it eats her and absorbs her energy, it will be indestructible," Mars shouted. "Nothing—not even a Great Elder—will be able to stop it.

Perenelle quickly raised her arm, but she had barely any power left. A handful of cold energy washed over the crab. It didn't even notice.

Mars threw himself at the Karkinos, his sword buzzing and whirling around him. The metal blade screamed off the creature's armored legs. He stabbed deep into the joints, trying to knock it over.

"Protect Billy," Black Hawk commanded the Italian. He crawled beneath the creature, then rose to stab at it with his spear. The crab reared up on its four hind legs while flailing the front four wildly. Its two giant claws snapped and clashed.

Black Hawk stabbed again, pushing the spear deep into the monster's flesh. The crab twisted away at the last moment, dragging the immortal up into the air with it. Black

Hawk clung tightly to the spear shaft as the Karkinos's front claws click-clacked inches from his head. And then one flailing leg caught a belt loop on the immortal's jeans. Dangling in midair, the American thrashed and twisted to get loose. Cloth tore, but the crab flicked its leg out and Black Hawk went sailing out over the wall. A moment later there was a splash as he hit the sea.

And they all knew the Nereids were waiting in the water.

The giant crab dropped back onto the ball of mud and resumed ripping it apart. Flamel threw spears of green light at the creature, and Perenelle washed it with ice and fire. But all to no effect.

"You've got to awaken the Old Spider!" Mars shouted.

Nicholas threw himself into the shell. Karkinos had torn away the outer layer of protective mud, revealing a second muddy ball within. This thin crust covered the enormous hairy form of the Areop-Enap, the Old Spider.

"Wake up, wake up, wake up!" Flamel's hands pounded on the shell, leaving pale green impressions on the coating of hardened saliva. "Nothing's happening," he said desperately. He had seen the crab punch through the outer shell with ease; it would have no difficulty shattering this inner crust.

And then Mars's aura blazed bright, filling the ruined building with crimson light, and the air was rich with the stench of burnt meat.

The Karkinos hesitated, huge claws trembling.

"Smell that," Mars shouted. "That's what you want, isn't it?" The Elder blazed brighter and brighter, bloodred armor flowing over his body and a metal helm appearing on his head, turning him into the ferocious warrior of legend. Sticky streamers of light blazed off his body. The Karkinos's mouth went into a frenzy trying to taste the energy.

Mars lowered his sword, then sheathed it. He walked up to the creature. "Here I am, beastie. Smell that—it is the scent of an Elder. You want some, don't you? Well, here I am."

"Mars, no!" Flamel shouted.

"Mars, you have to stop!" Perenelle shouted. "Stop it now."

"I have a little left," he said. "I can lead it away from here." He started moving toward the door and the crab tracked his movements with its enormous beady eyes.

"No, Mars, you can't," she whispered, realizing what was happening.

The Elder's odor had changed, becoming bitter and sour, and although the aura was still radiating off his flesh, it was flickering wildly. The crab lurched after him, following the rich smell.

"Come taste the aura of Mars Ultor, who was also Ares and Nergal and a dozen other names besides." Mars concentrated and his aura blazed higher, brighter, stronger. "But before I was Nergal, I was Huitzilopochtli, I was the Champion of Humankind. It is the name I have always been proudest of."

Then his aura died.

Abruptly, Mars turned and ran through the empty

doorway. He barely made it before he exploded into a fine white ash. When his aura had consumed all his energy, it had fed off his flesh.

Nicholas Flamel leaned his head against the shell protecting Areop-Enap. They had lost.

Another wall shattered as the Karkinos ripped apart the remainder of the building.

The Alchemyst looked up to find the orange crab looming over him, claws clicking. Nicholas desperately needed one more spell, one final transformation, one incantation to awaken the Old Spider, but his aura was spent. He had nothing left to give. He was just a tired old man and Perenelle an old, old woman, looking small and frail now, her life force almost finished. Their friends and allies were no more. They had come close, so very, very close, to defeating the Dark Elders. And they had failed.

"I'm sorry," Nicholas Flamel said to no one in particular. He looked down at the thin crust surrounding the Old Spider and discovered eight tiny bruise-colored eyes regarding him impassively.

Areop-Enap had awakened.

CHAPTER SEVENTY-FOUR

*T*sagaglalal and her brother had been brought to life by Prometheus's aura.

Prometheus and his sister Zephaniah had been sent to an abandoned city of black glass and glittering gold at the very edge of the world. The Nameless City sat on the cusp of many ley lines and at the confluence of seven Shadowrealms. There were stories that the city of black and gold existed simultaneously in all seven realms.

Legend had it that the city had been built by the Archons, but Abraham the Mage held that they had simply taken up residence in the massive buildings, which he believed dated from the Time Before Time. Eventually, even they abandoned it, and the forest quickly reclaimed what had once been a vast metropolis.

Every aspect of the Nameless City suggested that it had been built by inhuman creatures. The doors were too tall and too narrow, the windows were small, the steps were shallow, and the irregular angles of the buildings made them hard—almost disturbing—to look at. Most of the buildings were covered with intricately carved whorls and spirals. Elder lore was filled with the stories of individuals who had become entranced by the circles. They had stared wide-eyed and open-mouthed at the designs, refusing to move, taking neither food nor water, and when they did speak it was to report both wonders and horrors.

Abraham had sent Zephaniah and Prometheus to the Nameless City with instructions to search for any of the mysterious crystal skulls that sometimes turned up in Archon and Ancient ruins.

It was in an enormous chamber in the heart of the library that they had found the clay statues.

Intricately carved and delicately beautiful, the statues ranged in color from deep black to palest white. Every inch of their perfectly sculpted bodies was covered with archaic script, hieroglyphs from a forgotten language. But their faces were blank, unmarked and unfinished: little more than vague ovals, without eyes, ears, noses or mouths. Male and female stood side by side in identical positions, tall, elegant and otherworldly. They looked not unlike the Elders or even the legendary Archons but were obviously different from those races.

When Prometheus had stepped into the statue-filled chamber, his fiery aura had popped alight, washing over the closest statues. Red sparks ran across the curling script, bringing it to life, and his aura sank into the clay, which shifted and flowed with the heat. Features began to form on their blank faces: clay running off the foreheads into peaks that formed noses and chins, depressions shaping into eyes, cracks hinting at mouths. The ancient texts glowed orange, then red and finally blue, thickening and sinking below the surface like veins beneath skin.

Prometheus was ablaze. His aura streamed from his body in helixes of power, bathing the statues . . . bringing them to life.

Tsagaglalal had been the clay statue closest to Prometheus. One moment she was without consciousness, and the next she existed. Opening slate-gray eyes, she was instantly aware of her surroundings. The heat awakened memories, thoughts and implanted ideas—she knew who she was. She even knew the name of the figure feeding her raw burning energy.

She was Tsagaglalal.

She lifted her arm and a sliver of hardened clay fell away and shattered on the ground, revealing dark flesh beneath. She brought the hand to her face and flexed her fingers, dirt crumbling from them.

Behind her, a second statue, a male, shifted slightly, and a slab of clay fell away from his torso to expose rich golden skin beneath. She turned stiffly and looked at him. Memories that could never have been hers gave her his name. This was Gilgamesh, and together, they were the first of the First People.

Prometheus's aura had brought them to life. It had kept Tsagaglalal alive for many, many millennia.

And Prometheus's aura burned within her still.

Tsagaglalal sat cross-legged on the Golden Gate Bridge, with her back to the city. Prometheus and Niten lay stretched out by her side. She had arranged them with their feet pointing toward the city so that when she sat between them, she would be able to touch their foreheads.

Pressing both hands against her stomach, Tsagaglalal breathed deeply and felt heat bloom within her. Her white jasmine-scented aura was touched by a suggestion of anise and burned with the merest hint of red.

Tsagaglalal's age was not measured in centuries or millennia, but in hundreds of millennia. She had seen the rise and fall of countless civilizations and had explored endless Shadowrealms, lived entire lives on worlds where time flowed differently. There was so much she had witnessed, so much she had done, and yet there was one great mystery whose answer had always eluded her: who had created her? Prometheus had brought her to life, but who had carved the human-sized clay statues and then placed them in the Nameless City?

After millennia of searching, she was still no closer to the truth. Even her husband, the legendary Abraham the Mage, had been unable to answer the question. "And maybe you will never know," he'd told her once. "But what I do know is that you are here for a reason. You and your brother were meant to be found. You were meant to be brought to life by Prometheus. Perhaps one day you will discover the reason for your existence."

And now, sitting on a cold damp bridge on a summer's evening in San Francisco, Tsagaglalal believed she might have discovered that reason.

Intense heat flowed through her body, down her arms and into her hands, which were cupped, left hand atop right hand, in her lap. Her fingers glowed, the tips burning red, then yellow and finally white-hot. Her fingernails melted and a thin gelatinous fluid leaked from her fingertips and dribbled into her hands.

The smell of jasmine was gone now, replaced by the thick cloying odor of anise.

Tsagaglalal looked down. A puddle of rich bloodred aura shimmered in her palm. With infinite care, she lifted it . . . and then stopped. It was not enough. She'd used too much of her aura earlier, rejuvenating herself; she only had enough aura for one.

But which one?

Tsagaglalal looked from Niten to Prometheus and then back to the immortal. She liked him. He was quiet and unassuming, and yet she knew he had a reputation as a fearsome warrior and a man of honor. He was remarkable: he had gone into battle against the Spartoi, knowing that he would probably not return. He'd been prepared to sacrifice his life to save the city. He deserved to live.

Tsagaglalal looked to her right: Prometheus was an Elder. Surely in the battle ahead, his powers would prove more useful? And much more importantly, Prometheus was, in many respects, her father. His aura had given her life, and now it was only right and proper that she should return the gift to him.

Tsagaglalal blinked and suddenly there were tears on her face and the world dissolved into rainbow fractures. She had only ever cried once before, and that was when Danu Talis had fallen and she'd lost her husband.

"I'm sorry, Niten," she whispered, and poured the bloodred liquid aura down Prometheus's throat.

The effect was instantaneous.

The Elder's aura flared bright red around his body. He shuddered and coughed and his green eyes snapped open.

"Hello, Father."

Prometheus reached up to touch Tsagaglalal's face. "Just as I remember you," he whispered, "just as I first saw you, young and beautiful. The Spartoi?"

"Dead. All dead."

"And Niten?"

She dipped her head. "I could only save one."

Prometheus struggled to sit up and she caught his arm and eased him upright. "Tsagaglalal, what have you done?"

"Repaid the gift you gave me a long time ago. You brought me to life and now I've returned you to life."

He turned to look at her. "But at what cost to you?" Even as he was talking, her face was beginning to age, wrinkles appearing in her skin. A strand of white hair drifted to the ground between them.

"I think this is what I was meant to do," she said.

"Without my aura you will not be able to renew your flesh. You will age normally now, and die soon enough."

"Everything has a price," Tsagaglalal said. "And this is one I am willing to pay. It seems a small price for countless lifetimes of experiences."

Prometheus turned to look at Niten's still form. "But,

Tsagaglalal," he said quietly, "you have brought the wrong one back."

"No!"

"Yes," he insisted. "My time is done. My Shadowrealm is dust, and the First People are no more. There is nothing left for me here: it is time for me to go."

"No . . ." She shook her head.

"Yes," he said firmly. "Ten thousand years ago, your husband told me this was how it would end. He said I would die on a bridge wrapped in fog, in a city beyond comprehension, in a time out of time. I knew this when I set out tonight. I knew how it would end. Now let me go," he pleaded. "Take back my aura. Give it to Niten."

She shook her head, huge milk-colored tears on her face. "No, I cannot. I will not."

"Let me ask you as a friend. . . ."

She shook her head again, more hair curling and falling away from her face. Her tears sizzled on the bridge.

"I have never asked you for anything before. So let me ask you this as your father. Do this for me. Please."

Tsagaglalal bowed her head and wept. Then she placed her right hand on the Elder's chest and her left on Niten's.

Prometheus lay back down and looked up into the night, the light fading from his eyes. "I am tired now, so very, very tired. It will be good to rest. And if you come across my sister, tell her who did this; tell her who sent the Spartoi. I have recognized Bastet's and Quetzalcoatl's auras on the air. And perhaps you should tell my sister where to find them." He coughed a laugh. "They will not enjoy a visit from her."

Niten drew in a deep shuddering breath and the air was suffused with the delicate odor of green tea.

"And, Tsagaglalal . . ."

"Yes, Father?"

Prometheus closed his eyes. "Tell Niten to find Aoife and ask her the question. Tell him . . . tell him she will say yes."

CHAPTER SEVENTY-FIVE

Isis and Osiris changed.

The transformation was sudden, sending them from human to beast in a single heartbeat. Ceramic armor burst apart as their pale skin split to reveal something dark and foul beneath. They grew tall, and the human flesh peeled away like torn paper to expose hard scales, rigid with triangular armored plates. Their faces lengthened to long serpentine snouts, and angular mouths filled with teeth. Their eyes flattened along the sides of their faces and turned yellow, while wicked horns curled from their heads. Their fingers grew razor-tipped claws. Barbed tails uncoiled, and wings, huge black batlike wings, unfurled from their backs.

And Sophie suddenly knew what the Witch of Endor had only suspected but could never quite believe. "Earthlords," she whispered. She pulled out her swords. They shimmered, trembling in her hands. "That's why the Witch destroyed so much of the ancient knowledge. She was keeping it from you."

Josh stood frozen. Isis and Osiris had turned into huge lizardlike creatures, and he was terrified of snakes. They were his every nightmare made flesh.

"A hundred thousand years ago your ancestors nearly destroyed our race," one of the creatures said, speaking with Osiris's voice.

"But we survived, and we swore a terrible vengeance," the creature next to it continued in Isis's voice.

The two creatures advanced on the twins, and Sophie immediately moved in front of Josh, protecting him.

"With your powers—your vast, incalculable powers—at our command," Isis said, stamping her foot, "on this very spot, the very nexus of this Shadowrealm, we were going to open a portal into the past and bring our people through to this time. How they would have feasted on this world and all the other worlds."

The Earthlords stepped closer as they spoke.

They exuded a rancid odor, and tiny insects and fat fleas twisted through their scales. Saliva dripping from their fangs seared the stones like acid as it fell. Black wings rose and spread, blotting out the last of the light.

"We will kill you and go back into the Shadowrealms," Isis said. "We will find other Golds and Silvers. We will not make the same mistakes again."

"No, you will not," Sophie breathed. She threw herself forward, slashing out widely with the two swords. The movement caught the Earthlords by surprise, and the blades screamed off their thick plated skin, drawing thin lines of green blood. But the edge of a flailing tail caught Sophie across the back, shattering her gold armor, breaking ribs and an arm, sending her crashing to the ground, her swords spinning away.

One of the creatures stood over her and planted a clawed foot on her stomach, pinning her to the ground. Sophie grunted. Her left arm was completely numb, and the pain in her ribs was excruciating, breathtaking. When she tried to call up her aura, the pain across her back and in her stomach was too much.

Isis raised a claw and leaned forward to rub it against Sophie's face. "If only you had done what you were told."

The second Earthlord crowded in. "How did you ever think you could defeat us?" He choked out a liquid laugh. "You are just humani."

"We are the Gold and Silver!" Josh shouted. Blazing incandescent red and blue-white fire, he plunged Clarent and Excalibur into the Earthlords. "We are the twins of legend!"

A huge circle of white fire detonated off the top of the Pyramid of the Sun, and two vast columns of blinding flames were clearly visible in the night sky all across the island of Danu Talis.

CHAPTER SEVENTY-SIX

Sophie lay on the cold gold ground, and Josh sat cross-legged beside her.

They were both feeling sick and empty.

Excalibur and Clarent lay buzzing on the ground where Josh had dropped them, the blades of the two stone swords running with oily flame, sparkling, crackling and sizzling. Beside the swords were two bubbling pools of liquid gold where Isis and Osiris had been consumed.

Sophie was staring wide-eyed into distance. "Is it over?" she asked. She was focusing on healing her wounds, and the air was rich with the scent of vanilla.

"No," Josh said sadly. "There's still one thing to do. There is the prophecy."

She nodded. "The twins of legend," she whispered. "One to save the world, one to destroy it."

Josh leaned forward and felt something move under his

armor. He reached in and took out the emerald tablet Tsaga-glalal had given him. At first glance it was nothing more than a slab of slightly greasy stone. He turned it over and over in his hands. "It's blank," he said.

"Wait," Sophie advised.

Josh rubbed his thumb across the surface, cleaning it . . . and words formed, shimmering gold against the green.

I am Abraham of Danu Talis, sometimes called the Mage, and I send greetings to the Gold.

There is much that I know about you. I know your name and age, and I know you are male. I have followed your ancestors down through ten thousand years. You are a remarkable young man, the last of a line of equally remarkable men.

I am writing this sitting in a tower on the edge of the known world on the Isle of Danu Talis. Within a few hours the crystal tower and the island it stands upon will be no more. The pulse of energy that destroyed it is even now speeding toward the Pyramid of the Sun, toward you. You can choose to harness this energy and use it, or let it seep back into the earth.

This you need to know: your world begins with the death of mine.

Danu Talis needs to fall.

I have always known that the fate of our worlds—yours and mine—is at the mercy of individuals. The actions of a single person can change the course of a world and create history.

And you, like the Silver, are one of those individuals.

You are powerful. A Gold—as powerful as I have ever seen. And you are brave, too. That much is clear. You know what has to be done, and the swords will give you the power to do it, if you so choose, because even now, at this twilight hour, you still have a choice. And you do not need me to tell you that you will pay a price, a terrible price, no matter how you choose.

By now, you will have heard the prophecy time and again. The two that are one must become the one that is all. One to save the world, one to destroy it.

You know who you are, Josh Newman.

Do you know what you have to do?

Have you the courage to do it?

The words slowly faded from the tablet, leaving it nothing more than a blank green stone once more. Josh turned it over in his hand and then gently slipped it back beneath his armor.

Josh looked over at the girl who was not his sister but was still his twin, and they both nodded. "It's time," he whispered.

"Time for what?" she asked, groaning as she got up, arm pressed to her stomach.

"One to save the world," he said, "one to destroy it."

The pyramid groaned as another earthquake tremor rippled through it. The nearby volcano detonated in a long slow rumble, showering sparks onto the city below. There was a sudden patter of footsteps around them. Josh grabbed Clarent and Excalibur and scrambled to his feet . . . just as Prometheus and Tsagaglalal, then Scathach and Joan,

Saint-Germain and finally Palamedes, carrying a groaning Will Shakespeare, climbed onto the top of the pyramid. They were all bloodied and bruised, clothes torn, armor shattered, weapons broken. But they were alive.

"We need to get out of here," Prometheus said. "The earthquake will tear the pyramid apart." They started to climb into Isis and Osiris's gleaming vimana.

"I thought I said I was never getting into another vimana," Shakespeare muttered.

Josh helped Sophie to her feet and half carried her toward the vimana. Scathach and Joan were about to go to his aid, but Saint-Germain put a hand on their shoulders. "No. Leave them be," he said in French. "They need this moment together."

Sophie was crying. "Josh, we're powerful, we can do something else. . . ."

"You know what has to be done," he said simply. "That's why we're here. That's why all of us are here. We were brought here to do this one thing. This is what we were born for. This is our destiny."

"I should be the one to do it," she insisted. "I'm older."

"No you're not." He smiled. "Not anymore. I'm about thirty thousand years older than you. And you're injured. I'm not." There were tears on his face now, but he was unaware of them. "Besides, I think yours is going to be the harder job." He hugged her. "Let me do this," he said, "and if I can, I'll come find you."

"Promise?"

"I promise. Now go," he pleaded.

"I will never forget you," Sophie whispered.

"I will always remember you," Josh promised.

491

CHAPTER SEVENTY-SEVEN

*A*reop-Enap had awakened

Eight bruise-colored eyes looked at the Alchemyst, and then each blinked in turn. Although Areop-Enap had the body of a huge spider, set in the center of her body was a huge, almost human head. It was smooth and round, with no ears or nose, but with a horizontal slash for a mouth. Like a tarantula's, her tiny eyes were set close to the top of her skull. Beneath the thin shell, the Old Spider's mouth opened and two long spearlike fangs appeared. "You should probably move now," she said in a surprisingly sweet voice.

Nicholas scrambled away just as Areop-Enap erupted upward.

The Karkinos was huge.

But Areop-Enap was massive.

When Perenelle had first encountered the creature, the Old Spider had been large, but she had grown within the protective shell. She stretched, her massive body uncoiling out of the muddy shell. Areop-Enap was easily twice the size of the crab. Finger-thick purple hairs on her broad back waved to and fro.

"I am smelling Quetzalcoatl and that cat-headed monstrosity in this fog." She turned to look down at Perenelle. "Madam, would you care to explain just what is going on?"

The Sorceress pointed. "The crab is trying to eat you. It's just eaten Xolotl. We need you, Old Spider."

The creature shivered. "I have waited a lifetime to hear that."

And then she jumped straight up in the air and landed on top of the Karkinos, driving it into the ground. The crab squealed, snapping its massive claws, biting chunks out of the masonry, spraying stones everywhere. Areop-Enap plunged a razor-sharp stinger into the back of the crab and it froze, then started to spasm violently. Suddenly white threads blossomed around the claws, sealing them shut, and then the Old Spider's huge legs moved, lifting the crab off the ground, spinning it over and over, blindingly fast, completely enfolding it in gossamer-thin gray strands that quickly thickened to become a bulbous white package. The entire process took less than a minute.

"I'm going to save that for later," Areop-Enap said. "I'm quite peckish."

Slowly, almost delicately, she crouched before Perenelle, all eight eyes regarding her impassively. "How long have I slept?"

"A few days."

"Ah. But when I look at you, I see you have aged more than that."

"It has been a busy week," Perenelle murmured. "You remember my husband, Nicholas."

"I remember him dropping a mountain on me."

"Your followers were about to sacrifice my wife to a volcano," Nicholas said. "And it was only a small mountain."

"It was." Areop-Enap picked her way around the room, pausing to lean close to Machiavelli, who was cradling Billy the Kid's head in his lap. The Italian glared defiantly at the enormous spider.

Billy's nose twitched and then his eyes cracked open. He squinted up at the almost human head with the eight eyes. "I'm guessing this is not a nightmare," he rasped.

"It's not," Machiavelli said.

"I was afraid of that," Billy said, and closed his eyes. Then they snapped open. "Does this mean we've won?"

"We have," Machiavelli said quietly. "Though the cost has been heavy indeed."

Areop-Enap picked her way back to Nicholas and Perenelle. "So I am still on the island where Dee was storing the monsters. I can smell beasts in this filthy air."

"Not as many as there were," Nicholas said. "They have been killing one another throughout the night."

"I should go and clean up, then," Areop-Enap said as she turned to scuttle out of the building. "We don't want any of those trying to swim to shore."

"Tell her about the unicorns," Billy mumbled.

The spider froze.

"There may be a few monokerata unicorns running free," Machiavelli said.

"With or without horns?" Areop-Enap asked.

"With."

"Extra crunchy. My favorite."

CHAPTER SEVENTY-EIGHT

*T*he heavily laden vimana took off from the top of the Pyramid of the Sun into the night air, carrying the survivors to safety.

Josh Newman stood where it had perched and raised his right hand in farewell. He watched as Sophie, supported on either side by Scathach and Joan, raised a hand and pressed her fingers against the glass. She was not crying now—she had no tears left.

One to save the world . . .

Josh sat cross-legged in the center of the pyramid. Reaching under his armor, he pulled out the Codex, which Tsagaglalal had given him. He turned it over and over in his hands, feeling the metal surface slick and cool against his flesh. It fell open to the end, ragged edges showing where pages had been torn out . . . where he would tear them out in ten thousand years' time.

Dipping his head, Josh lifted the torn pages from where he carried them in a bag around his neck. He placed them in the book, slotting them back into place. The ancient pages shifted, and threadlike strands appeared, weaving and wrapping together like worms, mending the Codex, making it whole again.

Then, opening the book at random, Josh placed his index finger on the page and watched the words in endless languages twist beneath his fingernail. And as it scrolled before him, he read the history of the world after the Fall.

In the days and weeks to come, Sophie and the others would rally the survivors, lead them off the sundered island and take them out into the world.

The people of Danu Talis, Elder and human, would follow Aten and Virginia Dare, an Elder and a human, out across the globe. The couple would establish colonies in all the surrounding lands, and these would grow into the great nations that would one day rule the earth.

Sophie and Virginia, Joan and Scathach, too, would be given other names and come to be worshipped as goddesses, teachers and saviors of humankind.

And in time, Sophie Newman, after many adventures, would find a way to lead the other immortals through a series of sequenced leygates back home to their own time, arriving in San Francisco, where it all began.

Josh closed the Codex and shoved it back beneath his

armor. He didn't want to read any more. Not yet. He was going to have to keep this book safe for over nine and a half thousand years, until he sold it to a penniless French bookseller.

One to destroy the world.

Danu Talis had to fall for the modern world to rise.

And Josh would destroy it.

The four ancient swords lay on the ground before him. Abraham had told him that the swords would give him the power—all he had to do was to take them in his hand and focus the energy even now pulsing up through the pyramid.

He just had to pick them up.

Abraham had said he had a choice. But Josh knew he had no choice, not really. If he did not do this, then his sister—and everyone else—would die, and he would not allow that.

He sat down and arranged the four swords in front of him.

But which one . . . was there an order?

And suddenly he remembered something Dee had told him. He spoke the words aloud. " 'When in doubt, follow your heart. Words can be false, images and sounds can be manipulated. But this' "—he tapped his chest, over his heart—" 'this is always true.' "

Without hesitation, with his left hand, he immediately reached for Clarent, the Sword of Fire. He felt the shivering heat of the ancient blade as it settled into his palm, and wondered briefly at the origins of these Swords of Power. No matter, he thought; he would have plenty of time in the future to investigate.

With his right hand, he reached for Joyeuse, the Sword of Earth, and placed it in his left hand. It settled on top of Clarent and immediately broke up into flaking dry earth and dusty soil. It sizzled as it was absorbed into the Sword of Fire.

Clarent began to glow red-hot, and Josh smelled burning flesh. His flesh.

His aura began to smoke off him in orange-scented steam.

Quickly he pressed Durendal on top of Clarent. The Sword of Air instantly dissolved into a wispy white mist and evaporated onto the single blade.

And finally, Excalibur, the Sword of Ice.

Josh lifted it in his right hand, holding it for a second, knowing that the instant he brought them together, everything would change . . . and then he laughed. Everything had already changed. It had changed a long time ago.

Josh stood, Clarent in his left hand, Excalibur in his right. He held both swords aloft and the entire pyramid bellowed like a huge beast. Then he brought his hands together before his face and pressed the Sword of Ice into Clarent. It melted in an explosive plume that wrapped his left hand in steam. The four Swords of Power—Fire, Earth, Air and Water— combined to create a fifth power: Aether. It burned through him, filling him with knowledge, and with the knowledge came vast unimaginable power, hundreds of millennia of history and learning surging through him.

He knew . . . everything!

His aura raged, a solid spear of orange light blazing high into the heavens.

Josh looked at his hand. All four of the stone swords were

gone now. They had been swallowed into one another, becoming one bar of metal, which was slowly melting into his flesh, searing into it, becoming part of it, bending, twisting, curling into a flat metal hook.

And there was pain—the likes of which he had never experienced before. He screamed, and what started as pain ended in a cry of triumph as he held the shining silver hook to the sky. He could feel the incredible energy gathering in the pyramid, shaking it violently, just waiting to be released. He would tear this island apart and destroy the world of the Elders, and, in that moment, give birth to the world of man.

"Goodbye, Sophie," Josh Newman said, and then Marethyu plunged the hook into the pyramid at his feet. And he spoke aloud the last words he had seen in the Codex.

"Today, I am become Death, the destroyer of worlds."

FRIDAY, 8th June

CHAPTER SEVENTY-NINE

Arm in arm, Nicholas and Perenelle Flamel walked slowly around the island. They were incredibly aged, every one of their six hundred years etched into their flesh and bones.

The sun was rising in the east and a chill breeze was whipping in off the Pacific, clearing away the last of the foul-smelling fog, the stink of burnt meat, seared wood and melted stone. The air was beginning to smell of clean salt once again.

They walked past the wharf and followed the Agave Trail around the island, almost to the spot where they had come ashore less than twelve hours earlier. The bench was damp, and Nicholas bent to rub it clean with his sleeve before he would allow Perenelle to sit.

Nicholas sat beside his wife and she leaned into him. He put his arm around her, feeling her thin and delicate bones beneath his hand. Directly ahead of them, the city of San Francisco appeared ghostlike out of the early dawn.

"No mermaids in the water?" Perenelle asked.

"Without Nereus to keep them here, they've no reason to stay."

"Well, at least the city is still standing," Perenelle said in French, her voice a wispy thread. "I can see no smoke rising to the skies."

Nicholas looked right and then left. "And the bridges are unbroken. That's a good sign."

"Prometheus and Niten did not fail us. They must have survived," she said. "I surely hope so," she added sincerely. "We lost so many good people tonight."

"They gave their lives doing what they believed was right," he reminded her. "They gave their lives so that others might live and the world would go on. There is no greater sacrifice. And this morning the city survives, so they did not die in vain."

"And what of us, Nicholas? Did we always do what was right?"

"Perhaps not," he said softly. "But we always did what we believed was right. Is that the same thing?"

"Of late I have found myself wondering if we should ever have looked for the twins of legend."

"And if we had not, then we would never have found Sophie and Josh," Nicholas said simply. "From the moment I bought the Book of Abraham, our lives have been a journey which led us to this place and this time. It was our destiny— and no man can escape his destiny."

"I wonder where the twins are?" she whispered. "I would

504

like to know . . . to know before the end. I need to know that they survived."

"They are safe," he said confidently. "I have to believe that because this world goes on."

Perenelle nodded. "You must be right." She rested her cheek against Nicholas's arm. "It's peaceful," she said. "The island is so quiet this morning."

"No seagulls. The monsters either ate them or scared them away. They'll be back."

The long grass rasped in the light breeze, and waves lapped against the stones in a soothing rhythm. Perenelle closed her eyes. "The sun is warm," she murmured.

Nicholas rested the side of his face against the top of her head. "Very warm. It's going to be a glorious day."

As they sat, the sun rose slowly into the heavens, running golden along the Bay Bridge, bringing it to blazing light. The city of San Francisco came awake, the sounds of traffic faint and musical on the air.

"You know that I have always loved you," Nicholas said quietly.

There was a long silence, and then Perenelle replied in a whisper, "I know that. And you know that I love you?"

He nodded. "I have never doubted it for a moment."

"I would like to have been buried in Paris," Perenelle said suddenly. "In those empty graves we prepared for ourselves all those years ago."

"Does it matter where we lie, so long as it is together?" Nicholas asked, closing his eyes.

"Of course not," she said, and closed her eyes as well.

A shadow fell across the couple.

They opened their eyes to find a tall blue-eyed young man standing over them. He was wrapped in a long leather hooded cloak. The sun was behind him, throwing his hooded face into shadow. A gleaming half circle of metal took the place of his left hand.

"I wondered if you would come," Nicholas Flamel said quietly.

"I was there at the beginning when I sold you the Book all those years ago and started you on this great journey. It is only fitting that I should return at the end."

"Who are you?" the Alchemyst asked.

The hook-handed man pulled down his hood. He crouched before Nicholas and Perenelle, took both their hands in his and looked into their faces. "You know me," he said.

Nicholas searched the young man's lined and scarred face, and Perenelle reached up to run her fingers across his chin, tracing the plane of his forehead and the curve of his cheekbone. "Josh? Josh Newman?"

"You knew me as Josh Newman . . . ," he said very gently. "But that was before this"—he held up his hook—"which is a long story."

"What of Sophie?"

"A night has gone by for you. Almost seven hundred years have passed for her, but she has not aged. She's had a lot of adventures over the years, but this morning she returned safe and well to San Francisco and Aunt Agnes."

"And you, Josh? What of you?"

"Josh is no more. Now I am Marethyu. I am Death, and I am here to take you home." His hook moved and a golden arc appeared over the bench. The air suddenly smelled of oranges, and he smiled. "You did say Paris, didn't you?"

The leygate opened and then winked out of existence.

EPILOGUE

My Dearest Sister,

I cannot promise you too many letters—you know how bad I am at writing, and there aren't really phones where I've been.

I wanted you to know that I am safe and well and getting used to the hook. I did scratch my head with it, but that's a mistake you make only once. I've had a couple of offers to turn it into a proper silver hand or a golden glove, but to be honest, I've grown rather fond of it. And of course, it does have some wonderful advantages. I used it to make this most amazing Shadowrealm only last month. I put some great prehistoric animals in it and added two moons—and of course, there are no snakes.

I believe you are off to London shortly with Aunt Agnes. Give my regards to Gilgamesh. It's probably best not to tell him who I was/am/will be. He's confused enough as it is.

Please do not worry about me.

I know that is like telling you not to breathe, but I do need you to know that I am fine. More than fine. I am discovering more and more of my powers every day. I am immortal and eternal and I regret nothing. We did the right thing: one to save the world, one to destroy it.

You know that if you ever need me, all you have to do is look into a mirror and call my name three times. (Use the new name; I'm not sure calling Josh would have any impact.)

If you ever call me, I will come to you.

But even if you do not call, Sophie, know that I will watch over you all the days of your life.

It's what a brother is supposed to do, isn't it?

Marethyu
Writ this day, the 10th of Imbolc,
on the Shadowrealm Isle
of Tir na nOg

P.S. The Flamels send their love.
Marethyu

P.P.S. We were at Aoife and Niten's wedding last month. Scathach was her bridesmaid. Everyone cried.

—M

AUTHOR'S NOTE
ATLANTIS (DANU TALIS)

Did Atlantis really exist?

There are thousands of books that will tell you it did, and an equal number that will say it did not. Was it in the Atlantic? The Mediterranean? Off the west coast of Spain or Africa, or the east coast of America, or perhaps in Mexico? Was it south of India? Is it buried under Antarctica, or was it in the heart of Ireland?

The huge outpouring of research and speculation originates from a surprisingly small piece of text. Everything we know about Atlantis comes from the dialogues of Timaeus and Critias, written by Plato around 350 B.C. The word *Atlantis* is specifically used in Timaeus, where it is described as a vast island empire existing "beyond the Pillars of Hercules," which are the Straits of Gibraltar, between Spain and North Africa. Plato gives us a very clear description of Atlantis, including the rings of land and water and the canals, walls and bridges. Each bridge, for example, was described as being one hundred feet wide—a detail I used when creating the Danu Talis that appears in the Secrets of the Immortal Nicholas Flamel books.

In the second work, the unfinished *Critias,* there is a lengthier description of a catastrophic war and the ultimate destruction of the island in a single day and night by a combination of earthquakes, volcanoes and tsunamis.

Plato is supposed to have based his text on a story told to the Greek lawgiver Solon three hundred years earlier. An

Egyptian priest in the temple of Neith at Sais showed Solon the ancient story inscribed in stone. Some early Greek writers claimed to have seen those stones, but they have never been found.

Significantly, in Plato's own time, very few people believed he was writing about a real place—they considered Atlantis to be an idealized world that had been perfect in every way until it was destroyed by greed.

There is, sadly, no evidence for the advanced civilization of Atlantis; however, every year, there are new revelations about Earth's past, and we keep discovering that "primitive" peoples were not as primitive as we suspected. It is also true that around ten thousand years ago, at the end of the last ice age, the sea rose, and many shoreline communities would have been swamped. Recent research using supercomputers to replicate the melting of ice sheets suggests that water levels could have risen over sixty feet in two hundred years. Significantly, just about every culture on this planet has stories of a great flood that devastated the world, wiping away whole cities and tribes and instigating great migrations as people fled the rising waters. And as we know—at the heart of just about every legend is a grain of truth.

So perhaps there really is an Atlantis—an island kingdom destroyed by a series of natural disasters, waiting to be rediscovered. If there is, odds are that it will be nothing like we imagined.

And the name Danu Talis?

I had often said that the only characters I created for this series were the twins. Everything else was grounded in history or mythology. I did, however, take a little license with the name Danu Talis.

In a collection of Irish poems and stories called the *Lebor Gabála Érenn,* or *The Book of the Taking of Ireland,* there are the stories of the Tuatha De Danann, the People of Danu. They are the fifth invaders of Ireland, and unlike some of the others, whom we can ground firmly in history, the Tuatha De Danann are a magical and mysterious people, refugees from the west who sailed to Ireland on ships at a time of the "dark cloud."

So, for the purposes of this story, the Tuatha De Danann were the survivors of the fall of Atlantis, and Atlantis became Danu Talis.

ACKNOWLEDGMENTS

This book ends a very long journey, which began in May 1997 when I first wrote the word *Alchemyst* with a Υ in my notebook. A decade later, in May 2007, almost to the day, the first book of the Secrets of the Immortal Nicholas Flamel series, *The Alchemyst,* was published. Now, six years later, *The Enchantress* brings the series to a conclusion.

I am especially pleased that many of the same people who began that journey with me are here with me at the end.

This book, and indeed this series, would not have happened without the constant support and encouragement (and endless patience) of Beverly Horowitz and the wonderful Krista Marino at Delacorte Press.

A very special thanks goes out to Colleen Fellingham (who has kept me safe and out of trouble), Tim Terhune, and the entire team at Delacorte Press and Random House, especially Elizabeth Zajac, Jocelyn Lange and Andrea T. Sheridan, for taking care of me.

Thank you, as always, to Barry Krost at BKM, Frank Weimann at the Literary Group, Richard Thompson and Bernard Sidman.

Surrounding me as I wrote the series have been a number of people whose help, advice and support I have come to depend on. Claudette Sutherland is chief amongst them, but there are many others, and their thoughts, suggestions, ideas and criticisms have been more than invaluable: they have been essential. In alphabetical order (so there's no fighting), let me thank: Michael Carroll, Colette Freedman, Jumeaux (who are Antonio Gambale and Libby Lavella), Patrick Kavanagh (for too many things), Renee Lascala (and the flock, and especially Pookie, who taught me everything I know about parrots), Alfred Molina and Jill Gascoine (not alphabetical, I know, but I cannot separate them), Brooks and Maurizio Papalia, Melanie Rose, Mitch Ryan, Sonia Schorman, and Sherrod Turner and Jim Di Bella (equally inseparable).

This series has brought me into contact with many extraordinary and fascinating people. Again, in alphabetical order: Marilyn Anderson and Laysa Quintero, Lorenzo di Bonaventura, Topher Bradfield, LeVar Burton, Edie Ching, Jackie Collins, the Cooperkawa Clan, the Crooks Family, Simon Curtis, Jennifer Daugherty, Trista Delamere and Carleen Cappelletti, Roma Downey and Mark Burnett, Jim and Marissa Durham, Lynn Ferguson, Robin and Stephanie Gammell, Jerry Gelb, Melissa Gilbert, Alex Gogan, Andrea Goyan and Ron Freed, Bruce Hatton, Anne Kavanagh, Arnold and Anne Kopelson, Tina Lau, Gussie Lewis (and all her fabulous team, who were there right from the very beginning), Laura Lizer, Dwight L. MacPherson, Lisa Maxson, O. R. Melling, Chris Miller and Elaine Sir (and as I was completing this book, Eliana "Elle" Sir Miller appeared), Pat Neal, Mark Ordesky, Pierre O'Rourke, Christopher Paolini, Sidney and Joanna Poitier, Rick Riordan, Frank Sharp, Ronald Shepherd, Armin Shimerman and Kitty Swink, Becky Stewart, Simon and Wendy Wells, Cynthia True and Eric Wiese, Bill Young, and Hans and Suzanne Zimmer.

And of course, the team at Flamel's Immortal Portal, who know the books better than I do: Julie Blewett-Grant, Jeffrey

Smith, Jamie Krakover, Sean Gardell, Kristen Nolan Winsko, Rachel Carroll, Elena Charalambous, Bert Beattie, Genny Colby, Brittney Hauke and Joshua Ezekiel Crisanto.

I've forgotten someone. I know I have. If it is you—then I apologize.

ABOUT THE AUTHOR

An authority on mythology and folklore, Michael Scott is one of Ireland's most successful authors. A master of fantasy, science fiction, horror, and folklore, he has been hailed by the *Irish Times* as "the King of Fantasy in these isles." *The Enchantress* is the sixth book in the *New York Times* bestselling series The Secrets of the Immortal Nicholas Flamel. Look for book one, *The Alchemyst;* book two, *The Magician;* book three, *The Sorceress;* book four, *The Necromancer;* and book five, *The Warlock,* all available from Delacorte Press.

You can follow Michael Scott on Twitter @flamelauthor and visit him at dillonscott.com.